The Patrician by John Galsworthy

John Galsworthy was born at Kingston Upon Thames in Surrey, England, on August 14th 1867 to a wealthy and well established family. His schooling was at Harrow and New College, Oxford before training as a barrister and being called to the bar in 1890. However, Law was not attractive to him and he travelled abroad becoming great friends with the novelist Joseph Conrad, then a first mate on a sailing ship.

In 1895 Galsworthy began an affair with Ada Nemesis Pearson Cooper, the wife of his cousin Major Arthur Galsworthy. The affair was kept a secret for 10 years till she at last divorced and they married on 23rd September 1905.

Galsworthy first published in 1897 with a collection of short stories entitled "The Four Winds". For the next 7 years he published these and all works under his pen name John Sinjohn. It was only upon the death of his father and the publication of "The Island Pharisees" in 1904 that he published as John Galsworthy.

His first play, The Silver Box in 1906 was a success and was followed by "The Man of Property" later that same year and was the first in the Forsyte trilogy. Whilst today he is far more well know as a Nobel Prize winning novelist then he was considered a playwright dealing with social issues and the class system. Here we publish Villa Rubein, a very fine story that captures Galsworthy's unique narrative and take on life of the time.

He is now far better known for his novels, particularly The Forsyte Saga, his trilogy about the eponymous family of the same name. These books, as with many of his other works, deal with social class, upper-middle class lives in particular. Although always sympathetic to his characters, he reveals their insular, snobbish, and somewhat greedy attitudes and suffocating moral codes. He is now viewed as one of the first from the Edwardian era to challenge some of the ideals of society depicted in the literature of Victorian England.

In his writings he campaigns for a variety of causes, including prison reform, women's rights, animal welfare, and the opposition of censorship as well as a recurring theme of an unhappy marriage from the women's side. During World War I he worked in a hospital in France as an orderly after being passed over for military service.

He was appointed to the Order of Merit in 1929, after earlier turning down a knighthood, and awarded the Nobel Prize in 1932 though he was too ill to attend.

John Galsworthy died from a brain tumour at his London home, Grove Lodge, Hampstead on January 31st 1933. In accordance with his will he was cremated at Woking with his ashes then being scattered over the South Downs from an aeroplane.

Index of Contents

Chapter I

Light, entering the vast room—a room so high that its carved ceiling refused itself to exact scrutiny—travelled, with the wistful, cold curiosity of the dawn, over a fantastic storehouse of Time. Light, unaccompanied by the prejudice of human eyes, made strange revelation of incongruities, as though illuminating the dispassionate march of history.

For in this dining hall—one of the finest in England—the Caradoc family had for centuries assembled the trophies and records of their existence. Round about this dining hall they had built and pulled down and restored, until the rest of Monkland Court presented some aspect of homogeneity. Here alone they had left virgin the work of the old quasi-monastic builders, and within it unconsciously deposited their souls. For there were here, meeting the eyes of light, all those rather touching evidences of man's desire to persist for ever, those shells of his former bodies, the fetishes and queer proofs of his faiths, together with the remorseless demonstration of their treatment at the hands of Time.

The annalist might here have found all his needed confirmations; the analyst from this material formed the due equation of high birth; the philosopher traced the course of aristocracy, from its primeval rise in crude strength or subtlety, through centuries of power, to picturesque decadence, and the beginnings of its last stand. Even the artist might here, perchance, have seized on the dry ineffable pervading spirit, as one visiting an old cathedral seems to scent out the constriction of its heart.

From the legendary sword of that Welsh chieftain who by an act of high, rewarded treachery had passed into the favour of the conquering William, and received, with the widow of a Norman, many lands in Devonshire, to the Cup purchased for Geoffrey Caradoc; present Earl of Valleys, by subscription of his Devonshire tenants on the occasion of his marriage with the Lady Gertrude Semmering—no insignia were absent, save the family portraits in the gallery of Valleys House in London. There was even an ancient duplicate of that yellow tattered scroll royally, reconfirming lands and title to John, the most distinguished of all the Caradocs, who had unfortunately neglected to be born in wedlock, by one of those humorous omissions to be found in the genealogies of most old families. Yes, it was there, almost cynically hung in a corner; for this incident, though no doubt a burning question in the fifteenth century, was now but staple for an ironical little tale, in view of the fact that descendants of John's 'own' brother Edmund were undoubtedly to be found among the cottagers of a parish not far distant.

Light, glancing from the suits of armour to the tiger skins beneath them, brought from India but a year ago by Bertie Caradoc, the younger son, seemed recording, how those, who had once been foremost by virtue of that simple law of Nature which crowns the adventuring and strong, now being almost washed aside out of the main stream of national life, were compelled to devise adventure, lest they should lose belief in their own strength.

The unsparing light of that first half-hour of summer morning recorded many other changes, wandering from austere tapestries to the velvety carpets, and dragging from the contrast sure proof of a common sense which denied to the present Earl and Countess the asceticisms of the past. And then it seemed to lose interest in this critical journey, as though longing to clothe all in witchery. For the sun had risen, and through the Eastern windows came pouring its level and mysterious joy. And with it, passing in at an open lattice, came a wild bee to settle among the flowers on the table athwart the Eastern end, used when there was only a small party in the house. The hours fled on silent, till the sun was high, and the first visitors came—three maids, rosy, not silent, bringing brushes. They passed, and were followed by two footmen—scouts of the breakfast brigade, who stood for a moment professionally doing nothing, then soberly commenced to set the table. Then came a little girl of six, to see if there were anything exciting—little Ann Shropton, child of Sir William Shropton by his marriage with Lady Agatha, and eldest daughter of the house, the only one of the four young Caradocs as yet wedded. She came on tiptoe, thinking to surprise whatever was there. She had a broad little face, and wide frank hazel eyes over a little nose that came out straight and sudden. Encircled by a loose belt placed far below the waist of her holland frock, as if to symbolize freedom, she seemed to think everything in life good fun. And soon she found the exciting thing.

"Here's a bumble bee, William. Do you think I could tame it in my little glass bog?"

"No, I don't, Miss Ann; and look out, you'll be stung!"

"It wouldn't sting me."

"Why not?"

"Because it wouldn't."

"Of course—if you say so—"

"What time is the motor ordered?"

"Nine o'clock."

"I'm going with Grandpapa as far as the gate."

"Suppose he says you're not?"

"Well, then I shall go all the same."

"I see."

"I might go all the way with him to London! Is Auntie Babs going?"

"No, I don't think anybody is going with his lordship."

"I would, if she were. William!"

"Yes."

"Is Uncle Eustace sure to be elected?"

"Of course he is."

"Do you think he'll be a good Member of Parliament?"

"Lord Miltoun is very clever, Miss Ann."

"Is he?"

"Well, don't you think so?"

"Does Charles think so?"

"Ask him."

"William!"

"Yes."

"I don't like London. I like here, and I like Cotton, and I like home pretty well, and I love Pendridny—and—I like Ravensham."

"His lordship is going to Ravensham to-day on his way up, I heard say."

"Oh! then he'll see great-granny. William—"

"Here's Miss Wallace."

From the doorway a lady with a broad pale patient face said:

"Come, Ann."

"All right! Hallo, Simmons!"

The entering butler replied:

"Hallo, Miss Ann!"

"I've got to go."

"I'm sure we're very sorry."

"Yes."

The door banged faintly, and in the great room rose the busy silence of those minutes which precede repasts. Suddenly the four men by the breakfast fable stood back. Lord Valleys had come in.

He approached slowly, reading a blue paper, with his level grey eyes divided by a little uncharacteristic frown. He had a tanned yet ruddy, decisively shaped face, with crisp hair and moustache beginning to go iron-grey—the face of a man who knows his own mind and is contented with that knowledge. His figure too, well-braced and upright, with the back of the head carried like a soldier's, confirmed the impression, not so much of self-sufficiency, as of the sufficiency of his habits of life and thought. And there was apparent about all his movements that peculiar unconsciousness of his surroundings which comes to those who live a great deal in the public eye, have the material machinery of existence placed exactly to their hands, and never need to consider what others think of them. Taking his seat, and still perusing the paper, he at once began to eat what was put before him; then noticing that his eldest daughter had come in and was sitting down beside him, he said:

"Bore having to go up in such weather!"

"Is it a Cabinet meeting?"

"Yes. This confounded business of the balloons." But the rather anxious dark eyes of Agatha's delicate narrow face were taking in the details of a tray for keeping dishes warm on a sideboard, and she was thinking: "I believe that would be better than the ones I've got, after all. If William would only say whether he really likes these large trays better than single hot-water dishes!" She contrived how-ever to ask in her gentle voice—for all her words and movements were gentle, even a little timid, till anything appeared to threaten the welfare of her husband or children:

"Do you think this war scare good for Eustace's prospects, Father?"

But her father did not answer; he was greeting a new-comer, a tall, fine-looking young man, with dark hair and a fair moustache, between whom and himself there was no relationship, yet a certain negative resemblance. Claud Fresnay, Viscount Harbinger, was indeed also a little of what is called the 'Norman' type—having a certain firm regularity of feature, and a slight aquilinity of nose high up on the bridge—but that which in the elder man seemed to indicate only an unconscious acceptance of self as a standard, in the younger man gave an impression at once more assertive and more uneasy, as though he were a little afraid of not chaffing something all the time.

Behind him had come in a tall woman, of full figure and fine presence, with hair still brown—Lady Valleys herself. Though her eldest son was thirty, she was, herself, still little more than fifty. From her voice, manner, and whole personality, one might suspect that she had been an acknowledged beauty; but there was now more than a suspicion of maturity about her almost jovial face, with its full grey-blue eyes; and coarsened complexion. Good comrade, and essentially 'woman of the world,' was written on every line of her, and in every tone of her voice. She was indeed a figure suggestive of open air and generous living, endowed with abundant energy, and not devoid of humour. It was she who answered Agatha's remark.

"Of course, my dear, the very best thing possible."

Lord Harbinger chimed in:

"By the way, Brabrook's going to speak on it. Did you ever hear him, Lady Agatha? 'Mr. Speaker, Sir, I rise—and with me rises the democratic principle—'"

But Agatha only smiled, for she was thinking:

"If I let Ann go as far as the gate, she'll only make it a stepping-stone to something else to-morrow." Taking no interest in public affairs, her inherited craving for command had resorted for expression to a meticulous ordering of household matters. It was indeed a cult with her, a passion—as though she felt herself a sort of figurehead to national domesticity; the leader of a patriotic movement.

Lord Valleys, having finished what seemed necessary, arose.

"Any message to your mother, Gertrude?"

"No, I wrote last night."

"Tell Miltoun to keep—an eye on that Mr. Courtier. I heard him speak one day—he's rather good."

Lady Valleys, who had not yet sat down, accompanied her husband to the door.

"By the way, I've told Mother about this woman, Geoff."

"Was it necessary?"

"Well, I think so; I'm uneasy—after all, Mother has some influence with Miltoun."

Lord Valleys shrugged his shoulders, and slightly squeezing his wife's arm, went out.

Though himself vaguely uneasy on that very subject, he was a man who did not go to meet disturbance. He had the nerves which seem to be no nerves at all—especially found in those of his class who have much to do with horses. He temperamentally regarded the evil of the day as quite sufficient to it. Moreover, his eldest son was a riddle that he had long given up, so far as women were concerned.

Emerging into the outer hall, he lingered a moment, remembering that he had not seen his younger and favourite daughter.

"Lady Barbara down yet?" Hearing that she was not, he slipped into the motor coat held for him by Simmons, and stepped out under the white portico, decorated by the Caradoc hawks in stone.

The voice of little Ann reached him, clear and high above the smothered whirring of the car.

"Come on, Grandpapa!"

Lord Valleys grimaced beneath his crisp moustache—the word grandpapa always fell queerly on the ears of one who was but fifty-six, and by no means felt it—and jerking his gloved hand towards Ann, he said:

"Send down to the lodge gate for this."

The voice of little Ann answered loudly:

"No; I'm coming back by myself."

The car starting, drowned discussion.

Lord Valleys, motoring, somewhat pathetically illustrated the invasion of institutions by their destroyer, Science. A supporter of the turf, and not long since Master of Foxhounds, most of whose soul (outside politics) was in horses, he had been, as it were, compelled by common sense, not only to tolerate, but to take up and even press forward the cause of their supplanters. His instinct of self-preservation was secretly at work, hurrying him to his own destruction; forcing him to persuade himself that science and her successive victories over brute nature could be wooed into the service of a prestige which rested on a crystallized and stationary base. All this keeping pace with the times, this immersion in the results of modern discoveries, this speeding-up of existence so that it was all surface and little root—the increasing volatility, cosmopolitanism, and even commercialism of his life, on which he rather prided himself as a man of the world—was, with a secrecy too deep for his perception, cutting at the aloofness logically demanded of one in his position. Stubborn, and not spiritually subtle, though by no means dull in practical matters, he was resolutely letting the waters bear him on, holding the tiller firmly, without perceiving that he was in the vortex of a whirlpool. Indeed, his common sense continually impelled him, against the sort of reactionaryism of which his son Miltoun had so much, to that easier reactionaryism, which, living on its spiritual capital, makes what material capital it can out of its enemy, Progress.

He drove the car himself, shrewd and self-contained, sitting easily, with his cap well drawn over those steady eyes; and though this unexpected meeting of the Cabinet in the Whitsuntide recess was not only a nuisance, but gave food for anxiety, he was fully able to enjoy the swift smooth movement through the summer air, which met him with such friendly sweetness under the great trees of the long avenue. Beside him, little Ann was silent, with her legs stuck out rather wide apart. Motoring was a new excitement, for at home it was forbidden; and a meditative rapture shone in her wide eyes above her sudden little nose. Only once she spoke, when close to the lodge the car slowed down, and they passed the lodge-keeper's little daughter.

"Hallo, Susie!"

There was no answer, but the look on Susie's small pale face was so humble and adoring that Lord Valleys, not a very observant man, noticed it with a sort of satisfaction. "Yes," he thought, somewhat irrelevantly, "the country is sound at heart!"

Chapter II

At Ravensham House on the borders of Richmond Park, suburban seat of the Casterley family, ever since it became usual to have a residence within easy driving distance of Westminster—in a large conservatory adjoining the hall, Lady Casterley stood in front of some Japanese lilies. She was a slender, short old woman, with an ivory-coloured face, a thin nose, and keen eyes half-veiled by delicate wrinkled lids. Very still, in her grey dress, and with grey hair, she gave the impression of a little figure carved out of fine, worn steel. Her firm, spidery hand held a letter written in free somewhat sprawling style:

MONKLAND COURT,

"DEVON.

"MY DEAR, MOTHER,

"Geoffrey is motoring up to-morrow. He'll look in on you on the way if he can. This new war scare has taken him up. I shan't be in Town myself till Miltoun's election is over. The fact is, I daren't leave him down here alone. He sees his 'Anonyma' every day. That Mr. Courtier, who wrote the book against War—rather cool for a man who's been a soldier of fortune, don't you think?—is staying at the inn, working for the Radical. He knows her, too—and, one can only hope, for Miltoun's sake, too well—an attractive person, with red moustaches, rather nice and mad. Bertie has just come down; I must get him to have a talk with Miltoun, and see if he cant find out how the land lies. One can trust Bertie—he's really very astute. I must say, that she's quite a sweet-looking woman; but absolutely nothing's known of her here except that she divorced her husband. How does one find out about people? Miltoun's being so extraordinarily strait-laced makes it all the more awkward. The earnestness of this rising generation is most remarkable. I don't remember taking such a serious view of life in my youth."

Lady Casterley lowered the coronetted sheet of paper. The ghost of a grimace haunted her face—she had not forgotten her daughter's youth. Raising the letter again, she read on:

"I'm sure Geoffrey and I feel years younger than either Miltoun or Agatha, though we did produce them. One doesn't feel it with Bertie or Babs, luckily. The war scare is having an excellent effect on Miltoun's candidature. Claud Harbinger is with us, too, working for Miltoun; but, as a matter of fact, I think he's after Babs. It's rather melancholy, when you think that Babs isn't quite twenty—still, one can't expect anything else, I suppose, with her looks; and Claud is rather a fine specimen. They talk of him a lot now; he's quite coming to the fore among the young Tories."

Lady Casterley again lowered the letter, and stood listening. A prolonged, muffled sound as of distant cheering and groans had penetrated the great conservatory, vibrating among the pale petals of the lilies and setting free their scent in short waves of perfume. She passed into the hall; where, stood an old man with sallow face and long white whiskers.

"What was that noise, Clifton?"

"A posse of Socialists, my lady, on their way to Putney to hold a demonstration; the people are hooting them. They've got blocked just outside the gates."

"Are they making speeches?"

"They are talking some kind of rant, my lady."

"I'll go and hear them. Give me my black stick."

Above the velvet-dark, flat-toughed cedar trees, which rose like pagodas of ebony on either side of the drive, the sky hung lowering in one great purple cloud, endowed with sinister life by a single white beam striking up into it from the horizon. Beneath this canopy of cloud a small phalanx of dusty, dishevelled-looking men and women were drawn up in the road, guarding, and encouraging with cheers, a tall, black-coated orator. Before and behind this phalanx, a little mob of men and boys kept up an accompaniment of groans and jeering.

Lady Casterley and her 'major-domo' stood six paces inside the scrolled iron gates, and watched. The slight, steel-coloured figure with steel-coloured hair, was more arresting in its immobility than all the vociferations and gestures of the mob. Her eyes alone moved under their half-drooped lids; her right hand clutched tightly the handle of her stick. The speaker's voice rose in shrill protest against the exploitation of 'the people'; it sank in ironical comment on Christianity; it demanded passionately to be free from the continuous burden of 'this insensate militarist taxation'; it threatened that the people would take things into their own hands.

Lady Casterley turned her head:

"He is talking nonsense, Clifton. It is going to rain. I shall go in."

Under the stone porch she paused. The purple cloud had broken; a blind fury of rain was deluging the fast-scattering crowd. A faint smile came on Lady Casterley's lips.

"It will do them good to have their ardour damped a little. You will get wet, Clifton—hurry! I expect Lord Valleys to dinner. Have a room got ready for him to dress. He's motoring from Monkland."

Chapter III

In a very high, white-panelled room, with but little furniture, Lord Valleys greeted his mother-in-law respectfully.

"Motored up in nine hours, Ma'am—not bad going."

"I am glad you came. When is Miltoun's election?"

"On the twenty-ninth."

"Pity! He should be away from Monkland, with that—anonymous woman living there."

"Ah! yes; you've heard of her!"

Lady Casterley replied sharply:

"You're too easy-going, Geoffrey."

Lord Valleys smiled.

"These war scares," he said, "are getting a bore. Can't quite make out what the feeling of the country is about them."

Lady Casterley rose:

"It has none. When war comes, the feeling will be all right. It always is. Give me your arm. Are you hungry?"...

When Lord Valleys spoke of war, he spoke as one who, since he arrived at years of discretion, had lived within the circle of those who direct the destinies of States. It was for him—as for the lilies in the great glass house—impossible to see with the eyes, or feel with the feelings of a flower of the garden outside. Soaked in the best prejudices and manners of his class, he lived a life no more shut off from the general than was to be expected. Indeed, in some sort, as a man of facts and common sense, he was fairly in touch with the opinion of the average citizen. He was quite genuine when he said that he believed he knew what the people wanted better than those who prated on the subject; and no doubt he was right, for temperamentally he was nearer to them than their own leaders, though he would not perhaps have liked to be told so. His man-of-the-world, political shrewdness had been superimposed by life on a nature whose prime strength was its practicality and lack of imagination. It was his business to be efficient, but not strenuous, or desirous of pushing ideas to their logical conclusions; to be neither narrow nor puritanical, so long as the shell of 'good form' was preserved intact; to be a liberal landlord up to the point of not seriously damaging his interests; to be well-disposed towards the arts until those arts revealed that which he had not before perceived; it was his business to have light hands, steady eyes, iron nerves, and those excellent manners that have no mannerisms. It was his nature to be easy-going as a husband; indulgent as a father; careful and straightforward as a politician; and as a man, addicted to pleasure, to work, and to fresh air. He admired, and was fond of his wife, and had never regretted his marriage. He had never perhaps regretted anything, unless it were that he had not yet won the Derby, or quite succeeded in getting his special strain of blue-ticked pointers to breed absolutely true to type. His mother-in-law he respected, as one might respect a principle.

There was indeed in the personality of that little old lady the tremendous force of accumulated decision—the inherited assurance of one whose prestige had never been questioned; who, from long immunity, and a certain clear-cut matter-of-factness, bred by the habit of command, had indeed lost the power of perceiving that her prestige ever could be questioned. Her knowledge of her own mind was no ordinary piece of learning, had not, in fact, been learned at all, but sprang full-fledged from an active dominating temperament. Fortified by the necessity, common to her class, of knowing thoroughly the more patent side of public affairs; armoured by the tradition of a culture demanded by leadership; inspired by ideas, but always the same ideas; owning no master, but in servitude to her own custom of leading, she had a mind, formidable as the two-edged swords wielded by her ancestors the Fitz-Harolds, at Agincourt or Poitiers—a mind which had ever instinctively rejected that inner knowledge of herself or of the selves of others; produced by those foolish practices of introspection, contemplation, and understanding, so deleterious to authority. If Lord Valleys was the body of the aristocratic machine, Lady Casterley was the steel spring inside it. All her life studiously unaffected and simple in attire; of plain and frugal habit; an early riser; working at something or other from morning till night, and as little worn-out at seventy-eight as most women of fifty, she had only one weak spot—and that was her strength—blindness as to the nature and size of her place in the scheme of things. She was a type, a force.

Wonderfully well she went with the room in which they were dining, whose grey walls, surmounted by a deep frieze painted somewhat in the style of Fragonard, contained many nymphs and roses now rather dim; with the furniture, too, which had a look of having survived into times not its own. On the tables were no flowers, save five lilies in an old silver chalice; and on the wall over the great sideboard a portrait of the late Lord Casterley.

She spoke:

"I hope Miltoun is taking his own line?"

"That's the trouble. He suffers from swollen principles—only wish he could keep them out of his speeches."

"Let him be; and get him away from that woman as soon as his election's over. What is her real name?"

"Mrs. something Lees Noel."

"How long has she been there?"

"About a year, I think."

"And you don't know anything about her?"

Lord Valleys raised his shoulders.

"Ah!" said Lady Casterley; "exactly! You're letting the thing drift. I shall go down myself. I suppose Gertrude can have me? What has that Mr. Courtier to do with this good lady?"

Lord Valleys smiled. In this smile was the whole of his polite and easy-going philosophy. "I am no meddler," it seemed to say; and at sight of that smile Lady Casterley tightened her lips.

"He is a firebrand," she said. "I read that book of his against War—most inflammatory. Aimed at Grant-and Rosenstern, chiefly. I've just seen, one of the results, outside my own gates. A mob of anti-War agitators."

Lord Valleys controlled a yawn.

"Really? I'd no idea Courtier had any influence."

"He is dangerous. Most idealists are negligible-his book was clever."

"I wish to goodness we could see the last of these scares, they only make both countries look foolish," muttered Lord Valleys.

Lady Casterley raised her glass, full of a bloody red wine. "The war would save us," she said.

"War is no joke."

"It would be the beginning of a better state of things."

"You think so?"

"We should get the lead again as a nation, and Democracy would be put back fifty years."

Lord Valleys made three little heaps of salt, and paused to count them; then, with a slight uplifting of his eyebrows, which seemed to doubt what he was going to say, he murmured: "I should have said that we were all democrats nowadays.... What is it, Clifton?"

"Your chauffeur would like to know, what time you will have the car?"

"Directly after dinner."

Twenty minutes later, he was turning through the scrolled iron gates into the road for London. It was falling dark; and in the tremulous sky clouds were piled up, and drifted here and there with a sort of endless lack of purpose. No direction seemed to have been decreed unto their wings. They had met together in the firmament like a flock of giant magpies crossing and re-crossing each others' flight. The smell of rain was in the air. The car raised no dust, but bored swiftly on, searching out the road with its lamps. On Putney Bridge its march was stayed by a string of waggons. Lord Valleys looked to right and left. The river reflected the thousand lights of buildings piled along her sides, lamps of the embankments, lanterns of moored barges. The sinuous pallid body of this great Creature, for ever gliding down to the sea, roused in his mind no symbolic image. He had had to do with her, years back, at the Board of Trade, and knew her for what she was, extremely dirty, and getting abominably thin just where he would have liked her plump. Yet, as he lighted a cigar, there came to him a queer feeling—as if he were in the presence of a woman he was fond of.

"I hope to God," he thought, "nothing'll come of these scares!" The car glided on into the long road, swarming with traffic, towards the fashionable heart of London. Outside stationers' shops, however, the posters of evening papers were of no reassuring order.

      'THE PLOT THICKENS.'
      'MORE REVELATIONS.'
      'GRAVE SITUATION THREATENED.'

And before each poster could be seen a little eddy in the stream of the passers-by—formed by persons glancing at the news, and disengaging themselves, to press on again. The Earl of Valleys caught himself wondering what they thought of it! What was passing behind those pale rounds of flesh turned towards the posters?

Did they think at all, these men and women in the street? What was their attitude towards this vaguely threatened cataclysm? Face after face, stolid and apathetic, expressed nothing, no active desire, certainly no enthusiasm, hardly any dread. Poor devils! The thing, after all, was no more within their control than it was within the power of ants to stop the ruination of their ant-heap by some passing boy! It was no doubt quite true, that the people had never had much voice in the making of war. And the words of a Radical weekly, which as an impartial man he always forced himself to read, recurred to him. "Ignorant of the facts, hypnotized by the words 'Country' and 'Patriotism'; in the grip of mob-instinct and inborn prejudice against the foreigner; helpless by reason of his patience, stoicism, good faith, and confidence in those above him; helpless by reason of his snobbery, mutual distrust, carelessness for the morrow, and lack of public spirit-in the face of War how impotent and to be pitied is the man in the street!" That paper, though clever, always seemed to him intolerably hifalutin'!

It was doubtful whether he would get to Ascot this year. And his mind flew for a moment to his promising two-year-old Casetta; then dashed almost violently, as though in shame, to the Admiralty and the doubt whether they were fully alive to possibilities. He himself occupied a softer spot of Government, one of those almost nominal offices necessary to qualify into the Cabinet certain tried minds, for whom no more strenuous post can for the moment be found. From the Admiralty again his thoughts leaped to his mother-in-law. Wonderful old woman! What a statesman she would have made! Too reactionary! Deuce of a straight line she had taken about Mrs. Lees Noel! And with a connoisseur's twinge of pleasure he recollected that lady's face and figure seen that morning as he passed her cottage. Mysterious or not, the woman was certainly attractive! Very graceful head with its dark hair waved back from the middle over either temple—very charming figure, no lumber of any sort! Bouquet about her! Some story or other, no doubt—no affair of his! Always sorry for that sort of woman!

A regiment of Territorials returning from a march stayed the progress of his car. He leaned forward watching them with much the same contained, shrewd, critical look he would have bent on a pack of hounds. All the mistiness and speculation in his mind was gone now. Good stamp of man, would give a capital account of themselves! Their faces, flushed by a day in the open, were masked with passivity, or, with a half-aggressive, half-jocular self-consciousness; they were clearly not troubled by abstract doubts, or any visions of the horrors of war.

Someone raised a cheer 'for the Terriers!' Lord Valleys saw round him a little sea of hats, rising and falling, and heard a sound, rather shrill and tentative, swell into hoarse, high clamour, and suddenly die out. "Seem keen enough!" he thought. "Very little does it! Plenty of fighting spirit in the country." And again a thrill of pleasure shot through him.

Then, as the last soldier passed, his car slowly forged its way through the straggling crowd, pressing on behind the regiment—men of all ages, youths, a few women, young girls, who turned their eyes on him with a negligent stare as if their lives were too remote to permit them to take interest in this passing man at ease.

Chapter IV

At Monkland, that same hour, in the little whitewashed 'withdrawing-room' of a thatched, whitewashed cottage, two men sat talking, one on either side of the hearth; and in a low chair between them a dark-eyed woman leaned back, watching, the tips of her delicate thin fingers pressed together, or held out transparent towards the fire. A log, dropping now and then, turned up its glowing underside; and the firelight and the lamplight seemed so to have soaked into the white walls that a wan warmth exuded. Silvery dun moths, fluttering in from the dark garden, kept vibrating, like spun shillings, over a jade-green bowl of crimson roses; and there was a scent, as ever in that old thatched cottage, of woodsmoke, flowers, and sweetbriar.

The man on the left was perhaps forty, rather above middle height, vigorous, active, straight, with blue eyes and a sanguine face that glowed on small provocation. His hair was very bright, almost red, and his fiery moustaches which descended to the level of his chin, like Don Quixote's seemed bristling and charging.

The man on the right was nearer thirty, evidently tall, wiry, and very thin. He sat rather crumpled, in his low armchair, with hands clasped round a knee; and a little crucified smile haunted the lips of his lean face, which, with its parchmenty, tanned, shaven cheeks, and deep-set, very living eyes, had a certain beauty.

These two men, so extravagantly unlike, looked at each other like neighbouring dogs, who, having long decided that they are better apart, suddenly find that they have met at some spot where they cannot possibly have a fight. And the woman watched; the owner, as it were, of one, but who, from sheer love of dogs, had always stroked and patted the other.

"So, Mr. Courtier," said the younger man, whose dry, ironic voice, like his smile, seemed defending the fervid spirit in his eyes; "all you say only amounts, you see, to a defence of the so-called Liberal spirit; and, forgive my candour, that spirit, being an importation from the realms of philosophy and art, withers the moment it touches practical affairs."

The man with the red moustaches laughed; the sound was queer—at once so genial and so sardonic.

"Well put!" he said: "And far be it from me to gainsay. But since compromise is the very essence of politics, high-priests of caste and authority, like you, Lord Miltoun, are every bit as much out of it as any Liberal professor."

"I don't agree!"

"Agree or not, your position towards public affairs is very like the Church's attitude towards marriage and divorce; as remote from the realities of life as the attitude of the believer in Free Love, and not more likely to catch on. The death of your point of view lies in itself—it's too dried-up and far from things ever to understand them. If you don't understand you can never rule. You might just as well keep your hands in your pockets, as go into politics with your notions!"

"I fear we must continue to agree to differ."

"Well; perhaps I do pay you too high a compliment. After all, you are a patrician."

"You speak in riddles, Mr. Courtier."

The dark-eyed woman stirred; her hands gave a sort of flutter, as though in deprecation of acerbity.

Rising at once, and speaking in a deferential voice, the elder man said:

"We're tiring Mrs. Noel. Good-night, Audrey, It's high time I was off." Against the darkness of the open French window, he turned round to fire a parting shot.

"What I meant, Lord Miltoun, was that your class is the driest and most practical in the State—it's odd if it doesn't save you from a poet's dreams. Good-night!" He passed out on to the lawn, and vanished.

The young man sat unmoving; the glow of the fire had caught his face, so that a spirit seemed clinging round his lips, gleaming out of his eyes. Suddenly he said:

"Do you believe that, Mrs. Noel?"

For answer Audrey Noel smiled, then rose and went over to the window.

"Look at my dear toad! It comes here every evening!" On a flagstone of the verandah, in the centre of the stream of lamplight, sat a little golden toad. As Miltoun came to look, it waddled to one side, and vanished.

"How peaceful your garden is!" he said; then taking her hand, he very gently raised it to his lips, and followed his opponent out into the darkness.

Truly peace brooded over that garden. The Night seemed listening—all lights out, all hearts at rest. It watched, with a little white star for every tree, and roof, and slumbering tired flower, as a mother watches her sleeping child, leaning above him and counting with her love every hair of his head, and all his tiny tremors.

Argument seemed child's babble indeed under the smile of Night. And the face of the woman, left alone at her window, was a little like the face of this warm, sweet night. It was sensitive, harmonious; and its harmony was not, as in some faces, cold—but seemed to tremble and glow and flutter, as though it were a spirit which had found its place of resting.

In her garden,—all velvety grey, with black shadows beneath the yew-trees, the white flowers alone seemed to be awake, and to look at her wistfully. The trees stood dark and still. Not even the night birds stirred. Alone, the little stream down in the bottom raised its voice, privileged when day voices were hushed.

It was not in Audrey Noel to deny herself to any spirit that was abroad; to repel was an art she did not practise. But this night, though the Spirit of Peace hovered so near, she did not seem to know it. Her hands trembled, her cheeks were burning; her breast heaved, and sighs fluttered from her lips, just parted.

Chapter V

Eustace Cardoc, Viscount Miltoun, had lived a very lonely life, since he first began to understand the peculiarities of existence. With the exception of Clifton, his grandmother's 'majordomo,' he made, as a small child, no intimate friend. His nurses, governesses, tutors, by their own confession did not understand him, finding that he took himself with unnecessary seriousness; a little afraid, too, of one whom they discovered to be capable of pushing things to the point of enduring pain in silence. Much of that early time was passed at Ravensham, for he had always been Lady Casterley's favourite grandchild. She recognized in him the purposeful austerity which had somehow been omitted from the composition of her daughter. But only to Clifton, then a man of fifty with a great gravity and long black whiskers, did Eustace relieve his soul. "I tell you this, Clifton," he would say, sitting on the sideboard, or the arm of the big chair in Clifton's room, or wandering amongst the raspberries, "because you are my friend."

And Clifton, with his head a little on one side, and a sort of wise concern at his 'friend's' confidences, which were sometimes of an embarrassing description, would answer now and then: "Of course, my lord," but more often: "Of course, my dear."

There was in this friendship something fine and suitable, neither of these 'friends' taking or suffering liberties, and both being interested in pigeons, which they would stand watching with a remarkable attention.

In course of time, following the tradition of his family, Eustace went to Harrow. He was there five years—always one of those boys a little out at wrists and ankles, who may be seen slouching, solitary, along the pavement to their own haunts, rather dusty, and with one shoulder slightly raised above the other, from the habit of carrying something beneath one arm. Saved from being thought a 'smug,' by his title, his lack of any conspicuous scholastic ability, his obvious independence of what was thought of him, and a sarcastic tongue, which no one was eager to encounter, he remained the ugly duckling who refused to paddle properly in the green ponds of Public School tradition. He played games so badly that in sheer self-defence his fellows permitted him to play without them. Of 'fives' they made an exception, for in this he attained much proficiency, owing to a certain windmill-like quality of limb. He was noted too for daring chemical experiments, of which he usually had one or two brewing, surreptitiously at first, and afterwards by special permission of his house-master, on the principle that if a room must smell, it had better smell openly. He made few friendships, but these were lasting.

His Latin was so poor, and his Greek verse so vile, that all had been surprised when towards the finish of his career he showed a very considerable power of writing and speaking his own language. He left school without a pang. But when in the train he saw the old Hill and the old spire on the top of it fading away from him, a lump rose in his throat, he swallowed violently two or three times, and, thrusting himself far back into the carriage corner, appeared to sleep.

At Oxford, he was happier, but still comparatively lonely; remaining, so long as custom permitted, in lodgings outside his College, and clinging thereafter to remote, panelled rooms high up, overlooking the gardens and a portion of the city wall. It was at Oxford that he first developed that passion for self-discipline which afterwards distinguished him. He took up rowing; and, though thoroughly unsuited by nature to this pastime, secured himself a place in his College 'torpid.' At the end of a race he was usually supported from his stretcher in a state of extreme extenuation, due to having pulled the last quarter of the course entirely with his spirit. The same craving for self-discipline guided him in the choice of Schools; he went out in 'Greats,' for which, owing to his indifferent mastery of Greek and Latin, he was the least fitted. With enormous labour he took a very good degree. He carried off besides, the highest distinctions of the University for English Essays. The ordinary circles of College life knew nothing of him. Not once in the whole course of his University career, was he the better for wine. He, did not hunt; he never talked of women, and none talked of women in his presence. But now and then he was visited by those gusts which come to the ascetic, when all life seemed suddenly caught up and devoured by a flame burning night and day, and going out mercifully, he knew not why, like a blown candle. However unsocial in the proper sense of the word, he by no means lacked company in these Oxford days. He knew many, both dons and undergraduates. His long stride, and determined absence of direction, had severely tried all those who could stomach so slow a pastime as walking for the sake of talking. The country knew him—though he never knew the country—from Abingdon to Bablock Hythe. His name stood high, too, at the Union, where he made his mark during his first term in a debate on a 'Censorship of Literature' which he advocated with gloom, pertinacity, and a certain youthful brilliance that might well have carried the day, had not an Irishman got up and pointed out the danger hanging over the Old

Testament. To that he had retorted: "Better, sir, it should run a risk than have no risk to run." From which moment he was notable.

He stayed up four years, and went down with a sense of bewilderment and loss. The matured verdict of Oxford on this child of hers, was "Eustace Miltoun! Ah! Queer bird! Will make his mark!"

He had about this time an interview with his father which confirmed the impression each had formed of the other. It took place in the library at Monkland Court, on a late November afternoon.

The light of eight candles in thin silver candlesticks, four on either side of the carved stone hearth, illumined that room. Their gentle radiance penetrated but a little way into the great dark space lined with books, panelled and floored with black oak, where the acrid fragrance of leather and dried roseleaves seemed to drench the very soul with the aroma of the past. Above the huge fireplace, with light falling on one side of his shaven face, hung a portrait—painter unknown—of that Cardinal Caradoc who suffered for his faith in the sixteenth century. Ascetic, crucified, with a little smile clinging to the lips and deep-set eyes, he presided, above the bluefish flames of a log fire.

Father and son found some difficulty in beginning.

Each of those two felt as though he were in the presence of someone else's very near relation. They had, in fact, seen extremely little of each other, and not seen that little long.

Lord Valleys uttered the first remark:

"Well, my dear fellow, what are you going to do now? I think we can make certain of this seat down here, if you like to stand."

Miltoun had answered: "Thanks, very much; I don't think so at present."

Through the thin fume of his cigar Lord Valleys watched that long figure sunk deep in the chair opposite.

"Why not?" he said. "You can't begin too soon; unless you think you ought to go round the world."

"Before I can become a man of it?"

Lord Valleys gave a rather disconcerted laugh.

"There's nothing in politics you can't pick up as you go along," he said. "How old are you?"

"Twenty-four."

"You look older." A faint line, as of contemplation, rose between his eyes. Was it fancy that a little smile was hovering about Miltoun's lips?

"I've got a foolish theory," came from those lips, "that one must know the conditions first. I want to give at least five years to that."

Lord Valleys raised his eyebrows. "Waste of time," he said. "You'd know more at the end of it, if you went into the House at once. You take the matter too seriously."

"No doubt."

For fully a minute Lord Valleys made no answer; he felt almost ruffled. Waiting till the sensation had passed, he said: "Well, my dear fellow, as you please."

Miltoun's apprenticeship to the profession of politics was served in a slum settlement; on his father's estates; in Chambers at the Temple; in expeditions to Germany, America, and the British Colonies; in work at elections; and in two forlorn hopes to capture a constituency which could be trusted not to change its principles. He read much, slowly, but with conscientious tenacity, poetry, history, and works on philosophy, religion, and social matters.

Fiction, and especially foreign fiction, he did not care for. With the utmost desire to be wide and impartial, he sucked in what ministered to the wants of his nature, rejecting unconsciously all that by its unsuitability endangered the flame of his private spirit. What he read, in fact, served only to strengthen those profounder convictions which arose from his temperament. With a contempt of the vulgar gewgaws of wealth and rank he combined a humble but intense and growing conviction of his capacity for leadership, of a spiritual superiority to those whom he desired to benefit. There was no trace, indeed, of the common Pharisee in Miltoun, he was simple and direct; but his eyes, his gestures, the whole man, proclaimed the presence of some secret spring of certainty, some fundamental well into which no disturbing glimmers penetrated. He was not devoid of wit, but he was devoid of that kind of wit which turns its eyes inward, and sees something of the fun that lies in being what you are. Miltoun saw the world and all the things thereof shaped like spires—even when they were circles. He seemed to have no sense that the Universe was equally compounded of those two symbols, whose point of reconciliation had not yet been discovered.

Such was he, then, when the Member for his native division was made a peer.

He had reached the age of thirty without ever having been in love, leading a life of almost savage purity, with one solitary breakdown. Women were afraid of him. And he was perhaps a little afraid of woman. She was in theory too lovely and desirable—the half-moon in a summer sky; in practice too cloying, or too harsh. He had an affection for Barbara, his younger sister; but to his mother, his grandmother, or his elder sister Agatha, he had never felt close. It was indeed amusing to see Lady Valleys with her first-born. Her fine figure, the blown roses of her face, her grey-blue eyes which had a slight tendency to roll, as though amusement just touched with naughtiness bubbled behind them; were reduced to a queer, satirical decorum in Miltoun's presence. Thoughts and sayings verging on the risky were characteristic of her robust physique, of her soul which could afford to express almost all that occurred to it. Miltoun had never, not even as a child, given her his confidence. She bore him no resentment, being of that large, generous build in body and mind, rarely—never in her class—associated with the capacity for feeling aggrieved or lowered in any estimation, even its own. He was, and always had been, an odd boy, and there was an end of it! Nothing had perhaps so disconcerted Lady Valleys as his want of behaviour in regard to women. She felt it abnormal, just as she recognized the essential if duly veiled normality of her husband and younger son. It was this feeling which made her realize almost more vividly than she had time for, in the whirl of politics and fashion, the danger of his friendship with this lady to whom she alluded so discreetly as 'Anonyma.'

Pure chance had been responsible for the inception of that friendship. Going one December afternoon to the farmhouse of a tenant, just killed by a fall from his horse, Miltoun had found the widow in a state of bewildered grief, thinly cloaked in the manner of one who had almost lost the power to express her feelings, and quite lost it in presence of 'the gentry.' Having assured the poor soul that she need have no fear about her tenancy, he was just leaving, when he met, in the stone-flagged entrance, a lady in a fur cap and jacket, carrying in her arms a little crying boy, bleeding from a cut on the forehead. Taking him from her and placing him on a table in the parlour, Miltoun looked at this lady, and saw that she was extremely grave, and soft, and charming. He inquired of her whether the mother should be told.

She shook her head.

"Poor thing, not just now: let's wash it, and bind it up first."

Together therefore they washed and bound up the cut. Having finished, she looked at Miltoun, and seemed to say: "You would do the telling so much better than I."

He, therefore, told the mother and was rewarded by a little smile from the grave lady.

From that meeting he took away the knowledge of her name, Audrey Lees Noel, and the remembrance of a face, whose beauty, under a cap of squirrel's fur, pursued him. Some days later passing by the village green, he saw her entering a garden gate. On this occasion he had asked her whether she would like her cottage re-thatched; an inspection of the roof had followed; he had stayed talking a long time. Accustomed to women—over the best of whom, for all their grace and lack of affectation, high-caste life had wrapped the manner which seems to take all things for granted—there was a peculiar charm for Miltoun in this soft, dark-eyed lady who evidently lived quite out of the world, and had so poignant, and shy, a flavour. Thus from a chance seed had blossomed swiftly one of those rare friendships between lonely people, which can in short time fill great spaces of two lives.

One day she asked him: "You know about me, I suppose?" Miltoun made a motion of his head, signifying that he did. His informant had been the vicar.

"Yes, I am told, her story is a sad one—a divorce."

"Do you mean that she has been divorced, or—"

For the fraction of a second the vicar perhaps had hesitated.

"Oh! no—no. Sinned against, I am sure. A nice woman, so far as I have seen; though I'm afraid not one of my congregation."

With this, Miltoun, in whom chivalry had already been awakened, was content. When she asked if he knew her story, he would not for the world have had her rake up what was painful. Whatever that story, she could not have been to blame. She had begun already to be shaped by his own spirit; had become not a human being as it was, but an expression of his aspiration....

On the third evening after his passage of arms with Courtier, he was again at her little white cottage sheltering within its high garden walls. Smothered in roses, and with a black-brown thatch overhanging the old-fashioned leaded panes of the upper windows, it had an air of hiding from the world. Behind, as though on guard, two pine trees spread their dark boughs over the outhouses, and in any south-west wind could be heard speaking gravely about the weather. Tall lilac bushes flanked the garden, and a huge lime-tree in the adjoining field sighed and rustled, or on still days let forth the drowsy hum of countless small dusky bees who frequented that green hostelry.

He found her altering a dress, sitting over it in her peculiar delicate fashion—as if all objects whatsoever, dresses, flowers, books, music, required from her the same sympathy.

He had come from a long day's electioneering, had been heckled at two meetings, and was still sore from the experience. To watch her, to be soothed, and ministered to by her had never been so restful; and stretched out in a long chair he listened to her playing.

Over the hill a Pierrot moon was slowly moving up in a sky the colour of grey irises. And in a sort of trance Miltoun stared at the burnt-out star, travelling in bright pallor.

Across the moor a sea of shallow mist was rolling; and the trees in the valley, like browsing cattle, stood knee-deep in whiteness, with all the air above them wan from an innumerable rain as of moondust, falling into that white sea. Then the moon passed behind the lime-tree, so that a great lighted Chinese lantern seemed to hang blue-black from the sky.

Suddenly, jarring and shivering the music, came a sound of hooting. It swelled, died away, and swelled again.

Miltoun rose.

"That has spoiled my vision," he said. "Mrs. Noel, I have something I want to say." But looking down at her, sitting so still, with her hands resting on the keys, he was silent in sheer adoration.

A voice from the door ejaculated:

"Oh! ma'am—oh! my lord! They're devilling a gentleman on the green!"

Chapter VI

When the immortal Don set out to ring all the bells of merriment, he was followed by one clown. Charles Courtier on the other hand had always been accompanied by thousands, who really could not understand the conduct of this man with no commercial sense. But though he puzzled his contemporaries, they did not exactly laugh at him, because it was reported that he had really killed some men, and loved some women. They found such a combination irresistible, when coupled with an appearance both vigorous and gallant. The son of an Oxfordshire clergyman, and mounted on a lost cause, he had been riding through the world ever since he was eighteen, without once getting out of the saddle. The secret of this endurance lay perhaps in his unconsciousness that he was in the saddle at all. It was as much his natural seat as office stools to other mortals. He made no capital out of errantry, his temperament being far too like his red-gold hair, which people compared to flames, consuming all before them. His vices were patent; too incurable an optimism; an admiration for beauty such as must sometimes have caused him to forget which woman he was most in love with; too thin a skin; too hot a heart; hatred of humbug, and habitual neglect of his own interest. Unmarried, and with many friends, and many enemies, he kept his body like a sword-blade, and his soul always at white heat.

That one who admitted to having taken part in five wars should be mixing in a by-election in the cause of Peace, was not so inconsistent as might be supposed; for he had always fought on the losing side, and there seemed to him at the moment no side so losing as that of Peace. No great politician, he was not an orator, nor even a glib talker; yet a quiet mordancy of tongue, and the white-hot look in his eyes, never failed to make an impression of some kind on an audience.

There was, however, hardly a corner of England where orations on behalf of Peace had a poorer chance than the Bucklandbury division. To say that Courtier had made himself unpopular with its matter-of-fact, independent, stolid, yet quick-tempered population, would be inadequate. He had outraged their beliefs, and roused the most profound suspicions. They could not, for the life of them, make out what he was at. Though by his adventures and his book, "Peace-a lost Cause," he was, in London, a conspicuous figure, they had naturally never heard of him; and his adventure to these parts seemed to them an almost ludicrous example of pure idea poking its nose into plain facts—the idea that nations ought to, and could live in peace being so very pure; and the fact that they never had, so very plain!

At Monkland, which was all Court estate, there were naturally but few supporters of Miltoun's opponent, Mr. Humphrey Chilcox, and the reception accorded to the champion of Peace soon passed from curiosity to derision, from derision to menace, till Courtier's attitude became so defiant, and his sentences so heated that he was only saved from a rough handling by the influential interposition of the vicar.

Yet when he began to address them he had felt irresistibly attracted. They looked such capital, independent fellows. Waiting for his turn to speak, he had marked them down as men after his own heart. For though Courtier knew that against an unpopular idea there must always be a majority, he never thought so ill of any individual as to suppose him capable of belonging to that ill-omened body.

Surely these fine, independent fellows were not to be hoodwinked by the jingoes! It had been one more disillusion. He had not taken it lying down; neither had his audience. They dispersed without forgiving; they came together again without having forgotten.

The village Inn, a little white building whose small windows were overgrown with creepers, had a single guest's bedroom on the upper floor, and a little sitting-room where Courtier took his meals. The rest of the house was but stone-floored bar with a long wooden bench against the back wall, whence nightly a stream of talk would issue, all harsh a's, and sudden soft u's; whence too a figure, a little unsteady, would now and again emerge, to a chorus of 'Gude naights,' stand still under the ash-trees to light his pipe, then move slowly home.

But on that evening, when the trees, like cattle, stood knee-deep in the moon-dust, those who came out from the bar-room did not go away; they hung about in the shadows, and were joined by other figures creeping furtively through the bright moonlight, from behind the Inn. Presently more figures moved up from the lanes and the churchyard path, till thirty or more were huddled there, and their stealthy murmur of talk distilled a rare savour of illicit joy. Unholy hilarity, indeed, seemed lurking in the deep tree-shadow, before the wan Inn, whence from a single lighted window came forth the half-chanting sound of a man's voice reading out loud. Laughter was smothered, talk whispered.

"He'm a-practisin' his spaches." "Smoke the cunnin' old vox out!" "Red pepper's the proper stuff." "See men sneeze! We've a-screed up the door."

Then, as a face showed at the lighted window, a burst of harsh laughter broke the hush.

He at the window was seen struggling violently to wrench away a bar. The laughter swelled to hooting. The prisoner forced his way through, dropped to the ground, rose, staggered, and fell.

A voice said sharply:

"What's this?"

Out of the sounds of scuffling and scattering came the whisper: "His lordship!" And the shade under the ash-trees became deserted, save by the tall dark figure of a man, and a woman's white shape.

"Is that you, Mr. Courtier? Are you hurt?"

A chuckle rose from the recumbent figure.

"Only my knee. The beggars! They precious nearly choked me, though."

Chapter VII

Bertie Caradoc, leaving the smoking-room at Monkland Court that same evening,—on his way to bed, went to the Georgian corridor, where his pet barometer was hanging. To look at the glass had become the nightly habit of one who gave all the time he could spare from his profession to hunting in the winter and to racing in the summer.'

The Hon. Hubert Caradoc, an apprentice to the calling of diplomacy, more completely than any living Caradoc embodied the characteristic strength and weaknesses of that family. He was of fair height, and wiry build. His weathered face, under sleek, dark hair, had regular, rather small features, and wore an expression of alert resolution, masked by impassivity. Over his inquiring, hazel-grey eyes the lids were almost religiously kept half drawn. He had been born reticent, and great, indeed, was the emotion under which he suffered when the whole of his eyes were visible. His nose was finely chiselled, and had little flesh. His lips, covered by a small, dark moustache, scarcely opened to emit his speeches, which were uttered in a voice singularly muffled, yet unexpectedly quick. The whole personality was that of a man practical, spirited, guarded, resourceful, with great power of self-control, who looked at life as if she were a horse under him, to whom he must give way just so far as was necessary to keep mastery of her. A man to whom ideas were of no value, except when wedded to immediate action; essentially neat; demanding to be 'done well,' but capable of stoicism if necessary; urbane, yet always in readiness to thrust; able only to condone the failings and to compassionate the kinds of distress which his own experience had taught him to understand. Such was Miltoun's younger brother at the age of twenty-six.

Having noted that the glass was steady, he was about to seek the stairway, when he saw at the farther end of the entrance-hall three figures advancing arm-in-arm. Habitually both curious and wary, he waited till they came within the radius of a lamp; then, seeing them to be those of Miltoun and a footman, supporting between them a lame man, he at once hastened forward.

"Have you put your knee out, sir? Hold on a minute! Get a chair, Charles."

Seating the stranger in this chair, Bertie rolled up the trouser, and passed his fingers round the knee. There was a sort, of loving-kindness in that movement, as of a hand which had in its time felt the joints and sinews of innumerable horses.

"H'm!" he said; "can you stand a bit of a jerk? Catch hold of him behind, Eustace. Sit down on the floor, Charles, and hold the legs of the chair. Now then!" And taking up the foot, he pulled. There was a click, a little noise of teeth ground together; and Bertie said: "Good man—shan't have to have the vet. to you, this time."

Having conducted their lame guest to a room in the Georgian corridor hastily converted to a bedroom, the two brothers presently left him to the attentions of the footman.

"Well, old man," said Bertie, as they sought their rooms; "that's put paid to his name—won't do you any more harm this journey. Good plucked one, though!"

The report that Courtier was harboured beneath their roof went the round of the family before breakfast, through the agency of one whose practice it was to know all things, and to see that others partook of that knowledge, Little Ann, paying her customary morning visit to her mother's room, took her stand with face turned up and hands clasping her belt, and began at once.

"Uncle Eustace brought a man last night with a wounded leg, and Uncle Bertie pulled it out straight. William says that Charles says he only made a noise like this"—there was a faint sound of small chumping teeth: "And he's the man that's staying at the Inn, and the stairs were too narrow to carry him up, William says; and if his knee was put out he won't be able to walk without a stick for a long time. Can I go to Father?"

Agatha, who was having her hair brushed, thought:

"I'm not sure whether belts so low as that are wholesome," murmured:

"Wait a minute!"

But little Ann was gone; and her voice could be heard in the dressing-room climbing up towards Sir William, who from the sound of his replies, was manifestly shaving. When Agatha, who never could resist a legitimate opportunity of approaching her husband, looked in, he was alone, and rather thoughtful—a tall man with a solid, steady face and cautious eyes, not in truth remarkable except to his own wife.

"That fellow Courtier's caught by the leg," he said. "Don't know what your Mother will say to an enemy in the camp."

"Isn't he a freethinker, and rather—"

Sir William, following his own thoughts, interrupted:

"Just as well, of course, so far as Miltoun's concerned, to have got him here."

Agatha sighed: "Well, I suppose we shall have to be nice to him. I'll tell Mother."

Sir William smiled.

"Ann will see to that," he said.

Ann was seeing to that.

Seated in the embrasure of the window behind the looking-glass, where Lady Valleys was still occupied, she was saying:

"He fell out of the window because of the red pepper. Miss Wallace says he is a hostage—what does hostage mean, Granny?"

When six years ago that word had first fallen on Lady Valleys' ears, she had thought: "Oh! dear! Am I really Granny?" It had been a shock, had seemed the end of so much; but the matter-of-fact heroism of women, so much quicker to accept the inevitable than men, had soon come to her aid, and now, unlike her husband, she did not care a bit. For all that she answered nothing, partly because it was not necessary to speak in order to sustain a conversation with little Ann, and partly because she was deep in thought.

The man was injured! Hospitality, of course—especially since their own tenants had committed the outrage! Still, to welcome a man who had gone out of his way to come down here and stump the country against her own son, was rather a tall order. It might have been worse, no doubt. If; for instance, he had been some 'impossible' Nonconformist Radical! This Mr. Courtier was a free lance—rather a well-known man, an interesting creature. She must see that he felt 'at home' and comfortable. If he were pumped judiciously, no doubt one could find out about this woman. Moreover, the acceptance of their 'salt' would silence him politically if she knew anything of that type of man, who always had something in him of the Arab's creed. Her mind, that of a capable administrator, took in all the practical significance of this incident, which, although untoward, was not without its comic side to one disposed to find zest and humour in everything that did not absolutely run counter to her interests and philosophy.

The voice of little Ann broke in on her reflections.

"I'm going to Auntie Babs now."

"Very well; give me a kiss first."

Little Ann thrust up her face, so that its sudden little nose penetrated Lady Valleys' soft curving lips....

When early that same afternoon Courtier, leaning on a stick, passed from his room out on to the terrace, he was confronted by three sunlit peacocks marching slowly across a lawn towards a statue of Diana. With incredible dignity those birds moved, as if never in their lives had they been hurried. They seemed indeed to know that when they got there, there would be nothing for them to do but to come back again. Beyond them, through the tall trees, over some wooded foot-hills of the moorland and a promised land of pinkish fields, pasture, and orchards, the prospect stretched to the far sea. Heat clothed this view with a kind of opalescence, a fairy garment, transmuting all values, so that the four square walls and tall chimneys of the pottery-works a few miles down the valley seemed to Courtier like a vision of some old fortified Italian town. His sensations, finding himself in this galley, were peculiar. For his feeling towards Miltoun, whom he had twice met at Mrs. Noel's, was, in spite of disagreements, by no means unfriendly; while his feeling towards Miltoun's family was not yet in existence. Having lived from hand to mouth, and in many countries, since he left Westminster School, he had now practically no class feelings. An attitude of hostility to aristocracy because it was aristocracy, was as incomprehensible to him as an attitude of deference.

His sensations habitually shaped themselves in accordance with those two permanent requirements of his nature, liking for adventure, and hatred of tyranny. The labourer who beat his wife, the shopman who sweated his 'hands,' the parson who consigned his parishioners to hell, the peer who rode roughshod—all were equally odious to him. He thought of people as individuals, and it was, as it were, by accident that he had conceived the class generalization which he had fired back at Miltoun from Mrs. Noel's window. Sanguine, accustomed to queer environments, and always catching at the moment as it flew, he had not to fight with the timidities and irritations of a nervous temperament. His cheery courtesy was only disturbed when he became conscious of some sentiment which appeared to him mean or cowardly. On such occasions, not perhaps infrequent, his face looked as if his heart were physically fuming, and since his shell of stoicism was never quite melted by this heat, a very peculiar expression was the result, a sort of calm, sardonic, desperate, jolly look.

His chief feeling, then, at the outrage which had laid him captive in the enemy's camp, was one of vague amusement, and curiosity. People round about spoke fairly well of this Caradoc family. There did not seem to be any lack of kindly feeling between them and their tenants; there was said to be no griping destitution, nor any particular ill-housing on their estate. And if the inhabitants were not encouraged to improve themselves, they were at all events maintained at a certain level, by steady and not ungenerous supervision. When a roof required thatching it was thatched; when a man became too old to work, he was not suffered to lapse into the Workhouse. In bad years for wool, or beasts, or crops, the farmers received a graduated remission of rent. The pottery-works were run on a liberal if autocratic basis. It was true that though Lord Valleys was said to be a staunch supporter of a 'back to the land' policy, no disposition was shown to encourage people to settle on these particular lands, no doubt from a feeling that such settlers would not do them so much justice as their present owner. Indeed so firmly did this conviction seemingly obtain, that Lord Valleys' agent was not unfrequently observed to be buying a little bit more.

But, since in this life one notices only what interests him, all this gossip, half complimentary, half not, had fallen but lightly on the ears of the champion of Peace during his campaign, for he was, as has, been said, but a poor politician, and rode his own horse very much his own way.

While he stood there enjoying the view, he heard a small high voice, and became conscious of a little girl in a very shady hat so far back on her brown hair that it did not shade her; and of a small hand put out in front. He took the hand, and answered:

"Thank you, I am well—and you?" perceiving the while that a pair of wide frank eyes were examining his leg.

"Does it hurt?"

"Not to speak of."

"My pony's leg was blistered. Granny is coming to look at it."

"I see."

"I have to go now. I hope you'll soon be better. Good-bye!"

Then, instead of the little girl, Courtier saw a tall and rather florid woman regarding him with a sort of quizzical dignity. She wore a stiffish fawn-coloured dress that seemed to be cut a little too tight round her substantial hips, for it quite neglected to embrace her knees. She had on no hat, no gloves, no ornaments, except the rings on her fingers, and a little jewelled watch in a leather bracelet on her wrist. There was, indeed, about her whole figure an air of almost professional escape from finery.

Stretching out a well-shaped but not small hand, she said:

"I most heartily apologize to you, Mr. Courtier."

"Not at all."

"I do hope you're comfortable. Have they given you everything you want?"

"More than everything."

"It really was disgraceful! However it's brought us the pleasure of making your acquaintance. I've read your book, of course."

To Courtier it seemed that on this lady's face had come a look which seemed to say: Yes, very clever and amusing, quite enjoyable! But the ideas—What? You know very well they won't do—in fact they mustn't do!

"That's very nice of you."

But into Lady Valleys' answer, "I don't agree with it a bit, you know!" there had crept a touch of asperity, as though she knew that he had smiled inside. "What we want preached in these days are the warlike virtues—especially by a warrior."

"Believe me, Lady Valleys, the warlike virtues are best left to men of more virgin imagination."

He received a quick look, and the words: "Anyway, I'm sure you don't care a rap for politics. You know Mrs. Lees Noel, don't you? What a pretty woman she is!"

But as she spoke Courtier saw a young girl coming along the terrace. She had evidently been riding, for she wore high boots and a skirt which had enabled her to sit astride. Her eyes were blue, and her hair—the colour of beech-leaves in autumn with the sun shining through—was coiled up tight under a small soft hat. She was tall, and moved towards them like one endowed with great length from the hip joint to the knee. Joy of life, serene, unconscious vigour, seemed to radiate from her whole face and figure.

At Lady Valleys' words:

"Ah, Babs! My daughter Barbara—Mr. Courtier," he put out his hand, received within it some gauntleted fingers held out with a smile, and heard her say:

"Miltoun's gone up to Town, Mother; I was going to motor in to Bucklandbury with a message he gave me; so I can fetch Granny out from the station:"

"You had better take Ann, or she'll make our lives a burden; and perhaps Mr. Courtier would like an airing. Is your knee fit, do you think?"

Glancing at the apparition, Courtier replied:

"It is."

Never since the age of seven had he been able to look on feminine beauty without a sense of warmth and faint excitement; and seeing now perhaps the most beautiful girl he had ever beheld, he desired to be with her wherever she might be going. There was too something very fascinating in the way she smiled, as if she had a little seen through his sentiments.

"Well then," she said, "we'd better look for Ann."

After short but vigorous search little Ann was found—in the car, instinct having told her of a forward movement in which it was her duty to take part. And soon they had started, Ann between them in that peculiar state of silence to which she became liable when really interested.

From the Monkland estate, flowered, lawned, and timbered, to the open moor, was like passing to another world; for no sooner was the last lodge of the Western drive left behind, than there came into sudden view the most pagan bit of landscape in all England. In this wild parliament-house, clouds, rocks, sun, and winds met and consulted. The 'old' men, too, had left their spirits among the great stones, which lay couched like lions on the hill-tops, under the white clouds, and their brethren, the hunting buzzard hawks. Here the very rocks were restless, changing form, and sense, and colour from day to day, as though worshipping the unexpected, and refusing themselves to law. The winds too in their passage revolted against their courses, and came tearing down wherever there were combes or crannies, so that men in their shelters might still learn the power of the wild gods.

The wonders of this prospect were entirely lost on little Ann, and somewhat so on Courtier, deeply engaged in reconciling those two alien principles, courtesy, and the love of looking at a pretty face. He was wondering too what this girl of twenty, who had the self-possession of a woman of forty, might be thinking. It was little Ann who broke the silence.

"Auntie Babs, it wasn't a very strong house, was it?"

Courtier looked in the direction of her small finger. There was the wreck of a little house, which stood close to a stone man who had obviously possessed that hill before there were men of flesh. Over one corner of the sorry ruin, a single patch of roof still clung, but the rest was open.

"He was a silly man to build it, wasn't he, Ann? That's why they call it Ashman's Folly."

"Is he alive?"

"Not quite—it's just a hundred years ago."

"What made him build it here?"

"He hated women, and—the roof fell in on him."

"Why did he hate women?"

"He was a crank."

"What is a crank?"

"Ask Mr. Courtier."

Under this girl's calm quizzical glance, Courtier endeavoured to find an answer to that question.

"A crank," he said slowly, "is a man like me."

He heard a little laugh, and became acutely conscious of Ann's dispassionate examining eyes.

"Is Uncle Eustace a crank?"

"You know now, Mr. Courtier, what Ann thinks of you. You think a good deal of Uncle Eustace, don't you, Ann?"

"Yes," said Ann, and fixed her eyes before her. But Courtier gazed sideways—over her hatless head.

His exhilaration was increasing every moment. This girl reminded him of a two-year-old filly he had once seen, stepping out of Ascot paddock for her first race, with the sun glistening on her satin chestnut skin, her neck held high, her eyes all fire—as sure to win, as that grass was green. It was difficult to believe her Miltoun's sister. It was difficult to believe any of those four young Caradocs related. The grave ascetic Miltoun, wrapped in the garment of his spirit; mild, domestic, strait-laced Agatha; Bertie, muffled, shrewd, and steely; and this frank, joyful conquering Barbara—the range was wide.

But the car had left the moor, and, down a steep hill, was passing the small villas and little grey workmen's houses outside the town of Bucklandbury.

"Ann and I have to go on to Miltoun's headquarters. Shall I drop you at the enemy's, Mr. Courtier? Stop, please, Frith."

And before Courtier could assent, they had pulled up at a house on which was inscribed with extraordinary vigour: "Chilcox for Bucklandbury."

Hobbling into the Committee-room of Mr. Humphrey Chilcox, which smelled of paint, Courtier took with him the scented memory of youth, and ambergris, and Harris tweed.

In that room three men were assembled round a table; the eldest of whom, endowed with little grey eyes, a stubbly beard, and that mysterious something only found in those who have been mayors, rose at once and came towards him.

"Mr. Courtier, I believe," he said bluffly. "Glad to see you, sir. Most distressed to hear of this outrage. Though in a way, it's done us good. Yes, really. Grossly against fair play. Shouldn't be surprised if it turned a couple of hundred votes. You carry the effects of it about with you, I see."

A thin, refined man, with wiry hair, also came up, holding a newspaper in his hand.

"It has had one rather embarrassing effect," he said. "Read this

"'OUTRAGE ON A DISTINGUISHED VISITOR.

"'LORD MILTOUN'S EVENING ADVENTURE.'"

Courtier read a paragraph.

The man with the little eyes broke the ominous silence which ensued.

"One of our side must have seen the whole thing, jumped on his bicycle and brought in the account before they went to press. They make no imputation on the lady—simply state the facts. Quite enough," he added with impersonal grimness; "I think he's done for himself, sir."

The man with the refined face added nervously:

"We couldn't help it, Mr. Courtier; I really don't know what we can do. I don't like it a bit."

"Has your candidate seen this?" Courtier asked.

"Can't have," struck in the third Committee-man; "we hadn't seen it ourselves until an hour ago."

"I should never have permitted it," said the man with the refined face; "I blame the editor greatly."

"Come to that—" said the little-eyed man, "it's a plain piece of news. If it makes a stir, that's not our fault. The paper imputes nothing, it states. Position of the lady happens to do the rest. Can't help it, and moreover, sir, speaking for self, don't want to. We'll have no loose morals in public life down here, please God!" There was real feeling in his words; then, catching sight of Courtier's face, he added: "Do you know this lady?"

"Ever since she was a child. Anyone who speaks evil of her, has to reckon with me."

The man with the refined face said earnestly:

"Believe me, Mr. Courtier, I entirely sympathize. We had nothing to do with the paragraph. It's one of those incidents where one benefits against one's will. Most unfortunate that she came out on to the green with Lord Miltoun; you know what people are."

"It's the head-line that does it;" said the third Committee-man; "they've put what will attract the public."

"I don't know, I don't know," said the little-eyed man stubbornly; "if Lord Miltoun will spend his evenings with lonely ladies, he can't blame anybody but himself."

Courtier looked from face to face.

"This closes my connection with the campaign," he said: "What's the address of this paper?" And without waiting for an answer, he took up the journal and hobbled from the room. He stood a minute outside finding the address, then made his way down the street.

Chapter VIII

By the side of little Ann, Barbara sat leaning back amongst the cushions of the car. In spite of being already launched into high-caste life which brings with it an early knowledge of the world, she had still some of the eagerness in her face which makes children lovable. Yet she looked negligently enough at the citizens of Bucklandbury, being already a little conscious of the strange mixture of sentiment peculiar to her countrymen in presence of herself—that curious expression on their faces resulting from the continual attempt to look down their noses while slanting their eyes upwards. Yes, she was already alive to that mysterious glance which had built the national house and insured it afterwards—foe to cynicism, pessimism, and anything French or Russian; parent of all the national virtues, and all the national vices; of idealism and muddle-headedness, of independence and servility; fosterer of conduct, murderer of speculation; looking up, and looking down, but never straight at anything; most high, most deep, most queer; and ever bubbling-up from the essential Well of Emulation.

Surrounded by that glance, waiting for Courtier, Barbara, not less British than her neighbours, was secretly slanting her own eyes up and down over the absent figure of her new acquaintance. She too wanted something she could look up to, and at the same time see damned first. And in this knight-errant it seemed to her that she had got it.

He was a creature from another world. She had met many men, but not as yet one quite of this sort. It was rather nice to be with a clever man, who had none the less done so many outdoor things, been through so many bodily adventures. The mere writers, or even the 'Bohemians,' whom she occasionally met, were after all only 'chaplains to the Court,' necessary to keep aristocracy in touch with the latest developments of literature and art. But this Mr. Courtier was a man of action; he could not be looked on with the amused, admiring toleration suited to men remarkable only for ideas, and the way they put them into paint or ink. He had used, and could use, the sword, even in the cause of Peace. He could love, had loved, or so they said: If Barbara had been a girl of twenty in another class, she would probably never have heard of this, and if she had heard, it might very well have dismayed or shocked her. But she had heard, and without shock, because she had already learned that men were like that, and women too sometimes.

It was with quite a little pang of concern that she saw him hobbling down the street towards her; and when he was once more seated, she told the chauffeur: "To the station, Frith. Quick, please!" and began:

"You are not to be trusted a bit. What were you doing?"

But Courtier smiled grimly over the head of Ann, in silence.

At this, almost the first time she had ever yet encountered a distinct rebuff, Barbara quivered, as though she had been touched lightly with a whip. Her lips closed firmly, her eyes began to dance. "Very well, my dear," she thought. But presently stealing a look at him, she became aware of such a queer expression on his face, that she forgot she was offended.

"Is anything wrong, Mr. Courtier?"

"Yes, Lady Barbara, something is very wrong—that miserable mean thing, the human tongue."

Barbara had an intuitive knowledge of how to handle things, a kind of moral sangfroid, drawn in from the faces she had watched, the talk she had heard, from her youth up. She trusted those intuitions, and letting her eyes conspire with his over Ann's brown hair, she said:

"Anything to do with Mrs. N—?" Seeing "Yes" in his eyes, she added quickly: "And M—?"

Courtier nodded.

"I thought that was coming. Let them babble! Who cares?"

She caught an approving glance, and the word, "Good!"

But the car had drawn up at Bucklandbury Station.

The little grey figure of Lady Casterley, coming out of the station doorway, showed but slight sign of her long travel. She stopped to take the car in, from chauffeur to Courtier.

"Well, Frith!—Mr. Courtier, is it? I know your book, and I don't approve of you; you're a dangerous man—How do you do? I must have those two bags. The cart can bring the rest.... Randle, get up in front, and don't get dusty. Ann!" But Ann was already beside the chauffeur, having long planned this improvement. "H'm! So you've hurt your leg, sir? Keep still! We can sit three.... Now, my dear, I can kiss you! You've grown!"

Lady Casterley's kiss, once received, was never forgotten; neither perhaps was Barbara's. Yet they were different. For, in the case of Lady Casterley, the old eyes, bright and investigating, could be seen deciding the exact spot for the lips to touch; then the face with its firm chin was darted forward; the lips paused a second, as though to make quite certain, then suddenly dug hard and dry into the middle of the cheek, quavered for the fraction of a second as if trying to remember to be soft, and were relaxed like the elastic of a catapult. And in the case of Barbara, first a sort of light came into her eyes, then her chin tilted a little, then her lips pouted a little, her body quivered, as if it were getting a size larger, her hair breathed, there was a small sweet sound; it was over.

Thus kissing her grandmother, Barbara resumed her seat, and looked at Courtier. 'Sitting three' as they were, he was touching her, and it seemed to her somehow that he did not mind.

The wind had risen, blowing from the West, and sunshine was flying on it. The call of the cuckoos—a little sharpened—followed the swift-travelling car. And that essential sweetness of the moor, born of the heather roots and the South-West wind, was stealing out from under the young ferns.

With her thin nostrils distended to this scent, Lady Casterley bore a distinct resemblance to a small, fine game-bird.

"You smell nice down here," she said. "Now, Mr. Courtier, before I forget—who is this Mrs. Lees Noel that I hear so much of?"

At that question, Barbara could not help sliding her eyes round. How would he stand up to Granny? It was the moment to see what he was made of. Granny was terrific!

"A very charming woman, Lady Casterley."

"No doubt; but I am tired of hearing that. What is her story?"

"Has she one?"

"Ha!" said Lady Casterley.

Ever so slightly Barbara let her arm press against Courtiers. It was so delicious to hear Granny getting no forwarder.

"I may take it she has a past, then?"

"Not from me, Lady Casterley."

Again Barbara gave him that imperceptible and flattering touch.

"Well, this is all very mysterious. I shall find out for myself. You know her, my dear. You must take me to see her."

"Dear Granny! If people hadn't pasts, they wouldn't have futures."

Lady Casterley let her little claw-like hand descend on her grand-daughter's thigh.

"Don't talk nonsense, and don't stretch like that!" she said; "you're too large already...."

At dinner that night they were all in possession of the news. Sir William had been informed by the local agent at Staverton, where Lord Harbinger's speech had suffered from some rude interruptions. The Hon. Geoffrey Winlow; having sent his wife on, had flown over in his biplane from Winkleigh, and brought a copy of 'the rag' with him. The one member of the small house-party who had not heard the report before dinner was Lord Dennis Fitz-Harold, Lady Casterley's brother.

Little, of course, was said. But after the ladies had withdrawn, Harbinger, with that plain-spoken spontaneity which was so unexpected, perhaps a little intentionally so, in connection with his almost classically formed face, uttered words to the effect that, if they did not fundamentally kick that rumour, it was all up with Miltoun. Really this was serious! And the beggars knew it, and they were going to work it. And Miltoun had gone up to Town, no one knew what for. It was the devil of a mess!

In all the conversation of this young man there was that peculiar brand of voice, which seems ever rebutting an accusation of being serious—a brand of voice and manner warranted against anything save ridicule; and in the face of ridicule apt to disappear. The words, just a little satirically spoken: "What is, my dear young man?" stopped him at once.

Looking for the complement and counterpart of Lady Casterley, one would perhaps have singled out her brother. All her abrupt decision was negated in his profound, ironical urbanity. His voice and look and manner were like his velvet coat, which had here and there a whitish sheen, as if it had been touched by moonlight. His hair too had that sheen. His very delicate features were framed in a white beard and moustache of Elizabethan shape. His eyes, hazel and still clear, looked out very straight, with a certain dry kindliness. His face, though unweathered and unseamed, and much too fine and thin in texture, had a curious affinity to the faces of old sailors or fishermen who have lived a simple, practical life in the light of an overmastering tradition. It was the face of a man with a very set creed, and inclined to be satiric towards innovations, examined by him and rejected full fifty years ago. One felt that a brain not devoid either of subtlety or aesthetic quality had long given up all attempts to interfere with conduct; that all shrewdness of speculation had given place to shrewdness of practical judgment based on very definite experience. Owing to lack of advertising power, natural to one so conscious of his dignity as to have lost all care for it, and to his devotion to a certain lady, only closed by death, his life had been lived, as it were, in shadow. Still, he possessed a peculiar influence in Society, because it was known to be impossible to get him to look at things in a complicated way. He was regarded rather as a last resort, however. "Bad as that? Well, there's old Fitz-Harold! Try him! He won't advise you, but he'll say something."

And in the heart of that irreverent young man, Harbinger, there stirred a sort of misgiving. Had he expressed himself too freely? Had he said anything too thick? He had forgotten the old boy! Stirring Bertie up with his foot, he murmured "Forgot you didn't know, sir. Bertie will explain."

Thus called on, Bertie, opening his lips a very little way, and fixing his half-closed eyes on his great-uncle, explained. There was a lady at the cottage—a nice woman—Mr. Courtier knew her—old Miltoun went there sometimes—rather late the other evening—these devils were making the most of it—suggesting—lose him the election, if they didn't look out. Perfect rot, of course!

In his opinion, old Miltoun, though as steady as Time, had been a flat to let the woman come out with him on to the Green, showing clearly where he had been, when he ran to Courtier's rescue. You couldn't play about with women who had no form that anyone knew anything of, however promising they might look.

Then, out of a silence Winlow asked: What was to be done? Should Miltoun be wired for? A thing like this spread like wildfire! Sir William—a man not accustomed to underrate difficulties—was afraid it was going to be troublesome. Harbinger expressed the opinion that the editor ought to be kicked. Did anybody know what Courtier had done when he heard of it. Where was he—dining in his room? Bertie suggested that if Miltoun was at Valleys House, it mightn't be too late to wire to him. The thing ought to be stemmed at once! And in all this concern about the situation there kept cropping out quaint little outbursts of desire to disregard the whole thing as infernal insolence, and metaphorically to punch the beggars' heads, natural to young men of breeding.

Then, out of another silence came the voice of Lord Dennis:

"I am thinking of this poor lady."

Turning a little abruptly towards that dry suave voice, and recovering the self-possession which seldom deserted him, Harbinger murmured:

"Quite so, sir; of course!"

Chapter IX

In the lesser withdrawing room, used when there was so small a party, Mrs. Winlow had gone to the piano and was playing to herself, for Lady Casterley, Lady Valleys, and her two daughters had drawn together as though united to face this invading rumour.

It was curious testimony to Miltoun's character that, no more here than in the dining-hall, was there any doubt of the integrity of his relations with Mrs. Noel. But whereas, there the matter was confined to its electioneering aspect, here that aspect was already perceived to be only the fringe of its importance. Those feminine minds, going with intuitive swiftness to the core of anything which affected their own males, had already grasped the fact that the rumour would, as it were, chain a man of Miltoun's temper to this woman.

But they were walking on such a thin crust of facts, and there was so deep a quagmire of supposition beneath, that talk was almost painfully difficult. Never before perhaps had each of these four women realized so clearly how much Miltoun—that rather strange and unknown grandson, son, and brother—counted in the scheme of existence. Their suppressed agitation was manifested in very different ways. Lady Casterley, upright in her chair, showed it only by an added decision of speech, a continual restless movement of one hand, a thin line between her usually smooth brows. Lady Valleys wore a puzzled look, as if a little surprised that she felt serious. Agatha looked frankly anxious. She was in her quiet way a woman of much character, endowed with that natural piety, which accepts without questioning the established order in life and religion. The world to her being home and family, she had a real, if gently expressed, horror of all that she instinctively felt to be subversive of this ideal. People judged her a little quiet, dull, and narrow; they compared her to a hen for ever clucking round her chicks. The streak of heroism that lay in her nature was not perhaps of patent order. Her feeling about her brother's situation however was sincere and not to be changed or comforted. She saw him in danger of being damaged in the only sense in which she could conceive of a man—as a husband and a father. It was this that went to her heart, though her piety proclaimed to her also the peril of his soul; for she shared the High Church view of the indissolubility of marriage.

As to Barbara, she stood by the hearth, leaning her white shoulders against the carved marble, her hands behind her, looking down. Now and then her lips curled, her level brows twitched, a faint sigh came from her; then a little smile would break out, and be instantly suppressed. She alone was silent—Youth criticizing Life; her judgment voiced itself only in the untroubled rise and fall of her young bosom, the impatience of her brows, the downward look of her blue eyes, full of a lazy, inextinguishable light:

Lady Valleys sighed.

"If only he weren't such a queer boy! He's quite capable of marrying her from sheer perversity."

"What!" said Lady Casterley.

"You haven't seen her, my dear. A most unfortunately attractive creature—quite a charming face."

Agatha said quietly:

"Mother, if she was divorced, I don't think Eustace would."

"There's that, certainly," murmured Lady Valleys; "hope for the best!"

"Don't you even know which way it was?" said Lady Casterley.

"Well, the vicar says she did the divorcing. But he's very charitable; it may be as Agatha hopes."

"I detest vagueness. Why doesn't someone ask the woman?"

"You shall come with me, Granny dear, and ask her yourself; you will do it so nicely."

Lady Casterley looked up.

"We shall see," she said. Something struggled with the autocratic criticism in her eyes. No more than the rest of the world could she help indulging Barbara. As one who believed in the divinity of her order, she liked this splendid child. She even admired—though admiration was not what she excelled in—that warm joy in life, as of some great nymph, parting the waves with bare limbs, tossing from her the foam of breakers. She felt that in this granddaughter, rather than in the good Agatha, the patrician spirit was housed. There were points to Agatha, earnestness and high principle; but something morally narrow and over-Anglican slightly offended the practical, this-worldly temper of Lady Casterley. It was a weakness, and she disliked weakness. Barbara would never be squeamish over moral questions or matters such as were not really, essential to aristocracy. She might, indeed, err too much the other way from sheer high spirits. As the impudent child had said: "If people had no pasts, they would have no futures." And Lady Casterley could not bear people without futures. She was ambitious; not with the low ambition of one who had risen from nothing, but with the high passion of one on the top, who meant to stay there.

"And where have you been meeting this—er—anonymous creature?" she asked.

Barbara came from the hearth, and bending down beside Lady Casterley's chair, seemed to envelop her completely.

"I'm all right, Granny; she couldn't corrupt me."

Lady Casterley's face peered out doubtfully from that warmth, wearing a look of disapproving pleasure.

"I know your wiles!" she said. "Come, now!"

"I see her about. She's nice to look at. We talk."

Again with that hurried quietness Agatha said:

"My dear Babs, I do think you ought to wait."

"My dear Angel, why? What is it to me if she's had four husbands?"

Agatha bit her lips, and Lady Valleys murmured with a laugh:

"You really are a terror, Babs."

But the sound of Mrs. Winlow's music had ceased—the men had come in. And the faces of the four women hardened, as if they had slipped on masks; for though this was almost or quite a family party, the Winlows being second cousins, still the subject was one which each of these four in their very different ways felt to be beyond general discussion. Talk, now, began glancing from the war scare—Winlow had it very specially that this would be over in a week—to Brabrook's speech, in progress at that very moment, of which Harbinger provided an imitation. It sped to Winlow's flight—to Andrew Grant's articles in the 'Parthenon'—to the caricature of Harbinger in the 'Cackler', inscribed 'The New Tory. Lord H-rb-ng-r brings Social Reform beneath the notice of his friends,' which depicted him introducing a naked baby to a number of coroneted old ladies. Thence to a dancer. Thence to the Bill for Universal Assurance. Then back to the war scare; to the last book of a great French writer; and once more to Winlow's flight. It was all straightforward and outspoken, each seeming to say exactly what came into the head. For all that, there was a curious avoidance of the spiritual significances of these things; or was it perhaps that such significances were not seen?

Lord Dennis, at the far end of the room, studying a portfolio of engravings, felt a touch on his cheek; and conscious of a certain fragrance, said without turning his head:

"Nice things, these, Babs!"

Receiving no answer he looked up.

There indeed stood Barbara.

"I do hate sneering behind people's backs!"

There had always been good comradeship between these two, since the days when Barbara, a golden-haired child, astride of a grey pony, had been his morning companion in the Row all through the season. His riding days were past; he had now no outdoor pursuit save fishing, which he followed with the ironic persistence of a self-contained, high-spirited nature, which refuses to admit that the mysterious finger of old age is laid across it. But though she was no longer his companion, he still had a habit of expecting her confidences; and he looked after her, moving away from him to a window, with surprised concern.

It was one of those nights, dark yet gleaming, when there seems a flying malice in the heavens; when the stars, from under and above the black clouds, are like eyes frowning and flashing down at men with purposed malevolence. The great sighing trees even had caught this spirit, save one, a dark, spire-like cypress, planted three hundred and fifty years before, whose tall form incarnated the very spirit of tradition, and neither swayed nor soughed like the others. From her, too close-fibred, too resisting, to admit the breath of Nature, only a dry rustle came. Still almost exotic, in spite of her centuries of sojourn, and now brought to life by the eyes of night, she seemed almost terrifying, in her narrow, spear-like austerity, as though something had dried and died within her soul. Barbara came back from the window.

"We can't do anything in our lives, it seems to me," she said, "but play at taking risks!"

Lord Dennis replied dryly:

"I don't think I understand, my dear."

"Look at Mr. Courtier!" muttered Barbara. "His life's so much more risky altogether than any of our men folk lead. And yet they sneer at him."

"Let's see, what has he done?"

"Oh! I dare say not very much; but it's all neck or nothing. But what does anything matter to Harbinger, for instance? If his Social Reform comes to nothing, he'll still be Harbinger, with fifty thousand a year."

Lord Dennis looked up a little queerly.

"What! Is it possible you don't take the young man seriously, Babs?"

Barbara shrugged; a strap slipped a little off one white shoulder.

"It's all play really; and he knows it—you can tell that from his voice. He can't help its not mattering, of course; and he knows that too."

"I have heard that he's after you, Babs; is that true?"

"He hasn't caught me yet."

"Will he?"

Barbara's answer was another shrug; and, for all their statuesque beauty, the movement of her shoulders was like the shrug of a little girl in her pinafore.

"And this Mr. Courtier," said Lord Dennis dryly: "Are you after him?"

"I'm after everything; didn't you know that, dear?"

"In reason, my child."

"In reason, of course—like poor Eusty!" She stopped. Harbinger himself was standing there close by, with an air as nearly approaching reverence as was ever to be seen on him. In truth, the way in which he was looking at her was almost timorous.

"Will you sing that song I like so much, Lady Babs?"

They moved away together; and Lord Dennis, gazing after that magnificent young couple, stroked his beard gravely.

Chapter X

Miltoun's sudden journey to London had been undertaken in pursuance of a resolve slowly forming from the moment he met Mrs. Noel in the stone flagged passage of Burracombe Farm. If she would have him and since last evening he believed she would—he intended to marry her.

It has been said that except for one lapse his life had been austere, but this is not to assert that he had no capacity for passion. The contrary was the case. That flame which had been so jealously guarded smouldered deep within him—a smothered fire with but little air to feed on. The moment his spirit was touched by the spirit of this woman, it had flared up. She was the incarnation of all that he desired. Her hair, her eyes, her form; the tiny tuck or dimple at the corner of her mouth just where a child places its finger; her way of moving, a sort of unconscious swaying or yielding to the air; the tone in her voice, which seemed to come not so much from happiness of her own as from an innate wish to make others happy; and that natural, if not robust, intelligence, which belongs to the very sympathetic, and is rarely found in women of great ambitions or enthusiasms—all these things had twined themselves round his heart. He not only dreamed of her, and wanted her; he believed in her. She filled his thoughts as one who could never do wrong; as one who, though a wife would remain a mistress, and though a mistress, would always be the companion of his spirit.

It has been said that no one spoke or gossiped about women in Miltoun's presence, and the tale of her divorce was present to his mind simply in the form of a conviction that she was an injured woman. After his interview with the vicar, he had only once again alluded to it, and that in answer to the speech of a lady staying at the Court: "Oh! yes, I remember her case perfectly. She was the poor woman who—" "Did not, I am certain, Lady Bonington." The tone of his voice had made someone laugh uneasily; the subject was changed.

All divorce was against his convictions, but in a blurred way he admitted that there were cases where release was unavoidable. He was not a man to ask for confidences, or expect them to be given him. He himself had never confided his spiritual struggles to any living creature; and the unspiritual struggle had little interest for Miltoun. He was ready at any moment to stake his life on the perfection of the idol he had set up within his soul, as simply and straightforwardly as he would have placed his body in front of her to shield her from harm.

The same fanaticism, which looked on his passion as a flower by itself, entirely apart from its suitability to the social garden, was also the driving force which sent him up to London to declare his intention to his father before he spoke to Mrs. Noel. The thing should be done simply, and in right order. For he had the kind of moral courage found in those who live retired within the shell of their own aspirations. Yet it was not perhaps so much active moral courage as indifference to what others thought or did, coming from his inbred resistance to the appreciation of what they felt.

That peculiar smile of the old Tudor Cardinal—which had in it invincible self-reliance, and a sort of spiritual sneer—played over his face when he speculated on his father's reception of the coming news; and very soon he ceased to think of it at all, burying himself in the work he had brought with him for the journey. For he had in high degree the faculty, so essential to public life, of switching off his whole attention from one subject to another.

On arriving at Paddington he drove straight to Valleys House.

This large dwelling with its pillared portico, seemed to wear an air of faint surprise that, at the height of the season, it was not more inhabited. Three servants relieved Miltoun of his little luggage; and having washed, and learned that his father would be dining in, he went for a walk, taking his way towards his rooms in the Temple. His long figure, somewhat carelessly garbed, attracted the usual attention, of which he was as usual unaware. Strolling along, he meditated deeply on a London, an England, different from this flatulent hurly-burly, this 'omniuin gatherum', this great discordant symphony of sharps and flats. A London, an England, kempt and self-respecting; swept and garnished of slums, and plutocrats, advertisement, and jerry-building, of sensationalism, vulgarity, vice, and unemployment. An England where each man should know his place, and never change it, but serve in it loyally in his own caste. Where every man, from nobleman to labourer, should be an oligarch by faith, and a gentleman by practice. An England so steel-bright and efficient that the very sight should suffice to impose peace. An England whose soul should be stoical and fine with the stoicism and fineness of each soul amongst her many million souls; where the town should have its creed and the country its creed, and there should be contentment and no complaining in her streets.

And as he walked down the Strand, a little ragged boy cheeped out between his legs:

"Bloodee discoveree in a Bank—Grite sensytion! Pi-er!"

Miltoun paid no heed to that saying; yet, with it, the wind that blows where man lives, the careless, wonderful, unordered wind, had dispersed his austere and formal vision. Great was that wind—the myriad aspiration of men and women, the praying of the uncounted multitude to the goddess of Sensation—of Chance, and Change. A flowing from heart to heart, from lip to lip, as in Spring the wistful air wanders through a wood, imparting to every bush and tree the secrets of fresh life, the passionate resolve to grow, and become—no matter what! A sighing, as eternal as the old murmuring of the sea, as little to be hushed, as prone to swell into sudden roaring!

Miltoun held on through the traffic, not looking overmuch at the present forms of the thousands he passed, but seeing with the eyes of faith the forms he desired to see. Near St. Paul's he stopped in front of an old book-shop. His grave, pallid, not unhandsome face, was well-known to William Rimall, its small proprietor, who at once brought out his latest acquisition—a Mores 'Utopia.' That particular edition (he assured Miltoun) was quite unprocurable—he had never sold but one other copy, which had been literally, crumbling away. This copy was in even better condition. It could hardly last another twenty years—a genuine book, a bargain. There wasn't so much movement in More as there had been a little time back.

Miltoun opened the tome, and a small book-louse who had been sleeping on the word 'Tranibore,' began to make its way slowly towards the very centre of the volume.

"I see it's genuine," said Miltoun.

"It's not to read, my lord," the little man warned him: "Hardly safe to turn the pages. As I was saying—I've not had a better piece this year. I haven't really!"

"Shrewd old dreamer," muttered Miltoun; "the Socialists haven't got beyond him, even now."

The little man's eyes blinked, as though apologizing for the views of Thomas More.

"Well," he said, "I suppose he was one of them. I forget if your lordship's very strong on politics?"

Miltoun smiled.

"I want to see an England, Rimall, something like the England of Mores dream. But my machinery will be different. I shall begin at the top."

The little man nodded.

"Quite so, quite so," he said; "we shall come to that, I dare say."

"We must, Rimall." And Miltoun turned the page.

The little man's face quivered.

"I don't think," he said, "that book's quite strong enough for you, my lord, with your taste for reading. Now I've a most curious old volume here—on Chinese temples. It's rare—but not too old. You can peruse it thoroughly. It's what I call a book to browse on just suit your palate. Funny principle they built those things on," he added, opening the volume at an engraving, "in layers. We don't build like that in England."

Miltoun looked up sharply; the little man's face wore no signs of understanding.

"Unfortunately we don't, Rimall," he said; "we ought to, and we shall. I'll take this book."

Placing his finger on the print of the pagoda, he added: "A good symbol."

The little bookseller's eye strayed down the temple to the secret price mark.

"Exactly, my lord," he said; "I thought it'd be your fancy. The price to you will be twenty-seven and six."

Miltoun, pocketing the bargain, walked out. He made his way into the Temple, left the book at his Chambers, and passed on down to the bank of Mother Thames. The Sun was loving her passionately that afternoon; he had kissed her into warmth and light and colour. And all the buildings along her banks, as far as the towers at Westminster, seemed to be smiling. It was a great sight for the eyes of a lover. And another vision came haunting Miltoun, of a soft-eyed woman with a low voice, bending amongst her flowers. Nothing would be complete without her; no work bear fruit; no scheme could have full meaning.

Lord Valleys greeted his son at dinner with good fellowship and a faint surprise.

"Day off, my dear fellow? Or have you come up to hear Brabrook pitch into us? He's rather late this time—we've got rid of that balloon business no trouble after all."

And he eyed Miltoun with that clear grey stare of his, so cool, level, and curious. Now, what sort of bird is this? it seemed saying. Certainly not the partridge I should have expected from its breeding!

Miltoun's answer: "I came up to tell you some thing, sir," riveted his father's stare for a second longer than was quite urbane.

It would not be true to say that Lord Valleys was afraid of his son. Fear was not one of his emotions, but he certainly regarded him with a respectful curiosity that bordered on uneasiness. The oligarchic temper of Miltoun's mind and political convictions almost shocked one who knew both by temperament and experience how to wait in front. This instruction he had frequently had occasion to give his jockeys when he believed his horses could best get home first in that way. And it was an instruction he now longed to give his son. He himself had 'waited in front' for over fifty years, and he knew it to be the finest way of insuring that he would never be compelled to alter this desirable policy—for something in Lord Valleys' character made him fear that, in real emergency, he would exert himself to the point of the gravest discomfort sooner than be left to wait behind. A fellow like young Harbinger, of course, he understood—versatile, 'full of beans,' as he expressed it to himself in his more confidential moments, who had imbibed the new wine (very intoxicating it was) of desire for social reform. He would have to be given his head a little—but there would be no difficulty with him, he would never 'run out'—light handy build of horse that only required steadying at the corners. He would want to hear himself talk, and be let feel that he was doing something. All very well, and quite intelligible. But with Miltoun (and Lord Valleys felt this to be no, mere parental fancy) it was a very different business. His son had a way of forcing things to their conclusions which was dangerous, and reminded him of his mother-in-law. He was a baby in public affairs, of course, as yet; but as soon as he once got going, the intensity of his convictions, together with his position, and real gift—not of the gab, like Harbinger's—but of restrained, biting oratory, was sure to bring him to the front with a bound in the present state of parties. And what were those convictions? Lord Valleys had tried to understand them, but up to the present he had failed. And this did not surprise him exactly, since, as he often said, political convictions were not, as they appeared on the surface, the outcome of reason, but merely symptoms of temperament. And he could not comprehend, because he could not sympathize with, any attitude towards public affairs that was not essentially level, attached to the plain, common-sense factors of the case as they appeared to himself. Not that he could fairly be called a temporizer, for deep down in him there was undoubtedly a vein of obstinate, fundamental loyalty to the traditions of a caste which prized high spirit beyond all things. Still he did feel that Miltoun was altogether too much the 'pukka' aristocrat—no better than a Socialist, with his confounded way of seeing things all cut and dried; his ideas of forcing reforms down people's throats and holding them there with the iron hand! With his way too of acting on his principles! Why! He even admitted that he acted on his principles! This thought always struck a very discordant note in Lord Valleys' breast. It was almost indecent; worse-ridiculous! The fact was, the dear fellow had unfortunately a deeper habit of thought than was wanted in politics—dangerous—very! Experience might do something for him! And out of his own long experience the Earl of Valleys tried hard to recollect any politician whom the practice of politics had left where he was when he started. He could not think of one. But this gave him little comfort; and, above a piece of late asparagus his steady eyes sought his son's. What had he come up to tell him?

The phrase had been ominous; he could not recollect Miltoun's ever having told him anything. For though a really kind and indulgent father, he had—like so many men occupied with public and other lives—a little acquired towards his offspring the look and manner: Is this mine? Of his four children, Barbara alone he claimed with conviction. He admired her; and, being a man who savoured life, he was unable to love much except where he admired. But, the last person in the world to hustle any man or force a confidence, he waited to hear his son's news, betraying no uneasiness.

Miltoun seemed in no hurry. He described Courtier's adventure, which tickled Lord Valleys a good deal.

"Ordeal by red pepper! Shouldn't have thought them equal to that," he said. "So you've got him at Monkland now. Harbinger still with you?"

"Yes. I don't think Harbinger has much stamina.

"Politically?"

Miltoun nodded.

"I rather resent his being on our side—I don't think he does us any good. You've seen that cartoon, I suppose; it cuts pretty deep. I couldn't recognize you amongst the old women, sir."

Lord Valleys smiled impersonally.

"Very clever thing. By the way; I shall win the Eclipse, I think."

And thus, spasmodically, the conversation ran till the last servant had left the room.

Then Miltoun, without preparation, looked straight at his father and said:

"I want to marry Mrs. Noel, sir."

Lord Valleys received the shot with exactly the same expression as that with which he was accustomed to watch his horses beaten. Then he raised his wineglass to his lips; and set it down again untouched. This was the only sign he gave of interest or discomfiture.

"Isn't this rather sudden?"

Miltoun answered: "I've wanted to from the moment I first saw her."

Lord Valleys, almost as good a judge of a man and a situation as of a horse or a pointer dog, leaned back in his chair, and said with faint sarcasm:

"My dear fellow, it's good of you to have told me this; though, to be quite frank, it's a piece of news I would rather not have heard."

A dusky flush burned slowly up in Miltoun's cheeks. He had underrated his father; the man had coolness and courage in a crisis.

"What is your objection, sir?" And suddenly he noticed that a wafer in Lord Valleys' hand was quivering. This brought into his eyes no look of compunction, but such a smouldering gaze as the old Tudor Churchman might have bent on an adversary who showed a sign of weakness. Lord Valleys, too, noticed the quivering of that wafer, and ate it.

"We are men of the world," he said.

Miltoun answered: "I am not."

Showing his first real symptom of impatience Lord Valleys rapped out:

"So be it! I am."

"Yes?", said Miltoun.

"Eustace!"

Nursing one knee, Miltoun faced that appeal without the faintest movement. His eyes continued to burn into his father's face. A tremor passed over Lord Valleys' heart. What intensity of feeling there was in the fellow, that he could look like this at the first breath of opposition!

He reached out and took up the cigar-box; held it absently towards his son, and drew it quickly back.

"I forgot," he said; "you don't."

And lighting a cigar, he smoked gravely, looking straight before him, a furrow between his brows. He spoke at last:

"She looks like a lady. I know nothing else about her."

The smile deepened round Miltoun's mouth.

"Why should you want to know anything else?"

Lord Valleys shrugged. His philosophy had hardened.

"I understand for one thing," he said coldly; "that there is a matter of a divorce. I thought you took the Church's view on that subject."

"She has not done wrong."

"You know her story, then?"

"No."

Lord Valleys raised his brows, in irony and a sort of admiration.

"Chivalry the better part of discretion?"

Miltoun answered:

"You don't, I think, understand the kind of feeling I have for Mrs. Noel. It does not come into your scheme of things. It is the only feeling, however, with which I should care to marry, and I am not likely to feel it for anyone again."

Lord Valleys felt once more that uncanny sense of insecurity. Was this true? And suddenly he felt Yes, it is true! The face before him was the face of one who would burn in his own fire sooner than depart from his standards. And a sudden sense of the utter seriousness of this dilemma dumbed him.

"I can say no more at the moment," he muttered and got up from the table.

Chapter XI

Lady Casterley was that inconvenient thing—an early riser. No woman in the kingdom was a better judge of a dew carpet. Nature had in her time displayed before her thousands of those pretty fabrics, where all the stars of the past night, dropped to the dark earth, were waiting to glide up to heaven again on the rays of the sun. At Ravensham she walked regularly in her gardens between half-past seven and eight, and when she paid a visit, was careful to subordinate whatever might be the local custom to this habit.

When therefore her maid Randle came to Barbara's maid at seven o'clock, and said: "My old lady wants Lady Babs to get up," there was no particular pain in the breast of Barbara's maid, who was doing up her corsets. She merely answered "I'll see to it. Lady Babs won't be too pleased!" And ten minutes later she entered that white-walled room which smelled of pinks-a temple of drowsy sweetness, where the summer light was vaguely stealing through flowered chintz curtains.

Barbara was sleeping with her cheek on her hand, and her tawny hair, gathered back, streaming over the pillow. Her lips were parted; and the maid thought: "I'd like to have hair and a mouth like that!" She could not help smiling to herself with pleasure; Lady Babs looked so pretty—prettier asleep even than awake! And at sight of that beautiful creature, sleeping and smiling in her sleep, the earthy, hothouse fumes steeping the mind of one perpetually serving in an atmosphere unsuited to her natural growth, dispersed. Beauty, with its queer touching power of freeing the spirit from all barriers and thoughts of self, sweetened the maid's eyes, and kept her standing, holding her breath. For Barbara asleep was a symbol of that Golden Age in which she so desperately believed. She opened her eyes, and seeing the maid, said:

"Is it eight o'clock, Stacey?"

"No, but Lady Casterley wants you to walk with her."

"Oh! bother! I was having such a dream!"

"Yes; you were smiling."

"I was dreaming that I could fly."

"Fancy!"

"I could see everything spread out below me, as close as I see you; I was hovering like a buzzard hawk. I felt that I could come down exactly where I wanted. It was fascinating. I had perfect power, Stacey."

And throwing her neck back, she closed her eyes again. The sunlight streamed in on her between the half-drawn curtains.

The queerest impulse to put out a hand and stroke that full white throat shot through the maid's mind.

"These flying machines are stupid," murmured Barbara; "the pleasure's in one's body—wings!"

"I can see Lady Casterley in the garden."

Barbara sprang out of bed. Close by the statue of Diana Lady Casterley was standing, gazing down at some flowers, a tiny, grey figure. Barbara sighed. With her, in her dream, had been another buzzard hawk, and she was filled with a sort of surprise, and queer pleasure that ran down her in little shivers while she bathed and dressed.

In her haste she took no hat; and still busy with the fastening of her linen frock, hurried down the stairs and Georgian corridor, towards the garden. At the end of it she almost ran into the arms of Courtier.

Awakening early this morning, he had begun first thinking of Audrey Noel, threatened by scandal; then of his yesterday's companion, that glorious young creature, whose image had so gripped and taken possession of him. In the pleasure of this memory he had steeped himself. She was youth itself! That perfect thing, a young girl without callowness.

And his words, when she nearly ran into him, were: "The Winged Victory!"

Barbara's answer was equally symbolic: "A buzzard hawk! Do you know, I dreamed we were flying, Mr. Courtier."

Courtier gravely answered

"If the gods give me that dream—"

From the garden door Barbara turned her head, smiled, and passed through.

Lady Casterley, in the company of little Ann, who had perceived that it was novel to be in the garden at this hour, had been scrutinizing some newly founded colonies of a flower with which she was not familiar. On seeing her granddaughter approach, she said at once:

"What is this thing?"

"Nemesia."

"Never heard of it."

"It's rather the fashion, Granny."

"Nemesia?" repeated Lady Casterley. "What has Nemesis to do with flowers? I have no patience with gardeners, and these idiotic names. Where is your hat? I like that duck's egg colour in your frock. There's a button undone." And reaching up her little spidery hand, wonderfully steady considering its age, she buttoned the top button but one of Barbara's bodice.

"You look very blooming, my dear," she said. "How far is it to this woman's cottage? We'll go there now."

"She wouldn't be up."

Lady Casterley's eyes gleamed maliciously.

"You tell me she's so nice," she said. "No nice unencumbered woman lies in bed after half-past seven. Which is the very shortest way? No, Ann, we can't take you."

Little Ann, after regarding her great-grandmother rather too intently, replied:

"Well, I can't come, you see, because I've got to go."

"Very well," said Lady Casterley, "then trot along."

Little Ann, tightening her lips, walked to the next colony of Nemesia, and bent over the colonists with concentration, showing clearly that she had found something more interesting than had yet been encountered.

"Ha!" said Lady Casterley, and led on at her brisk pace towards the avenue.

All the way down the drive she discoursed on woodcraft, glancing sharply at the trees. Forestry—she said—like building, and all other pursuits which required faith and patient industry, was a lost art in this second-hand age. She had made Barbara's grandfather practise it, so that at Catton (her country place) and even at Ravensham, the trees were worth looking at. Here, at Monkland, they were monstrously neglected. To have the finest Italian cypress in the country, for example, and not take more care of it, was a downright scandal!

Barbara listened, smiling lazily. Granny was so amusing in her energy and precision, and her turns of speech, so deliberately homespun, as if she—than whom none could better use a stiff and polished phrase, or the refinements of the French language—were determined to take what liberties she liked. To the girl, haunted still by the feeling that she could fly, almost drunk on the sweetness of the air that summer morning, it seemed funny that anyone should be like that. Then for a second she saw her grandmother's face in repose, off guard, grim with anxious purpose, as if questioning its hold on life; and in one of those flashes of intuition which come to women—even when young and conquering like Barbara—she felt suddenly sorry, as though she had caught sight of the pale spectre never yet seen by her. "Poor old dear," she thought; "what a pity to be old!"

But they had entered the footpath crossing three long meadows which climbed up towards Mrs. Noel's. It was so golden-sweet here amongst the million tiny saffron cups frosted with lingering dewshine; there was such flying glory in the limes and ash-trees; so delicate a scent from the late whins and may-flower; and, on every tree a greybird calling to be sorry was not possible!

In the far corner of the first field a chestnut mare was standing, with ears pricked at some distant sound whose charm she alone perceived. On viewing the intruders, she laid those ears back, and a little vicious star gleamed out at the corner of her eye. They passed her and entered the second field. Half way across, Barbara said quietly:

"Granny, that's a bull!"

It was indeed an enormous bull, who had been standing behind a clump of bushes. He was moving slowly towards them, still distant about two hundred yards; a great red beast, with the huge development of neck and front which makes the bull, of all living creatures, the symbol of brute force.

Lady Casterley envisaged him severely.

"I dislike bulls," she said; "I think I must walk backward."

"You can't; it's too uphill."

"I am not going to turn back," said Lady Casterley. "The bull ought not to be here. Whose fault is it? I shall speak to someone. Stand still and look at him. We must prevent his coming nearer."

They stood still and looked at the bull, who continued to approach.

"It doesn't stop him," said Lady Casterley. "We must take no notice. Give me your arm, my dear; my legs feel rather funny."

Barbara put her arm round the little figure. They walked on.

"I have not been used to bulls lately," said Lady Casterley. The bull came nearer.

"Granny," said Barbara, "you must go quietly on to the stile. When you're over I'll come too."

"Certainly not," said Lady Casterley, "we will go together. Take no notice of him; I have great faith in that."

"Granny darling, you must do as I say, please; I remember this bull, he is one of ours."

At those rather ominous words Lady Casterley gave her a sharp glance.

"I shall not go," she said. "My legs feel quite strong now. We can run, if necessary."

"So can the bull," said Barbara.

"I'm not going to leave you," muttered Lady Casterley. "If he turns vicious I shall talk to him. He won't touch me. You can run faster than I; so that's settled."

"Don't be absurd, dear," answered Barbara; "I am not afraid of bulls."

Lady Casterley flashed a look at her which had a gleam of amusement.

"I can feel you," she said; "you're just as trembly as I am."

The bull was now distant some eighty yards, and they were still quite a hundred from the stile.

"Granny," said Barbara, "if you don't go on as I tell you, I shall just leave you, and go and meet him! You mustn't be obstinate!"

Lady Casterley's answer was to grip her granddaughter round the waist; the nervous force of that thin arm was surprising.

"You will do nothing of the sort," she said. "I refuse to have anything more to do with this bull; I shall simply pay no attention."

The bull now began very slowly ambling towards them.

"Take no notice," said Lady Casterley, who was walking faster than she had ever walked before.

"The ground is level now," said Barbara; "can you run?"

"I think so," gasped Lady Casterley; and suddenly she found herself half-lifted from the ground, and, as it were, flying towards the stile. She heard a noise behind; then Barbara's voice:

"We must stop. He's on us. Get behind me."

She felt herself caught and pinioned by two arms that seemed set on the wrong way. Instinct, and a general softness told her that she was back to back with her granddaughter.

"Let me go!" she gasped; "let me go!"

And suddenly she felt herself being propelled by that softness forward towards the stile.

"Shoo!" she said; "shoo!"

"Granny," Barbara's voice came, calm and breathless, "don't! You only excite him! Are we near the stile?"

"Ten yards," panted Lady Casterley.

"Look out, then!" There was a sort of warm flurry round her, a rush, a heave, a scramble; she was beyond the stile. The bull and Barbara, a yard or two apart, were just the other side. Lady Casterley raised her handkerchief and fluttered it. The bull looked up; Barbara, all legs and arms, came slipping down beside her.

Without wasting a moment Lady Casterley leaned forward and addressed the bull:

"You awful brute!" she said; "I will have you well flogged."

Gently pawing the ground, the bull snuffled.

"Are you any the worse, child?"

"Not a scrap," said Barbara's serene, still breathless voice.

Lady Casterley put up her hands, and took the girl's face between them.

"What legs you have!" she said. "Give me a kiss!"

Having received a hot, rather quivering kiss, she walked on, holding somewhat firmly to Barbara's arm.

"As for that bull," she murmured, "the brute—to attack women!"

Barbara looked down at her.

"Granny," she said, "are you sure you're not shaken?"

Lady Casterley, whose lips were quivering, pressed them together very hard.

"Not a b-b-bit."

"Don't you think," said Barbara, "that we had better go back, at once—the other way?"

"Certainly not. There are no more bulls, I suppose, between us and this woman?"

"But are you fit to see her?"

Lady Casterley passed her handkerchief over her lips, to remove their quivering.

"Perfectly," she answered.

"Then, dear," said Barbara, "stand still a minute, while I dust you behind."

This having been accomplished, they proceeded in the direction of Mrs. Noel's cottage.

At sight of it, Lady Casterley said:

"I shall put my foot down. It's out of the question for a man of Miltoun's prospects. I look forward to seeing him Prime Minister some day." Hearing Barbara's voice murmuring above her, she paused: "What's that you say?"

"I said: What is the use of our being what we are, if we can't love whom we like?"

"Love!" said Lady Casterley; "I was talking of marriage."

"I am glad you admit the distinction, Granny dear."

"You are pleased to be sarcastic," said Lady Casterley. "Listen to me! It's the greatest nonsense to suppose that people in our caste are free to do as they please. The sooner you realize that, the better, Babs. I am talking to you seriously. The preservation of our position as a class depends on our observing certain decencies. What do you imagine would happen to the Royal Family if they were allowed to marry as they liked? All this marrying with Gaiety girls, and American money, and people with pasts, and writers, and so forth, is most damaging. There's far too much of it, and it ought to be stopped. It may be tolerated for a few cranks, or silly young men, and these new women, but for Eustace—" Lady Casterley paused again, and her fingers pinched Barbara's arm, "or for you—there's only one sort of marriage possible. As for Eustace, I shall speak to this good lady, and see that he doesn't get entangled further."

Absorbed in the intensity of her purpose, she did not observe a peculiar little smile playing round Barbara's lips.

"You had better speak to Nature, too, Granny!"

Lady Casterley stopped short, and looked up in her granddaughter's face.

"Now what do you mean by that?" she said "Tell me!"

But noticing that Barbara's lips had closed tightly, she gave her arm a hard—if unintentional-pinch, and walked on.

Chapter XII

Lady Casterley's rather malicious diagnosis of Audrey Noel was correct. The unencumbered woman was up and in her garden when Barbara and her grandmother appeared at the Wicket gate; but being near the lime-tree at the far end she did not hear the rapid colloquy which passed between them.

"You are going to be good, Granny?"

"As to that—it will depend."

"You promised."

"H'm!"

Lady Casterley could not possibly have provided herself with a better introduction than Barbara, whom Mrs. Noel never met without the sheer pleasure felt by a sympathetic woman when she sees embodied in someone else that 'joy in life' which Fate has not permitted to herself.

She came forward with her head a little on one side, a trick of hers not at all affected, and stood waiting.

The unembarrassed Barbara began at once:

"We've just had an encounter with a bull. This is my grandmother, Lady Casterley."

The little old lady's demeanour, confronted with this very pretty face and figure was a thought less autocratic and abrupt than usual. Her shrewd eyes saw at once that she had no common adventuress to deal with. She was woman of the world enough, too, to know that 'birth' was not what it had been in her young days, that even money was rather rococo, and that good looks, manners, and a knowledge of literature, art, and music (and this woman looked like one of that sort), were often considered socially more valuable. She was therefore both wary and affable.

"How do you do?" she said. "I have heard of you. May we sit down for a minute in your garden? The bull was a wretch!"

But even in speaking, she was uneasily conscious that Mrs. Noel's clear eyes were seeing very well what she had come for. The look in them indeed was almost cynical; and in spite of her sympathetic murmurs, she did not somehow seem to believe in the bull. This was disconcerting. Why had Barbara condescended to mention the wretched brute? And she decided to take him by the horns.

"Babs," she said, "go to the Inn and order me a 'fly.' I shall drive back, I feel very shaky," and, as Mrs. Noel offered to send her maid, she added:

"No, no, my granddaughter will go."

Barbara having departed with a quizzical look, Lady Casterley patted the rustic seat, and said:

"Do come and sit down, I want to talk to you:"

Mrs. Noel obeyed. And at once Lady Casterley perceived that "she had a most difficult task before her. She had not expected a woman with whom one could take no liberties. Those clear dark eyes, and that soft, perfectly graceful manner—to a person so 'sympathetic' one should be able to say anything, and—one couldn't! It was awkward. And suddenly she noticed that Mrs. Noel was sitting perfectly upright, as upright—more upright, than she was herself. A bad, sign—a very bad sign! Taking out her handkerchief, she put it to her lips.

"I suppose you think," she said, "that we were not chased by a bull."

"I am sure you were."

"Indeed! Ah! But I've something else to talk to you about."

Mrs. Noel's face quivered back, as a flower might when it was going to be plucked; and again Lady Casterley put her handkerchief to her lips. This time she rubbed them hard. There was nothing to come off; to do so, therefore, was a satisfaction.

"I am an old woman," she said, "and you mustn't mind what I say."

Mrs. Noel did not answer, but looked straight at her visitor; to whom it seemed suddenly that this was another person. What was it about that face, staring at her! In a weird way it reminded her of a child that one had hurt—with those great eyes and that soft hair, and the mouth thin, in a line, all of a sudden. And as if it had been jerked out of her, she said:

"I don't want to hurt you, my dear. It's about my grandson, of course."

But Mrs. Noel made neither sign nor motion; and the feeling of irritation which so rapidly attacks the old when confronted by the unexpected, came to Lady Casterley's aid.

"His name," she said, "is being coupled with yours in a way that's doing him a great deal of harm. You don't wish to injure him, I'm sure."

Mrs. Noel shook her head, and Lady Casterley went on:

"I don't know what they're not saying since the evening your friend Mr. Courtier hurt his knee. Miltoun has been most unwise. You had not perhaps realized that."

Mrs. Noel's answer was bitterly distinct:

"I didn't know anyone was sufficiently interested in my doings."

Lady Casterley suffered a gesture of exasperation to escape her.

"Good heavens!" she said; "every common person is interested in a woman whose position is anomalous. Living alone as you do, and not a widow, you're fair game for everybody, especially in the country."

Mrs. Noel's sidelong glance, very clear and cynical, seemed to say: "Even for you."

"I am not entitled to ask your story," Lady Casterley went on, "but if you make mysteries you must expect the worst interpretation put on them. My grandson is a man of the highest principle; he does not see things with the eyes of the world, and that should have made you doubly careful not to compromise him, especially at a time like this."

Mrs. Noel smiled. This smile startled Lady Casterley; it seemed, by concealing everything, to reveal depths of strength and subtlety. Would the woman never show her hand? And she said abruptly:

"Anything serious, of course, is out of the question."

"Quite."

That word, which of all others seemed the right one, was spoken so that Lady Casterley did not know in the least what it meant. Though occasionally employing irony, she detested it in others. No woman should be allowed to use it as a weapon! But in these days, when they were so foolish as to want votes, one never knew what women would be at. This particular woman, however, did not look like one of that sort. She was feminine—very feminine—the sort of creature that spoiled men by being too nice to them. And though she had come determined to find out all about everything and put an end to it, she saw Barbara re-entering the wicket gate with considerable relief.

"I am ready to walk home now," she said. And getting up from the rustic seat, she made Mrs. Noel a satirical little bow.

"Thank you for letting me rest. Give me your arm, child."

Barbara gave her arm, and over her shoulder threw a swift smile at Mrs. Noel, who did not answer it, but stood looking quietly after them, her eyes immensely dark and large.

Out in the lane Lady Casterley walked on, very silent, digesting her emotions.

"What about the 'fly,' Granny?"

"What 'fly'?"

"The one you told me to order."

"You don't mean to say that you took me seriously?"

"No," said Barbara.

"Ha!"

They proceeded some little way farther before Lady Casterley said suddenly:

"She is deep."

"And dark," said Barbara. "I am afraid you were not good!"

Lady Casterley glanced upwards.

"I detest this habit," she said, "amongst you young people, of taking nothing seriously. Not even bulls," she added, with a grim smile.

Barbara threw back her head and sighed.

"Nor 'flys,'" she said.

Lady Casterley saw that she had closed her eyes and opened her lips. And she thought:

"She's a very beautiful girl. I had no idea she was so beautiful—but too big!" And she added aloud:

"Shut your mouth! You will get one down!"

They spoke no more till they had entered the avenue; then Lady Casterley said sharply:

"Who is this coming down the drive?"

"Mr. Courtier, I think."

"What does he mean by it, with that leg?"

"He is coming to talk to you, Granny."

Lady Casterley stopped short.

"You are a cat," she said; "a sly cat. Now mind, Babs, I won't have it!"

"No, darling," murmured Barbara; "you shan't have it—I'll take him off your hands."

"What does your mother mean," stammered Lady Casterley, "letting you grow up like this! You're as bad as she was at your age!"

"Worse!" said Barbara. "I dreamed last night that I could fly!"

"If you try that," said Lady Casterley grimly, "you'll soon come to grief. Good-morning, sir; you ought to be in bed!"

Courtier raised his hat.

"Surely it is not for me to be where you are not!" And he added gloomily: "The war scare's dead!"

"Ah!" said Lady Casterley: "your occupation's gone then. You'll go back to London now, I suppose." Looking suddenly at Barbara she saw that the girl's eyes were half-closed, and that she was smiling; it seemed to Lady Casterley too or was it fancy?—that she shook her head.

Chapter XIII

Thanks to Lady Valleys, a patroness of birds, no owl was ever shot on the Monkland Court estate, and those soft-flying spirits of the dusk hooted and hunted, to the great benefit of all except the creeping voles. By every farm, cottage, and field, they passed invisible, quartering the dark air. Their voyages of discovery stretched up on to the moor as far as the wild stone man, whose origin their wisdom perhaps knew. Round Audrey Noel's cottage they were as thick as thieves, for they had just there two habitations in a long, old, holly-grown wall, and almost seemed to be guarding the mistress of that thatched dwelling—so numerous were their fluttering rushes, so tenderly prolonged their soft sentinel callings. Now that the weather was really warm, so that joy of life was in the voles, they found those succulent creatures of an extraordinarily pleasant flavour, and on them each pair was bringing up a family of exceptionally fine little owls, very solemn, with big heads, bright large eyes, and wings as yet only able to fly downwards. There was scarcely any hour from noon of the day (for some of them had horns) to the small sweet hours when no one heard them, that they forgot to salute the very large, quiet, wingless owl whom they could espy moving about by day above their mouse-runs, or preening her white and sometimes blue and sometimes grey feathers morning and evening in a large square hole high up in the front wall. And they could not understand at all why no swift depredating graces nor any habit of long soft hooting belonged to that lady-bird.

On the evening of the day when she received that early morning call, as soon as dusk had fallen, wrapped in a long thin cloak, with black lace over her dark hair, Audrey Noel herself fluttered out into the lanes, as if to join the grave winged hunters of the invisible night. Those far, continual sounds, not stilled in the country till long after the sun dies, had but just ceased from haunting the air, where the late May-scent clung as close as fragrance clings to a woman's robe. There was just the barking of a dog, the boom of migrating chafers, the song of the stream, and of the owls, to proclaim the beating in the heart of this sweet Night. Nor was there any light by which Night's face could be seen; it was hidden, anonymous; so that when a lamp in a cottage threw a blink over the opposite bank, it was as if some wandering painter had wrought a picture of stones and leaves on the black air, framed it in purple, and left it hanging. Yet, if it could only have been come at, the Night was as full of emotion as this woman who wandered, shrinking away against the banks if anyone passed, stopping to cool her hot face with the dew on the ferns, walking swiftly to console her warm heart. Anonymous Night seeking for a symbol could have found none better than this errant figure, to express its hidden longings, the fluttering, unseen rushes of its dark wings, and all its secret passion of revolt against its own anonymity....

At Monkland Court, save for little Ann, the morning passed but dumbly, everyone feeling that something must be done, and no one knowing what. At lunch, the only allusion to the situation had been Harbinger's inquiry:

"When does Miltoun return?"

He had wired, it seemed, to say that he was motoring down that night.

"The sooner the better," Sir William murmured: "we've still a fortnight."

But all had felt from the tone in which he spoke these words, how serious was the position in the eyes of that experienced campaigner.

What with the collapse of the war scare, and this canard about Mrs. Noel, there was indeed cause for alarm.

The afternoon post brought a letter from Lord Valleys marked Express.

Lady Valleys opened it with a slight grimace, which deepened as she read. Her handsome, florid face wore an expression of sadness seldom seen there. There was, in fact, more than a touch of dignity in her reception of the unpalatable news.

"Eustace declares his intention of marrying this Mrs. Noel"—so ran her husband's letter—"I know, unfortunately, of no way in which I can prevent him. If you can discover legitimate means of dissuasion, it would be well to use them. My dear, it's the very devil."

It was the very devil! For, if Miltoun had already made up his mind to marry her, without knowledge of the malicious rumour, what would not be his determination now? And the woman of the world rose up in Lady Valleys. This marriage must not come off. It was contrary to almost every instinct of one who was practical not only by character, but by habit of life and training. Her warm and full-blooded nature had a sneaking sympathy with love and pleasure, and had she not been practical, she might have found this side of her a serious drawback to the main tenor of a life so much in view of the public eye. Her consciousness of this danger in her own case made her extremely alive to the risks of an undesirable connection—especially if it were a marriage—to any public man. At the same time the mother-heart in her was stirred. Eustace had never been so deep in her affection as Bertie, still he was her first-born; and in face of news which meant that he was lost to her—for this must indeed be 'the marriage of two minds' (or whatever that quotation was)—she felt strangely jealous of a woman, who had won her son's love, when she herself had never won it. The aching of this jealousy gave her face for a moment almost a spiritual expression, then passed away into impatience. Why should he marry her? Things could be arranged. People spoke of it already as an illicit relationship; well then, let people have what they had invented. If the worst came to the worst, this was not the only constituency in England; and a dissolution could not be far off. Better anything than a marriage which would handicap him all his life! But would it be so great a handicap? After all, beauty counted for much! If only her story were not too conspicuous! But what was her story? Not to know it was absurd! That was the worst of people who were not in Society, it was so difficult to find out! And there rose in her that almost brutal resentment, which ferments very rapidly in those who from their youth up have been hedged round with the belief that they and they alone are the whole of the world. In this mood Lady Valleys passed the letter to her daughters. They read, and in turn handed it to Bertie, who in silence returned it to his mother.

But that evening, in the billiard-room, having manoeuvred to get him to herself, Barbara said to Courtier:

"I wonder if you will answer me a question, Mr. Courtier?"

"If I may, and can."

Her low-cut dress was of yew-green, with, little threads of flame-colour, matching her hair, so that there was about her a splendour of darkness and whiteness and gold, almost dazzling; and she stood very still, leaning back against the lighter green of the billiard-table, grasping its edge so tightly that the smooth strong backs of her hands quivered.

"We have just heard that Miltoun is going to ask Mrs. Noel to marry him. People are never mysterious, are they, without good reason? I wanted you to tell me—who is she?"

"I don't think I quite grasp the situation," murmured Courtier. "You said—to marry him?"

Seeing that she had put out her hand, as if begging for the truth, he added: "How can your brother marry her—she's married!"

"Oh!"

"I'd no idea you didn't know that much."

"We thought there was a divorce."

The expression of which mention has been made—that peculiar white-hot sardonically jolly look—visited Courtier's face at once. "Hoist with their own petard! The usual thing. Let a pretty woman live alone—the tongues of men will do the rest."

"It was not so bad as that," said Barbara dryly; "they said she had divorced her husband."

Caught out thus characteristically riding past the hounds Courtier bit his lips.

"You had better hear the story now. Her father was a country parson, and a friend of my father's; so that I've known her from a child. Stephen Lees Noel was his curate. It was a 'snap' marriage—she was only twenty, and had met hardly any men. Her father was ill and wanted to see her settled before he died. Well, she found out almost directly, like a good many other people, that she'd made an utter mistake."

Barbara came a little closer.

"What was the man like?"

"Not bad in his way, but one of those narrow, conscientious pig-headed fellows who make the most trying kind of husband—bone egoistic. A parson of that type has no chance at all. Every mortal thing he has to do or say helps him to develop his worst points. The wife of a man like that's no better than a slave. She began to show the strain of it at last; though she's the sort who goes on till she snaps. It took him four years to realize. Then, the question was, what were they to do? He's a very High Churchman, with all their feeling about marriage; but luckily his pride was wounded. Anyway, they separated two years ago; and there she is, left high and dry. People say it was her fault. She ought to have known her own mind—at twenty! She ought to have held on and hidden it up somehow. Confound their thick-skinned charitable souls, what do they know of how a sensitive woman suffers? Forgive me, Lady Barbara—I get hot over this." He was silent; then seeing her eyes fixed on him, went on: "Her mother died when she was born, her father soon after her marriage. She's enough money of her own, luckily, to live on quietly. As for him, he changed his parish and runs one somewhere in the Midlands. One's sorry for the poor devil, too, of course! They never see each other; and, so far as I know, they don't correspond. That, Lady Barbara, is the simple history."

Barbara, said, "Thank you," and turned away; and he heard her mutter: "What a shame!"

But he could not tell whether it was Mrs. Noel's fate, or the husband's fate, or the thought of Miltoun that had moved her to those words.

She puzzled him by her self-possession, so almost hard, her way of refusing to show feeling.' Yet what a woman she would make if the drying curse of high-caste life were not allowed to stereotype and shrivel her! If enthusiasm were suffered to penetrate and fertilize her soul! She reminded him of a great tawny lily. He had a vision of her, as that flower, floating, freed of roots and the mould of its cultivated soil, in the liberty of the impartial air. What a passionate and noble thing she might become! What radiance and perfume she would exhale! A spirit Fleur-de-Lys! Sister to all the noble flowers of light that inhabited the wind!

Leaning in the deep embrasure of his window, he looked at anonymous Night. He could hear the owls hoot, and feel a heart beating out there somewhere in the darkness, but there came no answer to his wondering. Would she—this great tawny lily of a girl—ever become unconscious of her environment, not in manner merely, but in the very soul, so that she might be just a woman, breathing, suffering, loving, and rejoicing with the poet soul of all mankind? Would she ever be capable of riding out with the little company of big hearts, naked of advantage? Courtier had not been inside a church for twenty years, having long felt that he must not enter the mosques of his country without putting off the shoes of freedom, but he read the Bible, considering it a very great poem. And the old words came haunting him: 'Verily I say unto you, It is harder for a camel to pass through the eye of a needle than for a rich man to enter the kingdom of Heaven.' And now, looking into the Night, whose darkness seemed to hold the answer to all secrets, he tried to read the riddle of this girl's future, with which there seemed so interwoven that larger enigma, how far the spirit can free itself, in this life, from the matter that encompasseth.

The Night whispered suddenly, and low down, as if rising from the sea, came the moon, dropping a wan robe of light till she gleamed out nude against the sky-curtain. Night was no longer anonymous. There in the dusky garden the statue of Diana formed slowly before his eyes, and behind her—as it were, her temple—rose the tall spire of the cypress tree.

Chapter XIV

A copy of the Bucklandbury News, containing an account of his evening adventure, did not reach Miltoun till he was just starting on his return journey. It came marked with blue pencil together with a note.

"MY DEAR EUSTACE,

"The enclosed—however unwarranted and impudent—requires attention. But we shall do nothing till you come back.

"Yours ever,
"WILLIAM SHROPTON."

The effect on Miltoun might perhaps have been different had he not been so conscious of his intention to ask Audrey Noel to be his wife; but in any circumstances it is doubtful whether he would have done more than smile, and tear the paper up. Truly that sort of thing had so little power to hurt or disturb him personally, that he was incapable of seeing how it could hurt or disturb others. If those who read it were affected, so much the worse for them. He had a real, if unobtrusive, contempt for groundlings, of whatever class; and it never entered his head to step an inch out of his course in deference to their vagaries. Nor did it come home to him that Mrs. Noel, wrapped in the glamour which he cast about her, could possibly suffer from the meanness of vulgar minds. Shropton's note, indeed, caused him the more annoyance of those two documents. It was like his brother-in-law to make much of little!

He hardly dozed at all during his swift journey through the sleeping country; nor when he reached his room at Monkland did he go to bed. He had the wonderful, upborne feeling of man on the verge of achievement. His spirit and senses were both on fire—for that was the quality of this woman, she suffered no part of him to sleep, and he was glad of her exactions.

He drank some tea; went out, and took a path up to the moor. It was not yet eight o'clock when he reached the top of the nearest tor. And there, below him, around, and above, was a land and sky transcending even his exaltation. It was like a symphony of great music; or the nobility of a stupendous mind laid bare; it was God up there, in His many moods. Serenity was spread in the middle heavens, blue, illimitable, and along to the East, three huge clouds, like thoughts brooding over the destinies below, moved slowly toward the sea, so that great shadows filled the valleys. And the land that lay under all the other sky was gleaming, and quivering with every colour, as it were, clothed with the divine smile. The wind, from the North, whereon floated the white birds of the smaller clouds, had no voice, for it was above barriers, utterly free. Before Miltoun, turning to this wind, lay the maze of the lower lands, the misty greens, rose pinks, and browns of the fields, and white and grey dots and strokes of cottages and church towers, fading into the blue veil of distance, confined by a far range of hills. Behind him there was nothing but the restless surface of the moor, coloured purplish-brown. On that untamed sea of graven wildness could be seen no ship of man, save one, on the far horizon—the grim hulk, Dartmoor Prison. There was no sound, no scent, and it seemed to Miltoun as if his spirit had left his body, and become part of the solemnity of God. Yet, as he stood there, with his head bared, that strange smile which haunted him in moments of deep feeling, showed that he had not surrendered to the Universal, that his own spirit was but being fortified, and that this was the true and secret source of his delight. He lay down in a scoop of the stones. The sun entered there, but no wind, so that a dry sweet scent exuded from the young shoots of heather. That warmth and perfume crept through the shield of his spirit, and stole into his blood; ardent images rose before him, the vision of an unending embrace. Out of an embrace sprang Life, out of that the World was made, this World, with its innumerable forms, and natures—no two alike! And from him and her would spring forms to take their place in the great pattern. This seemed wonderful, and right-for they would be worthy forms, who would hand on those traditions which seemed to him so necessary and great. And then there broke on him one of those delirious waves of natural desire, against which he had so often fought, so often with great pain conquered. He got up, and ran downhill, leaping over the stones, and the thicker clumps of heather.

Audrey Noel, too, had been early astir, though she had gone late enough to bed. She dressed languidly, but very carefully, being one of those women who put on armour against Fate, because they are proud, and dislike the thought that their sufferings should make others suffer; because, too, their bodies are to them as it were sacred, having been given them in trust, to cause delight. When she had finished, she looked at herself in the glass rather more distrustfully than usual. She felt that her sort of woman was at a discount in these days, and being sensitive, she was never content either with her appearance, or her habits. But, for all that, she went on behaving in unsatisfactory ways, because she incorrigibly loved to look as charming as she could; and even if no one were going to see her, she never felt that she looked charming enough. She was—as Lady Casterley had shrewdly guessed—the kind of woman who spoils men by being too nice to them; of no use to those who wish women to assert themselves; yet having a certain passive stoicism, very disconcerting. With little or no power of initiative, she would do what she was set to do with a thoroughness that would shame an initiator; temperamentally unable to beg anything of anybody, she required love as a plant requires water; she could give herself completely, yet remain oddly incorruptible; in a word, hopeless, and usually beloved of those who thought her so.

With all this, however, she was not quite what is called a 'sweet woman—a phrase she detested—for there was in her a queer vein of gentle cynicism. She 'saw' with extraordinary clearness, as if she had been born in Italy and still carried that clear dry atmosphere about her soul. She loved glow and warmth and colour; such mysticism as she felt was pagan; and she had few aspirations—sufficient to her were things as they showed themselves to be.

This morning, when she had made herself smell of geraniums, and fastened all the small contrivances that hold even the best of women together, she went downstairs to her little dining-room, set the spirit lamp going, and taking up her newspaper, stood waiting to make tea.

It was the hour of the day most dear to her. If the dew had been brushed off her life, it was still out there every morning on the face of Nature, and on the faces of her flowers; there was before her all the pleasure of seeing how each of those little creatures in the garden had slept; how many children had been born since the Dawn; who was ailing, and needed attention. There was also the feeling, which renews itself every morning in people who live lonely lives, that they are not lonely, until, the day wearing on, assures them of the fact. Not that she was idle, for she had obtained through Courtier the work of reviewing music in a woman's paper, for which she was intuitively fitted. This, her flowers, her own music, and the affairs of certain families of cottagers, filled nearly all her time. And she asked no better fate than to have every minute occupied, having that passion for work requiring no initiation, which is natural to the owners of lazy minds.

Suddenly she dropped her newspaper, went to the bowl of flowers on the breakfast-table, and plucked forth two stalks of lavender; holding them away from her, she went out into the garden, and flung them over the wall.

This strange immolation of those two poor sprigs, born so early, gathered and placed before her with such kind intention by her maid, seemed of all acts the least to be expected of one who hated to hurt people's feelings, and whose eyes always shone at the sight of flowers. But in truth the smell of lavender—that scent carried on her husband's handkerchief and clothes—still affected her so strongly that she could not bear to be in a room with it. As nothing else did, it brought before her one, to live with whom had slowly become torture. And freed by that scent, the whole flood of memory broke in on her. The memory of three years when her teeth had been set doggedly, on her discovery that she was chained to unhappiness for life; the memory of the abrupt end, and of her creeping away to let her scorched nerves recover. Of how during the first year of this release which was not freedom, she had twice changed her abode, to get away from her own story—not because she was ashamed of it, but because it reminded her of wretchedness. Of how she had then come to Monkland, where the quiet life had slowly given her elasticity again. And then of her meeting with Miltoun; the unexpected delight of that companionship; the frank enjoyment of the first four months. And she remembered all her secret rejoicing, her silent identification of another life with her own, before she acknowledged or even suspected love. And just three weeks ago now, helping to tie up her roses, he had touched her, and she had known. But even then, until the night of Courtier's accident, she had not dared to realize. More concerned now for him than for herself, she asked herself a thousand times if she had been to blame. She had let him grow fond of her, a woman out of court, a dead woman! An unpardonable sin! Yet surely that depended on what she was prepared to give! And she was frankly ready to give everything, and ask for nothing. He knew her position, he had told her that he knew. In her love for him she gloried, would continue to glory; would suffer for it without regret. Miltoun was right in believing that newspaper gossip was incapable of hurting her, though her reasons for being so impervious were not what he supposed. She was not, like him, secured from pain because such insinuations about the private affairs of others were mean and vulgar and beneath notice; it had not as yet occurred to her to look at the matter in so lofty and general a light; she simply was not hurt, because she was already so deeply Miltoun's property in spirit, that she was almost glad that they should assign him all the rest of her. But for Miltoun's sake she was disturbed to the soul. She had tarnished his shield in the eyes of men; and (for she was oddly practical, and saw things in very clear proportion) perhaps put back his career, who knew how many years!

She sat down to drink her tea. Not being a crying woman, she suffered quietly. She felt that Miltoun would be coming to her. She did not know at all what she should say when he did come. He could not care for her so much as she cared for him! He was a man; men soon forget! Ah! but he was not like most men. One could not look at his eyes without feeling that he could suffer terribly! In all this her own reputation concerned her not at all. Life, and her clear way of looking at things, had rooted in her the conviction that to a woman the preciousness of her reputation was a fiction invented by men entirely for man's benefit; a second-hand fetish insidiously, inevitably set-up by men for worship, in novels, plays, and law-courts. Her instinct told her that men could not feel secure in the possession of their women unless they could believe that women set tremendous store by sexual reputation. What they wanted to believe, that they did believe! But she knew otherwise. Such great-minded women as she had met or read of had always left on her the impression that reputation for them was a matter of the spirit, having little to do with sex. From her own feelings she knew that reputation, for a simple woman, meant to stand well in the eyes of him or her whom she loved best. For worldly women—and there were so many kinds of those, besides the merely fashionable—she had always noted that its value was not intrinsic, but commercial; not a crown of dignity, but just a marketable asset. She did not dread in the least what people might say of her friendship with Miltoun; nor did she feel at all that her indissoluble marriage forbade her loving him. She had secretly felt free as soon as she had discovered that she had never really loved her husband; she had only gone on dutifully until the separation, from sheer passivity, and because it was against her nature to cause pain to anyone. The man who was still her husband was now as dead to her as if he had never been born. She could not marry again, it was true; but she could and did love. If that love was to be starved and die away, it would not be because of any moral scruples.

She opened her paper languidly; and almost the first words she read, under the heading of Election News, were these:

'Apropos of the outrage on Mr. Courtier, we are requested to state that the lady who accompanied Lord Miltoun to the rescue of that gentleman was Mrs. Lees Noel, wife of the Rev. Stephen Lees Noel, vicar of Clathampton, Warwickshire.'

This dubious little daub of whitewash only brought a rather sad smile to her lips. She left her tea, and went out into the air. There at the gate was Miltoun coming in. Her heart leaped. But she went forward quietly, and greeted him with cast-down eyes, as if nothing were out of the ordinary.

Chapter XV

Exaltation had not left Miltoun. His sallow face was flushed, his eyes glowed with a sort of beauty; and Audrey Noel who, better than most women, could read what was passing behind a face, saw those eyes with the delight of a moth fluttering towards a lamp. But in a very unemotional voice she said:

"So you have come to breakfast. How nice of you!"

It was not in Miltoun to observe the formalities of attack. Had he been going to fight a duel there would have been no preliminary, just a look, a bow, and the swords crossed. So in this first engagement of his with the soul of a woman!

He neither sat down nor suffered her to sit, but stood looking intently into her face, and said:

"I love you."

Now that it had come, with this disconcerting swiftness, she was strangely calm, and unashamed. The elation of knowing for sure that she was loved was like a wand waving away all tremors, stilling them to sweetness. Since nothing could take away that knowledge, it seemed that she could never again be utterly unhappy. Then, too, in her nature, so deeply, unreasoningly incapable of perceiving the importance of any principle but love, there was a secret feeling of assurance, of triumph. He did love her! And she, him! Well! And suddenly panic-stricken, lest he should take back those words, she put her hand up to his breast, and said:

"And I love you."

The feel of his arms round her, the strength and passion of that moment, were so terribly sweet, that she died to thought, just looking up at him, with lips parted and eyes darker with the depth of her love than he had ever dreamed that eyes could be. The madness of his own feeling kept him silent. And they stood there, so merged in one another that they knew and cared nothing for any other mortal thing. It was very still in the room; the roses and carnations in the lustre bowl, seeming to know that their mistress was caught up into heaven, had let their perfume steal forth and occupy every cranny of the abandoned air; a hovering bee, too, circled round the lovers' heads, scenting, it seemed, the honey in their hearts.

It has been said that Miltoun's face was not unhandsome; for Audrey Noel at this moment when his eyes were so near hers, and his lips touching her, he was transfigured, and had become the spirit of all beauty. And she, with heart beating fast against him, her eyes, half closing from delight, and her hair asking to be praised with its fragrance, her cheeks fainting pale with emotion, and her arms too languid with happiness to embrace him—she, to him, was the incarnation of the woman that visits dreams.

So passed that moment.

The bee ended it; who, impatient with flowers that hid their honey so deep, had entangled himself in Audrey's hair. And then, seeing that words, those dreaded things, were on his lips, she tried to kiss them back. But they came:

"When will you marry me?"

It all swayed a little. And with marvellous rapidity the whole position started up before her. She saw, with preternatural insight, into its nooks and corners. Something he had said one day, when they were talking of the Church view of marriage and divorce, lighted all up. So he had really never known about her! At this moment of utter sickness, she was saved from fainting by her sense of humour—her cynicism. Not content to let her be, people's tongues had divorced her; he had believed them! And the crown of irony was that he should want to marry her, when she felt so utterly, so sacredly his, to do what he liked with sans forms or ceremonies. A surge of bitter feeling against the man who stood between her and Miltoun almost made her cry out. That man had captured her before she knew the world or her own soul, and she was tied to him, till by some beneficent chance he drew his last breath when her hair was grey, and her eyes had no love light, and her cheeks no longer grew pale when they were kissed; when twilight had fallen, and the flowers, and bees no longer cared for her.

It was that feeling, the sudden revolt of the desperate prisoner, which steeled her to put out her hand, take up the paper, and give it to Miltoun.

When he had read the little paragraph, there followed one of those eternities which last perhaps two minutes.

He said, then:

"It's true, I suppose?" And, at her silence, added: "I am sorry."

This queer dry saying was so much more terrible than any outcry, that she remained, deprived even of the power of breathing, with her eyes still fixed on Miltoun's face.

The smile of the old Cardinal had come up there, and was to her like a living accusation. It seemed strange that the hum of the bees and flies and the gentle swishing of the limetree should still go on outside, insisting that there was a world moving and breathing apart from her, and careless of her misery. Then some of her courage came back, and with it her woman's mute power. It came haunting about her face, perfectly still, about her lips, sensitive and drawn, about her eyes, dark, almost mutinous under their arched brows. She stood, drawing him with silence and beauty.

At last he spoke:

"I have made a foolish mistake, it seems. I believed you were free."

Her lips just moved for the words to pass: "I thought you knew. I never, dreamed you would want to marry me."

It seemed to her natural that he should be thinking only of himself, but with the subtlest defensive instinct, she put forward her own tragedy:

"I suppose I had got too used to knowing I was dead."

"Is there no release?"

"None. We have neither of us done wrong; besides with him, marriage is—for ever."

"My God!"

She had broken his smile, which had been cruel without meaning to be cruel; and with a smile of her own that was cruel too, she said:

"I didn't know that you believed in release either."

Then, as though she had stabbed herself in stabbing him, her face quivered.

He looked at her now, conscious at last that she was suffering. And she felt that he was holding himself in with all his might from taking her again into his arms. Seeing this, the warmth crept back to her lips, and a little light into her eyes, which she kept hidden from him. Though she stood so proudly still, some wistful force was coming from her, as from a magnet, and Miltoun's hands and arms and face twitched as though palsied. This struggle, dumb and pitiful, seemed never to be coming to an end in the little white room, darkened by the thatch of the verandah, and sweet with the scent of pinks and of a wood fire just lighted somewhere out at the back. Then, without a word, he turned and went out. She heard the wicket gate swing to. He was gone.

Chapter XVI

Lord Denis was fly-fishing—the weather just too bright to allow the little trout of that shallow, never silent stream to embrace with avidity the small enticements which he threw in their direction. Nevertheless he continued to invite them, exploring every nook of their watery pathway with his soft-swishing line. In a rough suit and battered hat adorned with those artificial and other flies, which infest Harris tweed, he crept along among the hazel bushes and thorn-trees, perfectly happy. Like an old spaniel, who has once gloried in the fetching of hares, rabbits, and all manner of fowl, and is now glad if you will but throw a stick for him, so one, who had been a famous fisher before the Lord, who had harried the waters of Scotland and Norway, Florida and Iceland, now pursued trout no bigger than sardines. The glamour of a thousand memories hallowed the hours he thus spent by that brown water. He fished unhasting, religious, like some good Catholic adding one more to the row of beads already told, as though he would fish himself, gravely, without complaint, into the other world. With each fish caught he experienced a solemn satisfaction.

Though he would have liked Barbara with him that morning, he had only looked at her once after breakfast in such a way that she could not see him, and with a dry smile gone off by himself. Down by the stream it was dappled, both cool and warm, windless; the trees met over the river, and there were many stones, forming little basins which held up the ripple, so that the casting of a fly required much cunning. This long dingle ran for miles through the foot-growth of folding hills. It was beloved of jays; but of human beings there were none, except a chicken-farmer's widow, who lived in a house thatched almost to the ground, and made her livelihood by directing tourists, with such cunning that they soon came back to her for tea.

It was while throwing a rather longer line than usual to reach a little dark piece of crisp water that Lord Dennis heard the swishing and crackling of someone advancing at full speed. He frowned slightly, feeling for the nerves of his fishes, whom he did not wish startled. The invader was Miltoun, hot, pale, dishevelled, with a queer, hunted look on his face. He stopped on seeing his great-uncle, and instantly assumed the mask of his smile.

Lord Dennis was not the man to see what was not intended for him, and he merely said:

"Well, Eustace!" as he might have spoken, meeting his nephew in the hall of one of his London Clubs.

Miltoun, no less polite, murmured:

"Hope I haven't lost you anything."

Lord Dennis shook his head, and laying his rod on the bank, said:

"Sit down and have a chat, old fellow. You don't fish, I think?"

He had not, in the least, missed the suffering behind Miltoun's mask; his eyes were still good, and there was a little matter of some twenty years' suffering of his own on account of a woman—ancient history now—which had left him quaintly sensitive, for an old man, to signs of suffering in others.

Miltoun would not have obeyed that invitation from anyone else, but there was something about Lord Dennis which people did not resist; his power lay in a dry ironic suavity which could not but persuade people that impoliteness was altogether too new and raw a thing to be indulged in.

The two sat side by side on the roots of trees. At first they talked a little of birds, and then were dumb, so dumb that the invisible creatures of the woods consulted together audibly. Lord Dennis broke that silence.

"This place," he said, "always reminds me of Mark Twain's writings—can't tell why, unless it's the ever-greenness. I like the evergreen philosophers, Twain and Meredith. There's no salvation except through courage, though I never could stomach the 'strong man'—captain of his soul, Henley and Nietzsche and that sort—goes against the grain with me. What do you say, Eustace?"

"They meant well," answered Miltoun, "but they protested too much."

Lord Dennis moved his head in assent.

"To be captain of your soul!" continued Miltoun in a bitter voice; "it's a pretty phrase!"

"Pretty enough," murmured Lord Dennis.

Miltoun looked at him.

"And suitable to you," he said.

"No, my dear," Lord Dennis answered dryly, "a long way off that, thank God!"

His eyes were fixed intently on the place where a large trout had risen in the stillest toffee-coloured pool. He knew that fellow, a half-pounder at least, and his thoughts began flighting round the top of his head, hovering over the various merits of the flies. His fingers itched too, but he made no movement, and the ash-tree under which he sat let its leaves tremble, as though in sympathy.

"See that hawk?" said Miltoun.

At a height more than level with the tops of the hills a buzzard hawk was stationary in the blue directly over them. Inspired by curiosity at their stillness, he was looking down to see whether they were edible; the upcurved ends of his great wings flirted just once to show that he was part of the living glory of the air—a symbol of freedom to men and fishes.

Lord Dennis looked at his great-nephew. The boy—for what else was thirty to seventy-six?—was taking it hard, whatever it might be, taking it very hard! He was that sort—ran till he dropped. The worst kind to help—the sort that made for trouble—that let things gnaw at them! And there flashed before the old man's mind the image of Prometheus devoured by the eagle. It was his favourite tragedy, which he still read periodically, in the Greek, helping himself now and then out of his old lexicon to the meaning of some word which had flown to Erebus. Yes, Eustace was a fellow for the heights and depths!

He said quietly:

"You don't care to talk about it, I suppose?"

Miltoun shook his head, and again there was silence.

The buzzard hawk having seen them move, quivered his wings like a moth's, and deserted that plane of air. A robin from the dappled warmth of a mossy stone, was regarding them instead. There was another splash in the pool.

Lord Dennis said gently:

"That fellow's risen twice; I believe he'd take a 'Wistman's treasure.'" Extracting from his hat its latest fly, and binding it on, he began softly to swish his line.

"I shall have him yet!" he muttered. But Miltoun had stolen away....

The further piece of information about Mrs. Noel, already known by Barbara, and diffused by the 'Bucklandbury News', had not become common knowledge at the Court till after Lord Dennis had started out to fish. In combination with the report that Miltoun had arrived and gone out without breakfast, it had been received with mingled feelings. Bertie, Harbinger, and Shropton, in a short conclave, after agreeing that from the point of view of the election it was perhaps better than if she had been a divorcee, were still inclined to the belief that no time was to be lost—in doing what, however, they were unable to determine. Apart from the impossibility of knowing how a fellow like Miltoun would take the matter, they were faced with the devilish subtlety of all situations to which the proverb 'Least said, soonest mended' applies. They were in the presence of that awe-inspiring thing, the power of scandal. Simple statements of simple facts, without moral drawn (to which no legal exception could be taken) laid before the public as pieces of interesting information, or at the worst exposed in perfect good faith, lest the public should blindly elect as their representative one whose private life might not stand the inspection of daylight—what could be more justifiable! And yet Miltoun's supporters knew that this simple statement of where he spent his evenings had a poisonous potency, through its power of stimulating that side of the human imagination the most easily excited. They recognized only too well, how strong was a certain primitive desire, especially in rural districts, by yielding to which the world was made to go, and how remarkably hard it, was not to yield to it, and how interesting and exciting to see or hear of others yielding to it, and how (though here, of course, men might differ secretly) reprehensible of them to do so! They recognized, too well, how a certain kind of conscience would appreciate this rumour; and how the puritans would lick their lengthened chops. They knew, too, how irresistible to people of any imagination at all, was the mere combination of a member of a class, traditionally supposed to be inclined to having what it wanted, with a lady who lived alone! As Harbinger said: It was really devilish awkward! For, to take any notice of it would be to make more people than ever believe it true. And yet, that it was working mischief, they felt by the secret voice in their own souls, telling them that they would have believed it if they had not known better. They hung about, waiting for Miltoun to come in.

The news was received by Lady Valleys with a sigh of intense relief, and the remark that it was probably another lie. When Barbara confirmed it, she only said: "Poor Eustace!" and at once wrote off to her husband to say that 'Anonyma' was still married, so that the worst fortunately could not happen.

Miltoun came in to lunch, but from his face and manner nothing could be guessed. He was a thought more talkative than usual, and spoke of Brabrook's speech—some of which he had heard. He looked at Courtier meaningly, and after lunch said to him:

"Will you come round to my den?"

In that room, the old withdrawing-room of the Elizabethan wing—where once had been the embroideries, tapestries, and missals of beruffled dames were now books, pamphlets, oak-panels, pipes, fencing gear, and along one wall a collection of Red Indian weapons and ornaments brought back by Miltoun from the United States. High on the wall above these reigned the bronze death-mask of a famous Apache Chief, cast from a plaster taken of the face by a professor of Yale College, who had declared it to be a perfect specimen of the vanishing race. That visage, which had a certain weird resemblance to Dante's, presided over the room with cruel, tragic stoicism. No one could look on it without feeling that, there, the human will had been pushed to its farthest limits of endurance.

Seeing it for the first time, Courtier said:

"Fine thing—that! Only wants a soul."

Miltoun nodded:

"Sit down," he said.

Courtier sat down.

There followed one of those silences in which men whose spirits, though different, have a certain bigness in common—can say so much to one another:

At last Miltoun spoke:

"I have been living in the clouds, it seems. You are her oldest friend. The immediate question is how to make it easiest for her in face of this miserable rumour!"

Not even Courtier himself could have put such whip-lash sting into the word 'miserable.'

He answered:

"Oh! take no notice of that. Let them stew in their own juice. She won't care."

Miltoun listened, not moving a muscle of his face.

"Your friends here," went on Courtier with a touch of contempt, "seem in a flutter. Don't let them do anything, don't let them say a word. Treat the thing as it deserves to be treated. It'll die."

Miltoun, however, smiled.

"I'm not sure," he said, "that the consequences will be as you think, but I shall do as you say."

"As for your candidature, any man with a spark of generosity in his soul will rally to you because of it."

"Possibly," said Miltoun. "It will lose me the election, for all that."

Then, dimly conscious that their last words had revealed the difference of their temperaments and creeds, they stared at one another.

"No," said Courtier, "I never will believe that people can be so mean!"

"Until they are."

"Anyway, though we get at it in different ways, we agree."

Miltoun leaned his elbow on the mantelpiece, and shading his face with his hand, said:

"You know her story. Is there any way out of that, for her?"

On Courtier's face was the look which so often came when he was speaking for one of his lost causes—as if the fumes from a fire in his heart had mounted to his head.

"Only the way," he answered calmly, "that I should take if I were you."

"And that?"

"The law into your own hands."

Miltoun unshaded his face. His gaze seemed to have to travel from an immense distance before it reached Courtier. He answered:

"Yes, I thought you would say that."

Chapter XVII

When everything, that night, was quiet, Barbara, her hair hanging loose outside her dressing gown, slipped from her room into the dim corridor. With bare feet thrust into fur-crowned slippers which made no noise, she stole along looking at door after door. Through a long Gothic window, uncurtained, the mild moonlight was coming. She stopped just where that moonlight fell, and tapped. There came no answer. She opened the door a little way, and said:

"Are you asleep, Eusty?"

There still came no answer, and she went in.

The curtains were drawn, but a chink of moonlight peering through fell on the bed. This was empty. Barbara stood uncertain, listening. In the heart of that darkness there seemed to be, not sound, but, as it were, the muffled soul of sound, a sort of strange vibration, like that of a flame noiselessly licking the air. She put her hand to her heart, which beat as though it would leap through the thin silk covering. From what corner of the room was that mute tremor coming? Stealing to the window, she parted the curtains, and stared back into the shadows. There, on the far side, lying on the floor with his arms pressed tightly round his head and his face to the wall, was Miltoun. Barbara let fall the curtains, and stood breathless, with such a queer sensation in her breast as she had never felt; a sense of something outraged-of scarred pride. It was gone at once, in a rush of pity. She stepped forward quickly in the darkness, was visited by fear, and stopped. He had seemed absolutely himself all the evening. A little more talkative, perhaps, a little more caustic than usual. And now to find him like this! There was no great share of reverence in Barbara, but what little she possessed had always been kept for her eldest brother. He had impressed her, from a child, with his aloofness, and she had been proud of kissing him because he never seemed to let anybody else do so. Those caresses, no doubt, had the savour of conquest; his face had been the undiscovered land for her lips. She loved him as one loves that which ministers to one's pride; had for him, too, a touch of motherly protection, as for a doll that does not get on too well with the other dolls; and withal a little unaccustomed awe.

Dared she now plunge in on this private agony? Could she have borne that anyone should see herself thus prostrate? He had not heard her, and she tried to regain the door. But a board creaked; she heard him move, and flinging away her fears, said: "It's me! Babs!" and dropped on her knees beside him. If it had not been so pitch dark she could never have done that. She tried at once to take his head into her arms, but could not see it, and succeeded indifferently. She could but stroke his arm continually, wondering whether he would hate her ever afterwards, and blessing the darkness, which made it all seem as though it were not happening, yet so much more poignant than if it had happened. Suddenly she felt him slip away from her, and getting up, stole out. After the darkness of that room, the corridor seemed full of grey filmy light, as though dream-spiders had joined the walls with their cobwebs, in which innumerable white moths, so tiny that they could not be seen, were struggling. Small eerie noises crept about. A sudden frightened longing for warmth, and light, and colour came to Barbara. She fled back to her room. But she could not sleep. That terrible mute unseen vibration in the unlighted room-like the noiseless licking of a flame at bland air; the touch of Miltoun's hand, hot as fire against her cheek and neck; the whole tremulous dark episode, possessed her through and through. Thus had the wayward force of Love chosen to manifest itself to her in all its wistful violence. At this fiat sight of the red flower of passion her cheeks burned; up and down her, between the cool sheets, little hot cruel shivers ran; she lay, wide-eyed, staring at the ceiling. She thought, of the woman whom he so loved, and wondered if she too were lying sleepless, flung down on a bare floor, trying to cool her forehead and lips against a cold wall.

Not for hours did she fall asleep, and then dreamed of running desperately through fields full of tall spiky asphodel-like flowers, and behind her was running herself.

In the morning she dreaded to go down. Could she meet Miltoun now that she knew of the passion in him, and he knew that she knew it? She had her breakfast brought upstairs. Before she had finished Miltoun himself came in. He looked more than usually self-contained, not to say ironic, and only remarked: "If you're going to ride you might take this note for me over to old Haliday at Wippincott." By his coming she knew that he was saying all he ever meant to say about that dark incident. And sympathizing completely with a reticence which she herself felt to be the only possible way out for both of them, Barbara looked at him gratefully, took the note and said: "All right!"

Then, after glancing once or twice round the room, Miltoun went away.

He left her restless, divested of the cloak 'of course,' in a strange mood of questioning, ready as it were for the sight of the magpie wings of Life, and to hear their quick flutterings. Talk jarred on her that morning, with its sameness and attachment to the facts of the present and the future, its essential concern with the world as it was-she avoided all companionship on her ride. She wanted to be told of things that were not, yet might be, to peep behind the curtain, and see the very spirit of mortal happenings escaped from prison. And this was all so unusual with Barbara, whose body was too perfect, too sanely governed by the flow of her blood not to revel in the moment and the things thereof. She knew it was unusual. After her ride she avoided lunch, and walked out into the lanes. But about two o'clock, feeling very hungry, she went into a farmhouse, and asked for milk. There, in the kitchen, like young jackdaws in a row with their mouths a little open, were the three farm boys, seated on a bench gripped to the alcove of the great fire-way, munching bread and cheese. Above their heads a gun was hung, trigger upwards, and two hams were mellowing in the smoke. At the feet of a black-haired girl, who was slicing onions, lay a sheep dog of tremendous age, with nose stretched out on paws, and in his little blue eyes a gleam of approaching immortality. They all stared at, Barbara. And one of the boys, whose face had the delightful look of him who loses all sense of other things in what he is seeing at the moment, smiled, and continued smiling, with sheer pleasure. Barbara drank her milk, and wandered out again; passing through a gate at the bottom of a steep, rocky tor, she sat down on a sun-warmed stone. The sunlight fell greedily on her here, like an invisible swift hand touching her all over, and specially caressing her throat and face. A very gentle wind, which dived over the tor tops into the young fern; stole down at her, spiced with the fern sap. All was warmth and peace, and only the cuckoos on the far thorn trees—as though stationed by the Wistful Master himself—were there to disturb her heart: But all the sweetness and piping of the day did not soothe her. In truth, she could not have said what was the matter, except that she felt so discontented, and as it were empty of all but a sort of aching impatience with—what exactly she could not say. She had that rather dreadful feeling of something slipping by which she could not catch. It was so new to her to feel like that—for no girl was less given to moods and repinings. And all the time a sort of contempt for this soft and almost sentimental feeling made her tighten her lips and frown. She felt distrustful and sarcastic towards a mood so utterly subversive of that fetich 'Hardness,' to the unconscious worship of which she had been brought up. To stand no sentiment or nonsense either in herself or others was the first article of faith; not to slop-over anywhere. So that to feel as she did was almost horrible to Barbara. Yet she could not get rid of the sensation. With sudden recklessness she tried giving herself up to it entirely. Undoing the scarf at her throat, she let the air play on her bared neck, and stretched out her arms as if to hug the wind to her; then, with a sigh, she got up, and walked on. And now she began thinking of 'Anonyma'; turning her position over and over. The idea that anyone young and beautiful should thus be clipped off in her life, roused her impatient indignation. Let them try it with her! They would soon see! For all her cultivated 'hardness,' Barbara really hated anything to suffer. It seemed to her unnatural. She never went to that hospital where Lady Valleys had a ward, nor to their summer camp for crippled children, nor to help in their annual concert for sweated workers, without a feeling of such vehement pity that it was like being seized by the throat: Once, when she had been singing to them, the rows of wan, pinched faces below had been too much for her; she had broken down, forgotten her words, lost memory of the tune, and just ended her performance with a smile, worth more perhaps to her audience than those lost verses. She never came away from such sights and places without a feeling of revolt amounting almost to rage; and she only continued to go because she dimly knew that it was expected of her not to turn her back on such things, in her section of Society.

But it was not this feeling which made her stop before Mrs. Noel's cottage; nor was it curiosity. It was a quite simple desire to squeeze her hand.

'Anonyma' seemed taking her trouble as only those women who are no good at self-assertion can take things—doing exactly as she would have done if nothing had happened; a little paler than usual, with lips pressed rather tightly together.

They neither of them spoke at first, but stood looking, not at each other's faces, but at each other's breasts. At last Barbara stepped forward impulsively and kissed her.

After that, like two children who kiss first, and then make acquaintance, they stood apart, silent, faintly smiling. It had been given and returned in real sweetness and comradeship, that kiss, for a sign of womanhood making face against the world; but now that it was over, both felt a little awkward. Would that kiss have been given if Fate had been auspicious? Was it not proof of misery? So Mrs. Noel's smile seemed saying, and Barbara's smile unwillingly admitted. Perceiving that if they talked it could only be about the most ordinary things, they began speaking of music, flowers, and the queerness of bees' legs. But all the time, Barbara, though seemingly unconscious, was noting with her smiling eyes, the tiny movement's, by which one woman can tell what is passing in another. She saw a little quiver tighten the corner of the lips, the eyes suddenly grow large and dark, the thin blouse desperately rise and fall. And her fancy, quickened by last night's memory, saw this woman giving herself up to the memory of love in her thoughts. At this sight she felt a little of that impatience which the conquering feel for the passive, and perhaps just a touch of jealousy.

Whatever Miltoun decided, that would this woman accept! Such resignation, while it simplified things, offended the part of Barbara which rebelled against all inaction, all dictation, even from her favourite brother. She said suddenly:

"Are you going to do nothing? Aren't you going to try and free yourself? If I were in your position, I would never rest till I'd made them free me."

But Mrs. Noel did not answer; and sweeping her glance from that crown of soft dark hair, down the soft white figure, to the very feet, Barbara cried:

"I believe you are a fatalist."

Soon after that, not knowing what more to say, she went away. But walking home across the fields, where full summer was swinging on the delicious air and there was now no bull but only red cows to crop short the 'milk-maids' and buttercups, she suffered from this strange revelation of the strength of softness and passivity—as though she had seen in the white figure of 'Anonyma,' and heard in her voice something from beyond, symbolic, inconceivable, yet real.

Chapter XVIII

Lord Valleys, relieved from official pressure by subsidence of the war scare, had returned for a long week-end. To say that he had been intensely relieved by the news that Mrs. Noel was not free, would be to put it mildly. Though not old-fashioned, like his mother-in-law, in regard to the mixing of the castes, prepared to admit that exclusiveness was out of date, to pass over with a shrug and a laugh those numerous alliances by which his order were renewing the sinews of war, and indeed in his capacity of an expert, often pointing out the dangers of too much in-breeding—yet he had a peculiar personal feeling about his own family, and was perhaps a little extra sensitive because of Agatha; for Shropton, though a good fellow, and extremely wealthy, was only a third baronet, and had originally been made of iron. It was inadvisable to go outside the inner circle where there was no material necessity for so doing. He had not done it himself. Moreover there was a sentiment about these things!

On the morning after his arrival, visiting the kennels before breakfast, he stood chatting with his head man, and caressing the wet noses of his two favourite pointers,—with something of the feeling of a boy let out of school. Those pleasant creatures, cowering and quivering with pride against his legs, and turning up at him their yellow Chinese eyes, gave him that sense of warmth and comfort which visits men in the presence of their hobbies. With this particular pair, inbred to the uttermost, he had successfully surmounted a great risk. It was now touch and go whether he dared venture on one more cross to the original strain, in the hope of eliminating the last clinging of liver colour. It was a gamble—and it was just that which rendered it so vastly interesting.

A small voice diverted his attention; he looked round and saw little Ann. She had been in bed when he arrived the night before, and he was therefore the newest thing about.

She carried in her arms a guinea-pig, and began at once:

"Grandpapa, Granny wants you. She's on the terrace; she's talking to Mr. Courtier. I like him—he's a kind man. If I put my guinea-pig down, will they bite it? Poor darling—they shan't! Isn't it a darling!"

Lord Valleys, twirling his moustache, regarded the guinea-pig without favour; he had rather a dislike for all senseless kinds of beasts.

Pressing the guinea-pig between her hands, as it might be a concertina, little Ann jigged it gently above the pointers, who, wrinkling horribly their long noses, gazed upwards, fascinated.

"Poor darlings, they want it—don't they? Grandpapa."

"Yes."

"Do you think the next puppies will be spotted quite all over?"

Continuing to twirl his moustache, Lord Valleys answered:

"I think it is not improbable, Ann."

"Why do you like them spotted like that? Oh! they're kissing Sambo—I must go!"

Lord Valleys followed her, his eyebrows a little raised.

As he approached the terrace his wife came, towards him. Her colour was, deeper than usual, and she had the look, higher and more resolute, peculiar to her when she had been opposed. In truth she had just been through a passage of arms with Courtier, who, as the first revealer of Mrs. Noel's situation, had become entitled to a certain confidence on this subject. It had arisen from what she had intended as a perfectly natural and not unkind remark, to the effect that all the trouble had come from Mrs. Noel not having made her position clear to Miltoun from the first.

He had at once grown very red.

"It's easy, Lady Valleys, for those who have never been in the position of a lonely woman, to blame her."

Unaccustomed to be withstood, she had looked at him intently:

"I am the last person to be hard on a woman for conventional reasons. But I think it showed lack of character."

Courtier's reply had been almost rude.

"Plants are not equally robust, Lady Valleys. Some, as we know, are actually sensitive."

She had retorted with decision

"If you like to so dignify the simpler word 'weak'"

He had become very rigid at that, biting deeply into his moustache.

"What crimes are not committed under the sanctity of that creed 'survival of the fittest,' which suits the book of all you fortunate people so well!"

Priding herself on her restraint, Lady Valleys answered:

"Ah! we must talk that out. On the face of them your words sound a little unphilosophic, don't they?"

He had looked straight at her with a queer, unpleasant smile; and she had felt at once disturbed and angry. It was all very well to pet and even to admire these original sort of men, but there were limits. Remembering, however, that he was her guest, she had only said:

"Perhaps after all we had better not talk it out;" and moving away, she heard him answer: "In any case, I'm certain Audrey Noel never wilfully kept your son in the dark; she's much too proud."

Though rude, she could not help liking the way he stuck up for this woman; and she threw back at him the words:

"You and I, Mr. Courtier, must have a good fight some day!"

She went towards her husband conscious of the rather pleasurable sensation which combat always roused in her.

These two were very good comrades. Theirs had been a love match, and making due allowance for human nature beset by opportunity, had remained, throughout, a solid and efficient alliance. Taking, as they both did, such prominent parts in public and social matters, the time they spent together was limited, but productive of mutual benefit and reinforcement. They had not yet had an opportunity of discussing their son's affair; and, slipping her hand through his arm, Lady Valleys drew him away from the house.

"I want to talk to you about Miltoun, Geoff."

"H'm!" said Lord Valleys; "yes. The boy's looking worn. Good thing when this election's over."

"If he's beaten and hasn't something new and serious to concentrate himself on, he'll fret his heart out over that woman."

Lord Valleys meditated a little before replying.

"I don't think that, Gertrude. He's got plenty of spirit."

"Of course! But it's a real passion. And, you know, he's not like most boys, who'll take what they can."

She said this rather wistfully.

"I'm sorry for the woman," mused Lord Valleys; "I really am."

"They say this rumour's done a lot of harm."

"Our influence is strong enough to survive that."

"It'll be a squeak; I wish I knew what he was going to do. Will you ask him?"

"You're clearly the person to speak to him," replied Lord Valleys. "I'm no hand at that sort of thing."

But Lady Valleys, with genuine discomfort, murmured:

"My dear, I'm so nervous with Eustace. When he puts on that smile of his I'm done for, at once."

"This is obviously a woman's business; nobody like a mother."

"If it were only one of the others," muttered Lady Valleys: "Eustace has that queer way of making you feel lumpy."

Lord Valleys looked at her askance. He had that kind of critical fastidiousness which a word will rouse into activity. Was she lumpy? The idea had never struck him.

"Well, I'll do it, if I must," sighed Lady Valleys.

When after breakfast she entered Miltoun's 'den,' he was buckling on his spurs preparatory, to riding out to some of the remoter villages. Under the mask of the Apache chief, Bertie was standing, more inscrutable and neat than ever, in a perfectly tied cravatte, perfectly cut riding breeches, and boots worn and polished till a sooty glow shone through their natural russet. Not specially dandified in his usual dress, Bertie Caradoc would almost sooner have died than disgrace a horse. His eyes, the sharper because they had only half the space of the ordinary eye to glance from, at once took in the fact that his mother wished to be alone with 'old Miltoun,' and he discreetly left the room.

That which disconcerted all who had dealings with Miltoun was the discovery made soon or late, that they could not be sure how anything would strike him. In his mind, as in his face, there was a certain regularity, and then—impossible to say exactly where—it would, shoot off and twist round a corner. This was the legacy no doubt of the hard-bitten individuality, which had brought to the front so many of his ancestors; for in Miltoun was the blood not only of the Caradocs and Fitz-Harolds, but of most other prominent families in the kingdom, all of whom, in those ages before money made the man, must have had a forbear conspicuous by reason of qualities, not always fine, but always poignant.

And now, though Lady Valleys had the audacity of her physique, and was not customarily abashed, she began by speaking of politics, hoping her son would give her an opening. But he gave her none, and she grew nervous. At last, summoning all her coolness, she said:

"I'm dreadfully sorry about this affair, dear boy. Your father told me of your talk with him. Try not to take it too hard."

Miltoun did not answer, and silence being that which Lady Valleys habitually most dreaded, she took refuge in further speech, outlining for her son the whole episode as she saw it from her point of view, and ending with these words:

"Surely it's not worth it."

Miltoun heard her with his peculiar look, as of a man peering through a vizor. Then smiling, he said:

"Thank you;" and opened the door.

Lady Valleys, without quite knowing whether he intended her to do so, indeed without quite knowing anything at the moment, passed out, and Miltoun closed the door behind her.

Ten minutes later he and Bertie were seen riding down the drive.

Chapter XIX

That afternoon the wind, which had been rising steadily, brought a flurry of clouds up from the South-West. Formed out on the heart of the Atlantic, they sailed forward, swift and fleecy at first, like the skirmishing white shallops of a great fleet; then, in serried masses, darkened the sun. About four o'clock they broke in rain, which the wind drove horizontally with a cold whiffling murmur. As youth and glamour die in a face before the cold rains of life, so glory died on the moor. The tors, from being uplifted wild castles, became mere grey excrescences. Distance failed. The cuckoos were silent. There was none of the beauty that there is in death, no tragic greatness—all was moaning and monotony. But about seven the sun tore its way back through the swathe, and flared out. Like some huge star, whose rays were stretching down to the horizon, and up to the very top of the hill of air, it shone with an amazing murky glamour; the clouds splintered by its shafts, and tinged saffron, piled themselves up as if in wonder. Under the sultry warmth of this new great star, the heather began to steam a little, and the glitter of its wet unopened bells was like that of innumerable tiny smoking fires. The two brothers were drenched as they cantered silently home. Good friends always, they had never much to say to one another. For Miltoun was conscious that he thought on a different plane from Bertie; and Bertie grudged even to his brother any inkling of what was passing in his spirit, just as he grudged parting with diplomatic knowledge, or stable secrets, or indeed anything that might leave him less in command of life. He grudged it, because in a private sort of way it lowered his estimation of his own stoical self-sufficiency; it hurt something proud in the withdrawing-room of his soul. But though he talked little, he had the power of contemplation—often found in men of decided character, with a tendency to liver. Once in Nepal, where he had gone to shoot, he had passed a month quite happily with only a Ghoorka servant who could speak no English. To those who asked him if he had not been horribly bored, he had always answered: "Not a bit; did a lot of thinking."

With Miltoun's trouble he had the professional sympathy of a brother and the natural intolerance of a confirmed bachelor. Women were to him very kittle-cattle. He distrusted from the bottom of his soul those who had such manifest power to draw things from you. He was one of those men in whom some day a woman might awaken a really fine affection; but who, until that time, would maintain the perfectly male attitude to the entire sex, and, after it, to all the sex but one. Women were, like Life itself, creatures to be watched, carefully used, and kept duly subservient. The only allusion therefore that he made to Miltoun's trouble was very sudden.

"Old man, I hope you're going to cut your losses."

The words were followed by undisturbed silence: But passing Mrs. Noel's cottage Miltoun said:

"Take my horse on; I want to go in here."....

She was sitting at her piano with her hands idle, looking at a line of music.... She had been sitting thus for many minutes, but had not yet taken in the notes.

When Miltoun's shadow blotted the light by which she was seeing so little, she gave a slight start, and got up. But she neither went towards him, nor spoke. And he, without a word, came in and stood by the hearth, looking down at the empty grate. A tortoise-shell cat which had been watching swallows, disturbed by his entrance, withdrew from the window beneath a chair.

This silence, in which the question of their future lives was to be decided, seemed to both interminable; yet, neither could end it.

At last, touching his sleeve, she said: "You're wet!"

Miltoun shivered at that timid sign of possession. And they again stood in silence broken only by the sound of the cat licking its paws.

But her faculty for dumbness was stronger than his, and—he had to speak first.

"Forgive me for coming; something must be settled. This—rumour—"

"Oh! that!" she said. "Is there anything I can do to stop the harm to you?"

It was the turn of Miltoun's lips to curl. "God! no; let them talk!"

Their eyes had come together now, and, once together, seemed unable to part.

Mrs. Noel said at last:

"Will you ever forgive me?"

"What for—it was my fault."

"No; I should have known you better."

The depth of meaning in those words—the tremendous and subtle admission they contained of all that she had been ready to do, the despairing knowledge in them that he was not, and never had been, ready to 'bear it out even to the edge of doom'—made Miltoun wince away.

"It is not from fear—believe that, anyway."

"I do."

There followed another long, long silence! But though so close that they were almost touching, they no longer looked at one another. Then Miltoun said:

"There is only to say good-bye, then."

At those clear words spoken by lips which, though just smiling, failed so utterly to hide his misery, Mrs. Noel's face became colourless as her white gown. But her eyes, which had grown immense, seemed from the sheer lack of all other colour, to have drawn into them the whole of her vitality; to be pouring forth a proud and mournful reproach.

Shivering, and crushing himself together with his arms, Miltoun walked towards the window. There was not the faintest sound from her, and he looked back. She was following him with her eyes. He threw his hand up over his face, and went quickly out. Mrs. Noel stood for a little while where he had left her; then, sitting down once more at the piano, began again to con over the line of music. And the cat stole back to the window to watch the swallows. The sunlight was dying slowly on the top branches of the lime-tree; a drizzling rain began to fall.

Claud Fresnay, Viscount Harbinger was, at the age of thirty-one, perhaps the least encumbered peer in the United Kingdom. Thanks to an ancestor who had acquired land, and departed this life one hundred and thirty years before the town of Nettlefold was built on a small portion of it, and to a father who had died in his son's infancy, after judiciously selling the said town, he possessed a very large income independently of his landed interests. Tall and well-built, with handsome, strongly-marked features, he gave at first sight an impression of strength—which faded somewhat when he began to talk. It was not so much the manner of his speech—with its rapid slang, and its way of turning everything to a jest—as the feeling it produced, that the brain behind it took naturally the path of least resistance. He was in fact one of those personalities who are often enough prominent in politics and social life, by reason of their appearance, position, assurance, and of a certain energy, half genuine, and half mere inherent predilection for short cuts. Certainly he was not idle, had written a book, travelled, was a Captain of Yeomanry, a Justice of the Peace, a good cricketer, and a constant and glib speaker. It would have been unfair to call his enthusiasm for social reform spurious. It was real enough in its way, and did certainly testify that he was not altogether lacking either in imagination or good-heartedness. But it was over and overlaid with the public-school habit—that peculiar, extraordinarily English habit, so powerful and beguiling that it becomes a second nature stronger than the first—of relating everything in the Universe to the standards and prejudices of a single class. Since practically all his intimate associates were immersed in it, he was naturally not in the least conscious of this habit; indeed there was nothing he deprecated so much in politics as the narrow and prejudiced outlook, such as he had observed in the Nonconformist, or labour politician. He would never have admitted for a moment that certain doors had been banged-to at his birth, bolted when he went to Eton, and padlocked at Cambridge. No one would have denied that there was much that was valuable in his standards—a high level of honesty, candour, sportsmanship, personal cleanliness, and self-reliance, together with a dislike of such cruelty as had been officially (so to speak) recognized as cruelty, and a sense of public service to a State run by and for the public schools; but it would have required far more originality than he possessed ever to look at Life from any other point of view than that from which he had been born and bred to watch Her. To fully understand harbinger, one must, and with unprejudiced eyes and brain, have attended one of those great cricket matches in which he had figured conspicuously as a boy, and looking down from some high impartial spot have watched the ground at lunch time covered from rope to rope and stand to stand with a marvellous swarm, all walking in precisely the same manner, with precisely the same expression on their faces, under precisely the same hats—a swarm enshrining the greatest identity of, creed and habit ever known since the world began. No, his environment had not been favourable to originality. Moreover he was naturally rapid rather than deep, and life hardly ever left him alone or left him silent. Brought into contact day and night with people to whom politics were more or less a game; run after everywhere; subjected to no form of discipline—it was a wonder that he was as serious as he was. Nor had he ever been in love, until, last year, during her first season, Barbara had, as he might have expressed it—in the case of another 'bowled him middle stump. Though so deeply smitten, he had not yet asked her to marry him—had not, as it were, had time, nor perhaps quite the courage, or conviction. When he was near her, it seemed impossible that he could go on longer without knowing his fate; when he was away from her it was almost a relief, because there were so many things to be done and said, and so little time to do or say them in. But now, during this fortnight, which, for her sake, he had devoted to Miltoun's cause, his feeling had advanced beyond the point of comfort.

He did not admit that the reason of this uneasiness was Courtier, for, after all, Courtier was, in a sense, nobody, and 'an extremist' into the bargain, and an extremist always affected the centre of Harbinger's anatomy, causing it to give off a peculiar smile and tone of voice. Nevertheless, his eyes, whenever they fell on that sanguine, steady, ironic face, shone with a sort of cold inquiry, or were even darkened by the shade of fear. They met seldom, it is true, for most of his day was spent in motoring and speaking, and most of Courtier's in writing and riding, his leg being still too weak for walking. But once or twice in the smoking room late at night, he had embarked on some bantering discussion with the champion of lost causes; and very soon an ill-concealed impatience had crept into his voice. Why a man should waste his time, flogging dead horses on a journey to the moon, was incomprehensible! Facts were facts, human nature would never be anything but human nature! And it was peculiarly galling to see in Courtier's eye a gleam, to catch in his voice a tone, as if he were thinking: "My young friend, your soup is cold!"

On a morning after one of these encounters, seeing Barbara sally forth in riding clothes, he asked if he too might go round the stables, and started forth beside her, unwontedly silent, with an odd feeling about his heart, and his throat unaccountably dry.

The stables at Monkland Court were as large as many country houses. Accommodating thirty horses, they were at present occupied by twenty-one, including the pony of little Ann. For height, perfection of lighting, gloss, shine, and purity of atmosphere they were unequalled in the county. It seemed indeed impossible that any horse could ever so far forget himself in such a place as to remember that he was a horse. Every morning a little bin of carrots, apples, and lumps of sugar, was set close to the main entrance, ready for those who might desire to feed the dear inhabitants.

Reined up to a brass ring on either side of their stalls with their noses towards the doors, they were always on view from nine to ten, and would stand with their necks arched, ears pricked, and coats gleaming, wondering about things, soothed by the faint hissing of the still busy grooms, and ready to move their noses up and down the moment they saw someone enter.

In a large loose-box at the end of the north wing Barbara's favourite chestnut hunter, all but one saving sixteenth of whom had been entered in the stud book, having heard her footstep, was standing quite still with his neck turned. He had been crumping up an apple placed amongst his feed, and his senses struggled between the lingering flavour of that delicacy,—and the perception of a sound with which he connected carrots. When she unlatched his door, and said "Hal," he at once went towards his manger, to show his independence, but when she said: "Oh! very well!" he turned round and came towards her. His eyes, which were full and of a soft brilliance, under thick chestnut lashes, explored her all over. Perceiving that her carrots were not in front, he elongated his neck, let his nose stray round her waist, and gave her gauntletted hand a nip with his lips. Not tasting carrot, he withdrew his nose, and snuffled. Then stepping carefully so as not to tread on her foot, he bunted her gently with his shoulder, till with a quick manoeuvre he got behind her and breathed low and long on her neck. Even this did not smell of carrots, and putting his muzzle over her shoulder against her cheek, he slobbered a very little. A carrot appeared about the level of her waist, and hanging his head over, he tried to reach it. Feeling it all firm and soft under his chin, he snuffled again, and gave her a gentle dig with his knee. But still unable to reach the carrot, he threw his head up, withdrew, and pretended not to see her. And suddenly he felt two long substances round his neck, and something soft against his nose. He suffered this in silence, laying his ears back. The softness began puffing on his muzzle. Pricking his ears again, he puffed back a little harder, with more curiosity, and the softness was withdrawn. He perceived suddenly that he had a carrot in his mouth.

Harbinger had witnessed this episode, oddly pale, leaning against the loose-box wall. He spoke, as it came to an end:

"Lady Babs!"

The tone of his voice must have been as strange as it sounded to himself, for Barbara spun round.

"Yes?"

"How long am I going on like this?"

Neither changing colour nor dropping her eyes, she regarded him with a faintly inquisitive interest. It was not a cruel look, had not a trace of mischief, or sex malice, and yet it frightened him by its serene inscrutability. Impossible to tell what was going on behind it. He took her hand, bent over it, and said in a low voice:

"You know what I feel; don't be cruel to me!"

She did not pull away her hand; it was as if she had not thought of it.

"I am not a bit cruel."

Looking up, he saw her smiling.

"Then—Babs!"

His face was close to hers, but Barbara did not shrink back. She just shook her head; and Harbinger flushed up.

"Why?" he asked; and as though the enormous injustice of that rejecting gesture had suddenly struck him, he dropped her hand.

"Why?" he said again, sharply.

But the silence was only broken by the cheeping of sparrows outside the round window, and the sound of the horse, Hal, munching the last morsel of his carrot. Harbinger was aware in his every nerve of the sweetish, slightly acrid, husky odour of the loosebox, mingling with the scent of Barbara's hair and clothes. And rather miserably, he said for the third time:

"Why?"

But folding her hands away behind her back she answered gently:

"My dear, how should I know why?"

She was calmly exposed to his embrace if he had only dared; but he did not dare, and went back to the loose-box wall. Biting his finger, he stared at her gloomily. She was stroking the muzzle of her horse; and a sort of dry rage began whisking and rustling in his heart. She had refused him—Harbinger! He had not known, had not suspected how much he wanted her. How could there be anybody else for him, while that young, calm, sweet-scented, smiling thing lived, to make his head go round, his senses ache, and to fill his heart with longing! He seemed to himself at that moment the most unhappy of all men.

"I shall not give you up," he muttered.

Barbara's answer was a smile, faintly curious, compassionate, yet almost grateful, as if she had said:

"Thank you—who knows?"

And rather quickly, a yard or so apart, and talking of horses, they returned to the house.

It was about noon, when, accompanied by Courtier, she rode forth.

The Sou-Westerly spell—a matter of three days—had given way before radiant stillness; and merely to be alive was to feel emotion. At a little stream running beside the moor under the wild stone man, the riders stopped their horses, just to listen, and, inhale the day. The far sweet chorus of life was tuned to a most delicate rhythm; not one of those small mingled pipings of streams and the lazy air, of beasts, men; birds, and bees, jarred out too harshly through the garment of sound enwrapping the earth. It was noon—the still moment—but this hymn to the sun, after his too long absence, never for a moment ceased to be murmured. And the earth wore an under-robe of scent, delicious, very finely woven of the young fern sap, heather buds; larch-trees not yet odourless, gorse just going brown, drifted woodsmoke, and the breath of hawthorn. Above Earth's twin vestments of sound and scent, the blue enwrapping scarf of air, that wistful wide champaign, was spanned only by the wings of Freedom.

After that long drink of the day, the riders mounted almost in silence to the very top of the moor. There again they sat quite still on their horses, examining the prospect. Far away to South and East lay the sea, plainly visible. Two small groups of wild ponies were slowly grazing towards each other on the hillside below.

Courtier said in a low voice:

"'Thus will I sit and sing, with love in my arms; watching our two herds mingle together, and below us the far, divine, cerulean sea.'"

And, after another silence, looking steadily in Barbara's face, he added:

"Lady Barbara, I am afraid this is the last time we shall be alone together. While I have the chance, therefore, I must do homage.... You will always be the fixed star for my worship. But your rays are too bright; I shall worship from afar. From your seventh Heaven, therefore, look down on me with kindly eyes, and do not quite forget me:"

Under that speech, so strangely compounded of irony and fervour, Barbara sat very still, with glowing cheeks.

"Yes," said Courtier, "only an immortal must embrace a goddess. Outside the purlieus of Authority I shall sit cross-legged, and prostrate myself three times a day."

But Barbara answered nothing.

"In the early morning," went on Courtier, "leaving the dark and dismal homes of Freedom I shall look towards the Temples of the Great; there with the eye of faith I shall see you."

He stopped, for Barbara's lips were moving.

"Don't hurt me, please."

Courtier leaned over, took her hand, and put it to his lips. "We will now ride on...."

That night at dinner Lord Dennis, seated opposite his great-niece, was struck by her appearance.

"A very beautiful child," he thought, "a most lovely young creature!"

She was placed between Courtier and Harbinger. And the old man's still keen eyes carefully watched those two. Though attentive to their neighbours on the other side, they were both of them keeping the corner of an eye on Barbara and on each other. The thing was transparent to Lord Dennis, and a smile settled in that nest of gravity between his white peaked beard and moustaches. But he waited, the instinct of a fisherman bidding him to neglect no piece of water, till he saw the child silent and in repose, and watched carefully to see what would rise. Although she was so calmly, so healthily eating, her eyes stole round at Courtier. This quick look seemed to Lord Dennis perturbed, as if something were exciting her. Then Harbinger spoke, and she turned to answer him. Her face was calm now, faintly smiling, a little eager, provocative in its joy of life. It made Lord Dennis think of his own youth. What a splendid couple! If Babs married young Harbinger there would not be a finer pair in all England. His eyes travelled back to Courtier. Manly enough! They called him dangerous! There was a look of effervescence, carefully corked down—might perhaps be attractive to a girl! To his essentially practical and sober mind, a type like Courtier was puzzling. He liked the look of him, but distrusted his ironic expression, and that appearance of blood to the head. Fellow—no doubt—that would ride off on his ideas, humanitarian! To Lord Dennis there was something queer about humanitarians. They offended perhaps his dry and precise sense of form. They were always looking out for cruelty or injustice; seemed delighted when they found it—swelled up, as it were, when they scented it, and as there was a good deal about, were never quite of normal size. Men who lived for ideas were, in fact, to one for whom facts sufficed always a little worrying! A movement from Barbara brought him back to actuality. Was the possessor of that crown of hair and those divine young shoulders the little Babs who had ridden with him in the Row? Time was certainly the Devil! Her eyes were searching for something; and following the direction of that glance, Lord Dennis found himself observing Miltoun. What a difference between those two! Both no doubt in the great trouble of youth; which sometimes, as he knew too well, lasted on almost to old age. It was a curious look the child was giving her brother, as if asking him to help her. Lord Dennis had seen in his day many young creatures leave the shelter of their freedom and enter the house of the great lottery; many, who had drawn a prize and thereat lost forever the coldness of life; many too, the light of whose eyes had faded behind the shutters of that house, having drawn a blank. The thought of 'little' Babs on the threshold of that inexorable saloon, filled him with an eager sadness; and the sight of the two men watching for her, waiting for her, like hunters, was to him distasteful. In any case, let her not, for Heaven's sake, go ranging as far as that red fellow of middle age, who might have ideas, but had no pedigree; let her stick to youth and her own order, and marry the—young man, confound him, who looked like a Greek god, of the wrong period, having grown a moustache. He remembered her words the other evening about these two and the different lives they lived. Some romantic notion or other was working in her! And again he looked at Courtier. A Quixotic type—the sort that rode slap-bang at everything! All very well—but not for Babs! She was not like the glorious Garibaldi's glorious Anita! It was truly characteristic of Lord Dennis—and indeed of other people—that to him champions of Liberty when dead were far dearer than champions of Liberty when living. Yes, Babs would want more, or was it less, than just a life of sleeping under the stars for the man she loved, and the cause he fought for. She would want pleasure, and, not too much effort, and presently a little power; not the uncomfortable after-fame of a woman who went through fire, but the fame and power of beauty, and Society prestige. This, fancy of hers, if it were a fancy, could be nothing but the romanticism of a young girl. For the sake of a passing shadow, to give up substance? It wouldn't do! And again Lord Dennis fixed his shrewd glance on his great-niece. Those eyes, that smile! Yes! She would grow out of this. And take the Greek god, the dying Gaul—whichever that young man was!

Chapter XXI

It was not till the morning of polling day itself that Courtier left Monkland Court. He had already suffered for some time from bad conscience. For his knee was practically cured, and he knew well that it was Barbara, and Barbara alone, who kept him staying there. The atmosphere of that big house with its army of servants, the impossibility of doing anything for himself, and the feeling of hopeless insulation from the vivid and necessitous sides of life, galled him greatly. He felt a very genuine pity for these people who seemed to lead an existence as it were smothered under their own social importance. It was not their fault. He recognized that they did their best. They were good specimens of their kind; neither soft nor luxurious, as things went in a degenerate and extravagant age; they evidently tried to be simple—and this seemed to him to heighten the pathos of their situation. Fate had been too much for them. What human spirit could emerge untrammelled and unshrunken from that great encompassing host of material advantage? To a Bedouin like Courtier, it was as though a subtle, but very terrible tragedy was all the time being played before his eyes; and in, the very centre of this tragedy was the girl who so greatly attracted him. Every night when he retired to that lofty room, which smelt so good, and where, without ostentation, everything was so perfectly ordered for his comfort, he thought:

"My God, to-morrow I'll be off!"

But every morning when he met her at breakfast his thought was precisely the same, and there were moments when he caught himself wondering: "Am I falling under the spell of this existence—am I getting soft?" He recognized as never before that the peculiar artificial 'hardness' of the patrician was a brine or pickle, in which, with the instinct of self-preservation they deliberately soaked themselves, to prevent the decay of their overprotected fibre. He perceived it even in Barbara—a sort of sentiment-proof overall, a species of mistrust of the emotional or lyrical, a kind of contempt of sympathy and feeling. And every day he was more and more tempted to lay rude hands on this garment; to see whether he could not make her catch fire, and flare up with some emotion or idea. In spite of her tantalizing, youthful self-possession, he saw that she felt this longing in him, and now and then he caught a glimpse of a streak of recklessness in her which lured him on:

And yet, when at last he was saying good-bye on the night before polling day, he could not flatter himself that he had really struck any spark from her. Certainly she gave him no chance, at that final interview, but stood amongst the other women, calm and smiling, as if determined that he should not again mock her with his ironical devotion.

He got up very early the next morning, intending to pass away unseen. In the car put at his disposal; he found a small figure in a holland-frock, leaning back against the cushions so that some sandalled toes pointed up at the chauffeur's back. They belonged to little Ann, who in the course of business had discovered the vehicle before the door. Her sudden little voice under her sudden little nose, friendly but not too friendly, was comforting to Courtier.

"Are you going? I can come as, far as the gate." "That is lucky."

"Yes. Is that all your luggage?"

"I'm afraid it is."

"Oh! It's quite a lot, really, isn't it?"

"As much as I deserve."

"Of course you don't have to take guinea-pigs about with you?"

"Not as a rule."

"I always do. There's great-Granny!"

There certainly was Lady Casterley, standing a little back from the drive, and directing a tall gardener how to deal with an old oak-tree. Courtier alighted, and went towards her to say good-bye. She greeted him with a certain grim cordiality.

"So you are going! I am glad of that, though you quite understand that I like you personally."

"Quite!"

Her eyes gleamed maliciously.

"Men who laugh like you are dangerous, as I've told you before!"

Then, with great gravity; she added

"My granddaughter will marry Lord Harbinger. I mention that, Mr. Courtier, for your peace of mind. You are a man of honour; it will go no further."

Courtier, bowing over her hand, answered:

"He will be lucky."

The little old lady regarded him unflinchingly.

"He will, sir. Good-bye!"

Courtier smilingly raised his hat. His cheeks were burning. Regaining the car, he looked round. Lady Casterley was busy once more exhorting the tall gardener. The voice of little Ann broke in on his thoughts:

"I hope you'll come again. Because I expect I shall be here at Christmas; and my brothers will be here then, that is, Jock and Tiddy, not Christopher because he's young. I must go now. Good-bye! Hallo, Susie!"

Courtier saw her slide away, and join the little pale adoring figure of the lodge-keeper's daughter.

The car passed out into the lane.

If Lady Casterley had planned this disclosure, which indeed she had not, for the impulse had only come over her at the sound of Courtier's laugh, she could not have, devised one more effectual, for there was deep down in him all a wanderer's very real distrust, amounting almost to contempt, of people so settled and done for; as aristocrats or bourgeois, and all a man of action's horror of what he called puking and muling. The pursuit of Barbara with any other object but that of marriage had naturally not occurred to one who had little sense of conventional morality, but much self-respect; and a secret endeavour to cut out Harbinger, ending in a marriage whereat he would figure as a sort of pirate, was quite as little to the taste of a man not unaccustomed to think himself as good as other people.

He caused the car to deviate up the lane that led to Audrey Noel's, hating to go away without a hail of cheer to that ship in distress.

She came out to him on the verandah. From the clasp of her hand, thin and faintly browned—the hand of a woman never quite idle—he felt that she relied on him to understand and sympathize; and nothing so awakened the best in Courtier as such mute appeals to his protection. He said gently:

"Don't let them think you're down;" and, squeezing her hand hard: "Why should you be wasted like this? It's a sin and shame!"

But he stopped in what he felt to be an unlucky speech at sight of her face, which without movement expressed so much more than his words. He was protesting as a civilized man; her face was the protest of Nature, the soundless declaration of beauty wasted against its will, beauty that was life's invitation to the embrace which gave life birth.

"I'm clearing out, myself," he said: "You and I, you know, are not good for these people. No birds of freedom allowed!"

Pressing his hand, she turned away into the house, leaving Courtier gazing at the patch of air where her white figure had stood. He had always had a special protective feeling for Audrey Noel, a feeling which with but little encouragement might have become something warmer. But since she had been placed in her anomalous position, he would not for the world have brushed the dew off her belief that she could trust him. And, now that he had fixed his own gaze elsewhere, and she was in this bitter trouble, he felt on her account the rancour that a brother feels when Justice and Pity have conspired to flout his sister. The voice of Frith the chauffeur roused him from gloomy reverie.

"Lady Barbara, sir!"

Following the man's eyes, Courtier saw against the sky-line on the for above Ashman's Folly, an equestrian statue. He stopped the car at once, and got out.

He reached her at the ruin, screened from the road, by that divine chance which attends on men who take care that it shall. He could not tell whether she knew of his approach, and he would have given all he had, which was not much, to have seen through the stiff grey of her coat, and the soft cream of her body, into that mysterious cave, her heart. To have been for a moment, like Ashman, done for good and all with material things, and living the white life where are no barriers between man and woman. The smile on her lips so baffled him, puffed there by her spirit, as a first flower is puffed through the sur face of earth to mock at the spring winds. How tell what it signified! Yet he rather prided himself on his knowledge of women, of whom he had seen something. But all he found to say was:

"I'm glad of this chance."

Then suddenly looking up, he found her strangely pale and quivering.

"I shall see you in London!" she said; and, touching her horse with her whip, without looking back, she rode away over the hill.

Courtier returned to the moor road, and getting into the car, muttered:

"Faster, please, Frith!"....

Chapter XXII

Polling was already in brisk progress when Courtier arrived in Bucklandbury; and partly from a not unnatural interest in the result, partly from a half-unconscious clinging to the chance of catching another glimpse of Barbara, he took his bag to the hotel, determined to stay for the announcement of the poll. Strolling out into the High Street he began observing the humours of the day. The bloom of political belief had long been brushed off the wings of one who had so flown the world's winds. He had seen too much of more vivid colours to be capable now of venerating greatly the dull and dubious tints of blue and yellow. They left him feeling extremely philosophic. Yet it was impossible to get away from them, for the very world that day seemed blue and yellow, nor did the third colour of red adopted by both sides afford any clear assurance that either could see virtue in the other; rather, it seemed to symbolize the desire of each to have his enemy's blood. But Courtier soon observed by the looks cast at his own detached, and perhaps sarcastic, face, that even more hateful to either side than its antagonist, was the philosophic eye. Unanimous was the longing to heave half a brick at it whenever it showed itself. With its d—d impartiality, its habit of looking through the integument of things to see if there might be anything inside, he felt that they regarded it as the real adversary—the eternal foe to all the little fat 'facts,' who, dressed up in blue and yellow, were swaggering and staggering, calling each other names, wiping each other's eyes, blooding each other's noses. To these little solemn delicious creatures, all front and no behind, the philosophic eye, with its habit of looking round the corner, was clearly detestable. The very yellow and very blue bodies of these roistering small warriors with their hands on their tin swords and their lips on their tin trumpets, started up in every window and on every wall confronting each citizen in turn, persuading him that they and they alone were taking him to

Westminster. Nor had they apparently for the most part much trouble with electors, who, finding uncertainty distasteful, passionately desired to be assured that the country could at once be saved by little yellow facts or little blue facts, as the case might be; who had, no doubt, a dozen other good reasons for being on the one side or the other; as, for instance, that their father had been so before them; that their bread was buttered yellow or buttered blue; that they had been on the other side last time; that they had thought it over and made up their minds; that they had innocent blue or naive yellow beer within; that his lordship was the man; or that the words proper to their mouths were 'Chilcox for Bucklandbury'; and, above all, the one really creditable reason, that, so far as they could tell with the best of their intellect and feelings, the truth at the moment was either blue or yellow.

The narrow high street was thronged with voters. Tall policemen stationed there had nothing to do. The certainty of all, that they were going to win, seemed to keep everyone in good humour. There was as yet no need to break anyone's head, for though the sharpest lookout was kept for any signs of the philosophic eye, it was only to be found—outside Courtier—in the perambulators of babies, in one old man who rode a bicycle waveringly along the street and stopped to ask a policeman what was the matter in the town, and in two rather green-faced fellows who trundled barrows full of favours both blue and yellow.

But though Courtier eyed the 'facts' with such suspicion, the keenness of everyone about the business struck him as really splendid. They went at it with a will. Having looked forward to it for months, they were going to look back on it for months. It was evidently a religious ceremony, summing up most high feelings; and this seemed to one who was himself a man of action, natural, perhaps pathetic, but certainly no matter for scorn.

It was already late in the afternoon when there came debouching into the high street a long string of sandwichmen, each bearing before and behind him a poster containing these words beautifully situated in large dark blue letters against a pale blue ground:

"NEW COMPLICATIONS. DANGER NOT PAST. VOTE FOR MILTOUN AND THE GOVERNMENT, AND SAVE THE EMPIRE."

Courtier stopped to look at them with peculiar indignation. Not only did this poster tramp in again on his cherished convictions about Peace, but he saw in it something more than met the unphilosophic eye. It symbolized for him all that was catch-penny in the national life-an epitaph on the grave of generosity, unutterably sad. Yet from a Party point of view what could be more justifiable? Was it not desperately important that every blue nerve should be strained that day to turn yellow nerves, if not blue, at all events green, before night fell? Was it not perfectly true that the Empire could only be saved by voting blue? Could they help a blue paper printing the words, 'New complications,' which he had read that morning? No more than the yellows could help a yellow journal printing the words 'Lord Miltoun's Evening Adventure.' Their only business was to win, ever fighting fair. The yellows had not fought fair, they never did, and one of their most unfair tactics was the way they had of always accusing the blues of unfair fighting, an accusation truly ludicrous! As for truth! That which helped the world to be blue, was obviously true; that which didn't, as obviously not. There was no middle policy! The man who saw things neither was a softy, and no proper citizen. And as for giving the yellows credit for sincerity—the yellows never gave them credit! But though Courtier knew all that, this poster seemed to him particularly damnable, and he could not for the life of him resist striking one of the sandwich-boards with his cane. The resounding thwack startled a butcher's pony standing by the pavement. It reared, and bolted forward, with Courtier, who had naturally seized the rein, hanging on. A dog dashed past. Courtier tripped and fell. The pony, passing over, struck him on the head with a hoof. For a moment he lost consciousness; then coming to himself, refused assistance, and went to his hotel. He felt very giddy, and, after bandaging a nasty cut, lay down on his bed.

Miltoun, returning from that necessary exhibition of himself, the crowning fact, at every polling centre, found time to go and see him.

"That last poster of yours!" Courtier began, at once.

"I'm having it withdrawn."

"It's done the trick—congratulations—you'll get in!"

"I knew nothing of it."

"My dear fellow, I didn't suppose you did."

"When there is a desert, Courtier, between a man and the sacred city, he doesn't renounce his journey because he has to wash in dirty water on the way: The mob—how I loathe it!"

There was such pent-up fury in those words as to astonish even one whose life had been passed in conflict with majorities.

"I hate its mean stupidities, I hate the sound of its voice, and the look on its face—it's so ugly, it's so little. Courtier, I suffer purgatory from the thought that I shall scrape in by the votes of the mob. There is sin in using this creature and I am expiating it."

To this strange outburst, Courtier at first made no reply.

"You've been working too hard," he said at last, "you're off your balance. After all, the mob's made up of men like you and me."

"No, Courtier, the mob is not made up of men like you and me. If it were it would not be the mob."

"It looks," Courtier answered gravely, "as if you had no business in this galley. I've always steered clear of it myself."

"You follow your feelings. I have not that happiness."

So saying, Miltoun turned to the door.

Courtier's voice pursued him earnestly.

"Drop your politics—if you feel like this about them; don't waste your life following whatever it is you follow; don't waste hers!"

But Miltoun did not answer.

It was a wondrous still night, when, a few minutes before twelve, with his forehead bandaged under his hat, the champion of lost causes left the hotel and made his way towards the Grammar School for the declaration of the poll. A sound as of some monster breathing guided him, till, from a steep empty street he came in sight of a surging crowd, spread over the town square, like a dark carpet patterned by splashes of lamplight. High up above that crowd, on the little peaked tower of the Grammar School, a brightly lighted clock face presided; and over the passionate hopes in those thousands of hearts knit together by suspense the sky had lifted; and showed no cloud between them and the purple fields of air. To Courtier descending towards the square, the swaying white faces, turned all one way, seemed like the heads of giant wild flowers in a dark field, shivered by wind. The night had charmed away the blue and yellow facts, and breathed down into that throng the spirit of emotion. And he realized all at once the beauty and meaning of this scene—expression of the quivering forces, whose perpetual flux, controlled by the Spirit of Balance, was the soul of the world. Thousands of hearts with the thought of self lost in one over-mastering excitement!

An old man with a long grey beard, standing close to his elbow, murmured:

"'Tis anxious work—I wouldn't ha' missed this for anything in the world."

"Fine, eh?" answered Courtier.

"Aye," said the old man, "'tis fine. I've not seen the like o' this since the great year—forty-eight. There they are—the aristocrats!"

Following the direction of that skinny hand Courtier saw on a balcony Lord and Lady Valleys, side by side, looking steadily down at the crowd. There too, leaning against a window and talking to someone behind, was Barbara. The old man went on muttering, and Courtier could see that his eyes had grown very bright, his whole face transfigured by intense hostility; he felt drawn to this old creature, thus moved to the very soul. Then he saw Barbara looking down at him, with her hand raised to her temple to show that she saw his bandaged head. He had the presence of mind not to lift his hat.

The old man spoke again.

"You wouldn't remember forty-eight, I suppose. There was a feeling in the people then—we would ha' died for things in those days. I'm eighty-four," and he held his shaking hand up to his breast, "but the spirit's alive here yet! God send the Radical gets in!" There was wafted from him a scent as of potatoes.

Far behind, at the very edge of the vast dark throng, some voices began singing: "Way down upon the Swanee ribber." The tune floated forth, ceased, spurted up once more, and died.

Then, in the very centre of the square a stentorian baritone roared forth: "Should auld acquaintance be forgot!"

The song swelled, till every kind of voice, from treble to the old Chartist's quavering bass, was chanting it; here and there the crowd heaved with the movement of linked arms. Courtier found the soft fingers of a young woman in his right hand, the old Chartist's dry trembling paw in his left. He himself sang loudly. The grave and fearful music sprang straight up into they air, rolled out right and left, and was lost among the hills. But it had no sooner died away than the same huge baritone yelled "God save our gracious King!" The stature of the crowd seemed at once to leap up two feet, and from under that platform of raised hats rose a stupendous shouting.

"This," thought Courtier, "is religion!"

They were singing even on the balconies; by the lamplight he could see Lord Valleys mouth not opened quite enough, as though his voice were just a little ashamed of coming out, and Barbara with her head flung back against the pillar, pouring out her heart. No mouth in all the crowd was silent. It was as though the soul of the English people were escaping from its dungeon of reserve, on the pinions of that chant.

But suddenly, like a shot bird closing wings, the song fell silent and dived headlong back to earth. Out from under the clock-face had moved a thin dark figure. More figures came behind. Courtier could see Miltoun. A voice far away cried: "Up; Chilcox!" A huge: "Husill" followed; then such a silence, that the sound of an engine shunting a mile away could be heard plainly.

The dark figure moved forward, and a tiny square of paper gleamed out white against the black of his frock-coat.

"Ladies and gentlemen. Result of the Poll:

"Miltoun Four thousand eight hundred and ninety-eight. Chilcox Four thousand eight hundred and two."

The silence seemed to fall to earth, and break into a thousand pieces. Through the pandemonium of cheers and groaning, Courtier with all his strength forced himself towards the balcony. He could see Lord Valleys leaning forward with a broad smile; Lady Valleys passing her hand across her eyes; Barbara with her hand in Harbinger's, looking straight into his face. He stopped. The old Chartist was still beside him, tears rolling down his cheeks into his beard.

Courtier saw Miltoun come forward, and stand, unsmiling, deathly pale.

PART II

Chapter I

At three o'clock in the afternoon of the nineteenth of July little Ann Shropton commenced the ascent of the main staircase of Valleys House, London. She climbed slowly, in the very middle, an extremely small white figure on those wide and shining stairs, counting them aloud. Their number was never alike two days running, which made them attractive to one for whom novelty was the salt of life.

Coming to that spot where they branched, she paused to consider which of the two flights she had used last, and unable to remember, sat down. She was the bearer of a message. It had been new when she started, but was already comparatively old, and likely to become older, in view of a design now conceived by her of travelling the whole length of the picture gallery. And while she sat maturing this plan, sunlight flooding through a large window drove a white refulgence down into the heart of the wide polished space of wood and marble, whence she had come. The nature of little Ann habitually rejected fairies and all fantastic things, finding them quite too much in the air, and devoid of sufficient reality and 'go'; and this refulgence, almost unearthly in its travelling glory, passed over her small head and played strangely with the pillars in the hall, without exciting in her any fancies or any sentiment. The intention of discovering what was at the end of the picture gallery absorbed the whole of her essentially practical and active mind. Deciding on the left-hand flight of stairs, she entered that immensely long, narrow, and—with blinds drawn—rather dark saloon. She walked carefully, because the floor was very slippery here, and with a kind of seriousness due partly to the darkness and partly to the pictures. They were indeed, in this light, rather formidable, those old Caradocs black, armoured creatures, some of them, who seemed to eye with a sort of burning, grim, defensive greed the small white figure of their descendant passing along between them. But little Ann, who knew they were only pictures, maintained her course steadily, and every now and then, as she passed one who seemed to her rather uglier than the others, wrinkled her sudden little nose. At the end, as she had thought; appeared a door. She opened it, and passed on to a landing. There was a stone staircase in the corner, and there were two doors. It would be nice to go up the staircase, but it would also be nice to open the doors. Going towards the first door, with a little thrill, she turned the handle. It was one of those rooms, necessary in houses, for which she had no great liking; and closing this door rather loudly she opened the other one, finding herself in a chamber not resembling the rooms downstairs, which were all high and nicely gilded, but more like where she had lessons, low, and filled with books and leather chairs. From the end of the room which she could not see, she heard a sound as of someone kissing something, and instinct had almost made her turn to go away when the word: "Hallo!" suddenly opened her lips. And almost directly she saw that Granny and Grandpapa were standing by the fireplace. Not knowing quite whether they were glad to see her, she went forward and began at once:

"Is this where you sit, Grandpapa?"

"It is."

"It's nice, isn't it, Granny? Where does the stone staircase go to?"

"To the roof of the tower, Ann."

"Oh! I have to give a message, so I must go now."

"Sorry to lose you."

"Yes; good-bye!"

Hearing the door shut behind her, Lord and Lady Valleys looked at each other with a dubious smile.

The little interview which she had interrupted, had arisen in this way.

Accustomed to retire to this quiet and homely room, which was not his official study where he was always liable to the attacks of secretaries, Lord Valleys had come up here after lunch to smoke and chew the cud of a worry.

The matter was one in connection with his Pendridny estate, in Cornwall. It had long agitated both his agent and himself, and had now come to him for final decision. The question affected two villages to the north of the property, whose inhabitants were solely dependent on the working of a large quarry, which had for some time been losing money.

A kindly man, he was extremely averse to any measure which would plunge his tenants into distress, and especially in cases where there had been no question of opposition between himself and them. But, reduced to its essentials, the matter stood thus: Apart from that particular quarry the Pendridny estate was not only a going, but even a profitable concern, supporting itself and supplying some of the sinews of war towards Valleys House and the racing establishment at Newmarket and other general expenses; with this quarry still running, allowing for the upkeep of Pendridny, and the provision of pensions to superannuated servants, it was rather the other way.

Sitting there, that afternoon, smoking his favourite pipe, he had at last come to the conclusion that there was nothing for it but to close down. He had not made this resolution lightly; though, to do him justice, the knowledge that the decision would be bound to cause an outcry in the local, and perhaps the National Press, had secretly rather spurred him on to the resolve than deterred him from it. He felt as if he were being dictated to in advance, and he did not like dictation. To have to deprive these poor people of their immediate living was, he knew, a good deal more irksome to him than to those who would certainly make a fuss about it, his conscience was clear, and he could discount that future outcry as mere Party spite. He had very honestly tried to examine the thing all round; and had reasoned thus: If I keep this quarry open, I am really admitting the principle of pauperization, since I naturally look to each of my estates to support its own house, grounds, shooting, and to contribute towards the support of this house, and my family, and racing stable, and all the people employed about them both.

To allow any business to be run on my estates which does not contribute to the general upkeep, is to protect and really pauperize a portion of my tenants at the expense of the rest; it must therefore be false economics and a secret sort of socialism. Further, if logically followed out, it might end in my ruin, and to allow that, though I might not personally object, would be to imply that I do not believe that I am by virtue of my traditions and training, the best machinery through which the State can work to secure the welfare of the people....

When he had reached that point in his consideration of the question, his mind, or rather perhaps, his essential self, had not unnaturally risen up and said: Which is absurd!

Impersonality was in fashion, and as a rule he believed in thinking impersonally. There was a point, however, where the possibility of doing so ceased, without treachery to oneself, one's order, and the country. And to the argument which he was quite shrewd enough to put to himself, sooner than have it put by anyone else, that it was disproportionate for a single man by a stroke of the pen to be able to dispose of the livelihood of hundreds whose senses and feelings were similar to his own—he had answered: "If I didn't, some plutocrat or company would—or, worse still, the State!" Cooperative enterprise being, in his opinion, foreign to the spirit of the country, there was, so far as he could see, no other alternative. Facts were facts and not to be got over!

Notwithstanding all this, the necessity for the decision made him sorry, for if he had no great sense of proportion, he was at least humane.

He was still smoking his pipe and staring at a sheet of paper covered with small figures when his wife entered. Though she had come to ask his advice on a very different subject, she saw at once that he was vexed, and said:

"What's the matter, Geoff?"

Lord Valleys rose, went to the hearth, deliberately tapped out his pipe, then held out to her the sheet of paper.

"That quarry! Nothing for it—must go!"

Lady Valleys' face changed.

"Oh, no! It will mean such dreadful distress."

Lord Valleys stared at his nails. "It's putting a drag on the whole estate," he said.

"I know, but how could we face the people—I should never be able to go down there. And most of them have such enormous families."

Since Lord Valleys continued to bend on his nails that slow, thought-forming stare, she went on earnestly:

"Rather than that I'd make sacrifices. I'd sooner Pendridny were let than throw all those people out of work. I suppose it would let."

"Let? Best woodcock shooting in the world."

Lady Valleys, pursuing her thoughts, went on:

"In time we might get the people drafted into other things. Have you consulted Miltoun?"

"No," said Lord Valleys shortly, "and don't mean to—he's too unpractical."

"He always seems to know what he wants very well."

"I tell you," repeated Lord Valleys, "Miltoun's no good in a matter of this sort—he and his ideas throw back to the Middle Ages."

Lady Valleys went closer, and took him by the lapels of his collar.

"Geoff-really, to please me; some other way!"

Lord Valleys frowned, staring at her for some time; and at last answered:

"To please you—I'll leave it over another year."

"You think that's better than letting?"

"I don't like the thought of some outsider there. Time enough to come to that if we must. Take it as my Christmas present."

Lady Valleys, rather flushed, bent forward and kissed his ear.

It was at this moment that little Ann had entered.

When she was gone, and they had exchanged that dubious look, Lady Valleys said:

"I came about Babs. I don't know what to make of her since we came up. She's not putting her heart into things."

Lord Valleys answered almost sulkily:

"It's the heat probably—or Claud Harbinger." In spite of his easy-going parentalism, he disliked the thought of losing the child whom he so affectionately admired.

"Ah!" said Lady Valleys slowly, "I'm not so sure."

"How do you mean?"

"There's something queer about her. I'm by no means certain she hasn't got some sort of feeling for that Mr. Courtier."

"What!" said Lord Valleys, growing most unphilosophically red.

"Exactly!"

"Confound it, Gertrude, Miltoun's business was quite enough for one year."

"For twenty," murmured Lady Valleys. "I'm watching her. He's going to Persia, they say."

"And leaving his bones there, I hope," muttered Lord Valleys. "Really, it's too much. I should think you're all wrong, though."

Lady Valleys raised her eyebrows. Men were very queer about such things! Very queer and worse than helpless!

"Well," she said, "I must go to my meeting. I'll take her, and see if I can get at something," and she went away.

It was the inaugural meeting of the Society for the Promotion of the Birth Rate, over which she had promised to preside. The scheme was one in which she had been prominent from the start, appealing as it did to her large and full-blooded nature. Many movements, to which she found it impossible to refuse her name, had in themselves but small attraction; and it was a real comfort to feel something approaching enthusiasm for one branch of her public work. Not that there was any academic consistency about her in the matter, for in private life amongst her friends she was not narrowly dogmatic on the duty of wives to multiply exceedingly. She thought imperially on the subject, without bigotry. Large, healthy families, in all cases save individual ones! The prime idea at the back of her mind was—National Expansion! Her motto, and she intended if possible to make it the motto of the League, was: 'De l'audace, et encore de l'audace!' It was a question of the full realization of the nation. She had a true, and in a sense touching belief in 'the flag,' apart from what it might cover. It was her idealism. "You may talk," she would say, "as much as you like about directing national life in accordance with social justice! What does the nation care about social justice? The thing is much bigger than that. It's a matter of sentiment. We must expand!"

On the way to the meeting, occupied with her speech, she made no attempt to draw Barbara into conversation. That must wait. The child, though languid, and pale, was looking so beautiful that it was a pleasure to have her support in such a movement.

In a little dark room behind the hall the Committee were already assembled, and they went at once on to the platform.

Chapter II

Unmoved by the stares of the audience, Barbara sat absorbed in moody thoughts.

Into the three weeks since Miltoun's election there had been crowded such a multitude of functions that she had found, as it were, no time, no energy to know where she stood with herself. Since that morning in the stable, when he had watched her with the horse Hal, Harbinger had seemed to live only to be close to her. And the consciousness of his passion gave her a tingling sense of pleasure. She had been riding and dancing with him, and sometimes this had been almost blissful. But there were times too, when she felt—though always with a certain contempt of herself, as when she sat on that sunwarmed stone below the tor—a queer dissatisfaction, a longing for something outside a world where she had to invent her own starvations and simplicities, to make-believe in earnestness.

She had seen Courtier three times. Once he had come to dine, in response to an invitation from Lady Valleys worded in that charming, almost wistful style, which she had taught herself to use to those below her in social rank, especially if they were intelligent; once to the Valleys House garden party; and next day, having told him what time she would be riding, she had found him in the Row, not mounted, but standing by the rail just where she must pass, with that look on his face of mingled deference and ironic self-containment, of which he was a master. It appeared that he was leaving England; and to her questions why, and where, he had only shrugged his shoulders. Up on this dusty platform, in the hot bare hall, facing all those people, listening to speeches whose sense she was too languid and preoccupied to take in, the whole medley of thoughts, and faces round her, and the sound of the speakers' voices, formed a kind of nightmare, out of which she noted with extreme exactitude the colour of her mother's neck beneath a large black hat, and the expression on the face of a Committee man to the right, who was biting his fingers under cover of a blue paper. She realized that someone was speaking amongst the audience, casting forth, as it were, small bunches of words. She could see him—a little man in a black coat, with a white face which kept jerking up and down.

"I feel that this is terrible," she heard him say; "I feel that this is blasphemy. That we should try to tamper with the greatest force, the greatest and the most sacred and secret-force, that—that moves in the world, is to me horrible. I cannot bear to listen; it seems to make everything so small!" She saw him sit down, and her mother rising to answer.

"We must all sympathize with the sincerity and to a certain extent with the intention of our friend in the body of the hall. But we must ask ourselves:

"Have we the right to allow ourselves the luxury, of private feelings in a matter which concerns the national expansion. We must not give way to sentiment. Our friend in the body of the hall spoke—he will forgive me for saying so—like a poet, rather than a serious reformer. I am afraid that if we let ourselves drop into poetry, the birth rate of this country will very soon drop into poetry too. And that I think it is impossible for us to contemplate with folded hands. The resolution I was about to propose when our friend in the body of the hall—"

But Barbara's attention, had wandered off again into that queer medley of thoughts, and feelings, out of which the little man had so abruptly roused her. Then she realized that the meeting was breaking up, and her mother saying:

"Now, my dear, it's hospital day. We've just time."

When they were once more in the car, she leaned back very silent, watching the traffic.

Lady Valleys eyed her sidelong.

"What a little bombshell," she said, "from that small person! He must have got in by mistake. I hear Mr. Courtier has a card for Helen Gloucester's ball to-night, Babs."

"Poor man!"

"You will be there," said Lady Valleys dryly.

Barbara drew back into her corner.

"Don't tease me, Mother!"

An expression of compunction crossed Lady Valleys' face; she tried to possess herself of Barbara's hand. But that languid hand did not return her squeeze.

"I know the mood you're in, dear. It wants all one's pluck to shake it off; don't let it grow on you. You'd better go down to Uncle Dennis to-morrow. You've been overdoing it."

Barbara sighed.

"I wish it were to-morrow."

The car had stopped, and Lady Valleys said:

"Will you come in, or are you too tired? It always does them good to see you."

"You're twice as tired as me," Barbara answered; "of course I'll come."

At the entrance of the two ladies, there rose at once a faint buzz and murmur. Lady Valleys, whose ample presence radiated suddenly a businesslike and cheery confidence, went to a bedside and sat down. But Barbara stood in a thin streak of the July sunlight, uncertain where to begin, amongst the faces turned towards her. The poor dears looked so humble, and so wistful, and so tired. There was one lying quite flat, who had not even raised her head to see who had come in. That slumbering, pale, high cheek-boned face had a frailty as if a touch, a breath, would shatter it; a wisp of the blackest hair, finer than silk, lay across the forehead; the closed eyes were deep sunk; one hand, scarred almost to the bone with work, rested above her breast. She breathed between lips which had no colour. About her, sleeping, was a kind of beauty. And there came over the girl a queer rush of emotion. The sleeper seemed so apart from everything there, from all the formality and stiffness of the ward. To look at her swept away the languid, hollow feeling with which she had come in; it made her think of the tors at home, when the wind was blowing, and all was bare, and grand, and sometimes terrible. There was something elemental in that still sleep. And the old lady in the next led, with a brown wrinkled face and bright black eyes brimful of life, seemed almost vulgar beside such remote tranquillity, while she was telling Barbara that a little bunch of heather in the better half of a soap-dish on the window-sill had come from Wales, because, as she explained: "My mother was born in Stirling, dearie; so I likes a bit of heather, though I never been out o' Bethnal Green meself."

But when Barbara again passed, the sleeping woman was sitting up, and looked but a poor ordinary thing—her strange fragile beauty all withdrawn.

It was a relief when Lady Valleys said:

"My dear, my Naval Bazaar at five-thirty; and while I'm there you must go home and have a rest, and freshen yourself up for the evening. We dine at Plassey House."

The Duchess of Gloucester's Ball, a function which no one could very well miss, had been fixed for this late date owing to the Duchess's announced desire to prolong the season and so help the hackney cabmen; and though everybody sympathized, it had been felt by most that it would be simpler to go away, motor up on the day of the Ball, and motor down again on the following morning. And throughout the week by which the season was thus prolonged, in long rows at the railway stations, and on their stands, the hackney cabmen, unconscious of what was being done for them, waited, patient as their horses. But since everybody was making this special effort, an exceptionally large, exclusive, and brilliant company reassembled at Gloucester House.

In the vast ballroom over the medley of entwined revolving couples, punkahs had been fixed, to clear and freshen the languid air, and these huge fans, moving with incredible slowness, drove a faint refreshing draught down over the sea of white shirt-fronts and bare necks, and freed the scent from innumerable flowers.

Late in the evening, close by one of the great clumps of bloom, a very pretty woman stood talking to Bertie Caradoc. She was his cousin, Lily Malvezin, sister of Geoffrey Winlow, and wife of a Liberal peer, a charming creature, whose pink cheeks, bright eyes, quick lips, and rounded figure, endowed her with the prettiest air of animation. And while she spoke she kept stealing sly glances at her partner, trying as it were to pierce the armour of that self-contained young man.

"No, my dear," she said in her mocking voice, "you'll never persuade me that Miltoun is going to catch on. 'Il est trop intransigeant'. Ah! there's Babs!"

For the girl had come gliding by, her eyes wandering lazily, her lips just parted; her neck, hardly less pale than her white frock; her face pale, and marked with languor, under the heavy coil of her tawny hair; and her swaying body seeming with each turn of the waltz to be caught by the arms of her partner from out of a swoon.

With that immobility of lips, learned by all imprisoned in Society, Lily Malvezin murmured:

"Who's that she's dancing with? Is it the dark horse, Bertie?"

Through lips no less immobile Bertie answered:

"Forty to one, no takers."

But those inquisitive bright eyes still followed Barbara, drifting in the dance, like a great waterlily caught in the swirl of a mill pool; and the thought passed through that pretty head:

"She's hooked him. It's naughty of Babs, really!" And then she saw leaning against a pillar another whose eyes also were following those two; and she thought: "H'm! Poor Claud—no wonder he's looking like that. Oh! Babs!"

By one of the statues on the terrace Barbara and her partner stood, where trees, disfigured by no gaudy lanterns, offered the refreshment of their darkness and serenity.

Wrapped in her new pale languor, still breathing deeply from the waltz, she seemed to Courtier too utterly moulded out of loveliness. To what end should a man frame speeches to a vision! She was but an incarnation of beauty imprinted on the air, and would fade out at a touch-like the sudden ghosts of enchantment that came to one under the blue, and the starlit snow of a mountain night, or in a birch wood all wistful golden! Speech seemed but desecration! Besides, what of interest was there for him to say in this world of hers, so bewildering and of such glib assurance—this world that was like a building, whose every window was shut and had a blind drawn down. A building that admitted none who had not sworn, as it were, to believe it the world, the whole world, and nothing but the world, outside which were only the nibbled remains of what had built it. This, world of Society, in which he felt like one travelling through a desert, longing to meet a fellow-creature.

The voice of Harbinger behind them said:

"Lady-Babs!"

Long did the punkahs waft their breeze over that brave-hued wheel of pleasure, and the sound of the violins quaver and wail out into the morning. Then quickly, as the spangles of dew vanish off grass when the sun rises, all melted away; and in the great rooms were none but flunkeys presiding over the polished surfaces like flamingoes by some lakeside at dawn.

A brick dower-house of the Fitz-Harolds, just outside the little seaside town of Nettlefold, sheltered the tranquil days of Lord Dennis. In that south-coast air, sanest and most healing in all England, he raged very slowly, taking little thought of death, and much quiet pleasure in his life. Like the tall old house with its high windows and squat chimneys, he was marvellously self-contained. His books, for he somewhat passionately examined old civilizations, and described their habits from time to time with a dry and not too poignant pen in a certain old-fashioned magazine; his microscope, for he studied infusoria; and the fishing boat of his friend John Bogle, who had long perceived that Lord Dennis was the biggest fish he ever caught; all these, with occasional visitors, and little runs to London, to Monkland, and other country houses, made up the sum of a life which, if not desperately beneficial, was uniformly kind and harmless, and, by its notorious simplicity, had a certain negative influence not only on his own class but on the relations of that class with the country at large. It was commonly said in Nettlefold, that he was a gentleman; if they were all like him there wasn't much in all this talk against the Lords. The shop people and lodging-house keepers felt that the interests of the country were safer in his hands: than in the hands of people who wanted to meddle with everything for the good of those who were only anxious to be let alone. A man too who could so completely forget he was the son of a Duke, that other people never forgot it, was the man for their money. It was true that he had never had a say in public affairs; but this was overlooked, because he could have had it if he liked, and the fact that he did not like, only showed once more that he was a gentleman.

Just as he was the one personality of the little town against whom practically nothing was ever, said, so was his house the one house which defied criticism. Time had made it utterly suitable. The ivied walls, and purplish roof lichened yellow in places, the quiet meadows harbouring ponies and kine, reaching from it to the sea—all was mellow. In truth it made all the other houses of the town seem shoddy—standing alone beyond them, like its master, if anything a little too esthetically remote from common wants.

He had practically no near neighbours of whom he saw anything, except once in a way young Harbinger three miles distant at Whitewater. But since he had the faculty of not being bored with his own society, this did not worry him. Of local charity, especially to the fishers of the town, whose winter months were nowadays very bare of profit, he was prodigal to the verge of extravagance, for his income was not great. But in politics, beyond acting as the figure-head of certain municipal efforts, he took little or no part. His Toryism indeed was of the mild order, that had little belief in the regeneration of the country by any means but those of kindly feeling between the classes. When asked how that was to be brought about, he would answer with his dry, slightly malicious, suavity, that if you stirred hornets' nests with sticks the hornets would come forth. Having no land, he was shy of expressing himself on that vexed question; but if resolutely attacked would give utterance to some such sentiment as this: "The land's best in our hands on the whole, but we want fewer dogs-in-the-manger among us."

He had, as became one of his race, a feeling for land, tender and protective, and could not bear to think of its being put out to farm with that cold Mother, the State. He was ironical over the views of Radicals or Socialists, but disliked to hear such people personally abused behind their backs. It must be confessed, however, that if contradicted he increased considerably the ironical decision of his sentiments. Withdrawn from all chance in public life of enforcing his views on others, the natural aristocrat within him was forced to find some expression.

Each year, towards the end of July, he placed his house at the service of Lord Valleys, who found it a convenient centre for attending Goodwood.

It was on the morning after the Duchess of Gloucester's Ball, that he received this note:

"VALLEYS HOUSE.

"DEAREST UNCLE DENNIS,

"May I come down to you a little before time and rest? London is so terribly hot. Mother has three functions still to stay for, and I shall have to have come back again for our last evening, the political one—so I don't want to go all the way to Monkland; and anywhere else, except with you, would be rackety. Eustace looks so seedy. I'll try and bring him, if I may. Granny is terribly well.

"Best love, dear, from your
"BABS."

The same afternoon she came, but without Miltoun, driving up from the station in a fly. Lord Dennis met her at the gate; and, having kissed her, looked at her somewhat anxiously, caressing his white peaked beard. He had never yet known Babs sick of anything, except when he took her out in John Bogle's boat. She was certainly looking pale, and her hair was done differently—a fact disturbing to one who did not discover it. Slipping his arm through hers he led her out into a meadow still full of buttercups, where an old white pony, who had carried her in the Row twelve years ago, came up to them and rubbed his muzzle against her waist. And suddenly there rose in Lord Dennis the thoroughly discomforting and strange suspicion that, though the child was not going to cry, she wanted time to get over the feeling that she was. Without appearing to separate himself from her, he walked to the wall at the end of the field, and stood looking at the sea.

The tide was nearly up; the South wind driving over it brought him the scent of the sea-flowers, and the crisp rustle of little waves swimming almost to his feet. Far out, where the sunlight fell, the smiling waters lay white and mysterious in July haze, giving him a queer feeling. But Lord Dennis, though he had his moments of poetic sentiment, was on the whole quite able to keep the sea in its proper place—for after all it was the English Channel; and like a good Englishman he recognized that if you once let things get away from their names, they ceased to be facts, and if they ceased to be facts, they became—the devil! In truth he was not thinking much of the sea, but of Barbara. It was plain that she was in trouble of some kind. And the notion that Babs could find trouble in life was extraordinarily queer; for he felt, subconsciously, what a great driving force of disturbance was necessary to penetrate the hundred folds of the luxurious cloak enwrapping one so young and fortunate. It was not Death; therefore it must be Love; and he thought at once of that fellow with the red moustaches. Ideas were all very well—no one would object to as many as you liked, in their proper place—the dinner-table, for example. But to fall in love, if indeed it were so, with a man who not only had ideas, but an inclination to live up to them, and on them, and on nothing else, seemed to Lord Dennis 'outre'.

She had followed him to the wall, and he looked—at her dubiously.

"To rest in the waters of Lethe, Babs? By the way, seen anything of our friend Mr. Courtier? Very picturesque—that Quixotic theory of life!"

And in saying that, his voice (like so many refined voices which have turned their backs on speculation) was triple-toned-mocking at ideas, mocking at itself for mocking at ideas, yet showing plainly that at bottom it only mocked at itself for mocking at ideas, because it would be, as it were, crude not to do so.

But Barbara did not answer his question, and began to speak of other things. And all that afternoon and evening she talked away so lightly that Lord Dennis, but for his instinct, would have been deceived.

That wonderful smiling mask—the inscrutability of Youth—was laid aside by her at night. Sitting at her window, under the moon, 'a gold-bright moth slow-spinning up the sky,' she watched the darkness hungrily, as though it were a great thought into whose heart she was trying to see. Now and then she stroked herself, getting strange comfort out of the presence of her body. She had that old unhappy feeling of having two selves within her. And this soft night full of the quiet stir of the sea, and of dark immensity, woke in her a terrible longing to be at one with something, somebody, outside herself. At the Ball last night the 'flying feeling' had seized on her again; and was still there—a queer manifestation of her streak of recklessness. And this result of her contacts with Courtier, this 'cacoethes volandi', and feeling of clipped wings, hurt her—as being forbidden hurts a child.

She remembered how in the housekeeper's room at Monkland there lived a magpie who had once sought shelter in an orchid-house from some pursuer. As soon as they thought him wedded to civilization, they had let him go, to see whether he would come back. For hours he had sat up in a high tree, and at last come down again to his cage; whereupon, fearing lest the rooks should attack him when he next took this voyage of discovery, they clipped one of his wings. After that the twilight bird, though he lived happily enough, hopping about his cage and the terrace which served him for exercise yard, would seem at times restive and frightened, moving his wings as if flying in spirit, and sad that he must stay on earth.

So, too, at her window Barbara fluttered her wings; then, getting into bed, lay sighing and tossing. A clock struck three; and seized by an intolerable impatience at her own discomfort, she slipped a motor coat over her night-gown, put on slippers, and stole out into the passage. The house was very still. She crept downstairs, smothering her footsteps. Groping her way through the hall, inhabited by the thin ghosts of would-be light, she slid back the chain of the door, and fled towards the sea. She made no more noise running in the dew, than a bird following the paths of air; and the two ponies, who felt her figure pass in the darkness, snuffled, sending out soft sighs of alarm amongst the closed buttercups. She climbed the wall over to the beach. While she was running, she had fully meant to dash into the sea and cool herself, but it was so black, with just a thin edging scarf of white, and the sky was black, bereft of lights, waiting for the day!

She stood, and looked. And all the leapings and pulsings of flesh and spirit slowly died in that wide dark loneliness, where the only sound was the wistful breaking of small waves. She was well used to these dead hours—only last night, at this very time, Harbinger's arm had been round her in a last waltz! But here the dead hours had such different faces, wide-eyed, solemn, and there came to Barbara, staring out at them, a sense that the darkness saw her very soul, so that it felt little and timid within her. She shivered in her fur-lined coat, as if almost frightened at finding herself so marvellously nothing before that black sky and dark sea, which seemed all one, relentlessly great.... And crouching down, she waited for the dawn to break.

It came from over the Downs, sweeping a rush of cold air on its wings, flighting towards the sea. With it the daring soon crept back into her blood. She stripped, and ran down into the dark water, fast growing pale. It covered her jealously, and she set to work to swim. The water was warmer than the air. She lay on her back and splashed, watching the sky flush. To bathe like this in the half-dark, with her hair floating out, and no wet clothes clinging to her limbs, gave her the joy of a child doing a naughty thing. She swam out of her depth, then scared at her own adventure, swam in again as the sun rose.

She dashed into her two garments, climbed the wall, and scurried back to the house. All her dejection, and feverish uncertainty were gone; she felt keen, fresh, terribly hungry, and stealing into the dark dining-room, began rummaging for food. She found biscuits, and was still munching, when in the open doorway she saw Lord Dennis, a pistol in one hand and a lighted candle in the other. With his carved features and white beard above an old blue dressing-gown, he looked impressive, having at the moment a distinct resemblance to Lady Casterley, as though danger had armoured him in steel.

"You call this resting!" he said, dryly; then, looking at her drowned hair, added: "I see you have already entrusted your trouble to the waters of Lethe."

But without answer Barbara vanished into the dim hall and up the stairs.

Chapter IV

While Barbara was swimming to meet the dawn, Miltoun was bathing in those waters of mansuetude and truth which roll from wall to wall in the British House of Commons.

In that long debate on the Land question, for which he had waited to make his first speech, he had already risen nine times without catching the Speaker's eye, and slowly a sense of unreality was creeping over him. Surely this great Chamber, where without end rose the small sound of a single human voice, and queer mechanical bursts of approbation and resentment, did not exist at all but as a gigantic fancy of his own! And all these figures were figments of his brain! And when he at last spoke, it would be himself alone that he addressed! The torpid air tainted with human breath, the unwinking stare of the countless lights, the long rows of seats, the queer distant rounds of pale listening flesh perched up so high, they were all emanations of himself! Even the coming and going in the gangway was but the coming and going of little wilful parts of him! And rustling deep down in this Titanic creature of his fancy was 'the murmuration' of his own unspoken speech, sweeping away the puff balls of words flung up by that far-away, small, varying voice.

Then, suddenly all that dream creature had vanished; he was on his feet, with a thumping heart, speaking.

Soon he had no tremors, only a dim consciousness that his words sounded strange, and a queer icy pleasure in flinging them out into the silence. Round him there seemed no longer men, only mouths and eyes. And he had enjoyment in the feeling that with these words of his he was holding those hungry mouths and eyes dumb and unmoving. Then he knew that he had reached the end of what he had to say, and sat down, remaining motionless in the centre of a various sound; staring at the back of the head in front of him, with his hands clasped round his knee. And soon, when that little faraway voice was once more speaking, he took his hat, and glancing neither to right nor left, went out.

Instead of the sensation of relief and wild elation which fills the heart of those who have taken the first plunge, Miltoun had nothing in his deep dark well but the waters of bitterness. In truth, with the delivery of that speech he had but parted with what had been a sort of anodyne to suffering. He had only put the fine point on his conviction, of how vain was his career now that he could not share it with Audrey Noel. He walked slowly towards the Temple, along the riverside, where the lamps were paling into nothingness before that daily celebration of Divinity, the meeting of dark and light.

For Miltoun was not one of those who take things lying down; he took things desperately, deeply, and with revolt. He took them like a rider riding himself, plunging at the dig of his own spurs, chafing and wincing at the cruel tugs of his own bitt; bearing in his friendless, proud heart all the burden of struggles which shallower or more genial natures shared with others.

He looked hardly less haggard, walking home, than some of those homeless ones who slept nightly by the river, as though they knew that to lie near one who could so readily grant oblivion, alone could save them from seeking that consolation. He was perhaps unhappier than they, whose spirits, at all events, had long ceased to worry them, having oozed out from their bodies under the foot of Life:

Now that Audrey Noel was lost to him, her loveliness and that indescribable quality which made her lovable, floated before him, the very torture-flowers of a beauty never to be grasped—yet, that he could grasp, 'if he only would! That was the heart and fervour of his suffering. To be grasped if he only would! He was suffering, too, physically from a kind of slow fever, the result of his wetting on the day when he last saw her. And through that latent fever, things and feelings, like his sensations in the House before his speech, were all as it were muffled in a horrible way, as if they all came to him wrapped in a sort of flannel coating, through which he could not cut. And all the time there seemed to be within him two men at mortal grips with one another; the man of faith in divine sanction and authority, on which all his beliefs had hitherto hinged, and a desperate warm-blooded hungry creature. He was very miserable, craving strangely for the society of someone who could understand what he was feeling, and, from long habit of making no confidants, not knowing how to satisfy that craving.

It was dawn when he reached his rooms; and, sure that he would not sleep, he did not even go to bed, but changed his clothes, made himself some coffee, and sat down at the window which overlooked the flowered courtyard.

In Middle Temple Hall a Ball was still in progress, though the glamour from its Chinese lanterns was already darkened and gone. Miltoun saw a man and a girl, sheltered by an old fountain, sitting out their last dance. Her head had sunk on her partner's shoulder; their lips were joined. And there floated up to the window the scent of heliotrope, with the tune of the waltz that those two should have been dancing. This couple so stealthily enlaced, the gleam of their furtively turned eyes, the whispering of their lips, that stony niche below the twittering sparrows, so cunningly sought out—it was the world he had abjured! When he looked again, they—like a vision seen—had stolen away and gone; the music too had ceased, there was no scent of heliotrope. In the stony niche crouched a stray cat watching the twittering sparrows.

Miltoun went out, and, turning into the empty Strand, walked on—without heeding where, till towards five o'clock he found himself on Putney Bridge.

He rested there, leaning over the parapet, looking down at the grey water. The sun was just breaking through the heat haze; early waggons were passing, and already men were coming in to work. To what end did the river wander up and down; and a human river flow across it twice every day? To what end were men and women suffering? Of the full current of this life Miltoun could no more see the aim, than that of the wheeling gulls in the early sunlight.

Leaving the bridge he made towards Barnes Common. The night was still ensnared there on the gorse bushes grey with cobwebs and starry dewdrops. He passed a tramp family still sleeping, huddled all together. Even the homeless lay in each other's arms!

From the Common he emerged on the road near the gates of Ravensham; turning in there, he found his way to the kitchen garden, and sat down on a bench close to the raspberry bushes. They were protected from thieves, but at Miltoun's approach two blackbirds flustered out through the netting and flew away.

His long figure resting so motionless impressed itself on the eyes of a gardener, who caused a report to be circulated that his young lordship was in the fruit garden. It reached the ears of Clifton, who himself came out to see what this might mean. The old man took his stand in front of Miltoun very quietly.

"You have come to breakfast, my lord?"

"If my grandmother will have me, Clifton."

"I understood your lordship was speaking last night."

"I was."

"You find the House of Commons satisfactory, I hope."

"Fairly, thank you, Clifton."

"They are not what they were in the great days of your grandfather, I believe. He had a very good opinion of them. They vary, no doubt."

"Tempora mutantur."

"That is so. I find quite anew spirit towards public affairs. The ha'penny Press; one takes it in, but one hardly approves. I shall be anxious to read your speech. They say a first speech is a great strain."

"It is rather."

"But you had no reason to be anxious. I'm sure it was beautiful."

Miltoun saw that the old man's thin sallow cheeks had flushed to a deep orange between his snow-white whiskers.

"I have looked forward to this day," he stammered, "ever since I knew your lordship—twenty-eight years. It is the beginning."

"Or the end, Clifton."

The old man's face fell in a look of deep and concerned astonishment.

"No, no," he said; "with your antecedents, never."

Miltoun took his hand.

"Sorry, Clifton—didn't mean to shock you."

And for a minute neither spoke, looking at their clasped hands as if surprised.

"Would your lordship like a bath—breakfast is still at eight. I can procure you a razor."

When Miltoun entered the breakfast room, his grandmother, with a copy of the Times in her hands, was seated before a grape fruit, which, with a shredded wheat biscuit, constituted her first meal. Her appearance hardly warranted Barbara's description of 'terribly well'; in truth she looked a little white, as if she had been feeling the heat. But there was no lack of animation in her little steel-grey eyes, nor of decision in her manner.

"I see," she said, "that you've taken a line of your own, Eustace. I've nothing to say against that; in fact, quite the contrary. But remember this, my dear, however you may change you mustn't wobble. Only one thing counts in that place, hitting the same nail on the head with the same hammer all the time. You aren't looking at all well."

Miltoun, bending to kiss her, murmured:

"Thanks, I'm all right."

"Nonsense," replied Lady Casterley. "They don't look after you. Was your mother in the House?"

"I don't think so."

"Exactly. And what is Barbara about? She ought to be seeing to you."

"Barbara is down with Uncle Dennis."

Lady Casterley set her jaw; then looking her grandson through and through, said:

"I shall take you down there this very day. I shall have the sea to you. What do you say, Clifton?"

"His lordship does look pale."

"Have the carriage, and we'll go from Clapham Junction. Thomas can go in and fetch you some clothes. Or, better, though I dislike them, we can telephone to your mother for a car. It's very hot for trains. Arrange that, please, Clifton!"

To this project Miltoun raised no objection. And all through the drive he remained sunk in an indifference and lassitude which to Lady Casterley seemed in the highest degree ominous. For lassitude, to her, was the strange, the unpardonable, state. The little great lady—casket of the aristocratic principle—was permeated to the very backbone with the instinct of artificial energy, of that alert vigour which those who have nothing socially to hope for are forced to develop, lest they should decay and be again obliged to hope. To speak honest truth, she could not forbear an itch to run some sharp and foreign substance into her grandson, to rouse him somehow, for she knew the reason of his state, and was temperamentally out of patience with such a cause for backsliding. Had it been any other of her grandchildren she would not have hesitated, but there was that in Miltoun which held even Lady Casterley in check, and only once during the four hours of travel did she attempt to break down his reserve. She did it in a manner very soft for her—was he not of all living things the hope and pride of her heart? Tucking her little thin sharp hand under his arm, she said quietly:

"My dear, don't brood over it. That will never do."

But Miltoun removed her hand gently, and laid it back on the dust rug, nor did he answer, or show other sign of having heard.

And Lady Casterley, deeply wounded, pressed her faded lips together, and said sharply:

"Slower, please, Frith!"

Chapter V

It was to Barbara that Miltoun unfolded, if but little, the trouble of his spirit, lying that same afternoon under a ragged tamarisk hedge with the tide far out. He could never have done this if there had not been between them the accidental revelation of that night at Monkland; nor even then perhaps had he not felt in this young sister of his the warmth of life for which he was yearning. In such a matter as love Barbara was the elder of these two. For, besides the motherly knowledge of the heart peculiar to most women, she had the inherent woman-of-the-worldliness to be expected of a daughter of Lord and Lady Valleys. If she herself were in doubt as to the state of her affections, it was not as with Miltoun, on the score of the senses and the heart, but on the score of her spirit and curiosity, which Courtier had awakened and caused to flap their wings a little. She worried over Miltoun's forlorn case; it hurt her too to think of Mrs. Noel eating her heart out in that lonely cottage. A sister so—good and earnest as Agatha had ever inclined Barbara to a rebellious view of morals, and disinclined her altogether to religion. And so, she felt that if those two could not be happy apart, they should be happy together, in the name of all the joy there was in life!

And while her brother lay face to the sky under the tamarisks, she kept trying to think of how to console him, conscious that she did not in the least understand the way he thought about things. Over the fields behind, the larks were hymning the promise of the unripe corn; the foreshore was painted all colours, from vivid green to mushroom pink; by the edge of the blue sea little black figures stooped, gathering sapphire. The air smelled sweet in the shade of the tamarisk; there was ineffable peace. And Barbara, covered by the network of sunlight, could not help impatience with a suffering which seemed to her so corrigible by action. At last she ventured:

"Life is short, Eusty!"

Miltoun's answer, given without movement, startled her:

"Persuade me that it is, Babs, and I'll bless you. If the singing of these larks means nothing, if that blue up there is a morass of our invention, if we are pettily, creeping on furthering nothing, if there's no purpose in our lives, persuade me of it, for God's sake!"

Carried suddenly beyond her depth, Barbara could only put out her hand, and say: "Oh! don't take things so hard!"

"Since you say that life is short," Miltoun muttered, with his smile, "you shouldn't spoil it by feeling pity! In old days we went to the Tower for our convictions. We can stand a little private roasting, I hope; or has the sand run out of us altogether?"

Stung by his tone, Barbara answered in rather a hard voice:

"What we must bear, we must, I suppose. But why should we make trouble? That's what I can't stand!"

"O profound wisdom!"

Barbara flushed.

"I love Life!" she said.

The galleons of the westering sun were already sailing in a broad gold fleet straight for that foreshore where the little black stooping figures had not yet finished their toil, the larks still sang over the unripe corn—when Harbinger, galloping along the sands from Whitewater to Sea House, came on that silent couple walking home to dinner.

It would not be safe to say of this young man that he readily diagnosed a spiritual atmosphere, but this was the less his demerit, since everything from his cradle up had conspired to keep the spiritual thermometer of his surroundings at 60 in the shade. And the fact that his own spiritual thermometer had now run up so that it threatened to burst the bulb, rendered him less likely than ever to see what was happening with other people's. Yet, he did notice that Barbara was looking pale, and—it seemed—sweeter than ever.... With her eldest brother he always somehow felt ill at ease. He could not exactly afford to despise an uncompromising spirit in one of his own order, but he was no more impervious than others to Miltoun's caustic, thinly-veiled contempt for the commonplace; and having a full-blooded belief in himself—usual with men of fine physique, whose lots are so cast that this belief can never or almost never be really shaken—he greatly disliked the feeling of being a little looked down on. It was an intense relief, when, saying that he wanted a certain magazine, Miltoun strode off into the town.

To Harbinger, no less than to Miltoun and Barbara, last night had been bitter and restless. The sight of that pale swaying figure, with the parted lips, whirling round in Courtier's arms, had clung to his vision ever since, the Ball. During his own last dance with her he had been almost savagely silent; only by a great effort restraining his tongue from mordant allusions to that 'prancing, red-haired fellow,' as he secretly called the champion of lost causes. In fact, his sensations there and since had been a revelation, or would have teen if he could have stood apart to see them. True, he had gone about next day with his usual cool, off-hand manner, because one naturally did not let people see, but it was with such an inner aching and rage of want and jealousy as to really merit pity. Men of his physically big, rather rushing, type, are the last to possess their souls in patience. Walking home after the Ball he had determined to follow her down to the sea, where she had said, so maliciously; that she was going. After a second almost sleepless night he had no longer any hesitation. He must see her! After all, a man might go to his own 'place' with impunity; he did not care if it were a pointed thing to do.... Pointed! The more pointed the better! There was beginning to be roused in him an ugly stubbornness of male determination. She should not escape him!

But now that he was walking at her side, all that determination and assurance melted to perplexed humility. He marched along by his horse with his head down, just feeling the ache of being so close to her and yet so far; angry with his own silence and awkwardness, almost angry with her for her loveliness, and the pain it made him suffer. When they reached the house, and she left him at the stable-yard, saying she was going to get some flowers, he jerked the beast's bridle and swore at it for its slowness in entering the stable. He, was terrified that she would be gone before he could get into the garden; yet half afraid of finding her there. But she was still plucking carnations by the box hedge which led to the conservatories. And as she rose from gathering those blossoms, before he knew what he was doing, Harbinger had thrown his arm around her, held her as in a vice, kissed her unmercifully.

She seemed to offer no resistance, her smooth cheeks growing warmer and warmer, even her lips passive; but suddenly he recoiled, and his heart stood still at his own outrageous daring. What had he done? He saw her leaning back almost buried in the clipped box hedge, and heard her say with a sort of faint mockery: "Well!"

He would have flung himself down on his knees to ask for pardon but for the thought that someone might come. He muttered hoarsely: "By God, I was mad!" and stood glowering in sullen suspense between hardihood and fear. He heard her say, quietly:

"Yes, you were-rather."

Then seeing her put her hand up to her lips as if he had hurt them, he muttered brokenly:

"Forgive me, Babs!"

There was a full minute's silence while he stood there, no longer daring to look at her, beaten all over by his emotions. Then, with bewilderment, he heard her say:

"I didn't mind it—for once!"

He looked up at that. How could she love him, and speak so coolly! How could she not mind, if she did not love him! She was passing her hands over her face and neck and hair, repairing the damage of his kisses.

"Now shall we go in?" she said.

Harbinger took a step forward.

"I love you so," he said; "I will put my life in your hands, and you shall throw it away."

At those words, of whose exact nature he had very little knowledge, he saw her smile.

"If I let you come within three yards, will you be good?"

He bowed; and, in silence, they walked towards the house.

Dinner that evening was a strange, uncomfortable meal. But its comedy, too subtly played for Miltoun and Lord Dennis, seemed transparent to the eyes of Lady Casterley; for, when Harbinger had sallied forth to ride back along the sands, she took her candle and invited Barbara to retire. Then, having admitted her granddaughter to the apartment always reserved for herself, and specially furnished with practically nothing, she sat down opposite that tall, young, solid figure, as it were taking stock of it, and said:

"So you are coming to your senses, at all events. Kiss me!"

Barbara, stooping to perform this rite, saw a tear stealing down the carved fine nose. Knowing that to notice it would be too dreadful, she raised herself, and went to the window. There, staring out over the dark fields and dark sea, by the side of which Harbinger was riding home, she put her hand up to her, lips, and thought for the hundredth time:

"So that's what it's like!"

Chapter VI

Three days after his first, and as he promised himself, his last Society Ball, Courtier received a note from Audrey Noel, saying that she had left Monkland for the present, and come up to a little flat—on the riverside not far from Westminster.

When he made his way there that same July day, the Houses of Parliament were bright under a sun which warmed all the grave air emanating from their counsels of perfection: Courtier passed by dubiously. His feelings in the presence of those towers were always a little mixed. There was not so much of the poet in him as to cause him to see nothing there at all save only same lines against the sky, but there was enough of the poet to make him long to kick something; and in this mood he wended his way to the riverside.

Mrs. Noel was not at home, but since the maid informed him that she would be in directly, he sat down to wait. Her flat, which was on—the first floor, overlooked the river and had evidently been taken furnished, for there were visible marks of a recent struggle with an Edwardian taste which, flushed from triumph over Victorianism, had filled the rooms with early Georgian remains. On the only definite victory, a rose-coloured window seat of great comfort and little age, Courtier sat down, and resigned himself to doing nothing with the ease of an old soldier.

To the protective feeling he had once had for a very graceful, dark-haired child, he joined not only the championing pity of a man of warm heart watching a woman in distress, but the impatience of one, who, though temperamentally incapable of feeling oppressed himself, rebelled at sight of all forms of tyranny affecting others.

The sight of the grey towers, still just visible, under which Miltoun and his father sat, annoyed him deeply; symbolizing to him, Authority—foe to his deathless mistress, the sweet, invincible lost cause of Liberty. But presently the river; bringing up in flood the unbound water that had bathed every shore, touched all sands, and seen the rising and falling of each mortal star, so soothed him with its soundless hymn to Freedom, that Audrey Noel coming in with her hands full of flowers, found him sleeping firmly, with his mouth shut.

Noiselessly putting down the flowers, she waited for his awakening. That sanguine visage, with its prominent chin, flaring moustaches, and eyebrows raised rather V-shaped above his closed eyes, wore an expression of cheery defiance even in sleep; and perhaps no face in all London was so utterly its obverse, as that of this dark, soft-haired woman, delicate, passive, and tremulous with pleasure at sight of the only person in the world from whom she felt she might learn of Miltoun, without losing her self-respect.

He woke at last, and manifesting no discomfiture, said:

"It was like you not to wake me."

They sat for a long while talking, the riverside traffic drowsily accompanying their voices, the flowers drowsily filling the room with scent; and when Courtier left, his heart was sore. She had not spoken of herself at all, but had talked nearly all the time of Barbara, praising her beauty and high spirit; growing pale once or twice, and evidently drinking in with secret avidity every allusion to Miltoun. Clearly, her feelings had not changed, though she would not show them! Courtier's pity for her became well-nigh violent.

It was in such a mood, mingled with very different feelings, that he donned evening clothes and set out to attend the last gathering of the season at Valleys House, a function which, held so late in July, was perforce almost perfectly political.

Mounting the wide and shining staircase, that had so often baffled the arithmetic of little Ann, he was reminded of a picture entitled 'The Steps to Heaven' in his nursery four-and-thirty years before. At the top of this staircase, and surrounded by acquaintances, he came on Harbinger, who nodded curtly. The young man's handsome face and figure appeared to Courtier's jaundiced eye more obviously successful and complacent than ever; so that he passed him by sardonically, and manoeuvred his way towards Lady Valleys, whom he could perceive stationed, like a general, in a little cleared space, where to and fro flowed constant streams of people, like the rays of a star. She was looking her very best, going well with great and highly-polished spaces; and she greeted Courtier with a special cordiality of tone, which had in it, besides kindness towards one who must be feeling a strange bird, a certain diplomatic quality, compounded of desire, as it were, to 'warn him off,' and fear of saying something that might irritate and make him more dangerous. She had heard, she said, that he was bound for Persia; she hoped he was not going to try and make things more difficult there; then with the words: "So good of you to have come!" she became once more the centre of her battlefield.

Perceiving that he was finished with, Courtier stood back against a wall and watched. Thus isolated, he was like a solitary cuckoo contemplating the gyrations of a flock of rooks. Their motions seemed a little meaningless to one so far removed from all the fetishes and shibboleths of Westminster. He heard them discussing Miltoun's speech, the real significance of which apparently had only just been grasped. The words 'doctrinaire,' 'extremist,' came to his ears, together with the saying 'a new force.' People were evidently puzzled, disturbed, not pleased—as if some star not hitherto accounted for had suddenly appeared amongst the proper constellations.

Searching this crowd for Barbara, Courtier had all the time an uneasy sense of shame. What business had he to come amongst these people so strange to him, just for the sake of seeing her! What business had he to be hankering after this girl at all, knowing in his heart that he could not stand the atmosphere she lived in for a week, and that she was utterly unsuited for any atmosphere that he could give her; to say nothing of the unlikelihood that he could flutter the pulses of one half his age!

A voice, behind him said: "Mr. Courtier!"

He turned, and there was Barbara.

"I want to talk to you about something serious: Will you come into the picture gallery?"

When at last they were close to a family group of Georgian Caradocs, and could as it were shut out the throng sufficiently for private speech, she began:

"Miltoun's so horribly unhappy; I don't know what to do for him: He's making himself ill!"

And she suddenly looked up, in Courtier's face. She seemed to him very young, and touching, at that moment. Her eyes had a gleam of faith in them, like a child's eyes; as if she relied on him to straighten out this tangle, to tell her not only about Miltoun's trouble, but about all life, its meaning, and the secret of its happiness: And he said gently:

"What can I do? Mrs. Noel is in Town. But that's no good, unless—" Not knowing how to finish this sentence; he was silent.

"I wish I were Miltoun," she muttered.

At that quaint saying, Courtier was hard put to it not to take hold of the hands so close to him. This flash of rebellion in her had quickened all his blood. But she seemed to have seen what had passed in him, for her next speech was chilly.

"It's no good; stupid of me to be worrying you."

"It is quite impossible for you to worry me."

Her eyes lifted suddenly from her glove, and looked straight into his.

"Are you really going to Persia?"

"Yes."

"But I don't want you to, not yet!" and turning suddenly, she left him.

Strangely disturbed, Courtier remained motionless, consulting the grave stare of the group of Georgian Caradocs.

A voice said:

"Good painting, isn't it?"

Behind him was Lord Harbinger. And once more the memory of Lady Casterley's words; the memory of the two figures with joined hands on the balcony above the election crowd; all his latent jealousy of this handsome young Colossus, his animus against one whom he could, as it were, smell out to be always fighting on the winning side; all his consciousness too of what a lost cause his own was, his doubt whether he were honourable to look on it as a cause at all, flared up in Courtier, so that his answer was a stare. On Harbinger's face, too, there had come a look of stubborn violence slowly working up towards the surface.

"I said: 'Good, isn't it?' Mr. Courtier."

"I heard you."

"And you were pleased to answer?"

"Nothing."

"With the civility which might be expected of your habits."

Coldly disdainful, Courtier answered:

"If you want to say that sort of thing, please choose a place where I can reply to you," and turned abruptly on his heel.

But he ground his teeth as he made his way out into the street.

In Hyde Park the grass was parched and dewless under a sky whose stars were veiled by the heat and dust haze. Never had Courtier so bitterly wanted the sky's consolation—the blessed sense of insignificance in the face of the night's dark beauty, which, dwarfing all petty rage and hunger, made men part of its majesty, exalted them to a sense of greatness.

Chapter VII

It was past four o'clock the following day when Barbara issued from Valleys House on foot; clad in a pale buff frock, chosen for quietness, she attracted every eye. Very soon entering a taxi-cab, she drove to the Temple, stopped at the Strand entrance, and walked down the little narrow lane into the heart of the Law. Its votaries were hurrying back from the Courts, streaming up from their Chambers for tea, or escaping desperately to Lord's or the Park—young votaries, unbound as yet by the fascination of fame or fees. And each, as he passed, looked at Barbara, with his fingers itching to remove his hat, and a feeling that this was She. After a day spent amongst precedents and practice, after six hours at least of trying to discover what chance A had of standing on his rights, or B had of preventing him, it was difficult to feel otherwise about that calm apparition—like a golden slim tree walking. One of them, asked by her the way to Miltoun's staircase, preceded her with shy ceremony, and when she had vanished up those dusty stairs, lingered on, hoping that she might find her visitee out, and be obliged to return and ask him the way back. But she did not come, and he went sadly away, disturbed to the very bottom of all that he owned in fee simple.

In fact, no one answered Barbara's knock, and discovering that the door yielded, she walked through the lobby past the clerk's den, converted to a kitchen, into the sitting-room. It was empty. She had never been to Miltoun's rooms before, and she stared about her curiously. Since he did not practise, much of the proper gear was absent. The room indeed had a worn carpet, a few old chairs, and was lined from floor to ceiling with books. But the wall space between the windows was occupied by an enormous map of England, scored all over with figures and crosses; and before this map stood an immense desk, on which were piles of double foolscap covered with Miltoun's neat and rather pointed writing. Barbara examined them, puckering up her forehead; she knew that he was working at a book on the land question; but she had never realized that the making of a book requited so much writing. Papers, too, and Blue Books littered a large bureau on which stood bronze busts of AEschylus and Dante.

"What an uncomfortable place!" she thought. The room, indeed, had an atmosphere, a spirit, which depressed her horribly. Seeing a few flowers down in the court below, she had a longing to get out to them. Then behind her she heard the sound of someone talking. But there was no one in the room; and the effect of this disrupted soliloquy, which came from nowhere, was so uncanny, that she retreated to the door. The sound, as of two spirits speaking in one voice, grew louder, and involuntarily she glanced at the busts. They seemed quite blameless. Though the sound had been behind her when she was at the window, it was again behind her now that she was at the door; and she suddenly realized that it was issuing from a bookcase in the centre of the wall. Barbara had her father's nerve, and walking up to the bookcase she perceived that it had been affixed to, and covered, a door that was not quite closed. She pulled it towards her, and passed through. Across the centre of an unkempt bedroom Miltoun was striding, dressed only in his shirt and trousers. His feet were bare, and his head and hair dripping wet; the look on his thin dark face went to Barbara's heart. She ran forward, and took his hand. This was burning hot, but the sight of her seemed to have frozen his tongue and eyes. And the contrast of his burning hand with this frozen silence, frightened Barbara horribly. She could think of nothing but to put her other hand to his forehead. That too was burning hot!

"What brought you here?" he said.

She could only murmur:

"Oh! Eusty! Are you ill?"

Miltoun took hold of her wrists.

"It's all right, I've been working too hard; got a touch of fever."

"So I can feel," murmured Barbara. "You ought to be in bed. Come home with me."

Miltoun smiled. "It's not a case for leeches."

The look of his smile, the sound of his voice, sent a shudder through her.

"I'm not going to leave you here alone."

But Miltoun's grasp tightened on her wrists.

"My dear Babs, you will do what I tell you. Go home, hold your tongue, and leave me to burn out in peace."

Barbara sustained that painful grip without wincing; she had regained her calmness.

"You must come! You haven't anything here, not even a cool drink."

"My God! Barley water!"

The scorn he put into those two words was more withering than a whole philippic against redemption by creature comforts. And feeling it dart into her, Barbara closed her lips tight. He had dropped her wrists, and again, begun pacing up and down; suddenly he stopped:

"'The stars, sun, moon all shrink away,
A desert vast, without a bound,
And nothing left to eat or drink,
"And a dark desert all around.'

"You should read your Blake, Audrey."

Barbara turned quickly, and went out frightened. She passed through the sitting-room and corridor on to the staircase. He was ill-raving! The fever in Miltoun's veins seemed to have stolen through the clutch of his hands into her own veins. Her face was burning, she thought confusedly, breathed unevenly. She felt sore, and at the same time terribly sorry; and withal there kept rising in her the gusty memory of Harbingers kiss.

She hurried down the stairs, turned by instinct down-hill and found herself on the Embankment. And suddenly, with her inherent power of swift decision, she hailed a cab, and drove to the nearest telephone office.

Chapter VIII

To a woman like Audrey Noel, born to be the counterpart and complement of another,—whose occupations and effort were inherently divorced from the continuity of any stiff and strenuous purpose of her own, the uprooting she had voluntarily undergone was a serious matter.

Bereaved of the faces of her flowers, the friendly sighing of her lime-tree, the wants of her cottagers; bereaved of that busy monotony of little home things which is the stay and solace of lonely women, she was extraordinarily lost. Even music for review seemed to have failed her. She had never lived in London, so that she had not the refuge of old haunts and habits, but had to make her own—and to make habits and haunts required a heart that could at least stretch out feelers and lay hold of things, and her heart was not now able. When she had struggled with her Edwardian flat, and laid down her simple routine of meals, she was as stranded as ever was, convict let out of prison. She had not even that great support, the necessity of hiding her feelings for fear of disturbing others. She was planted there, with her longing and grief, and nothing, nobody, to take her out of herself. Having wilfully embraced this position, she tried to make the best of it, feeling it less intolerable, at all events, than staying on at Monkland, where she had made that grievous, and unpardonable error—falling in love.

This offence, on the part of one who felt within herself a great capacity to enjoy and to confer happiness, had arisen—like the other grievous and unpardonable offence, her marriage—from too much disposition to yield herself to the personality of another. But it was cold comfort to know that the desire to give and to receive love had twice over left her—a dead woman. Whatever the nature of those immature sensations with which, as a girl of twenty, she had accepted her husband, in her feeling towards Miltoun there was not only abandonment, but the higher flame of self-renunciation. She wanted to do the best for him, and had not even the consolation of the knowledge that she had sacrificed herself for his advantage. All had been taken out of her hands! Yet with characteristic fatalism she did not feel rebellious. If it were ordained that she should, for fifty, perhaps sixty years, repent in sterility and ashes that first error of her girlhood, rebellion was, none the less, too far-fetched. If she rebelled, it would not be in spirit, but in action. General principles were nothing to her; she lost no force brooding over the justice or injustice of her situation, but merely tried to digest its facts.

The whole day, succeeding Courtier's visit, was spent by her in the National Gallery, whose roof, alone of all in London, seemed to offer her protection. She had found one painting, by an Italian master, the subject of which reminded her of Miltoun; and before this she sat for a very long time, attracting at last the gouty stare of an official. The still figure of this lady, with the oval face and grave beauty, both piqued his curiosity, and stimulated certain moral qualms. She, was undoubtedly waiting for her lover. No woman, in his experience, had ever sat so long before a picture without ulterior motive; and he kept his eyes well opened to see what this motive would be like. It gave him, therefore, a sensation almost amounting to chagrin when coming round once more, he found they had eluded him and gone off together without coming under his inspection. Feeling his feet a good deal, for he had been on them all day, he sat down in the hollow which she had left behind her; and against his will found himself also looking at the picture. It was painted in a style he did not care for; the face of the subject, too, gave him the queer feeling that the gentleman was being roasted inside. He had not been sitting there long, however, before he perceived the lady standing by the picture, and the lips of the gentleman in the picture moving. It seemed to him against the rules, and he got up at once, and went towards it; but as he did so, he found that his eyes were shut, and opened them hastily. There was no one there.

From the National Gallery, Audrey had gone into an A.B.C. for tea, and then home. Before the Mansions was a taxi-cab, and the maid met her with the news that 'Lady Caradoc' was in the sitting-room.

Barbara was indeed standing in the middle of the room with a look on her face such as her father wore sometimes on the racecourse, in the hunting field, or at stormy Cabinet Meetings, a look both resolute and sharp. She spoke at once:

"I got your address from Mr. Courtier. My brother is ill. I'm afraid it'll be brain fever, I think you had better go and see him at his rooms in the Temple; there's no time to be lost."

To Audrey everything in the room seemed to go round; yet all her senses were preternaturally acute, so that she could distinctly smell the mud of the river at low tide. She said, with a shudder:

"Oh! I will go; yes, I will go at once."

"He's quite alone. He hasn't asked for you; but I think your going is the only chance. He took me for you. You told me once you were a good nurse."

"Yes."

The room was steady enough now, but she had lost the preternatural acuteness of her senses, and felt confused. She heard Barbara say: "I can take you to the door in my cab," and murmuring: "I will get ready," went into her bedroom. For a moment she was so utterly bewildered that she did nothing. Then every other thought was lost in a strange, soft, almost painful delight, as if some new instinct were being born in her; and quickly, but without confusion or hurry, she began packing. She put into a valise her own toilet things; then flannel, cotton-wool, eau de Cologne, hot-water bottle, Etna, shawls, thermometer, everything she had which could serve in illness. Changing to a plain dress, she took up the valise and returned to Barbara. They went out together to the cab. The moment it began to bear her to this ordeal at once so longed-for and so terrible, fear came over her again, so that she screwed herself into the corner, very white and still. She was aware of Barbara calling to the driver: "Go by the Strand, and stop at a poulterer's for ice!" And, when the bag of ice had been handed in, heard her saying: "I will bring you all you want—if he is really going to be ill."

Then, as the cab stopped, and the open doorway of the staircase was before her, all her courage came back.

She felt the girl's warm hand against her own, and grasping her valise and the bag of ice, got out, and hurried up the steps.

Chapter IX

On leaving Nettlefold, Miltoun had gone straight back to his rooms, and begun at once to work at his book on the land question. He worked all through that night—his third night without sleep, and all the following day. In the evening, feeling queer in the head, he went out and walked up and down the Embankment. Then, fearing to go to bed and lie sleepless, he sat down in his arm-chair. Falling asleep there, he had fearful dreams, and awoke unrefreshed. After his bath, he drank coffee, and again forced himself to work. By the middle of the day he felt dizzy and exhausted, but utterly disinclined to eat. He went out into the hot Strand, bought himself a necessary book, and after drinking more coffee, came back and again began to work. At four o'clock he found that he was not taking in the words. His head was burning hot, and he went into his bedroom to bathe it. Then somehow he began walking up and down, talking to himself, as Barbara had found him.

She had no sooner gone, than he felt utterly exhausted. A small crucifix hung over his bed, and throwing himself down before it, he remained motionless with his face buried in the coverlet, and his arms stretched out towards the wall. He did not pray, but merely sought rest from sensation. Across his half-hypnotized consciousness little threads of burning fancy kept shooting. Then he could feel nothing but utter physical sickness, and against this his will revolted. He resolved that he would not be ill, a ridiculous log for women to hang over. But the moments of sickness grew longer and more frequent; and to drive them away he rose from his knees, and for some time again walked up and down; then, seized with vertigo, he was obliged to sit on the bed to save himself from falling. From being burning hot he had become deadly cold, glad to cover himself with the bedclothes. The heat soon flamed up in him again; but with a sick man's instinct he did not throw off the clothes, and stayed quite still. The room seemed to have turned to a thick white substance like a cloud, in which he lay enwrapped, unable to move hand or foot. His sense of smell and hearing had become unnaturally acute; he smelled the distant streets, flowers, dust, and the leather of his books, even the scent left by Barbara's clothes, and a curious odour of river mud. A clock struck six, he counted each stroke; and instantly the whole world seemed full of striking clocks, the sound of horses' hoofs, bicycle bells, people's footfalls. His sense of vision, on the contrary, was absorbed in consciousness of this white blanket of cloud wherein he was lifted above the earth, in the midst of a dull incessant hammering. On the surface of the cloud there seemed to be forming a number of little golden spots; these spots were moving, and he saw that they were toads. Then, beyond them, a huge face shaped itself, very dark, as if of bronze, with eyes burning into his brain. The more he struggled to get away from these eyes, the more they bored and burned into him. His voice was gone, so that he was unable to cry out, and suddenly the face marched over him.

When he recovered consciousness his head was damp with moisture trickling from something held to his forehead by a figure leaning above him. Lifting his hand he touched a cheek; and hearing a sob instantly suppressed, he sighed. His hand was gently taken; he felt kisses on it.

The room was so dark, that he could scarcely see her face—his sight too was dim; but he could hear her breathing and the least sound of her dress and movements—the scent too of her hands and hair seemed to envelop him, and in the midst of all the acute discomfort of his fever, he felt the band round his brain relax. He did not ask how long she had been there, but lay quite still, trying to keep his eyes on her, for fear of that face, which seemed lurking behind the air, ready to march on him again. Then feeling suddenly that he could not hold it back, he beckoned, and clutched at her, trying to cover himself with the protection of her breast. This time his swoon was not so deep; it gave way to delirium, with intervals when he knew that she was there, and by the shaded candle light could see her in a white garment, floating close to him, or sitting still with her hand on his; he could even feel the faint comfort of the ice cap, and of the scent of eau de Cologne. Then he would lose all consciousness of her presence, and pass through into the incoherent world, where the crucifix above his bed seemed to bulge and hang out, as if it must fall on him. He conceived a violent longing to tear it down, which grew till he had struggled up in bed and wrenched it from off the wall. Yet a mysterious consciousness of her presence permeated even his darkest journeys into the strange land; and once she seemed to be with him, where a strange light showed them fields and trees, a dark line of moor, and a bright sea, all whitened, and flashing with sweet violence.

Soon after dawn he had a long interval of consciousness, and took in with a sort of wonder her presence in the low chair by his bed. So still she sat in a white loose gown, pale with watching, her eyes immovably fixed on him, her lips pressed together, and quivering at his faintest motion. He drank in desperately the sweetness of her face, which had so lost remembrance of self.

Chapter X

Barbara gave the news of her brother's illness to no one else, common sense telling her to run no risk of disturbance. Of her own initiative, she brought a doctor, and went down twice a day to hear reports of Miltoun's progress.

As a fact, her father and mother had gone to Lord Dennis, for Goodwood, and the chief difficulty had been to excuse her own neglect of that favourite Meeting. She had fallen back on the half-truth that Eustace wanted her in Town; and, since Lord and Lady Valleys had neither of them shaken off a certain uneasiness about their son, the pretext sufficed:

It was not until the sixth day, when the crisis was well past and Miltoun quite free from fever, that she again went down to Nettlefold.

On arriving she at once sought out her mother, whom she found in her bedroom, resting. It had been very hot at Goodwood.

Barbara was not afraid of her—she was not, indeed, afraid of anyone, except Miltoun, and in some strange way, a little perhaps of Courtier; yet, when the maid had gone, she did not at once begin her tale. Lady Valleys, who at Goodwood had just heard details of a Society scandal, began a carefully expurgated account of it suitable to her daughter's ears—for some account she felt she must give to somebody.

"Mother," said Barbara suddenly, "Eustace has been ill. He's out of danger now, and going on all right." Then, looking hard at the bewildered lady, she added: "Mrs. Noel is nursing him."

The past tense in which illness had been mentioned, checking at the first moment any rush of panic in Lady Valleys, left her confused by the situation conjured up in Barbara's last words. Instead of feeding that part of man which loves a scandal, she was being fed, always an unenviable sensation. A woman did not nurse a man under such circumstances without being everything to him, in the world's eyes. Her daughter went on:

"I took her to him. It seemed the only thing to do—since it's all through fretting for her. Nobody knows, of course, except the doctor, and—Stacey."

"Heavens!" muttered Lady Valleys.

"It has saved him."

The mother instinct in Lady Valleys took sudden fright. "Are you telling me the truth, Babs? Is he really out of danger? How wrong of you not to let me know before?"

But Barbara did not flinch; and her mother relapsed into rumination.

"Stacey is a cat!" she said suddenly. The expurgated details of the scandal she had been retailing to her daughter had included the usual maid. She could not find it in her to enjoy the irony of this coincidence. Then, seeing Barbara smile, she said tartly:

"I fail to see the joke."

"Only that I thought you'd enjoy my throwing Stacey in, dear."

"What! You mean she doesn't know?"

"Not a word."

Lady Valleys smiled.

"What a little wretch you are, Babs!" Maliciously she added: "Claud and his mother are coming over from Whitewater, with Bertie and Lily Malvezin, you'd better go and dress;" and her eyes searched her daughter's so shrewdly, that a flush rose to the girl's cheeks.

When she had gone, Lady Valleys rang for her maid again, and relapsed into meditation. Her first thought was to consult her husband; her second that secrecy was strength. Since no one knew but Barbara, no one had better know.

Her astuteness and experience comprehended the far-reaching probabilities of this affair. It would not do to take a single false step. If she had no one's action to control but her own and Barbara's, so much the less chance of a slip. Her mind was a strange medley of thoughts and feelings, almost comic, well-nigh tragic; of worldly prudence, and motherly instinct; of warm-blooded sympathy with all love-affairs, and cool-blooded concern for her son's career. It was not yet too late perhaps to prevent real mischief; especially since it was agreed by everyone that the woman was no adventuress. Whatever was done, they must not forget that she had nursed him—saved him, Barbara had said! She must be treated with all kindness and consideration.

Hastening her toilette, she in turn went to her daughter's room.

Barbara was already dressed, leaning out of her window towards the sea.

Lady Valleys began almost timidly:

"My dear, is Eustace out of bed yet?"

"He was to get up to-day for an hour or two."

"I see. Now, would there be any danger if you and I went up and took charge over from Mrs. Noel?"

"Poor Eusty!"

"Yes, yes! But, exercise your judgment. Would it harm him?"

Barbara was silent. "No," she said at last, "I don't suppose it would, now; but it's for the doctor to say."

Lady Valleys exhibited a manifest relief.

"We'll see him first, of course. Eustace will have to have an ordinary nurse, I suppose, for a bit."

Looking stealthily at Barbara, she added:

"I mean to be very nice to her; but one mustn't be romantic, you know, Babs."

From the little smile on Barbara's lips she derived no sense of certainty; indeed she was visited by all her late disquietude about her young daughter, by all the feeling that she, as well as Miltoun, was hovering on the verge of some folly.

"Well, my dear," she said, "I am going down."

But Barbara lingered a little longer in that bedroom where ten nights ago she had lain tossing, till in despair she went and cooled herself in the dark sea.

Her last little interview with Courtier stood between her and a fresh meeting with Harbinger, whom at the Valleys House gathering she had not suffered to be alone with her. She came down late.

That same evening, out on the beach road, under a sky swarming with stars, the people were strolling—folk from the towns, down for their fortnight's holiday. In twos and threes, in parties of six or eight, they passed the wall at the end of Lord Dennis's little domain; and the sound of their sparse talk and laughter, together with the sighing of the young waves, was blown over the wall to the ears of Harbinger, Bertie, Barbara, and Lily Malvezin, when they strolled out after dinner to sniff the sea. The holiday-makers stared dully at the four figures in evening dress looking out above their heads; they had other things than these to think of, becoming more and more silent as the night grew dark. The four young people too were rather silent. There was something in this warm night, with its sighing, and its darkness, and its stars, that was not favourable to talk, so that presently they split into couples, drifting a little apart.

Standing there, gripping the wall, it seemed to Harbinger that there were no words left in the world. Not even his worst enemy could have called this young man romantic; yet that figure beside him, the gleam of her neck and her pale cheek in the dark, gave him perhaps the most poignant glimpse of mystery that he had ever had. His mind, essentially that of a man of affairs, by nature and by habit at home amongst the material aspects of things, was but gropingly conscious that here, in this dark night, and the dark sea, and the pale figure of this girl whose heart was dark to him and secret, there was perhaps something—yes, something—which surpassed the confines of his philosophy, something beckoning him on out of his snug compound into the desert of divinity. If so, it was soon gone in the aching of his senses at the scent of her hair, and the longing to escape from this weird silence.

"Babs," he said; "have you forgiven me?"

Her answer came, without turn of head, natural, indifferent:

"Yes—I told you so."

"Is that all you have to say to a fellow?"

"What shall we talk about—the running of Casetta?"

Deep down within him Harbinger uttered a noiseless oath. Something sinister was making her behave like this to him! It was that fellow—that fellow! And suddenly he said:

"Tell me this—" then speech seemed to stick in his throat. No! If there were anything in that, he preferred not to hear it. There was a limit!

Down below, a pair of lovers passed, very silent, their arms round each other's waists.

Barbara turned and walked away towards the house.

Chapter XI

The days when Miltoun was first allowed out of bed were a time of mingled joy and sorrow to her who had nursed him. To see him sitting up, amazed at his own weakness, was happiness, yet to think that he would be no more wholly dependent, no more that sacred thing, a helpless creature, brought her the sadness of a mother whose child no longer needs her. With every hour he would now get farther from her, back into the fastnesses of his own spirit. With every hour she would be less his nurse and comforter, more the woman he loved. And though that thought shone out in the obscure future like a glamorous flower, it brought too much wistful uncertainty to the present. She was very tired, too, now that all excitement was over—so tired that she hardly knew what she did or where she moved. But a smile had become so faithful to her eyes that it clung there above the shadows of fatigue, and kept taking her lips prisoner.

Between the two bronze busts she had placed a bowl of lilies of the valley; and every free niche in that room of books had a little vase of roses to welcome Miltoun's return.

He was lying back in his big leather chair, wrapped in a Turkish gown of Lord Valleys'—on which Barbara had laid hands, having failed to find anything resembling a dressing-gown amongst her brother's austere clothing. The perfume of lilies had overcome the scent of books, and a bee, dusky, adventurer, filled the room with his pleasant humming.

They did not speak, but smiled faintly, looking at one another. In this still moment, before passion had returned to claim its own, their spirits passed through the sleepy air, and became entwined, so that neither could withdraw that soft, slow, encountering glance. In mutual contentment, each to each, close as music to the strings of a violin, their spirits clung—so lost, the one in the other, that neither for that brief time seemed to know which was self.

In fulfilment of her resolution, Lady Valleys, who had returned to Town by a morning train, started with Barbara for the Temple about three in the after noon, and stopped at the doctor's on the way. The whole thing would be much simpler if Eustace were fit to be moved at once to Valleys House; and with much relief she found that the doctor saw no danger in this course. The recovery had been remarkable—touch and go for bad brain fever just avoided! Lord Miltoun's constitution was extremely sound. Yes, he would certainly favour a removal. His rooms were too confined in this weather. Well nursed—(decidedly) Oh; yes! Quite! And the doctor's eyes became perhaps a trifle more intense. Not a professional, he understood. It might be as well to have another nurse, if they were making the change. They would have this lady knocking up. Just so! Yes, he would see to that. An ambulance carriage he thought advisable. That could all be arranged for this afternoon—at once—he himself would look to it. They might take Lord Miltoun off just as he was; the men would know what to do. And when they had him at Valleys House, the moment he showed interest in his food, down to the sea-down to the sea! At this time of year nothing like it! Then with regard to nourishment, he would be inclined already to shove in a leetle stimulant, a thimbleful perhaps four times a day with food—not without—mixed with an egg, with arrowroot, with custard. A week would see him on his legs, a fortnight at the sea make him as good a man as ever. Overwork—burning the candle—a leetlemore would have seen a very different state of things! Quite so! quite so! Would come round himself before dinner, and make sure. His patient might feel it just at first! He bowed Lady Valleys out; and when she had gone, sat down at his telephone with a smile flickering on his clean-cut lips.

Greatly fortified by this interview, Lady Valleys rejoined her daughter in the ear; but while it slid on amongst the multitudinous traffic, signs of unwonted nervousness began to start out through the placidity of her face.

"I wish, my dear," she said suddenly, "that someone else had to do this. Suppose Eustace refuses!"

"He won't," Barbara answered; "she looks so tired, poor dear. Besides—"

Lady Valleys gazed with curiosity at that young face, which had flushed pink. Yes, this daughter of hers was a woman already, with all a woman's intuitions. She said gravely:

"It was a rash stroke of yours, Babs; let's hope it won't lead to disaster."

Barbara bit her lips.

"If you'd seen him as I saw him! And, what disaster? Mayn't they love each other, if they want?"

Lady Valleys swallowed a grimace. It was so exactly her own point of view. And yet—!

"That's only the beginning," she said; "you forget the sort of boy Eustace is."

"Why can't the poor thing be let out of her cage?" cried Barbara. "What good does it do to anyone? Mother, if ever, when I am married, I want to get free, I will!"

The tone of her voice was so quivering, and unlike the happy voice of Barbara, that Lady Valleys involuntarily caught hold of her hand and squeezed it hard.

"My dear sweet," she said, "don't let's talk of such gloomy things."

"I mean it. Nothing shall stop me."

But Lady Valleys' face had suddenly become rather grim.

"So we think, child; it's not so simple."

"It can't be worse, anyway," muttered Barbara, "than being buried alive as that wretched woman is."

For answer Lady Valleys only murmured:

"The doctor promised that ambulance carriage at four o'clock. What am I going to say?"

"She'll understand when you look at her. She's that sort."

The door was opened to them by Mrs. Noel herself.

It was the first time Lady Valleys had seen her in a house, and there was real curiosity mixed with the assurance which masked her nervousness. A pretty creature, even lovely! But the quite genuine sympathy in her words: "I am truly grateful. You must be quite worn out," did not prevent her adding hastily: "The doctor says he must be got home out of these hot rooms. We'll wait here while you tell him."

And then she saw that it was true; this woman was the sort who understood.

Left in the dark passage, she peered round at Barbara.

The girl was standing against the wall with her head thrown back. Lady Valleys could not see her face; but she felt all of a sudden exceedingly uncomfortable, and whispered:

"Two murders and a theft, Babs; wasn't it 'Our Mutual Friend'?"

"Mother!"

"What?"

"Her face! When you're going to throw away a flower, it looks at you!"

"My dear!" murmured Lady Valleys, thoroughly distressed, "what things you're saying to-day!"

This lurking in a dark passage, this whispering girl—it was all queer, unlike an experience in proper life.

And then through the reopened door she saw Miltoun, stretched out in a chair, very pale, but still with that look about his eyes and lips, which of all things in the world had a chastening effect on Lady Valleys, making her feel somehow incurably mundane.

She said rather timidly:

"I'm so glad you're better, dear. What a time you must have had! It's too bad that I knew nothing till yesterday!"

But Miltoun's answer was, as usual, thoroughly disconcerting.

"Thanks, yes! I have had a perfect time—and have now to pay for it, I suppose."

Held back by his smile from bending to kiss him, poor Lady Valleys fidgeted from head to foot. A sudden impulse of sheer womanliness caused a tear to fall on his hand.

When Miltoun perceived that moisture, he said:

"It's all right, mother. I'm quite willing to come."

Still wounded by his voice, Lady Valleys hardened instantly. And while preparing for departure she watched the two furtively. They hardly looked at one another, and when they did, their eyes baffled her. The expression was outside her experience, belonging as it were to a different world, with its faintly smiling, almost shining, gravity.

Vastly relieved when Miltoun, covered with a fur, had been taken down to the carriage, she lingered to speak to Mrs. Noel.

"We owe you a great debt. It might have been so much worse. You mustn't be disconsolate. Go to bed and have a good long rest." And from the door, she murmured again: "He will come and thank you, when he's well."

Descending the stone stairs, she thought: "'Anonyma'—'Anonyma'—yes, it was quite the name." And suddenly she saw Barbara come running up again.

"What is it, Babs?"

Barbara answered:

"Eustace would like some of those lilies." And, passing Lady Valleys, she went on up to Miltoun's chambers.

Mrs. Noel was not in the sitting-room, and going to the bedroom door, the girl looked in.

She was standing by the bed, drawing her hand over and over the white surface of the pillow. Stealing noiselessly back, Barbara caught up the bunch of lilies, and fled.

Chapter XII

Miltoun, whose constitution, had the steel-like quality of Lady Casterley's, had a very rapid convalescence. And, having begun to take an interest in his food, he was allowed to travel on the seventh day to Sea House in charge of Barbara.

The two spent their time in a little summer-house close to the sea; lying out on the beach under the groynes; and, as Miltoun grew stronger, motoring and walking on the Downs.

To Barbara, keeping a close watch, he seemed tranquilly enough drinking in from Nature what was necessary to restore balance after the struggle, and breakdown of the past weeks. Yet she could never get rid of a queer feeling that he was not really there at all; to look at him was like watching an uninhabited house that was waiting for someone to enter.

During a whole fortnight he did not make a single allusion to Mrs. Noel, till, on the very last morning, as they were watching the sea, he said with his queer smile:

"It almost makes one believe her theory, that the old gods are not dead. Do you ever see them, Babs; or are you, like me, obtuse?"

Certainly about those lithe invasions of the sea-nymph waves, with ashy, streaming hair, flinging themselves into the arms of the land, there was the old pagan rapture, an inexhaustible delight, a passionate soft acceptance of eternal fate, a wonderful acquiescence in the untiring mystery of life.

But Barbara, ever disconcerted by that tone in his voice, and by this quick dive into the waters of unaccustomed thought, failed to find an answer.

Miltoun went on:

"She says, too, we can hear Apollo singing. Shall we try."

But all that came was the sigh of the sea, and of the wind in the tamarisk.

"No," muttered Miltoun at last, "she alone can hear it."

And Barbara saw, once more on his face that look, neither sad nor impatient, but as of one uninhabited and waiting.

She left Sea House next day to rejoin her mother, who, having been to Cowes, and to the Duchess of Gloucester's, was back in Town waiting for Parliament to rise, before going off to Scotland. And that same afternoon the girl made her way to Mrs. Noel's flat. In paying this visit she was moved not so much by compassion, as by uneasiness, and a strange curiosity. Now that Miltoun was well again, she was seriously disturbed in mind. Had she made a mistake in summoning Mrs. Noel to nurse him?

When she went into the little drawing-room Audrey was sitting in the deep-cushioned window-seat with a book on her knee; and by the fact that it was open at the index, Barbara judged that she had not been reading too attentively. She showed no signs of agitation at the sight of her visitor, nor any eagerness to hear news of Miltoun. But the girl had not been five minutes in the room before the thought came to her: "Why! She has the same look as Eustace!" She, too, was like an empty tenement; without impatience, discontent, or grief—waiting! Barbara had scarcely realized this with a curious sense of discomposure, when Courtier was announced. Whether there was in this an absolute coincidence or just that amount of calculation which might follow on his part from receipt of a note written from Sea House—saying that Miltoun was well again, that she was coming up and meant to go and thank Mrs. Noel—was not clear, nor were her own sensations; and she drew over her face that armoured look which she perhaps knew Courtier could not bear to see. His face, at all events, was very red when he shook hands. He had come, he told Mrs. Noel, to say good-bye. He was definitely off next week. Fighting had broken out; the revolutionaries were greatly outnumbered. Indeed he ought to have been there long before!

Barbara had gone over to the window; she turned suddenly, and said:

"You were preaching peace two months ago!"

Courtier bowed.

"We are not all perfectly consistent, Lady Barbara. These poor devils have a holy cause."

Barbara held out her hand to Mrs. Noel.

"You only think their cause holy because they happen to be weak. Good-bye, Mrs. Noel; the world is meant for the strong, isn't it!"

She intended that to hurt him; and from the tone of his voice, she knew it had.

"Don't, Lady Barbara; from your mother, yes; not from you!"

"It's what I believe. Good-bye!" And she went out.

She had told him that she did not want him to go—not yet; and he was going!

But no sooner had she got outside, after that strange outburst, than she bit her lips to keep back an angry, miserable feeling. He had been rude to her, she had been rude to him; that was the way they had said good-bye! Then, as she emerged into the sunlight, she thought: "Oh! well; he doesn't care, and I'm sure I don't!"

She heard a voice behind her.

"May I get you a cab?" and at once the sore feeling began to die away; but she did not look round, only smiled, and shook her head, and made a little room for him on the pavement.

But though they walked, they did not at first talk. There was rising within Barbara a tantalizing devil of desire to know the feelings that really lay behind that deferential gravity, to make him show her how much he really cared. She kept her eyes demurely lowered, but she let the glimmer of a smile flicker about her lips; she knew too that her cheeks were glowing, and for that she was not sorry. Was she not to have any—any—was he calmly to go away—without—And she thought: "He shall say something! He shall show me, without that horrible irony of his!"

She said suddenly:

"Those two are just waiting—something will happen!"

"It is probable," was his grave answer.

She looked at him then—it pleased her to see him quiver as if that glance had gone right into him; and she said softly:

"And I think they will be quite right."

She knew those were reckless words, nor cared very much what they meant; but she knew the revolt in them would move him. She saw from his face that it had; and after a little pause, said:

"Happiness is the great thing," and with soft, wicked slowness: "Isn't it, Mr. Courtier?"

But all the cheeriness had gone out of his face, which had grown almost pale. He lifted his hand, and let it drop. Then she felt sorry. It was just as if he had asked her to spare him.

"As to that," he said: "The rough, unfortunately, has to be taken with the smooth. But life's frightfully jolly sometimes."

"As now?"

He looked at her with firm gravity, and answered

"As now."

A sense of utter mortification seized on Barbara. He was too strong for her—he was quixotic—he was hateful! And, determined not to show a sign, to be at least as strong as he, she said calmly:

"Now I think I'll have that cab!"

When she was in the cab, and he was standing with his hat lifted, she looked at him in the way that women can, so that he did not realize that she had looked.

Chapter XIII

When Miltoun came to thank her, Audrey Noel was waiting in the middle of the room, dressed in white, her lips smiling, her dark eyes smiling, still as a flower on a windless day.

In that first look passing between them, they forgot everything but happiness. Swallows, on the first day of summer, in their discovery of the bland air, can neither remember that cold winds blow, nor imagine the death of sunlight on their feathers, and, flitting hour after hour over the golden fields, seem no longer birds, but just the breathing of a new season—swallows were no more forgetful of misfortune than were those two. His gaze was as still as her very self; her look at him had in at the quietude of all emotion.

When they' sat down to talk it was as if they had gone back to those days at Monkland, when he had come to her so often to discuss everything in heaven and earth. And yet, over that tranquil eager drinking—in of each other's presence, hovered a sort of awe. It was the mood of morning before the sun has soared. The dew-grey cobwebs enwrapped the flowers of their hearts—yet every prisoned flower could be seen. And he and she seemed looking through that web at the colour and the deep-down forms enshrouded so jealously; each feared too much to unveil the other's heart. They were like lovers who, rambling in a shy wood, never dare stay their babbling talk of the trees and birds and lost bluebells, lest in the deep waters of a kiss their star of all that is to come should fall and be drowned. To each hour its familiar—and the spirit of that hour was the spirit of the white flowers in the bowl on the window-sill above her head.

They spoke of Monk-land, and Miltoun's illness; of his first speech, his impressions of the House of Commons; of music, Barbara, Courtier, the river. He told her of his health, and described his days down by the sea. She, as ever, spoke little of herself, persuaded that it could not interest even him; but she described a visit to the opera; and how she had found a picture in the National Gallery which reminded her of him. To all these trivial things and countless others, the tone of their voices—soft, almost murmuring, with a sort of delighted gentleness—gave a high, sweet importance, a halo that neither for the world would have dislodged from where it hovered.

It was past six when he got up to go, and there had not been a moment to break the calm of that sacred feeling in both their hearts. They parted with another tranquil look, which seemed to say: 'It is well with us—we have drunk of happiness.'

And in this same amazing calm Miltoun remained after he had gone away, till about half-past nine in the evening, he started forth, to walk down to the House. It was now that sort of warm, clear night, which in the country has firefly magic, and even over the Town spreads a dark glamour. And for Miltoun, in the delight of his new health and well-being, with every sense alive and clean, to walk through the warmth and beauty of this night was sheer pleasure. He passed by way of St. James's Park, treading down the purple shadows of plane-tree leaves into the pools of lamplight, almost with remorse—so beautiful, and as if alive, were they. There were moths abroad, and gnats, born on the water, and scent of new-mown grass drifted up from the lawns. His heart felt light as a swallow he had seen that morning; swooping at a grey feather, carrying it along, letting it flutter away, then diving to seize it again. Such was his elation, this beautiful night! Nearing the House of Commons, he thought he would walk a little longer, and turned westward to the river: On that warm evening the water, without movement at turn of tide, was like the black, snake-smooth hair of Nature streaming out on her couch of Earth, waiting for the caress of a divine hand. Far away on the further; bank throbbed some huge machine, not stilled as yet. A few stars were out in the dark sky, but no moon to invest with pallor the gleam of the lamps. Scarcely anyone passed. Miltoun strolled along the river wall, then crossed, and came back in front of the Mansions where she lived. By the railing he stood still. In the sitting-room of her little flat there was no light, but the casement window was wide open, and the crown of white flowers in the bowl on the window-sill still gleamed out in the darkness like a crescent moon lying on its face. Suddenly, he saw two pale hands rise—one on either side of that bowl, lift it, and draw it in. And he quivered, as though they had touched him. Again those two hands came floating up; they were parted now by darkness; the moon of flowers was gone, in its place had been set handfuls of purple or crimson blossoms. And a puff of warm air rising quickly out of the night drifted their scent of cloves into his face, so that he held his breath for fear of calling out her name.

Again the hands had vanished—through the open window there was nothing to be seen but darkness; and such a rush of longing seized on Miltoun as stole from him all power of movement. He could hear her playing, now. The murmurous current of that melody was like the night itself, sighing, throbbing, languorously soft. It seemed that in this music she was calling him, telling him that she, too, was longing; her heart, too, empty. It died away; and at the window her white figure appeared. From that vision he could not, nor did he try to shrink, but moved out into the lamplight. And he saw her suddenly stretch out her hands to him, and withdraw them to her breast. Then all save the madness of his longing deserted Miltoun. He ran down the little garden, across the hall, up the stairs.

The door was open. He passed through. There, in the sitting-room, where the red flowers in the window scented all the air, it was dark, and he could not at first see her, till against the piano he caught the glimmer of her white dress. She was sitting with hands resting on the pale notes. And falling on his knees, he buried his face against her. Then, without looking up, he raised his hands. Her tears fell on them covering her heart, that throbbed as if the passionate night itself were breathing in there, and all but the night and her love had stolen forth.

On a spur of the Sussex Downs, inland from Nettle-Cold, there stands a beech-grove. The traveller who enters it out of the heat and brightness, takes off the shoes of his spirit before its, sanctity; and, reaching the centre, across the clean beech-mat, he sits refreshing his brow with air, and silence. For the flowers of sunlight on the ground under those branches are pale and rare, no insects hum, the birds are almost mute. And close to the border trees are the quiet, milk-white sheep, in congregation, escaping from noon heat. Here, above fields and dwellings, above the ceaseless network of men's doings, and the vapour of their talk, the traveller feels solemnity. All seems conveying divinity—the great white clouds moving their wings above him, the faint longing murmur of the boughs, and in far distance, the sea.... And for a space his restlessness and fear know the peace of God.

So it was with Miltoun when he reached this temple, three days after that passionate night, having walked for hours, alone and full of conflict. During those three days he had been borne forward on the flood tide; and now, tearing himself out of London, where to think was impossible, he had come to the solitude of the Downs to walk, and face his new position.

For that position he saw to be very serious. In the flush of full realization, there was for him no question of renunciation. She was his, he hers; that was determined. But what, then, was he to do? There was no chance of her getting free. In her husband's view, it seemed, under no circumstances was marriage dissoluble. Nor, indeed, to Miltoun would divorce have made things easier, believing as he did that he and she were guilty, and that for the guilty there could be no marriage. She, it was true, asked nothing but just to be his in secret; and that was the course he knew most men would take, without further thought. There was no material reason in the world why he should not so act, and maintain unchanged every other current of his life. It would be easy, usual. And, with her faculty for self-effacement, he knew she would not be unhappy. But conscience, in Miltoun, was a terrible and fierce thing. In the delirium of his illness it had become that Great Face which had marched over him. And, though during the weeks of his recuperation, struggle of all kind had ceased, now that he had yielded to his passion, conscience, in a new and dismal shape, had crept up again to sit above his heart: He must and would let this man, her husband, know; but even if that caused no open scandal, could he go on deceiving those who, if they knew of an illicit love, would no longer allow him to be their representative? If it were known that she was his mistress, he could no longer maintain his position in public life—was he not therefore in honour bound; of his own accord, to resign it? Night and day he was haunted by the thought: How can I, living in defiance of authority, pretend to authority over my fellows? How can I remain in public life? But if he did not remain in public life, what was he to do? That way of life was in his blood; he had been bred and born into it; had thought of nothing else since he was a boy. There was no other occupation or interest that could hold him for a moment—he saw very plainly that he would be cast away on the waters of existence.

So the battle raged in his proud and twisted spirit, which took everything so hard—his nature imperatively commanding him to keep his work and his power for usefulness; his conscience telling him as urgently that if he sought to wield authority, he must obey it.

He entered the beech-grove at the height of this misery, flaming with rebellion against the dilemma which Fate had placed before him; visited by gusts of resentment against a passion, which forced him to pay the price, either of his career, or of his self-respect; gusts, followed by remorse that he could so for one moment regret his love for that tender creature. The face of Lucifer was not more dark, more tortured, than Miltoun's face in the twilight of the grove, above those kingdoms of the world, for which his ambition and his conscience fought. He threw himself down among the trees; and stretching out his arms, by chance touched a beetle trying to crawl over the grassless soil. Some bird had maimed it. He took the little creature up. The beetle truly could no longer work, but it was spared the fate lying before himself. The beetle was not, as he would be, when his power of movement was destroyed, conscious of his own wasted life. The world would not roll away down there. He would still see himself cumbering the ground, when his powers were taken, from him. This thought was torture. Why had he been suffered to meet her, to love her, and to be loved by her? What had made him so certain from the first moment, if she were not meant for him? If he lived to be a hundred, he would never meet another. Why, because of his love, must he bury the will and force of a man? If there were no more coherence in God's scheme than this, let him too be incoherent! Let him hold authority, and live outside authority! Why stifle his powers for the sake of a coherence which did not exist! That would indeed be madness greater than that of a mad world!

There was no answer to his thoughts in the stillness of the grove, unless it were the cooing of a dove, or the faint thudding of the sheep issuing again into sunlight. But slowly that stillness stole into Miltoun's spirit. "Is it like this in the grave?" he thought. "Are the boughs of those trees the dark earth over me? And the sound in them the sound the dead hear when flowers are growing, and the wind passing through them? And is the feel of this earth how it feels to lie looking up for ever at nothing? Is life anything but a nightmare, a dream; and is not this the reality? And why my fury, my insignificant flame, blowing here and there, when there is really no wind, only a shroud of still air, and these flowers of sunlight that have been dropped on me! Why not let my spirit sleep, instead of eating itself away with rage; why not resign myself at once to wait for the substance, of which this is but the shadow!"

And he lay scarcely breathing, looking up at the unmoving branches setting with their darkness the pearls of the sky.

"Is not peace enough?" he thought. "Is not love enough? Can I not be reconciled, like a woman? Is not that salvation, and happiness? What is all the rest, but 'sound and fury, signifying nothing?"

And as though afraid to lose his hold of that thought, he got up and hurried from the grove.

The whole wide landscape of field and wood, cut by the pale roads, was glimmering under the afternoon sun, Here was no wild, wind-swept land, gleaming red and purple, and guarded by the grey rocks; no home of the winds, and the wild gods. It was all serene and silver-golden. In place of the shrill wailing pipe of the hunting buzzard-hawks half lost up in the wind, invisible larks were letting fall hymns to tranquillity; and even the sea—no adventuring spirit sweeping the shore with its wing—seemed to lie resting by the side of the land.

Chapter XV

When on the afternoon of that same day Miltoun did not come, all the chilly doubts which his presence alone kept away, crowded thick and fast into the mind of one only too prone to distrust her own happiness. It could not last—how could it?

His nature and her own were so far apart! Even in that giving of herself which had been such happiness, she had yet doubted; for there was so much in him that was to her mysterious. All that he loved in poetry and nature, had in it something craggy and culminating. The soft and fiery, the subtle and harmonious, seemed to leave him cold. He had no particular love for all those simple natural things, birds, bees, animals, trees, and flowers, that seemed to her precious and divine.

Though it was not yet four o'clock she was already beginning to droop like a flower that wants water. But she sat down to her piano, resolutely, till tea came; playing on and on with a spirit only half present, the other half of her wandering in the Town, seeking for Miltoun. After tea she tried first to read, then to sew, and once more came back to her piano. The clock struck six; and as if its last stroke had broken the armour of her mind, she felt suddenly sick with anxiety. Why was he so long? But she kept on playing, turning the pages without taking in the notes, haunted by the idea that he might again have fallen ill. Should she telegraph? What good, when she could not tell in the least where he might be? And all the unreasoning terror of not knowing where the loved one is, beset her so that her hands, in sheer numbness, dropped from the keys. Unable to keep still, now, she wandered from window to door, out into the little hall, and back hastily to the window. Over her anxiety brooded a darkness, compounded of vague growing fears. What if it were the end? What if he had chosen this as the most merciful way of leaving her? But surely he would never be so cruel! Close on the heels of this too painful thought came reaction; and she told herself that she was a fool. He was at the House; something quite ordinary was keeping him. It was absurd to be anxious! She would have to get used to this now. To be a drag on him would be dreadful. Sooner than that she would rather—yes—rather he never came back! And she took up her book, determined to read quietly till he came. But the moment she sat down her fears returned with redoubled force-the cold sickly horrible feeling of uncertainty, of the knowledge that she could do nothing but wait till she was relieved by something over which she had no control. And in the superstition that to stay there in the window where she could see him come, was keeping him from her, she went into her bedroom. From there she could watch the sunset clouds wine-dark over the river. A little talking wind shivered along the houses; the dusk began creeping in. She would not turn on the light, unwilling to admit that it was really getting late, but began to change her dress, lingering desperately over every little detail of her toilette, deriving therefrom a faint, mysterious comfort, trying to make herself feel beautiful. From sheer dread of going back before he came, she let her hair fall, though it was quite smooth and tidy, and began brushing it. Suddenly she thought with horror of her efforts at adornment—by specially preparing for him, she must seem presumptuous to Fate. At any little sound she stopped and stood listening—save for her hair and eyes, as white from head to foot as a double narcissus flower in the dusk, bending towards some faint tune played to it somewhere oft in the fields. But all those little sounds ceased, one after another—they had meant nothing; and each time, her spirit returning—within the pale walls of the room, began once more to inhabit her lingering fingers. During that hour in her bedroom she lived through years. It was dark when she left it.

Chapter XVI

When Miltoun at last came it was past nine o'clock.

Silent, but quivering all over; she clung to him in the hall; and this passion of emotion, without sound to give it substance, affected him profoundly. How terribly sensitive and tender she was! She seemed to have no armour. But though so stirred by her emotion, he was none the less exasperated. She incarnated at that moment the life to which he must now resign himself—a life of unending tenderness, consideration, and passivity.

For a long time he could not bring himself to speak of his decision. Every look of her eyes, every movement of her body, seemed pleading with him to keep silence. But in Miltoun's character there was an element of rigidity, which never suffered him to diverge from an objective once determined.

When he had finished telling her, she only said:

"Why can't we go on in secret?"

And he felt with a sort of horror that he must begin his struggle over again. He got up, and threw open the window. The sky was dark above the river; the wind had risen. That restless murmuration, and the width of the night with its scattered stars, seemed to come rushing at his face. He withdrew from it, and leaning on the sill looked down at her. What flower-like delicacy she had! There flashed across him the memory of a drooping blossom, which, in the Spring, he had seen her throw into the flames; with the words: "I can't bear flowers to fade, I always want to burn them." He could see again those waxen petals yield to the fierce clutch of the little red creeping sparks, and the slender stalk quivering, and glowing, and writhing to blackness like a live thing. And, distraught, he began:

"I can't live a lie. What right have I to lead, if I can't follow? I'm not like our friend Courtier who believes in Liberty. I never have, I never shall. Liberty? What is Liberty? But only those who conform to authority have the right to wield authority. A man is a churl who enforces laws, when he himself has not the strength to observe them. I will not be one of whom it can be said: 'He can rule others, himself—!'"

"No one will know."

Miltoun turned away.

"I shall know," he said; but he saw clearly that she did not understand him. Her face had a strange, brooding, shut-away look, as though he had frightened her. And the thought that she could not understand, angered him.

He said, stubbornly: "No, I can't remain in public life."

"But what has it to do with politics? It's such a little thing."

"If it had been a little thing to me, should I have left you at Monkland, and spent those five weeks in purgatory before my illness? A little thing!"

She exclaimed with sudden fire:

"Circumstances aye the little thing; it's love that's the great thing."

Miltoun stared at her, for the first time understanding that she had a philosophy as deep and stubborn as his own. But he answered cruelly:

"Well! the great thing has conquered me!"

And then he saw her looking at him, as if, seeing into the recesses of his soul, she had made some ghastly discovery. The look was so mournful, so uncannily intent that he turned away from it.

"Perhaps it is a little thing," he muttered; "I don't know. I can't see my way. I've lost my bearings; I must find them again before I can do anything."

But as if she had not heard, or not taken in the sense of his words, she said again:

"Oh! don't let us alter anything; I won't ever want what you can't give."

And this stubbornness, when he was doing the very thing that would give him to her utterly, seemed to him unreasonable.

"I've had it out with myself," he said. "Don't let's talk about it any more."

Again, with a sort of dry anguish, she murmured:

"No, no! Let us go on as we are!"

Feeling that he had borne all he could, Miltoun put his hands on her shoulders, and said: "That's enough!"

Then, in sudden remorse, he lifted her, and clasped her to him.

But she stood inert in his arms, her eyes closed, not returning his kisses.

Chapter XVII

On the last day before Parliament rose, Lord Valleys, with a light heart, mounted his horse for a gallop in the Row. Though she was a blood mare he rode her with a plain snaffle, having the horsemanship of one who has hunted from the age of seven, and been for twenty years a Colonel of Yeomanry. Greeting affably everyone he knew, he maintained a frank demeanour on all subjects, especially of Government policy, secretly enjoying the surmises and prognostications, so pleasantly wide of the mark, and the way questions and hints perished before his sphinx-like candour. He spoke cheerily too of Miltoun, who was 'all right again,' and 'burning for the fray' when the House met again in the autumn. And he chaffed Lord Malvezin about his wife. If anything—he said—could make Bertie take an interest in politics, it would be she. He had two capital gallops, being well known to the police: The day was bright, and he was sorry to turn home. Falling in with Harbinger, he asked him to come back to lunch. There had seemed something different lately, an almost morose look, about young Harbinger; and his wife's disquieting words about Barbara came back to Lord Valleys with a shock. He had seen little of the child lately, and in the general clearing up of this time of year had forgotten all about the matter.

Agatha, who was still staying at Valleys House with little Ann, waiting to travel up to Scotland with her mother, was out, and there was no one at lunch except Lady Valleys and Barbara herself. Conversation flagged; for the young people were extremely silent, Lady Valleys was considering the draft of a report which had to be settled before she left, and Lord Valleys himself was rather carefully watching his daughter. The news that Lord Miltoun was in the study came as a surprise, and somewhat of a relief to all. To an exhortation to luring him in to lunch; the servant replied that Lord Miltoun had lunched, and would wait.

"Does he know there's no one here?"

"Yes, my lady."

Lady Valleys pushed back her plate, and rose:

"Oh, well!" she said, "I've finished."

Lord Valleys also got up, and they went out together, leaving Barbara, who had risen, looking doubtfully at the door.

Lord Valleys had recently been told of the nursing episode, and had received the news with the dubious air of one hearing something about an eccentric person, which, heard about anyone else, could have had but one significance. If Eustace had been a normal young man his father would have shrugged his shoulder's, and thought: "Oh, well! There it is!" As it was, he had literally not known what to think.

And now, crossing the saloon which intervened between the dining-room and the study, he said to his wife uneasily:

"Is it this woman again, Gertrude—or what?"

Lady Valleys answered with a shrug:

"Goodness knows, my dear."

Miltoun was standing in the embrasure of a window above the terrace. He looked well, and his greeting was the same as usual.

"Well, my dear fellow," said Lord Valleys, "you're all right again evidently—what's the news?"

"Only that I've decided to resign my seat."

Lord Valleys stared.

"What on earth for?"

But Lady Valleys, with the greater quickness of women, divining already something of the reason, had flushed a deep pink.

"Nonsense, my dear," she said; "it can't possibly be necessary, even if—" Recovering herself, she added dryly:

"Give us some reason."

"The reason is simply that I've joined my life to Mrs. Noel's, and I can't go on as I am, living a lie. If it were known I should obviously have to resign at once."

"Good God!" exclaimed Lord Valleys.

Lady Valleys made a rapid movement. In the face of what she felt to be a really serious crisis between these two utterly different creatures of the other sex, her husband and her son, she had dropped her mask and become a genuine woman. Unconsciously both men felt this change, and in speaking, turned towards her.

"I can't argue it," said Miltoun; "I consider myself bound in honour."

"And then?" she asked.

Lord Valleys, with a note of real feeling, interjected:

"By Heaven! I did think you put your country above your private affairs."

"Geoff!" said Lady Valleys.

But Lord Valleys went on:

"No, Eustace, I'm out of touch with your view of things altogether. I don't even begin to understand it."

"That is true," said Miltoun.

"Listen to me, both of you!" said Lady Valleys: "You two are altogether different; and you must not quarrel. I won't have that. Now, Eustace, you are our son, and you have got to be kind and considerate. Sit down, and let's talk it over."

And motioning her husband to a chair, she sat down in the embrasure of a window. Miltoun remained standing. Visited by a sudden dread, Lady Valleys said:

"Is it—you've not—there isn't going to be a scandal?"

Miltoun smiled grimly.

"I shall tell this man, of course, but you may make your minds easy, I imagine; I understand that his view of marriage does not permit of divorce in any case whatever."

Lady Valleys sighed with an utter and undisguised relief.

"Well, then, my dear boy," she began, "even if you do feel you must tell him, there is surely no reason why it should not otherwise be kept secret."

Lord Valleys interrupted her:

"I should be glad if you would point out the connection between your honour and the resignation of your seat," he said stiffly.

Miltoun shook his head.

"If you don't see already, it would be useless."

"I do not see. The whole matter is—is unfortunate, but to give up your work, so long as there is no absolute necessity, seems to me far-fetched and absurd. How many men are, there into whose lives there has not entered some such relation at one time or another? This idea would disqualify half the nation." His eyes seemed in that crisis both to consult and to avoid his wife's, as though he were at once asking her endorsement of his point of view, and observing the proprieties. And for a moment in the midst of her anxiety, her sense of humour got the better of Lady Valleys. It was so funny that Geoff should have to give himself away; she could not for the life of her help fixing him with her eyes.

"My dear," she murmured, "you underestimate three-quarters, at the very least!"

But Lord Valleys, confronted with danger, was growing steadier.

"It passes my comprehension;" he said, "why you should want to mix up sex and politics at all."

Miltoun's answer came very slowly, as if the confession were hurting his lips:

"There is—forgive me for using the word—such a thing as one's religion. I don't happen to regard life as divided into public and private departments. My vision is gone—broken—I can see no object before me now in public life—no goal—no certainty."

Lady Valleys caught his hand:

"Oh! my dear," she said, "that's too dreadfully puritanical!" But at Miltoun's queer smile, she added hastily: "Logical—I mean."

"Consult your common sense, Eustace, for goodness' sake," broke in Lord Valleys. "Isn't it your simple duty to put your scruples in your pocket, and do the best you can for your country with the powers that have been given you?"

"I have no common sense."

"In that case, of course, it may be just as well that you should leave public life."

Miltoun bowed.

"Nonsense!" cried Lady Valleys. "You don't understand, Geoffrey. I ask you again, Eustace, what will you do afterwards?"

"I don't know."

"You will eat your heart out."

"Quite possibly."

"If you can't come to a reasonable arrangement with your conscience," again broke in Lord Valleys, "for Heaven's sake give her up, like a man, and cut all these knots."

"I beg your pardon, sir!" said Miltoun icily.

Lady Valleys laid her hand on his arm. "You must allow us a little logic too, my dear. You don't seriously imagine that she would wish you to throw away your life for her? I'm not such a bad judge of character as that."

She stopped before the expression on Miltoun's face.

"You go too fast," he said; "I may become a free spirit yet."

To this saying, which seemed to her cryptic and sinister, Lady Valleys did not know what to answer.

"If you feel, as you say," Lord Valleys began once more, "that the bottom has been knocked out of things for you by this—this affair, don't, for goodness' sake, do anything in a hurry. Wait! Go abroad! Get your balance back! You'll find the thing settle itself in a few months. Don't precipitate matters; you can make your health an excuse to miss the Autumn session."

Lady Valleys chimed in eagerly

"You really are seeing the thing out of all proportion. What is a love-affair. My dear boy, do you suppose for a moment anyone would think the worse of you, even if they knew? And really not a soul need know."

"It has not occurred to me to consider what they would think."

"Then," cried Lady Valleys, nettled, "it's simply your own pride."

"You have said."

Lord Valleys, who had turned away, spoke in an almost tragic voice

"I did not think that on a point of honour I should differ from my son."

Catching at the word honour, Lady Valleys cried suddenly:

"Eustace, promise me, before you do anything, to consult your Uncle Dennis."

Miltoun smiled.

"This becomes comic," he said.

At that word, which indeed seemed to them quite wanton, Lord and Lady Valleys turned on their son, and the three stood staring, perfectly silent. A little noise from the doorway interrupted them.

Chapter XVIII

Left by her father and mother to the further entertainment of Harbinger, Barbara had said:

"Let's have coffee in here," and passed into the withdrawing room.

Except for that one evening, when together by the sea wall they stood contemplating the populace, she had not been alone with him since he kissed her under the shelter of the box hedge. And now, after the first moment, she looked at him calmly, though in her breast there was a fluttering, as if an imprisoned bird were struggling ever so feebly against that soft and solid cage. Her last jangled talk with Courtier had left an ache in her heart. Besides, did she not know all that Harbinger could give her?

Like a nymph pursued by a faun who held dominion over the groves, she, fugitive, kept looking back. There was nothing in that fair wood of his with which she was not familiar, no thicket she had not travelled, no stream she had not crossed, no kiss she could not return. His was a discovered land, in which, as of right, she would reign. She had nothing to hope from him but power, and solid pleasure. Her eyes said: How am I to know whether I shall not want more than you; feel suffocated in your arms; be surfeited by all that you will bring me? Have I not already got all that?

She knew, from his downcast gloomy face, how cruel she seemed, and was sorry. She wanted to be good to him, and said almost shyly:

"Are you angry with me, Claud?"

Harbinger looked up.

"What makes you so cruel?"

"I am not cruel."

"You are. Where is your heart?"

"Here!" said Barbara, touching her breast.

"Ah!" muttered Harbinger; "I'm not joking."

She said gently:'

"Is it as bad as that, my dear?"

But the softness of her voice seemed to fan the smouldering fires in him.

"There's something behind all this," he stammered, "you've no right to make a fool of me!"

"And what is the something, please?"

"That's for you to say. But I'm not blind. What about this fellow Courtier?"

At that moment there was revealed to Barbara a new acquaintance—the male proper. No, to live with him would not be quite lacking in adventure!

His face had darkened; his eyes were dilated, his whole figure seemed to have grown. She suddenly noticed the hair which covered his clenched fists. All his suavity had left him. He came very close.

How long that look between them lasted, and of all there was in it, she had no clear knowledge; thought after thought, wave after wave of feeling, rushed through her. Revolt and attraction, contempt and admiration, queer sensations of disgust and pleasure, all mingled—as on a May day one may see the hail fall, and the sun suddenly burn through and steam from the grass.

Then he said hoarsely:

"Oh! Babs, you madden me so!"

Smoothing her lips, as if to regain control of them, she answered:

"Yes, I think I have had enough," and went out into her father's study.

The sight of Lord and Lady Valleys so intently staring at Miltoun restored hex self-possession.

It struck her as slightly comic, not knowing that the little scene was the outcome of that word. In truth, the contrast between Miltoun and his parents at this moment was almost ludicrous.

Lady Valleys was the first to speak.

"Better comic than romantic. I suppose Barbara may know, considering her contribution to this matter. Your brother is resigning his seat, my dear; his conscience will not permit him to retain it, under certain circumstances that have arisen."

"Oh!" cried Barbara: "but surely—"

"The matter has been argued, Babs," Lord Valleys said shortly; "unless you have some better reason to advance than those of ordinary common sense, public spirit, and consideration for one's family, it will hardly be worth your while to reopen the discussion."

Barbara looked up at Miltoun, whose face, all but the eyes, was like a mask.

"Oh, Eusty!" she said, "you're not going to spoil your life like this! Just think how I shall feel."

Miltoun answered stonily:

"You did what you thought right; as I am doing."

"Does she want you to?"

"No."

"There is, I should imagine," put in Lord Valleys, "not a solitary creature in the whole world except your brother himself who would wish for this consummation. But with him such a consideration does not weigh!"

"Oh!" sighed Barbara; "think of Granny!"

"I prefer not to think of her," murmured Lady Valleys.

"She's so wrapped up in you, Eusty. She always has believed in you intensely."

Miltoun sighed. And, encouraged by that sound, Barbara went closer.

It was plain enough that, behind his impassivity, a desperate struggle was going on in Miltoun. He spoke at last:

"If I have not already yielded to one who is naturally more to me than anything, when she begged and entreated, it is because I feel this in a way you don't realize. I apologize for using the word comic just now, I should have said tragic. I'll enlighten Uncle Dennis, if that will comfort you; but this is not exactly a matter for anyone, except myself." And, without another look or word, he went out.

As the door closed, Barbara ran towards it; and, with a motion strangely like the wringing of hands, said:

"Oh, dear! Oh! dear!" Then, turning away to a bookcase, she began to cry.

This ebullition of feeling, surpassing even their own, came as a real shock to Lady and Lord Valleys, ignorant of how strung-up she had been before she entered the room. They had not seen Barbara cry since she was a tiny girl. And in face of her emotion any animus they might have shown her for having thrown Miltoun into Mrs. Noel's arms, now melted away. Lord Valleys, especially moved, went up to his daughter, and stood with her in that dark corner, saying nothing, but gently stroking her hand. Lady Valleys, who herself felt very much inclined to cry, went out of sight into the embrasure of the window.

Barbara's sobbing was soon subdued.

"It's his face," she said: "And why? Why? It's so unnecessary!"

Lord Valleys, continually twisting his moustache, muttered:

"Exactly! He makes things for himself!"

"Yes," murmured Lady Valleys from the window, "he was always uncomfortable, like that. I remember him as a baby. Bertie never was."

And then the silence was only broken by the little angry sounds of Barbara blowing her nose.

"I shall go and see mother," said Lady Valleys, suddenly: "The boy's whole life may be ruined if we can't stop this. Are you coming, child?"

But Barbara refused.

She went to her room, instead. This crisis in Miltoun's life had strangely shaken her. It was as if Fate had suddenly revealed all that any step out of the beaten path might lead to, had brought her sharply up against herself. To wing out into the blue! See what it meant! If Miltoun kept to his resolve, and gave up public life, he was lost! And she herself! The fascination of Courtier's chivalrous manner, of a sort of innate gallantry, suggesting the quest of everlasting danger—was it not rather absurd? And—was she fascinated? Was it not simply that she liked the feeling of fascinating him? Through the maze of these thoughts, darted the memory of Harbinger's face close to her own, his clenched hands, the swift revelation of his dangerous masculinity. It was all a nightmare of scaring queer sensations, of things that could never be settled. She was stirred for once out of all her normal conquering philosophy. Her thoughts flew back to Miltoun. That which she had seen in their faces, then, had come to pass! And picturing Agatha's horror, when she came to hear of it, Barbara could not help a smile. Poor Eustace! Why did he take things so hardly? If he really carried out his resolve—and he never changed his mind—it would be tragic! It would mean the end of everything for him!

Perhaps now he would get tired of Mrs. Noel. But she was not the sort of woman a man would get tired of. Even Barbara in her inexperience felt that. She would always be too delicately careful never to cloy him, never to exact anything from him, or let him feel that he was bound to her by so much as a hair. Ah! why couldn't they go on as if nothing had happened? Could nobody persuade him? She thought again of Courtier. If he, who knew them both, and was so fond of Mrs. Noel, would talk to Miltoun, about the right to be happy, the right to revolt? Eustace ought to revolt! It was his duty. She sat down to write; then, putting on her hat, took the note and slipped downstairs.

Chapter XIX

The flowers of summer in the great glass house at Ravensham were keeping the last afternoon-watch when Clifton summoned Lady Casterley with the words:

"Lady Valleys in the white room."

Since the news of Miltoun's illness, and of Mrs. Noel's nursing, the little old lady had possessed her soul in patience; often, it is true, afflicted with poignant misgivings as to this new influence in the life of her favourite, affected too by a sort of jealousy, not to be admitted, even in her prayers, which, though regular enough, were perhaps somewhat formal. Having small liking now for leaving home, even for Catton, her country place, she was still at Ravensham, where Lord Dennis had come up to stay with her as soon as Miltoun had left Sea House. But Lady Casterley was never very dependent on company. She retained unimpaired her intense interest in politics, and still corresponded freely with prominent men. Of late, too, a slight revival of the June war scare had made its mark on her in a certain rejuvenescence, which always accompanied her contemplation of national crises, even when such were a little in the air. At blast of trumpet her spirit still leaped forward, unsheathed its sword, and stood at the salute. At such times, she rose earlier, went to bed later, was far less susceptible to draughts, and refused with asperity any food between meals. She wrote too with her own hand letters which she would otherwise have dictated to her secretary. Unfortunately the scare had died down again almost at once; and the passing of danger always left her rather irritable. Lady Valleys' visit came as a timely consolation.

She kissed her daughter critically; for there was that about her manner which she did not like.

"Yes, of course I am well!" she said. "Why didn't you bring Barbara?"

"She was tired!"

"H'm! Afraid of meeting me, since she committed that piece of folly over Eustace. You must be careful of that child, Gertrude, or she will be doing something silly herself. I don't like the way she keeps Claud Harbinger hanging in the wind."

Her daughter cut her short:

"There is bad news about Eustace."

Lady Casterley lost the little colour in her cheeks; lost, too, all her superfluity of irritable energy.

"Tell me, at once!"

Having heard, she said nothing; but Lady Valleys noticed with alarm that over her eyes had come suddenly the peculiar filminess of age.

"Well, what do you advise?" she asked.

Herself tired, and troubled, she was conscious of a quite unwonted feeling of discouragement before this silent little figure, in the silent white room. She had never before seen her mother look as if she heard Defeat passing on its dark wings. And moved by sudden tenderness for the little frail body that had borne her so long ago, she murmured almost with surprise:

"Mother, dear!"

"Yes," said Lady Casterley, as if speaking to herself, "the boy saves things up; he stores his feelings—they burst and sweep him away. First his passion; now his conscience. There are two men in him; but this will be the death of one of them." And suddenly turning on her daughter, she said:

"Did you ever hear about him at Oxford, Gertrude? He broke out once, and ate husks with the Gadarenes. You never knew. Of course—you never have known anything of him."

Resentment rose in Lady Valleys, that anyone should knew her son better than herself; but she lost it again looking at the little figure, and said, sighing:

"Well?"

Lady Casterley murmured:

"Go away, child; I must think. You say he's to consult' Dennis? Do you know her address? Ask Barbara when you get back and telephone it to me. And at her daughter's kiss, she added grimly:

"I shall live to see him in the saddle yet, though I am seventy-eight."

When the sound of her daughter's car had died away, she rang the bell.

"If Lady Valleys rings up, Clifton, don't take the message, but call me." And seeing that Clifton did not move she added sharply: "Well?"

"There is no bad news of his young lordship's health, I hope?"

"No."

"Forgive me, my lady, but I have had it on my mind for some time to ask you something."

And the old man raised his hand with a peculiar dignity, seeming to say: You will excuse me that for the moment I am a human being speaking to a human being.

"The matter of his attachment," he went on, "is known to me; it has given me acute anxiety, knowing his lordship as I do, and having heard him say something singular when he was here in July. I should be grateful if you would assure—me that there is to be no hitch in his career, my lady."

The expression on Lady Casterley's face was strangely compounded of surprise, kindliness, defence, and impatience as with a child.

"Not if I can prevent it, Clifton," she said shortly; "in fact, you need not concern yourself."

Clifton bowed.

"Excuse me mentioning it, my lady;" a quiver ran over his face between its long white whiskers, "but his young lordship's career is more to me than my own."

When he had left her, Lady Casterley sat down in a little low chair—long she sat there by the empty hearth, till the daylight, was all gone.

Chapter XX

Not far from the dark-haloed indeterminate limbo where dwelt that bugbear of Charles Courtier, the great Half-Truth Authority, he himself had a couple of rooms at fifteen shillings a week. Their chief attraction was that the great Half-Truth Liberty had recommended them. They tied him to nothing, and were ever at his disposal when he was in London; for his landlady, though not bound by agreement so to do, let them in such a way, that she could turn anyone else out at a week's notice. She was a gentle soul, married to a socialistic plumber twenty years her senior. The worthy man had given her two little boys, and the three of them kept her in such permanent order that to be in the presence of Courtier was the greatest pleasure she knew. When he disappeared on one of his nomadic missions, explorations, or adventures, she enclosed the whole of his belongings in two tin trunks and placed them in a cupboard which smelled a little of mice. When he reappeared the trunks were reopened, and a powerful scent of dried rose-leaves would escape. For, recognizing the mortality of things human, she procured every summer from her sister, the wife of a market gardener, a consignment of this commodity, which she passionately sewed up in bags, and continued to deposit year by year, in Courtier's trunks.

This, and the way she made his toast—very crisp—and aired his linen—very dry, were practically the only things she could do for a man naturally inclined to independence, and accustomed from his manner of life to fend for himself.

At first signs of his departure she would go into some closet or other, away from the plumber and the two marks of his affection, and cry quietly; but never in Courtier's presence did she dream of manifesting grief—as soon weep in the presence of death or birth, or any other fundamental tragedy or joy. In face of the realities of life she had known from her youth up the value of the simple verb 'sto—stare-to stand fast.'

And to her Courtier was a reality, the chief reality of life, the focus of her aspiration, the morning and the evening star.

The request, then five days after his farewell visit to Mrs. Noel—for the elephant-hide trunk which accompanied his rovings, produced her habitual period of seclusion, followed by her habitual appearance in his sitting-room bearing a note, and some bags of dried rose—leaves on a tray. She found him in his shirt sleeves, packing.

"Well, Mrs. Benton; off again!"

Mrs. Benton, plaiting her hands, for she had not yet lost something of the look and manner of a little girl, answered in her flat, but serene voice:

"Yes, sir; and I hope you're not going anywhere very dangerous this time. I always think you go to such dangerous places."

"To Persia, Mrs. Benton, where the carpets come from."

"Oh! yes, sir. Your washing's just come home."

Her, apparently cast-down, eyes stored up a wealth of little details; the way his hair grew, the set of his back, the colour of his braces. But suddenly she said in a surprising voice:

"You haven't a photograph you could spare, sir, to leave behind? Mr. Benton was only saying to me yesterday, we've nothing to remember him by, in case he shouldn't come back."

"Here's an old one."

Mrs. Benton took the photograph.

"Oh!" she said; "you can see who it is." And holding it perhaps too tightly, for her fingers trembled, she added:

"A note, please, sir; and the messenger boy is waiting for—an answer."

While he read the note she noticed with concern how packing had brought the blood into his head....

When, in response to that note, Courtier entered the well-known confectioner's called Gustard's, it was still not quite tea-time, and there seemed to him at first no one in the room save three middle-aged women packing sweets; then in the corner he saw Barbara. The blood was no longer in his head; he was pale, walking down that mahogany-coloured room impregnated with the scent of wedding-cake. Barbara, too, was pale.

So close to her that he could count her every eyelash, and inhale the scent of her hair and clothes to listen to her story of Miltoun, so hesitatingly, so wistfully told, seemed very like being kept waiting with the rope already round his neck, to hear about another person's toothache. He felt this to have been unnecessary on the part of Fate! And there came to him perversely the memory of that ride over the sun-warmed heather, when he had paraphrased the old Sicilian song: 'Here will I sit and sing.' He was a long way from singing now; nor was there love in his arms. There was instead a cup of tea; and in his nostrils the scent of cake, with now and then a whiff of orange-flower water.

"I see," he said, when she had finished telling him: "'Liberty's a glorious feast!' You want me to go to your brother, and quote Bums? You know, of course, that he regards me as dangerous."

"Yes; but he respects and likes you."

"And I respect and like him," answered Courtier.

One of the middle-aged females passed, carrying a large white card-board box; and the creaking of her stays broke the hush.

"You have been very sweet to me," said Barbara, suddenly.

Courtier's heart stirred, as if it were turning over within him; and gazing into his teacup, he answered—

"All men are decent to the evening star. I will go at once and find your brother. When shall I bring you news?"

"To-morrow at five I'll be at home."

And repeating, "To-morrow at five," he rose.

Looking back from the door, he saw her face puzzled, rather reproachful, and went out gloomily. The scent of cake, and orange-flower water, the creaking of the female's stays, the colour of mahogany, still clung to his nose and ears, and eyes; but within him it was all dull baffled rage. Why had he not made the most of this unexpected chance; why had he not made desperate love to her? A conscientious ass! And yet—the whole thing was absurd! She was so young! God knew he would be glad to be out of it. If he stayed he was afraid that he would play the fool. But the memory of her words: "You have been very sweet to me!" would not leave him; nor the memory of her face, so puzzled, and reproachful. Yes, if he stayed he would play the fool! He would be asking her to marry a man double her age, of no position but that which he had carved for himself, and without a rap. And he would be asking her in such a way that she might possibly have some little difficulty in refusing. He would be letting himself go. And she was only twenty—for all her woman-of-the-world air, a child! No! He would be useful to her, if possible, this once, and then clear out!

Chapter XXI

When Miltoun left Valleys House he walked in the direction of Westminster. During the five days that he had been back in London he had not yet entered the House of Commons. After the seclusion of his illness, he still felt a yearning, almost painful, towards the movement and stir of the town. Everything he heard and saw made an intensely vivid impression. The lions in Trafalgar Square, the great buildings of Whitehall, filled him with a sort of exultation. He was like a man, who, after a long sea voyage, first catches sight of land, and stands straining his eyes, hardly breathing, taking in one by one the lost features of that face. He walked on to Westminster Bridge, and going to an embrasure in the very centre, looked back towards the towers.

It was said that the love of those towers passed into the blood. It was said that he who had sat beneath them could never again be quite the same. Miltoun knew that it was true—desperately true, of himself. In person he had sat there but three weeks, but in soul he seemed to have been sitting there hundreds of years. And now he would sit there no more! An almost frantic desire to free himself from this coil rose up within him. To be held a prisoner by that most secret of all his instincts, the instinct for authority! To be unable to wield authority because to wield authority was to insult authority. God! It was hard! He turned his back on the towers; and sought distraction in the faces of the passers-by.

Each of these, he knew, had his struggle to keep self-respect! Or was it that they were unconscious of struggle or of self-respect, and just let things drift? They looked like that, most of them! And all his inherent contempt for the average or common welled up as he watched them. Yes, they looked like that! Ironically, the sight of those from whom he had desired the comfort of compromise, served instead to stimulate that part of him which refused to let him compromise. They looked soft, soggy, without pride or will, as though they knew that life was too much for them, and had shamefully accepted the fact. They so obviously needed to be told what they might do, and which way they should, go; they would accept orders as they accepted their work, or pleasures: And the thought that he was now debarred from the right to give them orders, rankled in him furiously. They, in their turn, glanced casually at his tall figure leaning against the parapet, not knowing how their fate was trembling in the balance. His thin, sallow face, and hungry eyes gave one or two of them perhaps a feeling of interest or discomfort; but to most he was assuredly no more than any other man or woman in the hurly-burly. That dark figure of conscious power struggling in the fetters of its own belief in power, was a piece of sculpture they had neither time nor wish to understand, having no taste for tragedy—for witnessing the human spirit driven to the wall.

It was five o'clock before Miltoun left the Bridge, and passed, like an exile, before the gates of Church and State, on his way to his uncle's Club. He stopped to telegraph to Audrey the time he would be coming to-morrow afternoon; and on leaving the Post-Office, noticed in the window of the adjoining shop some reproductions of old Italian masterpieces, amongst them one of Botticelli's 'Birth of Venus.' He had never seen that picture; and, remembering that she had told him it was her favourite, he stopped to look at it. Averagely well versed in such matters, as became one of his caste, Miltoun had not the power of letting a work of art insidiously steal the private self from his soul, and replace it with the self of all the world; and he examined this far-famed presentment of the heathen goddess with aloofness, even irritation. The drawing of the body seemed to him crude, the whole picture a little flat and Early; he did not like the figure of the Flora. The golden serenity, and tenderness, of which she had spoken, left him cold. Then he found himself looking at the face, and slowly, but with uncanny certainty, began to feel that he was looking at the face of Audrey herself. The hair was golden and different, the eyes grey and different, the mouth a little fuller; yet—it was her face; the same oval shape, the same far-apart, arched brows, the same strangely tender, elusive spirit. And, as though offended, he turned and walked on. In the window of that little shop was the effigy of her for whom he had bartered away his life—the incarnation of passive and entwining love, that gentle creature, who had given herself to him so utterly, for whom love, and the flowers, and trees, and birds, music, the sky, and the quick-flowing streams, were all-sufficing; and who, like the goddess in the picture, seemed wondering at her own existence. He had a sudden glimpse of understanding, strange indeed in one who had so little power of seeing into others' hearts: Ought she ever to have been born into a world like this? But the flash of insight yielded quickly to that sickening consciousness of his own position, which never left him now. Whatever else he did, he must get rid of that malaise! But what could he do in that coming life? Write books? What sort of books could he write? Only such as expressed his views of citizenship, his political and social beliefs. As well remain sitting and speaking beneath those towers! He could never join the happy band of artists, those soft and indeterminate spirits, for whom barriers had no meaning, content-to understand, interpret, and create. What should he be doing in that galley? The thought was inconceivable. A career at the Bar—yes, he might take that up; but to what end? To become a judge! As well continue to sit beneath those towers! Too late for diplomacy. Too late for the Army; besides, he had not the faintest taste for military glory. Bury himself in the country like Uncle Dennis, and administer one of his father's estates? It would be death. Go amongst the poor? For a moment he thought he had found a new vocation. But in what capacity—to order their lives, when he himself could not order his own; or, as a mere conduit pipe for money, when he believed that charity was rotting the nation to its core? At the head of every avenue stood an angel or devil with drawn sword. And then there came to him another thought. Since he was being cast forth from Church and State, could he not play the fallen spirit like a man—be Lucifer, and destroy! And instinctively he at once saw himself returning to those towers, and beneath them crossing the floor; joining the revolutionaries, the Radicals, the freethinkers, scourging his present Party, the party of authority and institutions. The idea struck him as supremely comic, and he laughed out loud in the street....

The Club which Lord Dennis frequented was in St. James's untouched by the tides of the waters of fashion—steadily swinging to its moorings in a quiet backwater, and Miltoun found his uncle in the library. He was reading a volume of Burton's travels, and drinking tea.

"Nobody comes here," he said, "so, in spite of that word on the door, we shall talk. Waiter, bring some more tea, please."

Impatiently, but with a sort of pity, Miltoun watched Lord Dennis's urbane movements, wherein old age was, pathetically, trying to make each little thing seem important, if only to the doer. Nothing his great-uncle could say would outweigh the warning of his picturesque old figure! To be a bystander; to see it all go past you; to let your sword rust in its sheath, as this poor old fellow had done! The notion of explaining what he had come about was particularly hateful to Miltoun; but since he had given his word, he nerved himself with secret anger, and began:

"I promised my mother to ask you a question, Uncle Dennis. You know of my attachment, I believe?"

Lord Dennis nodded.

"Well, I have joined my life to this lady's. There will be no scandal, but I consider it my duty to resign my seat, and leave public life alone. Is that right or wrong according to, your view?"

Lord Dennis looked at his nephew in silence. A faint flush coloured his brown cheeks. He had the appearance of one travelling in mind over the past.

"Wrong, I think," he said, at last.

"Why, if I may ask?"

"I have not the pleasure of knowing this lady, and am therefore somewhat in the dark; but it appears to me that your decision is not fair to her."

"That is beyond me," said Miltoun.

Lord Dennis answered firmly:

"You have asked me a frank question, expecting a frank answer, I suppose?"

Miltoun nodded.

"Then, my dear, don't blame me if what I say is unpalatable."

"I shall not."

"Good! You say you are going to give up public life for the sake of your conscience. I should have no criticism to make if it stopped there."

He paused, and for quite a minute remained silent, evidently searching for words to express some intricate thread of thought.

"But it won't, Eustace; the public man in you is far stronger than the other. You want leadership more than you want love. Your sacrifice will kill your affection; what you imagine is your loss and hurt, will prove to be this lady's in the end."

Miltoun smiled.

Lord Dennis continued very dryly and with a touch of malice:

"You are not listening to me; but I can see very well that the process has begun already underneath. There's a curious streak of the Jesuit in you, Eustace. What you don't want to see, you won't look at."

"You advise me, then, to compromise?"

"On the contrary, I point out that you will be compromising if you try to keep both your conscience and your love. You will be seeking to have, it both ways."

"That is interesting."

"And you will find yourself having it neither," said Lord Dennis sharply.

Miltoun rose. "In other words, you, like the others, recommend me to desert this lady who loves me, and whom I love. And yet, Uncle, they say that in your own case—"

But Lord Dennis had risen, too, having lost all the appanage and manner of old age.

"Of my own case," he said bluntly, "we won't talk. I don't advise you to desert anyone; you quite mistake me. I advise you to know yourself. And I tell you my opinion of you—you were cut out by Nature for a statesman, not a lover! There's something dried-up in you, Eustace; I'm not sure there isn't something dried-up in all our caste. We've had to do with forms and ceremonies too long. We're not good at taking the lyrical point of view."

"Unfortunately," said Miltoun, "I cannot, to fit in with a theory of yours, commit a baseness."

Lord Dennis began pacing up and down. He was keeping his lips closed very tight.

"A man who gives advice," he said at last, "is always something of a fool. For all that, you have mistaken mine. I am not so presumptuous as to attempt to enter the inner chamber of your spirit. I have merely told you that, in my opinion, it would be more honest to yourself, and fairer to this lady, to compound with your conscience, and keep both your love and your public life, than to pretend that you were capable of sacrificing what I know is the stronger element in you for the sake of the weaker. You remember the saying, Democritus I think: 'each man's nature or character is his fate or God'. I recommend it to you."

For a full minute Miltoun stood without replying, then said:

"I am sorry to have troubled you, Uncle Dennis. A middle policy is no use to me. Good-bye!" And without shaking hands, he went out.

Chapter XXII

In the hall someone rose from a sofa, and came towards him. It was Courtier.

"Run you to earth at last," he said; "I wish you'd come and dine with me. I'm leaving England to-morrow night, and there are things I want to say."

There passed through Miltoun's mind the rapid thought: 'Does he know?' He assented, however, and they went out together.

"It's difficult to find a quiet place," said Courtier; "but this might do."

The place chosen was a little hostel, frequented by racing men, and famed for the excellence of its steaks. And as they sat down opposite each other in the almost empty room, Miltoun thought: Yes, he does know! Can I stand any more of this? He waited almost savagely for the attack he felt was coming.

"So you are going to give up your seat?" said Courtier.

Miltoun looked at him for some seconds, before replying.

"From what town-crier did you hear that?"

But there was that in Courtier's face which checked his anger; its friendliness was transparent.

"I am about her only friend," Courtier proceeded earnestly; "and this is my last chance—to say nothing of my feeling towards you, which, believe me, is very cordial."

"Go on, then," Miltoun muttered.

"Forgive me for putting it bluntly. Have you considered what her position was before she met you?"

Miltoun felt the blood rushing to his face, but he sat still, clenching his nails into the palms of his hands.

"Yes, yes," said Courtier, "but that attitude of mind—you used to have it yourself—which decrees either living death, or spiritual adultery to women, makes my blood boil. You can't deny that those were the alternatives, and I say you had the right fundamentally to protest against them, not only in words but deeds. You did protest, I know; but this present decision of yours is a climb down, as much as to say that your protest was wrong."

Miltoun rose from his seat. "I cannot discuss this," he said; "I cannot."

"For her sake, you must. If you give up your public work, you'll spoil her life a second time."

Miltoun again sat down. At the word 'must' a steely feeling had come to his aid; his eyes began to resemble the old Cardinal's. "Your nature and mine, Courtier," he said, "are too far apart; we shall never understand each other."

"Never mind that," answered Courtier. "Admitting those two alternatives to be horrible, which you never would have done unless the facts had been brought home to you personally—"

"That," said Miltoun icily, "I deny your right to say."

"Anyway, you do admit them—if you believe you had not the right to rescue her, on what principle do you base that belief?"

Miltoun placed his elbow on the table, and leaning his chin on his hand, regarded the champion of lost causes without speaking. There was such a turmoil going on within him that with difficulty he could force his lips to obey him.

"By what right do you ask me that?" he said at last. He saw Courtier's face grow scarlet, and his fingers twisting furiously at those flame-like moustaches; but his answer was as steadily ironical as usual.

"Well, I can hardly sit still, my last evening in England, without lifting a finger, while you immolate a woman to whom I feel like a brother. I'll tell you what your principle is: Authority, unjust or just, desirable or undesirable, must be implicitly obeyed. To break a law, no matter on what provocation, or for whose sake, is to break the commandment."

"Don't hesitate—say, of God."

"Of an infallible fixed Power. Is that a true definition of your principle?"

"Yes," said Miltoun, between his teeth, "I think so."

"Exceptions prove the rule."

"Hard cases make bad law."

Courtier smiled: "I knew you were coming out with that. I deny that they do with this law, which is altogether behind the times. You had the right to rescue this woman."

"No, Courtier, if we must fight, let us fight on the naked facts. I have not rescued anyone. I have merely stolen sooner than starve. That is why I cannot go on pretending to be a pattern. If it were known, I could not retain my seat an hour; I can't take advantage of an accidental secrecy. Could you?"

Courtier was silent; and with his eyes Miltoun pressed on him, as though he would despatch him with that glance.

"I could," said Courtier at last. "When this law, by enforcing spiritual adultery on those who have come to hate their mates, destroys the sanctity of the married state—the very sanctity it professes to uphold, you must expect to have it broken by reasoning men and women without their feeling shame, or losing self-respect."

In Miltoun there was rising that vast and subtle passion for dialectic combat, which was of his very fibre. He had almost lost the feeling that this was his own future being discussed. He saw before him in this sanguine man, whose voice and eyes had such a white-hot sound and look, the incarnation of all that he temperamentally opposed.

"That," he said, "is devil's advocacy. I admit no individual as judge in his own case."

"Ah! Now we're coming to it. By the way, shall we get out of this heat?"

They were no sooner in the cooler street, than the voice of Courtier began again:

"Distrust of human nature, fear—it's the whole basis of action for men of your stamp. You deny the right of the individual to judge, because you've no faith in the essential goodness of men; at heart you believe them bad. You give them no freedom, you allow them no consent, because you believe that their decisions would move downwards, and not upwards. Well, it's the whole difference between the aristocratic and the democratic view of life. As you once told me, you hate and fear the crowd."

Miltoun eyed that steady sanguine face askance:

"Yes," he said, "I do believe that men are raised in spite of themselves."

"You're honest. By whom?"

Again Miltoun felt rising within him a sort of fury. Once for all he would slay this red-haired rebel; he answered with almost savage irony:

"Strangely enough, by that Being to mention whom you object—working through the medium of the best."

"High-Priest! Look at that girl slinking along there, with her eye on us; suppose, instead of withdrawing your garment, you went over and talked to her, got her to tell you what she really felt and thought, you'd find things that would astonish you. At bottom, mankind is splendid. And they're raised, sir, by the aspiration that's in all of them. Haven't you ever noticed that public sentiment is always in advance of the Law?"

"And you," said Miltoun, "are the man who is never on the side of the majority?"

The champion of lost causes uttered a short laugh.

"Not so logical as all that," he answered; "the wind still blows; and Life's not a set of rules hung up in an office. Let's see, where are we?" They had been brought to a stand-still by a group on the pavement in front of the Queen's Hall: "Shall we go in, and hear some music, and cool our tongues?"

Miltoun nodded, and they went in.

The great lighted hall, filled with the faint bluefish vapour from hundreds of little rolls of tobacco leaf, was crowded from floor to ceiling.

Taking his stand among the straw-hatted throng, Miltoun heard that steady ironical voice behind him:

"Profanum vulgus! Come to listen to the finest piece of music ever written! Folk whom you wouldn't trust a yard to know what was good for them! Deplorable sight, isn't it?"

He made no answer. The first slow notes of the seventh Symphony of Beethoven had begun to steal forth across the bank of flowers; and, save for the steady rising of that bluefish vapour, as it were incense burnt to the god of melody, the crowd had become deathly still, as though one mind, one spirit, possessed each pale face inclined towards that music rising and falling like the sighing of the winds, that welcome from death the freed spirits of the beautiful.

When the last notes had died away, he turned and walked out.

"Well," said the voice behind him, "hasn't that shown you how things swell and grow; how splendid the world is?"

Miltoun smiled.

"It has shown me how beautiful the world can be made by a great man."

And suddenly, as if the music had loosened some band within him, he began to pour forth words:

"Look at the crowd in this street, Courtier, which of all crowds in the whole world can best afford to be left to itself; secure from pestilence, earthquake, cyclone, drought, from extremes of heat and cold, in the heart of the greatest and safest city in the world; and yet-see the figure of that policeman! Running through all the good behaviour of this crowd, however safe and free it looks, there is, there always must be, a central force holding it together. Where does that central force come from? From the crowd itself, you say. I answer: No. Look back at the origin of human States. From the beginnings of things, the best man has been the unconscious medium of authority, of the controlling principle, of the divine force; he felt that power within him—physical, at first—he used it to take the lead, he has held the lead ever since, he must always hold it. All your processes of election, your so-called democratic apparatus, are only a blind to the inquiring, a sop to the hungry, a salve to the pride of the rebellious. They are merely surface machinery; they cannot prevent the best man from coming to the top; for the best man stands nearest to the Deity, and is the first to receive the waves that come from Him. I'm not speaking of heredity. The best man is not necessarily born in my class, and I, at all events, do not believe he is any more frequent there than in other classes."

He stopped as suddenly as he had begun.

"You needn't be afraid," answered Courtier, "that I take you for an average specimen. You're at one end, and I at the other, and we probably both miss the golden mark. But the world is not ruled by power, and the fear which power produces, as you think, it's ruled by love. Society is held together by the natural decency in man, by fellow-feeling. The democratic principle, which you despise, at root means nothing at all but that. Man left to himself is on the upward lay. If it weren't so, do you imagine for a moment your 'boys in blue' could keep order? A man knows unconsciously what he can and what he can't do, without losing his self-respect. He sucks that knowledge in with every breath. Laws and authority are not the be-all and end-all, they are conveniences, machinery, conduit pipes, main roads. They're not of the structure of the building—they're only scaffolding."

Miltoun lunged out with the retort

"Without which no building could be built."

Courtier parried.

"That's rather different, my friend, from identifying them with the building. They are things to be taken down as fast as ever they can be cleared away, to make room for an edifice that begins on earth, not in the sky. All the scaffolding of law is merely there to save time, to prevent the temple, as it mounts, from losing its way, and straying out of form."

"No," said Miltoun, "no! The scaffolding, as you call it, is the material projection of the architect's conception, without which the temple does not and cannot rise; and the architect is God, working through the minds and spirits most akin to Himself."

"We are now at the bed-rock," cried Courtier, "your God is outside this world. Mine within it."

"And never the twain shall meet!"

In the silence that followed Miltoun saw that they were in Leicester Square, all quiet as yet before the theatres had disgorged; quiet yet waiting, with the lights, like yellow stars low-driven from the dark heavens, clinging to the white shapes of music-halls and cafes, and a sort of flying glamour blanching the still foliage of the plane trees.

"A 'whitely wanton'—this Square!" said Courtier: "Alive as a face; no end to its queer beauty! And, by Jove, if you went deep enough, you'd find goodness even here."

"And you'd ignore the vice," Miltoun answered.

He felt weary all of a sudden, anxious to get to his rooms, unwilling to continue this battle of words, that brought him no nearer to relief. It was with strange lassitude that he heard the voice still speaking:

"We must make a night of it, since to-morrow we die.... You would curb licence from without—I from within. When I get up and when I go to bed, when I draw a breath, see a face, or a flower, or a tree—if I didn't feel that I was looking on the Deity, I believe I should quit this palace of varieties, from sheer boredom. You, I understand, can't look on your God, unless you withdraw into some high place. Isn't it a bit lonely there?"

"There are worse things than loneliness." And they walked on, in silence; till suddenly Miltoun broke out:

"You talk of tyranny! What tyranny could equal this tyranny of your freedom? What tyranny in the world like that of this 'free' vulgar, narrow street, with its hundred journals teeming like ants' nests, to produce-what? In the entrails of that creature of your freedom, Courtier, there is room neither for exaltation, discipline, nor sacrifice; there is room only for commerce, and licence."

There was no answer for a moment; and from those tall houses, whose lighted windows he had apostrophized, Miltoun turned away towards the river. "No," said the voice beside him, "for all its faults, the wind blows in that street, and there's a chance for everything. By God, I would rather see a few stars struggle out in a black sky than any of your perfect artificial lighting."

And suddenly it seemed to Miltoun that he could never free himself from the echoes of that voice—it was not worth while to try. "We are repeating ourselves," he said, dryly.

The river's black water was making stilly, slow recessional under a half-moon. Beneath the cloak of night the chaos on the far bank, the forms of cranes, high buildings, jetties, the bodies of the sleeping barges, a—million queer dark shapes, were invested with emotion. All was religious out there, all beautiful, all strange. And over this great quiet friend of man, lamps—those humble flowers of night, were throwing down the faint continual glamour of fallen petals; and a sweet-scented wind stole along from the West, very slow as yet, bringing in advance the tremor and perfume of the innumerable trees and fields which the river had loved as she came by.

A murmur that was no true sound, but like the whisper of a heart to a heart, accompanied this voyage of the dark water.

Then a small blunt skiff—manned by two rowers came by under the wall, with the thudding and the creak of oars.

"So 'To-morrow we die'?" said Miltoun: "You mean, I suppose, that 'public life' is the breath of my nostrils, and I must die, because I give it up?"

Courtier nodded.

"Am I right in thinking that it was my young sister who sent you on this crusade?"

Courtier did not answer.

"And so," Miltoun went on, looking him through and through; "to-morrow is to be your last day, too? Well, you're right to go. She is not an ugly duckling, who can live out of the social pond; she'll always want her native element. And now, we'll say goodbye! Whatever happens to us both, I shall remember this evening." Smiling, he put out his hand 'Moriturus te saluto.'

Chapter XXIII

Courtier sat in Hyde Park waiting for five o'clock. The day had recovered somewhat from a grey morning, as though the glow of that long hot summer were too burnt-in on the air to yield to the first assault. The sun, piercing the crisped clouds, those breast feathers of heavenly doves, darted its beams at the mellowed leaves, and showered to the ground their delicate shadow stains. The first, too early, scent from leaves about to fall, penetrated to the heart. And sorrowful sweet birds were tuning their little autumn pipes, blowing into them fragments of Spring odes to Liberty.

Courtier thought of Miltoun and his mistress. By what a strange fate had those two been thrown together; to what end was their love coming? The seeds of grief were already sown, what flowers of darkness, or of tumult would come up? He saw her again as a little, grave, considering child, with her soft eyes, set wide apart under the dark arched brows, and the little tuck at the corner of her mouth that used to come when he teased her. And to that gentle creature who would sooner die than force anyone to anything, had been given this queer lover; this aristocrat by birth and nature, with the dried fervent soul, whose every fibre had been bred and trained in and to the service of Authority; this rejecter of the Unity of Life; this worshipper of an old God! A God that stood, whip in hand, driving men to obedience. A God that even now Courtier could conjure up staring at him from the walls of his nursery. The God his own father had believed in. A God of the Old Testament, knowing neither sympathy nor understanding. Strange that He should be alive still; that there should still be thousands who worshipped Him. Yet, not so very strange, if, as they said, man made God in his own image! Here indeed was a curious mating of what the philosophers would call the will to Love, and the will to Power!

A soldier and his girl came and sat down on a bench close by. They looked askance at this trim and upright figure with the fighting face; then, some subtle thing informing them that he was not of the disturbing breed called officer, they ceased to regard him, abandoning themselves to dumb and inexpressive felicity. Arm in arm, touching each other, they seemed to Courtier very jolly, having that look of living entirely in the moment, which always especially appealed to one whose blood ran too fast to allow him to speculate much upon the future or brood much over the past.

A leaf from the bough above him, loosened by the sun's kisses, dropped, and fell yellow at his feet. The leaves were turning very soon?

It was characteristic of this man, who could be so hot over the lost causes of others, that, sitting there within half an hour of the final loss of his own cause, he could be so calm, so almost apathetic. This apathy was partly due to the hopelessness, which Nature had long perceived, of trying to make him feel oppressed, but also to the habits of a man incurably accustomed to carrying his fortunes in his hand, and that hand open. It did not seem real to him that he was actually going to suffer a defeat, to have to confess that he had hankered after this girl all these past weeks, and that to-morrow all would be wasted, and she as dead to him as if he had never seen her. No, it was not exactly resignation, it was rather sheer lack of commercial instinct. If only this had been the lost cause of another person. How gallantly he would have rushed to the assault, and taken her by storm! If only he himself could have been that other person, how easily, how passionately could he not have pleaded, letting forth from him all those words which had knocked at his teeth ever since he knew her, and which would have seemed so ridiculous and so unworthy, spoken on his own behalf. Yes, for that other person he could have cut her out from under the guns of the enemy; he could have taken her, that fairest prize. And in queer, cheery-looking apathy—not far removed perhaps from despair—he sat, watching the leaves turn over and fall, and now and then cutting with his stick at the air, where autumn was already riding. And, if in imagination he saw himself carrying her away into the wilderness, and with his devotion making her happiness to grow, it was so far a flight, that a smile crept about his lips, and once or twice he snapped his jaws.

The soldier and his girl rose, passing in front of him down the Row. He watched their scarlet and blue figures, moving slowly towards the sun, and another couple close to the rails, crossing those receding forms. Very straight and tall, there was something exhilarating in the way this new couple swung along, holding their heads up, turning towards each other, to exchange words or smiles. Even at that distance they could be seen to be of high fashion; in their gait was the almost insolent poise of those who are above doubts and cares, certain of the world and of themselves. The girl's dress was tawny brown, her hair and hat too of the same hue, and the pursuing sunlight endowed her with a hazy splendour. Then, Courtier saw who they were—that couple!

Except for an unconscious grinding of his teeth, he made no sound or movement, so that they went by without seeing him. Her voice, though not the words, came to him distinctly. He saw her hand slip up under Harbinger's arm and swiftly down again. A smile, of whose existence he was unaware, settled on his lips. He got up, shook himself, as a dog shakes off a beating, and walked away, with his mouth set very firm.

Chapter XXIV

Left alone among the little mahogany tables of Gustard's, where the scent of cake and of orange-flower water made happy all the air, Barbara had sat for some minutes, her eyes cast down—as a child from whom a toy has been taken contemplates the ground, not knowing precisely what she is feeling. Then, paying one of the middle-aged females, she went out into the Square. There a German band was playing Delibes' Coppelia; and the murdered tune came haunting her, a very ghost of incongruity.

She went straight back to Valleys House. In the room where three hours ago she had been left alone after lunch with Harbinger, her sister was seated in the window, looking decidedly upset. In fact, Agatha had just spent an awkward hour. Chancing, with little Ann, into that confectioner's where she could best obtain a particularly gummy sweet which she believed wholesome for her children, she had been engaged in purchasing a pound, when looking down, she perceived Ann standing stock-still, with her sudden little nose pointed down the shop, and her mouth opening; glancing in the direction of those frank, enquiring eyes, Agatha saw to her amazement her sister, and a man whom she recognized as Courtier. With a readiness which did her complete credit, she placed a sweet in Ann's mouth, and saying to the middle-aged female: "Then you'll send those, please. Come, Ann!" went out. Shocks never coming singly, she had no sooner reached home, than from her father she learned of the development of Miltoun's love affair. When Barbara returned, she was sitting, unfeignedly disturbed and grieved; unable to decide whether or no she ought to divulge what she herself had seen, but withal buoyed-up by that peculiar indignation of the essentially domestic woman, whose ideals have been outraged.

Judging at once from the expression of her face that she must have heard the news of Miltoun, Barbara said:

"Well, my dear Angel, any lecture for me?"

Agatha answered coldly:

"I think you were quite mad to take Mrs. Noel to him."

"The whole duty of woman," murmured Barbara, "includes a little madness."

Agatha looked at her in silence.

"I can't make you out," she said at last; "you're not a fool!"

"Only a knave."

"You may think it right to joke over the ruin of Miltoun's life," murmured Agatha; "I don't."

Barbara's eyes grew bright; and in a hard voice she answered:

"The world is not your nursery, Angel!"

Agatha closed her lips very tightly, as who should imply: "Then it ought to be!" But she only answered:

"I don't think you know that I saw you just now in Gustard's."

Barbara eyed her for a moment in amazement, and began to laugh.

"I see," she said; "monstrous depravity—poor old Gustard's!" And still laughing that dangerous laugh, she turned on her heel and went out.

At dinner and afterwards that evening she was very silent, having on her face the same look that she wore out hunting, especially when in difficulties of any kind, or if advised to 'take a pull.' When she got away to her own room she had a longing to relieve herself by some kind of action that would hurt someone, if only herself. To go to bed and toss about in a fever—for she knew herself in these thwarted moods—was of no use! For a moment she thought of going out. That would be fun, and hurt them, too; but it was difficult. She did not want to be seen, and have the humiliation of an open row. Then there came into her head the memory of the roof of the tower, where she had once been as a little girl. She would be in the air there, she would be able to breathe, to get rid of this feverishness. With the unhappy pleasure of a spoiled child taking its revenge, she took care to leave her bedroom door open, so that her maid would wonder where she was, and perhaps be anxious, and make them anxious. Slipping through the moonlit picture gallery on to the landing, outside her father's sanctum, whence rose the stone staircase leading to the roof, she began to mount. She was breathless when, after that unending flight of stairs she emerged on to the roof at the extreme northern end of the big house, where, below her, was a sheer drop of a hundred feet. At first she stood, a little giddy, grasping the rail that ran round that garden of lead, still absorbed in her brooding, rebellious thoughts. Gradually she lost consciousness of everything save the scene before her. High above all neighbouring houses, she was almost appalled by the majesty of what she saw. This night-clothed city, so remote and dark, so white-gleaming and alive, on whose purple hills and valleys grew such myriad golden flowers of light, from whose heart came this deep incessant murmur—could it possibly be the same city through which she had been walking that very day! From its sleeping body the supreme wistful spirit had emerged in dark loveliness, and was low-flying down there, tempting her. Barbara turned round, to take in all that amazing prospect, from the black glades of Hyde Park, in front, to the powdery white ghost of a church tower, away to the East. How marvellous was this city of night! And as, in presence of that wide darkness of the sea before dawn, her spirit had felt little and timid within her—so it felt now, in face of this great, brooding, beautiful creature, whom man had made. She singled out the shapes of the Piccadilly hotels, and beyond them the palaces and towers of Westminster and Whitehall; and everywhere the inextricable loveliness of dim blue forms and sinuous pallid lines of light, under an indigo-dark sky. Near at hand, she could see plainly the still-lighted windows, the motorcars gliding by far down, even the tiny shapes of people walking; and the thought that each of them meant someone like herself, seemed strange.

Drinking of this wonder-cup, she began to experience a queer intoxication, and lost the sense of being little; rather she had the feeling of power, as in her dream at Monkland. She too, as well as this great thing below her, seemed to have shed her body, to be emancipated from every barrier-floating deliciously identified with air. She seemed to be one with the enfranchised spirit of the city, drowned in perception of its beauty. Then all that feeling went, and left her frowning, shivering, though the wind from the West was warm. Her whole adventure of coming up here seemed bizarre, ridiculous. Very stealthily she crept down, and had reached once more the door into 'the picture gallery, when she heard her mother's voice say in amazement: "That you, Babs?" And turning, saw her coming from the doorway of the sanctum.

Of a sudden very cool, with all her faculties about her, Barbara smiled, and stood looking at Lady Valleys, who said with hesitation:

"Come in here, dear, a minute, will you?"

In that room resorted to for comfort, Lord Valleys was standing with his back to the hearth, and an expression on his face that wavered between vexation and decision. The doubt in Agatha's mind whether she should tell or no, had been terribly resolved by little Ann, who in a pause of conversation had announced: "We saw Auntie Babs and Mr. Courtier in Gustard's, but we didn't speak to them."

Upset by the events of the afternoon, Lady Valleys had not shown her usual 'savoir faire'. She had told her husband. A meeting of this sort in a shop celebrated for little save its wedding cakes was in a sense of no importance; but, being disturbed already by the news of Miltoun, it seemed to them both nothing less than sinister, as though the heavens were in league for the demolition of their house. To Lord Valleys it was peculiarly mortifying, because of his real admiration for his daughter, and because he had paid so little attention to his wife's warning of some weeks back. In consultation, however, they had only succeeded in deciding that Lady Valleys should talk with her. Though without much spiritual insight, they had, each of them, a certain cool judgment; and were fully alive to the danger of thwarting Barbara. This had not prevented Lord Valleys from expressing himself strongly on the 'confounded unscrupulousness of that fellow,' and secretly forming his own plan for dealing with this matter. Lady Valleys, more deeply conversant with her daughter's nature, and by reason of femininity more lenient towards the other sex, had not tried to excuse Courtier, but had thought privately: 'Babs is rather a flirt.' For she could not altogether help remembering herself at the same age.

Summoned thus unexpectedly, Barbara, her lips very firmly pressed together, took her stand, coolly enough, by her father's writing-table.

Seeing her suddenly appear, Lord Valleys instinctively relaxed his frown; his experience of men and things, his thousands of diplomatic hours, served to give him an air of coolness and detachment which he was very far from feeling. In truth he would rather have faced a hostile mob than his favourite daughter in such circumstances. His tanned face with its crisp grey moustache, his whole head indeed, took on, unconsciously, a more than ordinarily soldier-like appearance. His eyelids drooped a little, his brows rose slightly.

She was wearing a blue wrap over her evening frock, and he seized instinctively on that indifferent trifle to begin this talk.

"Ah! Babs, have you been out?"

Alive to her very finger-nails, with every nerve tingling, but showing no sign, Barbara answered:

"No; on the roof of the tower."

It gave her a real malicious pleasure to feel the perplexity beneath her father's dignified exterior. And detecting that covert mockery, Lord Valleys said dryly:

"Star-gazing?"

Then, with that sudden resolution peculiar to him, as though he were bored with having to delay and temporize, he added:

"Do you know, I doubt whether it's wise to make appointments in confectioner's shops when Ann is in London."

The dangerous little gleam in Barbara's eyes escaped his vision but not that of Lady Valleys, who said at once:

"No doubt you had the best of reasons, my dear."

Barbara curled her lip. Had it not been for the scene they had been through that day with Miltoun, and for their very real anxiety, both would have seen, then, that while their daughter was in this mood, least said was soonest mended. But their nerves were not quite within control; and with more than a touch of impatience Lord Valleys ejaculated:

"It doesn't appear to you, I suppose, to require any explanation?"

Barbara answered:

"No."

"Ah!" said Lord Valleys: "I see. An explanation can be had no doubt from the gentleman whose sense of proportion was such as to cause him to suggest such a thing."

"He did not suggest it. I did."

Lord Valleys' eyebrows rose still higher.

"Indeed!" he said.

"Geoffrey!" murmured Lady Valleys, "I thought I was to talk to Babs."

"It would no doubt be wiser."

In Barbara, thus for the first time in her life seriously reprimanded, there was at work the most peculiar sensation she had ever felt, as if something were scraping her very skin—a sick, and at the same time devilish, feeling. At that moment she could have struck her father dead. But she showed nothing, having lowered the lids of her eyes.

"Anything else?" she said.

Lord Valleys' jaw had become suddenly more prominent.

"As a sequel to your share in Miltoun's business, it is peculiarly entrancing."

"My dear," broke in Lady Valleys very suddenly, "Babs will tell me. It's nothing, of course."

Barbara's calm voice said again:

"Anything else?"

The repetition of this phrase in that maddening, cool voice almost broke down her father's sorely tried control.

"Nothing from you," he said with deadly coldness. "I shall have the honour of telling this gentleman what I think of him."

At those words Barbara drew herself together, and turned her eyes from one face to the other.

Under that gaze, which for all its cool hardness, was so furiously alive, neither Lord nor Lady Valleys could keep quite still. It was as if she had stripped from them the well-bred mask of those whose spirits, by long unquestioning acceptance of themselves, have become inelastic, inexpansive, commoner than they knew. In fact a rather awful moment! Then Barbara said:

"If there's nothing else, I'm going to bed. Goodnight!"

And as calmly as she had come in, she went out.

When she had regained her room, she locked the door, threw off her cloak, and looked at herself in the glass. With pleasure she saw how firmly her teeth were clenched, how her breast was heaving, and how her eyes seemed to be stabbing herself. And all the time she thought:

"Very well! My dears! Very well!"

Chapter XXV

In that mood of rebellious mortification she fell asleep. And, curiously enough, dreamed not of him whom she had in mind been so furiously defending, but of Harbinger. She fancied herself in prison, lying in a cell fashioned like the drawing-room at Sea house; and in the next cell, into which she could somehow look, Harbinger was digging at the wall with his nails. She could distinctly see the hair on the back of his hands, and hear him breathing. The hole he was making grew larger and larger. Her heart began to beat furiously; she awoke.

She rose with a new and malicious resolution to show no sign of rebellion, to go through the day as if nothing had happened, to deceive them all, and then—! Exactly what 'and then' meant, she did not explain even to herself.

In accordance with this plan of action she presented an untroubled front at breakfast, went out riding with little Ann, and shopping with her mother afterwards. Owing to this news of Miltoun the journey to Scotland had been postponed. She parried with cool ingenuity each attempt made by Lady Valleys to draw her into conversation on the subject of that meeting at Gustard's, nor would she talk of her brother; in every other way she was her usual self. In the afternoon she even volunteered to accompany her mother to old Lady Harbinger's in the neighbourhood of Prince's Gate. She knew that Harbinger would be there, and with the thought of meeting that other at 'five o'clock,' had a cynical pleasure in thus encountering him. It was so complete a blind to them all! Then, feeling that she was accomplishing a masterstroke; she even told him, in her mother's hearing, that she would walk home, and he might come if he cared. He did care.

But when once she had begun to swing along in the mellow afternoon, under the mellow trees, where the air was sweetened by the South-West wind, all that mutinous, reckless mood of hers vanished, she felt suddenly happy and kind, glad to be walking with him. To-day too he was cheerful, as if determined not to spoil her gaiety; and she was grateful for this. Once or twice she even put her hand up and touched his sleeve, calling his attention to birds or trees, friendly, and glad, after all those hours of bitter feelings, to be giving happiness. When they parted at the door of Valleys House, she looked back at him with a queer, half-rueful smile. For, now the hour had come!

In a little unfrequented ante-room, all white panels and polish, she sat down to wait. The entrance drive was visible from here; and she meant to encounter Courtier casually in the hall. She was excited, and a little scornful of her own excitement. She had expected him to be punctual, but it was already past five; and soon she began to feel uneasy, almost ridiculous, sitting in this room where no one ever came. Going to the window, she looked out.

A sudden voice behind her, said:

"Auntie Babs!".

Turning, she saw little Ann regarding her with those wide, frank, hazel eyes. A shiver of nerves passed through Barbara.

"Is this your room? It's a nice room, isn't it?"

She answered:

"Quite a nice room, Ann."

"Yes. I've never been in here before. There's somebody just come, so I must go now."

Barbara involuntarily put her hands up to her cheeks, and quickly passed with her niece into the hall. At the very door the footman William handed her a note. She looked at the superscription. It was from Courtier. She went back into the room. Through its half-closed door the figure of little Ann could be seen, with her legs rather wide apart, and her hands clasped on her low-down belt, pointing up at William her sudden little nose. Barbara shut the door abruptly, broke the seal, and read:

"DEAR LADY BARBARA,

"I am sorry to say my interview with your brother was fruitless.

"I happened to be sitting in the Park just now, and I want to wish you every happiness before I go. It has been the greatest pleasure to know you. I shall never have a thought of you that will not be my pride; nor a memory that will not help me to believe that life is good. If I am tempted to feel that things are dark, I shall remember that you are breathing this same mortal air. And to beauty and joy' I shall take off my hat with the greater reverence, that once I was permitted to walk and talk, with you. And so, good-bye, and God bless you.

"Your faithful servant,
"CHARLES COURTIER."

Her cheeks burned, quick sighs escaped her lips; she read the letter again, but before getting to the end could not see the words for mist. If in that letter there had been a word of complaint or even of regret! She could not let him go like this, without good-bye, without any explanation at all. He should not think of her as a cold, stony flirt, who had been merely stealing a few weeks' amusement out of him. She would explain to him at all events that it had not been that. She would make him understand that it was not what he thought—that something in her wanted—wanted—! Her mind was all confused. "What was it?" she thought: "What did I do?" And sore with anger at herself, she screwed the letter up in her glove, and ran out. She walked swiftly down to Piccadilly, and crossed into the Green Park. There she passed Lord Malvezin and a friend strolling up towards Hyde Park Corner, and gave them a very faint bow. The composure of those two precise and well-groomed figures sickened her just then. She wanted to run, to fly to this meeting that should remove from him the odious feelings he must have, that she, Barbara Caradoc, was a vulgar enchantress, a common traitress and coquette! And his letter—without a syllable of reproach! Her cheeks burned so, that she could not help trying to hide them from people who passed.

As she drew nearer to his rooms she walked slower, forcing herself to think what she should do, what she should let him do! But she continued resolutely forward. She would not shrink now—whatever came of it! Her heart fluttered, seemed to stop beating, fluttered again. She set her teeth; a sort of desperate hilarity rose in her. It was an adventure! Then she was gripped by the feeling that had come to her on the roof. The whole thing was bizarre, ridiculous! She stopped, and drew the letter from her glove. It might be ridiculous, but it was due from her; and closing her lips very tight, she walked on. In thought she was already standing close to him, her eyes shut, waiting, with her heart beating wildly, to know what she would feel when his lips had spoken, perhaps touched her face or hand. And she had a sort of mirage vision of herself, with eyelashes resting on her cheeks, lips a little parted, arms helpless at her sides. Yet, incomprehensibly, his figure was invisible. She discovered then that she was standing before his door.

She rang the bell calmly, but instead of dropping her hand, pressed the little bare patch of palm left open by the glove to her face, to see whether it was indeed her own cheek flaming so.

The door had been opened by some unseen agency, disclosing a passage and flight of stairs covered by a red carpet, at the foot of which lay an old, tangled, brown-white dog full of fleas and sorrow. Unreasoning terror seized on Barbara; her body remained rigid, but her spirit began flying back across the Green Park, to the very hall of Valleys House. Then she saw coming towards her a youngish woman in a blue apron, with mild, reddened eyes.

"Is this where Mr. Courtier lives?"

"Yes, miss." The teeth of the young woman were few in number and rather black; and Barbara could only stand there saying nothing, as if her body had been deserted between the sunlight and this dim red passage, which led to-what?

The woman spoke again:

"I'm sorry if you was wanting him, miss, he's just gone away."

Barbara felt a movement in her heart, like the twang and quiver of an elastic band, suddenly relaxed. She bent to stroke the head of the old dog, who was smelling her shoes. The woman said:

"And, of course, I can't give you his address, because he's gone to foreign parts."

With a murmur, of whose sense she knew nothing, Barbara hurried out into the sunshine. Was she glad? Was she sorry? At the corner of the street she turned and looked back; the two heads, of the woman and the dog, were there still, poked out through the doorway.

A horrible inclination to laugh seized her, followed by as horrible a desire to cry.

Chapter XXVI

By the river the West wind, whose murmuring had visited Courtier and Miltoun the night before, was bringing up the first sky of autumn. Slow-creeping and fleecy grey, the clouds seemed trying to overpower a sun that shone but fitfully even thus early in the day. While Audrey Noel was dressing sunbeams danced desperately on the white wall, like little lost souls with no to-morrow, or gnats that wheel and wheel in brief joy, leaving no footmarks on the air. Through the chinks of a side window covered by a dark blind some smoky filaments of light were tethered to the back of her mirror. Compounded of trembling grey spirals, so thick to the eye that her hand felt astonishment when it failed to grasp them, and so jealous as ghosts of the space they occupied, they brought a moment's distraction to a heart not happy. For how could she be happy, her lover away from her now thirty hours, without having overcome with his last kisses the feeling of disaster which had settled on her when he told her of his resolve. Her eyes had seen deeper than his; her instinct had received a message from Fate.

To be the dragger-down, the destroyer of his usefulness; to be not the helpmate, but the clog; not the inspiring sky, but the cloud! And because of a scruple which she could not understand! She had no anger with that unintelligible scruple; but her fatalism, and her sympathy had followed it out into his future. Things being so, it could not be long before he felt that her love was maiming him; even if he went on desiring her, it would be only with his body. And if, for this scruple, he were capable of giving up his public life, he would be capable of living on with her after his love was dead! This thought she could not bear. It stung to the very marrow of her nerves. And yet surely Life could not be so cruel as to have given her such happiness meaning to take it from her! Surely her love was not to be only one summer's day; his love but an embrace, and then—for ever nothing!

This morning, fortified by despair, she admitted her own beauty. He would, he must want her more than that other life, at the very thought of which her face darkened. That other life so hard, and far from her! So loveless, formal, and yet—to him so real, so desperately, accursedly real! If he must indeed give up his career, then surely the life they could live together would make up to him—a life among simple and sweet things, all over the world, with music and pictures, and the flowers and all Nature, and friends who sought them for themselves, and in being kind to everyone, and helping the poor and the unfortunate, and loving each other! But he did not want that sort of life! What was the good of pretending that he did? It was right and natural he should want, to use his powers! To lead and serve! She would not have him otherwise: With these thoughts hovering and darting within her, she went on twisting and coiling her dark hair, and burying her heart beneath its lace defences. She noted too, with her usual care, two fading blossoms in the bowl of flowers on her dressing-table, and, removing them, emptied out the water and refilled the bowl.

Before she left her bedroom the sunbeams had already ceased to dance, the grey filaments of light were gone. Autumn sky had come into its own. Passing the mirror in the hall which was always rough with her, she had not courage to glance at it. Then suddenly a woman's belief in the power of her charm came to her aid; she felt almost happy—surely he must love her better than his conscience! But that confidence was very tremulous, ready to yield to the first rebuff. Even the friendly fresh—cheeked maid seemed that morning to be regarding her with compassion; and all the innate sense, not of 'good form,' but of form, which made her shrink from anything that should disturb or hurt another, or make anyone think she was to be pitied, rose up at once within her; she became more than ever careful to show nothing even to herself. So she passed the morning, mechanically doing the little usual things. An overpowering longing was with her all the time, to get him away with her from England, and see whether the thousand beauties she could show him would not fire him with love of the things she loved. As a girl she had spent nearly three years abroad. And Eustace had never been to Italy, nor to her beloved mountain valleys! Then, the remembrance of his rooms at the Temple broke in on that vision, and shattered it. No Titian's feast of gentian, tawny brown, and alpen-rose could intoxicate the lover of those books, those papers, that great map. And the scent of leather came to her now as poignantly as if she were once more flitting about noiselessly on her business of nursing. Then there rushed through her again the warm wonderful sense that had been with her all those precious days—of love that knew secretly of its approaching triumph and fulfilment; the delicious sense of giving every minute of her time, every thought, and movement; and all the sweet unconscious waiting for the divine, irrevocable moment when at last she would give herself and be his. The remembrance too of how tired, how sacredly tired she had been, and of how she had smiled all the time with her inner joy of being tired for him.

The sound of the bell startled her. His telegram had said, the afternoon! She determined to show nothing of the trouble darkening the whole world for her, and drew a deep breath, waiting for his kiss.

It was not Miltoun, but Lady Casterley.

The shock sent the blood buzzing into her temples. Then she noticed that the little figure before her was also trembling; drawing up a chair, she said: "Won't you sit down?"

The tone of that old voice, thanking her, brought back sharply the memory of her garden, at Monkland, bathed in the sweetness and shimmer of summer, and of Barbara standing at her gate towering above this little figure, which now sat there so silent, with very white face. Those carved features, those keen, yet veiled eyes, had too often haunted her thoughts; they were like a bad dream come true.

"My grandson is not here, is he?"

Audrey shook her head.

"We have heard of his decision. I will not beat about the bush with you. It is a disaster for me a calamity. I have known and loved him since he was born, and I have been foolish enough to dream, dreams about him. I wondered perhaps whether you knew how much we counted on him. You must forgive an old woman's coming here like this. At my age there are few things that matter, but they matter very much."

And Audrey thought: "And at my age there is but one thing that matters, and that matters worse than death." But she did not speak. To whom, to what should she speak? To this hard old woman, who personified the world? Of what use, words?

"I can say to you," went on the voice of the little figure, that seemed so to fill the room with its grey presence, "what I could not bring myself to say to others; for you are not hard-hearted."

A quiver passed up from the heart so praised to the still lips. No, she was not hard-hearted! She could even feel for this old woman from whose voice anxiety had stolen its despotism.

"Eustace cannot live without his career. His career is himself, he must be doing, and leading, and spending his powers. What he has given you is not his true self. I don't want to hurt you, but the truth is the truth, and we must all bow before it. I may be hard, but I can respect sorrow."

To respect sorrow! Yes, this grey visitor could do that, as the wind passing over the sea respects its surface, as the air respects the surface of a rose, but to penetrate to the heart, to understand her sorrow, that old age could not do for youth! As well try to track out the secret of the twistings in the flight of those swallows out there above the river, or to follow to its source the faint scent of the lilies in that bowl! How should she know what was passing in here—this little old woman whose blood was cold? And Audrey had the sensation of watching someone pelt her with the rind and husks of what her own spirit had long devoured. She had a longing to get up, and take the hand, the chill, spidery hand of age, and thrust it into her breast, and say: "Feel that, and cease!"

But, withal, she never lost her queer dull compassion for the owner of that white carved face. It was not her visitor's fault that she had come! Again Lady Casterley was speaking.

"It is early days. If you do not end it now, at once, it will only come harder on you presently. You know how determined he is. He will not change his mind. If you cut him off from his work in life, it will but recoil on you. I can only expect your hatred, for talking like this, but believe me, it's for your good, as well as his, in the long run."

A tumultuous heart-beating of ironical rage seized on the listener to that speech. Her good! The good of a corse that the breath is just abandoning; the good of a flower beneath a heel; the good of an old dog whose master leaves it for the last time! Slowly a weight like lead stopped all that fluttering of her heart. If she did not end it at once! The words had now been spoken that for so many hours, she knew, had lain unspoken within her own breast. Yes, if she did not, she could never know a moment's peace, feeling that she was forcing him to a death in life, desecrating her own love and pride! And the spur had been given by another! The thought that someone—this hard old woman of the hard world—should have shaped in words the hauntings of her love and pride through all those ages since Miltoun spoke to her of his resolve; that someone else should have had to tell her what her heart had so long known it must do—this stabbed her like a knife! This, at all events, she could not bear!

She stood up, and said:

"Please leave me now! I have a great many things to do, before I go."

With a sort of pleasure she saw a look of bewilderment cover that old face; with a sort of pleasure she marked the trembling of the hands raising their owner from the chair; and heard the stammering in the voice: "You are going? Before-before he comes? You-you won't be seeing him again?" With a sort of pleasure she marked the hesitation, which did not know whether to thank, or bless, or just say nothing and creep away. With a sort of pleasure she watched the flush mount in the faded cheeks, the faded lips pressed together. Then, at the scarcely whispered words: "Thank you, my dear!" she turned, unable to bear further sight or sound. She went to the window and pressed her forehead against the glass, trying to think of nothing. She heard the sound of wheels-Lady Casterley had gone. And then, of all the awful feelings man or woman can know, she experienced the worst: She could not cry!

At this most bitter and deserted moment of her life, she felt strangely calm, foreseeing clearly, exactly; what she must do, and where go. Quickly it must be done, or it would never be done! Quickly! And without fuss! She put some things together, sent the maid out for a cab, and sat down to write.

She must do and say nothing that could excite him, and bring back his illness. Let it all be sober, reasonable! It would be easy to let him know where she was going, to write a letter that would bring him flying after her. But to write the calm, reasonable words that would keep him waiting and thinking, till he never again came to her, broke her heart.

When she had finished and sealed the letter, she sat motionless with a numb feeling in hands and brain, trying to realize what she had next to do. To go, and that was all!

Her trunks had been taken down already. She chose the little hat that he liked her best in, and over it fastened her thickest veil. Then, putting on her travelling coat and gloves, she looked in the long mirror, and seeing that there was nothing more to keep her, lifted her dressing bag, and went down.

Over on the embankment a child was crying; and the passionate screaming sound, broken by the gulping of tears, made her cover her lips, as though she had heard her own escaped soul wailing out there.

She leaned out of the cab to say to the maid:

"Go and comfort that crying, Ella."

Only when she was alone in the train, secure from all eyes, did she give way to desperate weeping. The white smoke rolling past the windows was not more evanescent than her joy had been. For she had no illusions—it was over! From first to last—not quite a year! But even at this moment, not for all the world would she have been without her love, gone to its grave, like a dead child that evermore would be touching her breast with its wistful fingers.

Chapter XXVII

Barbara returning from her visit to Courtier's deserted rooms, was met at Valleys House with the message: Would she please go at once to Lady Casterley?

When, in obedience, she reached Ravensham, she found her grandmother and Lord-Dennis in the white room. They were standing by one of the tall windows, apparently contemplating the view. They turned indeed at sound of Barbara's approach, but neither of them spoke or nodded. Not having seen her grandfather since before Miltoun's illness, Barbara found it strange to be so treated; she too took her stand silently before the window. A very large wasp was crawling up the pane, then slipping down with a faint buzz.

Suddenly Lady Casterley spoke.

"Kill that thing!"

Lord Dennis drew forth his handkerchief.

"Not with that, Dennis. It will make a mess. Take a paper knife."

"I was going to put it out," murmured Lord Dennis.

"Let Barbara with her gloves."

Barbara moved towards the pane.

"It's a hornet, I think," she said.

"So he is!" said Lord Dennis, dreamily:

"Nonsense," murmured Lady Casterley, "it's a common wasp."

"I know it's a hornet, Granny. The rings are darker."

Lady Casterley bent down; when she raised herself she had a slipper in her hand.

"Don't irritate him!" cried Barbara, catching her wrist. But Lady Casterley freed her hand.

"I will," she said, and brought the sole of the slipper down on the insect, so that it dropped on the floor, dead. "He has no business in here."

And, as if that little incident had happened to three other people, they again stood silently looking through the window.

Then Lady Casterley turned to Barbara.

"Well, have you realized the mischief that you've done?"

"Ann!" murmured Lord Dennis.

"Yes, yes; she is your favourite, but that won't save her. This woman—to her great credit—I say to her great credit—has gone away, so as to put herself out of Eustace's reach, until he has recovered his senses."

With a sharp-drawn breath Barbara said:

"Oh! poor thing!"

But on Lady Casterley's face had come an almost cruel look.

"Ah!" she said: "Exactly. But, curiously enough, I am thinking of Eustace." Her little figure was quivering from head to foot: "This will be a lesson to you not to play with fire!"

"Ann!" murmured Lord Dennis again, slipping his arm through Barbara's.

"The world," went on Lady Casterley, "is a place of facts, not of romantic fancies. You have done more harm than can possibly be repaired. I went to her myself. I was very much moved.' If it hadn't been for your foolish conduct—"

"Ann!" said Lord Dennis once more.

Lady Casterley paused, tapping the floor with her little foot. Barbara's eyes were gleaming.

"Is there anything else you would like to squash, dear?"

"Babs!" murmured Lord Dennis; but, unconsciously pressing his hand against her heart, the girl went on.

"You are lucky to be abusing me to-day—if it had been yesterday—"

At these dark words Lady Casterley turned away, her shoes leaving little dull stains on the polished floor.

Barbara raised to her cheek the fingers which she had been so convulsively embracing. "Don't let her go on, uncle," she whispered, "not just now!"

"No, no, my dear," Lord Dennis murmured, "certainly not—it is enough."

"It has been your sentimental folly," came Lady Casterley's voice from a far corner, "which has brought this on the boy."

Responding to the pressure of the hand, back now at her waist, Barbara did not answer; and the sound of the little feet retracing their steps rose in the stillness. Neither of those two at the window turned their heads; once more the feet receded, and again began coming back.

Suddenly Barbara, pointing to the floor, cried:

"Oh! Granny, for Heaven's sake, stand still; haven't you squashed the hornet enough, even if he did come in where he hadn't any business?"

Lady Casterley looked down at the debris of the insect.

"Disgusting!" she said; but when she next spoke it was in a less hard, more querulous voice.

"That man—what was his name—have you got rid of him?"

Barbara went crimson.

"Abuse my friends, and I will go straight home and never speak to you again."

For a moment Lady Casterley looked almost as if she might strike her granddaughter; then a little sardonic smile broke out on her face.

"A creditable sentiment!" she said.

Letting fall her uncle's hand, Barbara cried:

"In any case, I'd better go. I don't know why you sent for me."

Lady Casterley answered coldly:

"To let you and your mother know of this woman's most unselfish behaviour; to put you on the 'qui vive' for what Eustace may do now; to give you a chance to make up for your folly. Moreover to warn you against—" she paused.

"Yes?"

"Let me—" interrupted Lord Dennis.

"No, Uncle Dennis, let Granny take her shoe!"

She had withdrawn against the wall, tall, and as it were, formidable, with her head up. Lady Casterley remained silent.

"Have you got it ready?" cried Barbara: "Unfortunately he's flown!"

A voice said:

"Lord Miltoun."

He had come in quietly and quickly, preceding the announcement, and stood almost touching that little group at the window before they caught sight of him. His face had the rather ghastly look of sunburnt faces from which emotion has driven the blood; and his eyes, always so much the most living part of him, were full of such stabbing anger, that involuntarily they all looked down.

"I want to speak to you alone," he said to Lady Casterley.

Visibly, for perhaps the first time in her life, that indomitable little figure flinched. Lord Dennis drew Barbara away, but at the door he whispered:

"Stay here quietly, Babs; I don't like the look of this."

Unnoticed, Barbara remained hovering.

The two voices, low, and so far off in the long white room, were uncannily distinct, emotion charging each word with preternatural power of penetration; and every movement of the speakers had to the girl's excited eyes a weird precision, as of little figures she had once seen at a Paris puppet show. She could hear Miltoun reproaching his grandmother in words terribly dry and bitter. She edged nearer and nearer, till, seeing that they paid no more heed to her than if she were an attendant statue, she had regained her position by the window.

Lady Casterley was speaking.

"I was not going to see you ruined before my eyes, Eustace. I did what I did at very great cost. I did my best for you."

Barbara saw Miltoun's face transfigured by a dreadful smile—the smile of one defying his torturer with hate. Lady Casterley went on:

"Yes, you stand there looking like a devil. Hate me if you like—but don't betray us, moaning and moping because you can't have the moon. Put on your armour, and go down into the battle. Don't play the coward, boy!"

Miltoun's answer cut like the lash of a whip.

"By God! Be silent!"

And weirdly, there was silence. It was not the brutality of the words, but the sight of force suddenly naked of all disguise—like a fierce dog let for a moment off its chain—which made Barbara utter a little dismayed sound. Lady Casterley had dropped into a chair, trembling. And without a look Miltoun passed her. If their grandmother had fallen dead, Barbara knew he would not have stopped to see. She ran forward, but the old woman waved her away.

"Go after him," she said, "don't let him go alone."

And infected by the fear in that wizened voice, Barbara flew.

She caught her brother as he was entering the taxi-cab in which he had come, and without a word slipped in beside him. The driver's face appeared at the window, but Miltoun only motioned with his head, as if to say: Anywhere, away from here!

The thought flashed through Barbara: "If only I can keep him in here with me!"

She leaned out, and said quietly:

"To Nettlefold, in Sussex—never mind your petrol—get more on the road. You can have what fare you like. Quick!"

The man hesitated, looked in her face, and said:

"Very well; miss. By Dorking, ain't it?"

Barbara nodded.

Chapter XXVIII

The clock over the stables was chiming seven when Miltoun and Barbara passed out of the tall iron gates, in their swift-moving small world, that smelled faintly of petrol. Though the cab was closed, light spurts of rain drifted in through the open windows, refreshing the girl's hot face, relieving a little her dread of this drive. For, now that Fate had been really cruel, now that it no longer lay in Miltoun's hands to save himself from suffering, her heart bled for him; and she remembered to forget herself. The immobility with which he had received her intrusion, was ominous. And though silent in her corner, she was desperately working all her woman's wits to discover a way of breaking into the house of his secret mood. He appeared not even to have noticed that they had turned their backs on London, and passed into Richmond Park.

Here the trees, made dark by rain, seemed to watch gloomily the progress of this whirring-wheeled red box, unreconciled even yet to such harsh intruders on their wind-scented tranquillity. And the deer, pursuing happiness on the sweet grasses, raised disquieted noses, as who should say: Poisoners of the fern, defilers of the trails of air!

Barbara vaguely felt the serenity out there in the clouds, and the trees, and wind. If it would but creep into this dim, travelling prison, and help her; if it would but come, like sleep, and steal away dark sorrow, and in one moment make grief-joy. But it stayed outside on its wistful wings; and that grand chasm which yawns between soul and soul remained unbridged. For what could she say? How make him speak of what he was going to do? What alternatives indeed were now before him? Would he sullenly resign his seat, and wait till he could find Audrey Noel again? But even if he did find her, they would only be where they were. She had gone, in order not to be a drag on him—it would only be the same thing all over again! Would he then, as Granny had urged him, put on his armour, and go down into the fight? But that indeed would mean the end, for if she had had the strength to go away now, she would surely never come back and break in on his life a second time. And a grim thought swooped down on Barbara. What if he resigned everything! Went out into the dark! Men did sometimes—she knew—caught like this in the full flush of passion. But surely not Miltoun, with his faith! 'If the lark's song means nothing—if that sky is a morass of our invention—if we are pettily creeping on, furthering nothing—persuade me of it, Babs, and I'll bless you.' But had he still that anchorage, to prevent him slipping out to sea? This sudden thought of death to one for whom life was joy, who had never even seen the Great Stillness, was very terrifying. She fixed her eyes on the back of the chauffeur, in his drab coat with the red collar, finding some comfort in its solidity. They were in a taxi-cab, in Richmond Park! Death—incongruous, incredible death! It was stupid to be frightened! She forced herself to look at Miltoun. He seemed to be asleep; his eyes were closed, his arms folded—only a quivering of his eyelids betrayed him. Impossible to tell what was going on in that grim waking sleep, which made her feel that she was not there at all, so utterly did he seem withdrawn into himself!

He opened his eyes, and said suddenly:

"So you think I'm going to lay hands on myself, Babs?"

Horribly startled by this reading of her thoughts, Barbara could only edge away and stammer:

"No; oh, no!"

"Where are we going in this thing?"

"Nettlefold. Would you like him stopped?"

"It will do as well as anywhere."

Terrified lest he should relapse into that grim silence, she timidly possessed herself of his hand.

It was fast growing dark; the cab, having left the villas of Surbiton behind, was flying along at great speed among pine-trees and stretches of heather gloomy with faded daylight.

Miltoun said presently, in a queer, slow voice "If I want, I have only to open that door and jump. You who believe that 'to-morrow we die'—give me the faith to feel that I can free myself by that jump, and out I go!" Then, seeming to pity her terrified squeeze of his hand, he added: "It's all right, Babs; we, shall sleep comfortably enough in our beds tonight."

But, so desolate to the girl was his voice, that she hoped now for silence.

"Let us be skinned quietly," muttered Miltoun, "if nothing else. Sorry to have disturbed you."

Pressing close up to him, Barbara murmured:

"If only—Talk to me!".

But Miltoun, though he stroked her hand, was silent.

The cab, moving at unaccustomed speed along these deserted roads, moaned dismally; and Barbara was possessed now by a desire which she dared not put in practice, to pull his head down, and rock it against her. Her heart felt empty, and timid; to have something warm resting on it would have made all the difference. Everything real, substantial, comforting, seemed to have slipped away. Among these flying dark ghosts of pine-trees—as it were the unfrequented borderland between two worlds—the feeling of a cheek against her breast alone could help muffle the deep disquiet in her, lost like a child in a wood.

The cab slackened speed, the driver was lighting his lamps; and his red face appeared at the window.

"We'll 'ave to stop here, miss; I'm out of petrol. Will you get some dinner, or go through?"

"Through," answered Barbara:

While they were passing the little time, buying then petrol, asking the way, she felt less miserable, and even looked about her with a sort of eagerness. Then when they had started again, she thought: If I could get him to sleep—the sea will comfort him! But his eyes were staring, wide-open. She feigned sleep herself; letting her head slip a little to one side, causing small sounds of breathing to escape. The whirring of the wheels, the moaning of the cab joints, the dark trees slipping by, the scent of the wet fern drifting in, all these must surely help! And presently she felt that he was indeed slipping into darkness—and then-she felt nothing.

When she awoke from the sleep into which she had seen Miltoun fall, the cab was slowly mounting a steep hill, above which the moon had risen. The air smelled strong and sweet, as though it had passed over leagues of grass.

"The Downs!" she thought; "I must have been asleep!"

In sudden terror, she looked round for Miltoun. But he was still there, exactly as before, leaning back rigid in his corner of the cab, with staring eyes, and no other signs of life. And still only half awake, like a great warm sleepy child startled out of too deep slumber, she clutched, and clung to him. The thought that he had been sitting like that, with his spirit far away, all the time that she had been betraying her watch in sleep, was dreadful. But to her embrace there was no response, and awake indeed now, ashamed, sore, Barbara released him, and turned her face to the air.

Out there, two thin, dense-black, long clouds, shaped like the wings of a hawk, had joined themselves together, so that nothing of the moon showed but a living brightness imprisoned, like the eyes and life of a bird, between those swift sweeps of darkness. This great uncanny spirit, brooding malevolent over the high leagues of moon-wan grass, seemed waiting to swoop, and pluck up in its talons, and devour, all that intruded on the wild loneness of these far-up plains of freedom. Barbara almost expected to hear coming from it the lost whistle of the buzzard hawks. And her dream came back to her. Where were her wings-the wings that in sleep had borne her to the stars; the wings that would never lift her—waking—from the ground? Where too were Miltoun's wings? She crouched back into her corner; a tear stole up and trickled out between her closed lids-another and another followed. Faster and faster they came. Then she felt Miltoun's arm round her, and heard him say: "Don't cry, Babs!" Instinct telling her what to do, she laid her head against his chest, and sobbed bitterly. Struggling with those sobs, she grew less and less unhappy—knowing that he could never again feel quite so desolate, as before he tried to give her comfort. It was all a bad dream, and they would soon wake from it! And they would be happy; as happy as they had been before—before these last months! And she whispered:

"Only a little while, Eusty!"

Chapter XXIX

Old Lady Harbinger dying in the early February of the following year, the marriage of Barbara with her son was postponed till June.

Much of the wild sweetness of Spring still clung to the high moor borders of Monkland on the early morning of the wedding day.

Barbara was already up and dressed for riding when her maid came to call her; and noting Stacey's astonished eyes fix themselves on her boots, she said:

"Well, Stacey?"

"It'll tire you."

"Nonsense; I'm not going to be hung."

Refusing the company of a groom, she made her way towards the stretch of high moor where she had ridden with Courtier a year ago. Here over the short, as yet unflowering, heather, there was a mile or more of level galloping ground. She mounted steadily, and her spirit rode, as it were, before her, longing to get up there among the peewits and curlew, to feel the crisp, peaty earth slip away under her, and the wind drive in her face, under that deep blue sky. Carried by this warm-blooded sweetheart of hers, ready to jump out of his smooth hide with pleasure, snuffling and sneezing in sheer joy, whose eye she could see straying round to catch a glimpse of her intentions, from whose lips she could hear issuing the sweet bitt-music, whose vagaries even seemed designed to startle from her a closer embracing—she was filled with a sort of delicious impatience with everything that was not this perfect communing with vigour.

Reaching the top, she put him into a gallop. With the wind furiously assailing her face and throat, every muscle crisped; and all her blood tingling—this was a very ecstasy of motion!

She reined in at the cairn whence she and Courtier had looked down at the herds of ponies. It was the merest memory now, vague and a little sweet, like the remembrance of some exceptional Spring day, when trees seem to flower before your eyes, and in sheer wantonness exhale a scent of lemons. The ponies were there still, and in distance the shining sea. She sat thinking of nothing, but how good it was to be alive. The fullness and sweetness of it all, the freedom and strength! Away to the West over a lonely farm she could see two buzzard hawks hunting in wide circles. She did not envy them—so happy was she, as happy as the morning. And there came to her suddenly the true, the overmastering longing of mountain tops.

"I must," she thought; "I simply must!"

Slipping off her horse she lay down on her back, and at once everything was lost except the sky. Over her body, supported above solid earth by the warm, soft heather, the wind skimmed without sound or touch. Her spirit became one with that calm unimaginable freedom. Transported beyond her own contentment, she no longer even knew whether she was joyful.

The horse Hal, attempting to eat her sleeve, aroused her. She mounted him, and rode down. Near home she took a short cut across a meadow, through which flowed two thin bright streams, forming a delta full of lingering 'milkmaids,' mauve marsh orchis, and yellow flags. From end to end of this long meadow, so varied, so pied with trees and stones, and flowers, and water, the last of the Spring was passing.

Some ponies, shyly curious of Barbara and her horse, stole up, and stood at a safe distance, with their noses dubiously stretched out, swishing their lean tails. And suddenly, far up, following their own music, two cuckoos flew across, seeking the thorn-trees out on the moor. While she was watching the arrowy birds, she caught sight of someone coming towards her from a clump of beech-trees, and suddenly saw that it was Mrs. Noel!

She rode forward, flushing. What dared she say? Could she speak of her wedding, and betray Miltoun's presence? Could she open her mouth at all without rousing painful feeling of some sort? Then, impatient of indecision, she began:

"I'm so glad to see you again. I didn't know you were still down here."

"I only came back to England yesterday, and I'm just here to see to the packing of my things."

"Oh!" murmured Barbara. "You know what's happening to me, I suppose?"

Mrs. Noel smiled, looked up, and said: "I heard last night. All joy to you!"

A lump rose in Barbara's throat.

"I'm so glad to have seen you," she murmured once more; "I expect I ought to be getting on," and with the word "Good-bye," gently echoed, she rode away.

But her mood of delight was gone; even the horse Hal seemed to tread unevenly, for all that he was going back to that stable which ever appeared to him desirable ten minutes after he had left it.

Except that her eyes seemed darker, Mrs. Noel had not changed. If she had shown the faintest sign of self-pity, the girl would never have felt, as she did now, so sorry and upset.

Leaving the stables, she saw that the wind was driving up a huge, white, shining cloud. "Isn't it going to be fine after all!" she thought.

Re-entering the house by an old and so-called secret stairway that led straight to the library, she had to traverse that great dark room. There, buried in an armchair in front of the hearth she saw Miltoun with a book on his knee, not reading, but looking up at the picture of the old Cardinal. She hurried on, tiptoeing over the soft carpet, holding her breath, fearful of disturbing the queer interview, feeling guilty, too, of her new knowledge, which she did not mean to impart. She had burnt her fingers once at the flame between them; she would not do so a second time!

Through the window at the far end she saw that the cloud had burst; it was raining furiously. She regained her bedroom unseen. In spite of her joy out there on the moor, this last adventure of her girlhood had not been all success; she had again the old sensations, the old doubts, the dissatisfaction which she had thought dead. Those two! To shut one's eyes, and be happy—was it possible! A great rainbow, the nearest she had ever seen, had sprung up in the park, and was come to earth again in some fields close by. The sun was shining out already through the wind-driven bright rain. Jewels of blue had begun to star the black and white and golden clouds. A strange white light-ghost of Spring passing in this last violent outburst-painted the leaves of every tree; and a hundred savage hues had come down like a motley of bright birds on moor and fields.

The moment of desperate beauty caught Barbara by the throat. Its spirit of galloping wildness flew straight into her heart. She clasped her hands across her breast to try and keep that moment. Far out, a cuckoo hooted-and the immortal call passed on the wind. In that call all the beauty, and colour, and rapture of life seemed to be flying by. If she could only seize and evermore have it in her heart, as the buttercups out there imprisoned the sun, or the fallen raindrops on the sweetbriars round the windows enclosed all changing light! If only there were no chains, no walls, and finality were dead!

Her clock struck ten. At this time to-morrow! Her cheeks turned hot; in a mirror she could see them burning, her lips scornfully curved, her eyes strange. Standing there, she looked long at herself, till, little by little, her face lost every vestige of that disturbance, became solid and resolute again. She ceased to have the galloping wild feeling in her heart, and instead felt cold. Detached from herself she watched, with contentment, her own calm and radiant beauty resume the armour it had for that moment put off.

After dinner that night, when the men left the dining-hall, Miltoun slipped away to his den. Of all those present in the little church he had seemed most unemotional, and had been most moved. Though it had been so quiet and private a wedding, he had resented all cheap festivity accompanying the passing of his young sister. He would have had that ceremony in the little dark disused chapel at the Court; those two, and the priest alone. Here, in this half-pagan little country church smothered hastily in flowers, with the raw singing of the half-pagan choir, and all the village curiosity and homage-everything had jarred, and the stale aftermath sickened him. Changing his swallow-tail to an old smoking jacket, he went out on to the lawn. In the wide darkness he could rid himself of his exasperation.

Since the day of his election he had not once been at Monkland; since Mrs. Noel's flight he had never left London. In London and work he had buried himself; by London and work he had saved himself! He had gone down into the battle.

Dew had not yet fallen, and he took the path across the fields. There was no moon, no stars, no wind; the cattle were noiseless under the trees; there were no owls calling, no night-jars churring, the fly-by-night chafers were not abroad. The stream alone was alive in the quiet darkness. And as Miltoun followed the wispy line of grey path cleaving the dim glamour of daisies and buttercups, there came to him the feeling that he was in the presence, not of sleep, but of eternal waiting. The sound of his footfalls seemed desecration. So devotional was that hush, burning the spicy incense of millions of leaves and blades of grass.

Crossing the last stile he came out, close to her deserted cottage, under her lime-tree, which on the night of Courtier's adventure had hung blue-black round the moon. On that side, only a rail, and a few shrubs confined her garden.

The house was all dark, but the many tall white flowers, like a bright vapour rising from earth, clung to the air above the beds. Leaning against the tree Miltoun gave himself to memory.

From the silent boughs which drooped round his dark figure, a little sleepy bird uttered a faint cheep; a hedgehog, or some small beast of night, rustled away in the grass close by; a moth flew past, seeking its candle flame. And something in Miltoun's heart took wings after it, searching for the warmth and light of his blown candle of love. Then, in the hush he heard a sound as of a branch ceaselessly trailed through long grass, fainter and fainter, more and more distinct; again fainter; but nothing could he see that should make that homeless sound. And the sense of some near but unseen presence crept on him, till the hair moved on his scalp. If God would light the moon or stars, and let him see! If God would end the expectation of this night, let one wan glimmer down into her garden, and one wan glimmer into his breast! But it stayed dark, and the homeless noise never ceased. The weird thought came to Miltoun that it was made by his own heart, wandering out there, trying to feel warm again. He closed his eyes and at once knew that it was not his heart, but indeed some external presence, unconsoled. And stretching his hands out he moved forward to arrest that sound. As he reached the railing, it ceased. And he saw a flame leap up, a pale broad pathway of light blanching the grass.

And, realizing that she was there, within, he gasped. His fingernails bent and broke against the iron railing without his knowing. It was not as on that night when the red flowers on her windowsill had wafted their scent to him; it was no sheer overpowering rush of passion. Profounder, more terrible, was this rising up within him of yearning for love—as if, now defeated, it would nevermore stir, but lie dead on that dark grass beneath those dark boughs. And if victorious—what then? He stole back under the tree.

He could see little white moths travelling down that path of lamplight; he could see the white flowers quite plainly now, a pale watch of blossoms guarding the dark sleepy ones; and he stood, not reasoning, hardly any longer feeling; stunned, battered by struggle. His face and hands were sticky with the honey-dew, slowly, invisibly distilling from the lime-tree. He bent down and felt the grass. And suddenly there came over him the certainty of her presence. Yes, she was there—out on the verandah! He could see her white figure from head to foot; and, not realizing that she could not see him, he expected her to utter some cry. But no sound came from her, no gesture; she turned back into the house. Miltoun ran forward to the railing. But there, once more, he stopped—unable to think, unable to feel; as it were abandoned by himself. And he suddenly found his hand up at his mouth, as though there were blood there to be staunched that had escaped from his heart.

Still holding that hand before his mouth, and smothering the sound of his feet in the long grass, he crept away.

Chapter XXX

In the great glass house at Ravensham, Lady Casterley stood close to some Japanese lilies, with a letter in her hand. Her face was very white, for it was the first day she had been allowed down after an attack of influenza; nor had the hand in which she held the letter its usual steadiness. She read:

"Monkland Court.

"Just a line, dear, before the post goes, to tell you that Babs has gone off happily. The child looked beautiful. She sent you her love, and some absurd message—that you would be glad to hear, she was perfectly safe, with both feet firmly on the ground."

A grim little smile played on Lady Casterley's pale lips:—Yes, indeed, and time too! The child had been very near the edge of the cliffs! Very near committing a piece of romantic folly! That was well over! And raising the letter again, she read on:

"We were all down for it, of course, and come back tomorrow. Geoffrey is quite cut up. Things can't be what they were without our Babs. I've watched Eustace very carefully, and I really believe he's safely over that affair at last. He is doing extraordinarily well in the House just now. Geoffrey says his speech on the Poor Law was head and shoulders the best made."

Lady Casterley let fall the hand which held the letter. Safe? Yes, he was safe! He had done the right—the natural thing! And in time he would be happy! He would rise now to that pinnacle of desired authority which she had dreamed of for him, ever since he was a tiny thing, ever since his little thin brown hand had clasped hers in their wanderings amongst the flowers, and the furniture of tall rooms. But, as she stood—crumpling the letter, grey-white as some small resolute ghost, among her tall lilies that filled with their scent the great glass house-shadows flitted across her face. Was it the fugitive noon sunshine? Or was it some glimmering perception of the old Greek saying—'Character is Fate;' some sudden sense of the universal truth that all are in bond to their own natures, and what a man has most desired shall in the end enslave him?

John Galsworthy – A Short Biography

John Galsworthy, eldest son of John Galsworthy (1817-1904), a solicitor and company director of Old Jewry, London, and Blanche Bailey (1835-1915), daughter of Charles Bartleet, a needlemaker in Redditch. His father's ancestors originated in Wembury, near Plymouth in England, and Galsworthy, for whom family origins were of significant importance, maintained a close connection with Devon. His more immediate family were considerably wealthy and well established in the shipping industry, and owned a fine estate in Kingston-upon-Thames called Parkfield, where Galsworthy was born on the 14th August 1867. At the age of nine he began education at Saugeen, a Bournemouth preparatory school, before starting at Harrow school in 1881 where he remained until 1886, distinguishing himself as an athlete.

His education at Harrow being successful enough to gain him entrance to Oxford, he began at New College to read law and gained a second-class degree with honours in 1889. Following Lincoln's Inn he was called to the bar in 1890. Despite this recognition he realised that he was not keen to actually begin practising law and so he resolved instead to look after the family's shipping business while specialising himself in Marine Law. This decision saw him take to the seas to destinations such as Vancouver, Island and South AFrica, though it was at the age of twenty-five on one particular journey to Australia, motivated by an (unfulfilled) intention to meet Robert Louis Stevenson on Samoa that he would being to realise fully his literary interests: though he was not considering becoming a writer at this time, his enjoyment of literature was enough to encourage an attempt at meeting a great writer and eventually enabled one of the most significant encounters of his life. He made the journey with his friend Edward Sanderson and, though he missed Stevenson, he met Joseph Conrad, a fellow future author famed for his novels which were often nautically themed. At the time Conrad was the first mate of the sailing-ship Torrens moored in the harbour of Adelaide, Australia; still very much focused on his ship-borne career, he was yet to begin his writing in earnest.

Indeed, though neither knew at the time, both Conrad and Galsworthy were at similar junctures in their lives, their time spent as sea acting as a transitional period during which each found their literary calling. It is perhaps owning to this unknown common ground that they became close friends. During his time on the Torrens Galsworthy recorded several details, offering a frank and valuable characterisation of Conrad while also illuminating his own experiences as a student of Marine Law.

"I supposed to be studying navigation for the Admiralty Bar, would every day work out the position of the ship with the captain. On one side of the saloon table we would sit and check our observations with those of Conrad, who from the other side of the table would look at us a little quizzically."

On his return to England and the cessation of his nautical voyaging, Galsworthy began an affair with the wife of his first cousin, Major Arthur John Galsworthy. Ada Nemesis Pearson Cooper (1864-1956), the daughter of Emanuel Copper, an obstetrician from Norwich, remained married to the Major for ten years and the affair remained secret for its duration. In order to conceal the affair they took considerable pains to avoid suspicion. One such tactic was to stay in a secluded farmhouse called Wingstone in the village on Manaton on Dartmoor, in Devon. In Galsworthy's decision to choose Devon as the location for their clandestine rendezvous we see evidence of Galsworthy's affection for the place of his father's origin. It was only when, in 1905, she divorced the Major that their affair became known following their marriage on 23rd September of that year.

Galsworthy now took to writing sometime after having met Conrad and his career began in earnest when, in 1897, his first work, From the Four Winds, a volume of short stories, was published under the pseudonym John Sinjohn. He succeeded this in 1898 with Jocelyn, his first novel, and then his second in 1900, Villa Rubein. In 1901 he published a second volume of short stories, A Man of Devon, which was the last of his work to be published under pseudonym. The first of his work to be published under his own name was The Island Pharisees in 1904, a novel of social observation, seasoned with flashes of satire and propaganda. His decision to write under his own name is arguably owing to the recent death of his father, either as a mark of respect to his name or because now he was able to publish freely without incurring the possibility of paternal disappointment at his choice of career. It also marked a shift in his professionalism; he had hitherto published with small, independent publishers, but The Island Pharisees was published by Heinemann, a far more established House and one with whom he remained for the duration of his writing career.

He arguably cemented his position and maturity as a writer when, in 1906, he saw the publication of both his first major play, The Silver Box, and the novel The Man of Property. Each was published to considerable critical acclaim, and to achieve both in such a short space of time was impressive. the Silver Box concerns the imbalance in the justice system with regards to criminals of differing class by contrasting the treatment of a poor thief and a rich thief, both of whom stole silver cigarette cases but for very different reasons. The complexity of individual experience when not dealt with in public is highlighted and questioned in a bravely critical manner; despite the clear issues it raises with class and privilege, the final night was attended by the Price and Princess of Wales. The Man of Property was the first novel in the famous The Forsyte Saga, a trilogy of novels with an 'interlude' between each one, written between 1906 and 1921. Dealing with the questions of status, class and materialism, The Man of Property introduces us to the Forsyte family, particularly Soames Forsyte, who is acutely aware of his status as 'new money' and equally keen to assert himself as a wealthy man. Jealous of his wife and desperate to own things in order to confirm his wealth to those observing him, he engineers a plan to keep his wife from her friends which backfires spectacularly when, instead of cutting her off, all Soames achieves is enabling her to have an affair. This drives Soames to terrible actions with terrible consequences, which Galsworthy depicts with confidence.

Very typically Edwardian, the novel focuses on conflict between property and art, and to a certain degree much of its emotional power is drawn from Galsworthy's own life, particularly his affair with Ada. Their rendezvous in the countryside of Devon mirror the manner in which Forsyte seeks to relocate his wife and; though theirs was a much healthier relationship, there are clear similarities. By examining the fragile nature of the class system and those moving within it Galsworthy offered an important perspective on the relationships between material wealth, personal happiness and obsession, and the manner in which these change over time. His contemporaries widely regarded the publication of this novel as marking the end of Victorianism. His friend Conrad praised it as "indubitably a piece of art" and, though the notoriously risqué D.H. Lawrence lamented the novel's timidity in the face of sexuality and sensuality, he considered it potentially "a very great novel, a very great satire".

Though he continued to write both plays and novels, it was his work as a playwright for which he was most celebrated by his contemporaries. Indeed, his next novel, The Country House, seems uncharacteristically unfocused, its satirical view of those belonging to the country set comparatively unremarkable and weakly characterised, while at times the tone of satire becomes one of ironic detachment. In 1909 he published Fraternity, an exploration of of the various connections between urban society and the social classes therein, though its representation of lower-class Londoners is utterly unconvincing and ill-informed. Remaining with the subject of the landed gentry and the society surrounding it, in 1915 he published The Freelands, which does not stray far from conservative discussions of capitalism, the rural economy and their interrelationship.

His drama, however, featured a convincingly muted realism, directed at a relatively small, educated and politically-aware audience. His social agenda is prevalent here too, and is represented in a simple and static manner producing arresting instances of high drama. This talent for creating moments of captivating theatre is complimented by an instinctual sense of balance enabling his narratives to vacillate between their emotional high- and low-points, ultimately reaching conclusive equilibrium. This is particularly evident in one of his most popular plays, Strife, published in 1909 and examining the antagonists in a strike at a Cornish tin mine. In this, and in 1910's Justice, he approaches his subject with sympathy, irony and balance, which establishes a position of narrative authority while garnering the audiences trust that he is representing his characters and their motives justly. Justice condemns the use of solitary confinement in prisons, a reformist agenda which caught the liberality of his contemporary audiences along with the home secretary, Winston Churchill. Despite he was careful to disassociate himself with politics and professed himself apolitical, he and his work were nevertheless aligned with the views of the Liberal establishment. He spent much of the duration of the First World War working in a field hospital in France as an orderly having been passed over for military service.

Despite the popularity and brilliance of his work, it was only in 1920 that he had his first true commercial success with The Skin Game, a melodrama dealing with ethics, property and class. The play was adapted by Alfred Hitchcock in 1931. Galsworthy, meanwhile, had turned down a knighthood in 1918, considering his work not sufficient to be made a knight of the realm. He did, however, accept the Belgian Palmes d'Or in the following year. In 1920 he published the second novel in the Forsyte Saga, In Chancery, in which he resumes many of the themes of the first novel, focusing on the marital disharmony between Soames Forsyte and his wife. Katherine Mansfield considered it "a fascinating, brilliant book" in her review in The Atheneum. Then, in 1921, he was elected as the PEN International Literary Club's first president. The concluding novel to The Forsyte Saga, To Let was published in 1921 with a kind of peace being found between Forsyte and his now-ex wife, though he is left contemplating his losses and his greed. More ironic treatment of class confusions followed in Loyalties, bringing with it more popular success which lasted until 1926 and Escape, the last of his popular plays. Though he enjoyed popular success it was inconsistent and relatively small. His Collected Plays was published in 1929.

Over the course of time the appreciation of his work has gradually shifted from his plays to his novels, and particularly the detail and intricacy of his chronicle of English social difference, tension and pretension in The Forsyte Saga. Its success encouraged Galsworthy to revisit Soames Forsyte in a second trilogy, A Modern Comedy, which follows Soames's obsessive love of his daughter Fleur. In its three volumes, The White Monkey (1924), The Silver Spoon (1936) and Swan Song (1928) he examines the English commercial upper-middle class and its ideologies, its instinct to possess as its only way of distinguishing itself manifested in the poisonous materialism of Soames. Interestingly, this emergent social class which he so vehemently criticises is the very class from which he emerged. He witnessed first-hand its insularity, its chauvinism, its restrictive and oppressive morality, its stubborn imperialism and its materialism, and it is this experience which enables him to write so comfortably about it. Swan Song is widely considered among the best of Galsworthy's writing for the depth of its exploration of society and its heightened emotional subtlety. In 1929 he was appointed to the Order of Merit, despite having turned down a knighthood earlier. He spent his last years writing a third trilogy, End of the Chapter, beginning in 1931 with Maid in Waiting, Flowering Wilderness in 1932 and concluding with Over The River in 1933. These are significantly less coherent works and are indicative of his deteriorating health. Indeed, in 1932 he was awarded the Nobel Prize, though he was too ill to attend the ceremony.

Throughout the course of his career he received honorary degrees from the universities of St Andrews (1922), Manchester (1927), Dublin (1929), Cambridge (1930), Sheffield (1930), Oxford (1931), and Princeton (1931). In 1926 New College, Oxford, elected him as an honourary fellow. In photographs he is portrayed as handsome, fastidiously dressed and dignified. He was unusually compassionate and this saw him involved in several charitable and humane causes throughout the course of his life, including penal reforms, attacks on theatrical censorship and campaigning for animal rights. Though he spent the majority of the final seven years of his life at his home in Bury, West Sussex, it was at his home in Hampstead, London, that he died of a brain tumour on 31st January, 1933, six weeks after having been too ill to attend the ceremony in honour of his receiving the Nobel Prize. According to demands made in his will he was cremated and his ashes scattered over the South Downs from an aeroplane. Also in his will was his wish to leave cottages to several of his astonished tenants. He is memorialised in Highgate 'New' Cemetery and in the cloisters of New College, Oxford, where he was an honourary fellow.

John Galsworthy – A Concise Bibliography

From the Four Winds, 1897 (as John Sinjohn)
Jocelyn, 1898 (as John Sinjohn)
Villa Rubein, 1900 (as John Sinjohn)
A Man of Devon, 1901 (as John Sinjohn)
The Island Pharisees, 1904
The Silver Box, 1906 (his first play)
The Man of Property, 1906 – First book of The Forsyte Saga (1922)
The Country House, 1907
A Commentary, 1908
Fraternity, 1909
A Justification for the Censorship of Plays, 1909
Strife, 1909
Fraternity, 1909
Joy, 1909
Justice, 1910
A Motley, 1910
The Spirit of Punishment, 1910
Horses in Mines, 1910
The Patrician, 1911

The Little Dream, 1911
The Pigeon, 1912
The Eldest Son, 1912
Quality, 1912
Moods, Songs, and Doggerels, 1912
For Love of Beasts, 1912
The Inn of Tranquillity, 1912
The Dark Flower, 1913
The Fugitive, 1913
The Mob, 1914
The Freelands, 1915
The Little Man, 1915
A Bit o' Love, 1915
A Sheaf, 1916
The Apple Tree, 1916
The Foundations, 1917
Beyond, 1917
Five Tales, 1918
Indian Summer of a Forsyte, 1918 – First interlude of The Forsyte Saga
Saint's Progress, 1919
Addresses in America, 1912
In Chancery, 1920 – Second book of The Forsyte Saga
Awakening, 1920 – Second interlude of The Forsyte Saga
The Skin Game, 1920
To Let, 1921 – Third book of The Forsyte Saga
A Family Man, 1922
The Little Man, 1922
Loyalties, 1922
Windows, 1922
Captures, 1923
Abracadabra, 1924
The Forest, 1924
Old English, 1924
The White Monkey, 1924 – First book of A Modern Comedy
The Show, 1925
Escape, 1926
The Silver Spoon, 1926 – Second book of A Modern Comedy
Verses New and Old, 1926
Castles in Spain, 1927
A Silent Wooing, 1927 – First Interlude of A Modern Comedy
Passers By, 1927 – Second Interlude of A Modern Comedy
Swan Song, 1928 – Third book of A Modern Comedy
The Manaton Edition, 1923–26 (collection, 30 vols.)
Exiled, 1929
The Roof, 1929
On Forsyte 'Change, 1930
Two Essays on Conrad, 1930
Soames and the Flag, 1930

The Creation of Character in Literature, 1931 (The Romanes Lecture for 1931).
Maid in Waiting, 1931 – First book of End of the Chapter (1934)
Forty Poems, 1932
Flowering Wilderness, 1932 – Second book of End of the Chapter
Autobiographical Letters of Galsworthy: A Correspondence with Frank Harris, 1933
One More River (originally Over the River), 1933 – Third book of End of the Chapter
The Grove Edition, 1927–34 (collection, 27 Vols.)
Collected Poems, 1934
Punch and Go, 1935
The Life and Letters, 1935
The Winter Garden, 1935
Forsytes, Pendyces and Others, 1935
Selected Short Stories, 1935
Glimpses and Reflections, 1937

www.ingramcontent.com/pod-product-compliance
Lightning Source LLC
Chambersburg PA
CBHW051514170626
46811CB00002B/822